The Device

The Device

Dale C. George

Idea Creations Press
www.ideacreationspress.com

IC Idea Creations Press
www.ideacreationspress.com

Copyright © Dale C. George, 2017.

This is a work of fiction. Any resemblance of characters to actual persons, living or dead, is purely coincidental.

978-0-9978904-9-5

Publisher's Catalog-In-Publishing Data

Name: George, Dale C., author
Title: The Device / Dale C. George
Description: First trade paperback original edition. | Salt Lake City: Idea Creations Press, 2017.
Identifiers: ISBN 978-0-9978904-9-5 | LCCN 2017953609
Subjects: Science Fiction. – Time Travel | Historical-Fiction. | BISAC: FICTION / Science Fiction / Time Travel

Printed in the U. S. A

To the victims of the Holocaust
whose names have been forgotten.

And to those whose lives have been affected by
Parkinson's disease –
may you never lose hope!

Acknowledgements

I would like to thank my wife Cindy for steadfastly supporting me throughout this endeavor. For more than two-and-a-half years she listened to me read segments of The Device, and gave me suggestions that helped shape the storyline. She was also the first to volunteer to be a beta (test) reader. My love, you will never know the full extent of your contributions.

I would also like to thank Ms. Kathryn Jones of Idea Creations Press for her editorial review and constructive criticism, and the rest of my awesome beta-reading team: Brad Andes, Marla Avner, Donna Magana, Shannon Seymour, and Gale & Stan Sjols. All of you contributed significantly in making my book more authentic and easier to read.

Additional thanks to Mr. Gregg Wixom for his stellar photography.

Lastly, a very special thank you to the men and women of the Davis County Parkinson's Support Group for inspiring the plot. In my eyes, you are all heroes.

Preface

It is hard for me to comprehend what has happened. When I think about it now, I still second-guess myself and wonder if I saw what I saw, experienced the remarkable journey, or whether I have crossed over from the real world to an imaginary one. But after reviewing my actions and rechecking my facts (several times, I might add) I have concluded that I have not imagined anything! I have survived an incredible adventure, and it is only by the actions of one remarkable man and a great deal of luck that I was able to return and tell my story.

I also explored many different methods to recount the events, such as making a video recording, but the affliction I have been cursed with sometimes causes me to struggle to find the right word, making even the easiest of sentences hard for me to repeat aloud. In addition, I've never really felt comfortable in front of a camera, and such feelings increase the severity of my Parkinson's symptoms. Therefore, after a great deal of urging from my wife Madison, I have decided to write my story in the form of a novel.

It is not without a great deal of trepidation that I place my adventure in a book. I know that by doing so, I will open myself up to a great deal of scrutiny and criticism. As far as that goes, I have no doubt that the so-called "great minds" of the world will be the first to nit-pick my account to the point of absurdity, and then follow up with a salvo of personal attacks aimed at discrediting me. These close-minded intellectuals will undoubtedly remain unconvinced no matter how much evidence I present in my narrative.

Before you begin, however, let me write candidly to you and convey this simple message: to close your mind means ignoring facts that cannot logically be explained away, nor can they be dismissed as mere figments of my imagination. I *know* the events and experiences I have put forth in this novel are true. So I challenge whoever may read this to suspend your disbelief until you read the story in its entirety, then decide whether it is credible or if you think it is a well-meaning (albeit fictitious) tale.

I have, admittedly, changed the names of the primary players so as not to cause them unnecessary embarrassment or unwanted publicity. With a few exceptions (for dramatic effect) I've also added sections of how I *believe* the events transpired and dialog of what *might have* been said. Everything else of what you are about to read I have recounted truthfully and to the best of my recollection. With everything that has happened, however, there will no doubt be some minor inaccuracies where I simply could not recall exact actions or words at precise moments in time.

And even if you decide my story is implausible, it is my sincere wish that you enjoy it nonetheless.

George d'Clare

Prologue

Nazi Germany
Monday, 30 April 1945, 15:00hrs
Inside the *Führerbunker, Berlin*

Adolph Hitler had just finished another one of his infamous temper tantrums. The tension inside the crowded underground conference room following his latest rant seemed to smother the atmosphere like a giant pillow. Adding to the grim mood was the lone light bulb hanging down from the ceiling which cast a dim light on the proceedings, and the unspoken truth that the war was now lost. Those in attendance, which not only included high-ranking Nazi officers, but also his new wife Eva Braun, stood motionless after his latest eruption, no one daring to say a word lest they incur his wrath.

What began fifteen minutes ago as another raging outburst against the advancing Russian Army was now a vitriolic personal attack directed squarely at one of his most trusted senior officers, *SS-Obergruppenführer* (Lieutenant General of the SS) Karl Berger. If the general had seen fit to attend this final meeting of the German high command, Hitler would've ordered him shot.

"When the Third Reich needs him most," he fumed, "he is nowhere to be found!"

At first, the frantic Nazi leader thought his underground headquarters had been breached by elite Russian commandos, bent on removing his senior officers first before coming to kill him. Adding credence to this belief was the power outage that occurred in the bunker approximately three hours ago, when the entire underground complex went dark for almost five minutes. After the electricity was restored and the lights came back on, Hitler ordered a thorough security check. Aside from Berger's two Jewish assistants, who were found dead with their necks broken, the general was nowhere to be found. Over the course of the last three hours, additional checks were made in and around the complex, but the results were the same: search teams found no evidence of intruders entering the bunker from the outside, nor any clues as to the whereabouts of General Berger.

A single fact remained: one of the Nazi's most powerful generals, who oversaw the Third Reich's top-secret weapon development programs, was missing. And now, in his increasingly paranoid state of mind, Hitler was beginning to believe that Berger (like Heinrich Himmler proved himself to be two days ago) was a traitor to the Nazi cause.

~ Then ~

Less than one year ago, Hitler transferred General Berger from the *Waffen-Schultzstaffel* (Waffen-SS) to his current position as Deputy Director of the Reich Research Council. His meteoric rise through the Nazi officer ranks had previously raised more than a few eyebrows among the staff of the German high command, but this appointment, at the still-young age of thirty-three, came as a surprise to no one. This was because Berger's good friend, Albert Speer, was the Minister of Armaments and War Production for the Third Reich, and advised the Führer who to select for the position.

Adding to his political connections was the general's higher-than-normal intelligence quotient, which was both exceptional and shrewd. His brilliant mental power, in turn, led to many of the successes he achieved in his previous duty assignments, some of which included working as either an assistant or understudy to some of Germany's most notable scientists. His high IQ also served him well while playing his favorite pastime, the game of chess, of which he often exhibited his champion-level prowess whenever challenged.

General Berger first proved himself to be an asset to the Third Reich when he assisted Heinrich Himmler with the design, construction and oversight of the system of Nazi concentration camps throughout Eastern Europe. He received notoriety yet again when he oversaw the development of Zyklon-B gas (a newer form of hydrogen cyanide) to use at several of the death camps, thus making the method of killing "more efficient" for the Nazis. A review of his dossier included page after page of glittering accolades from his former commanders, one of which read, "The talented SS officer with a proven record of getting results." His record, however, omitted his dark side and the method of how he obtained those results, which was on the backs of dead or near-dead concentration camp prisoners he used for either experimental purposes or slave labor.

He was a tyrannical sadist who took pleasure in torturing and killing people. The seeds of his unique personality were planted early in his life by his domineering mother and cultivated in the disquieting backdrop of the place where he grew to manhood. Born in Munich on February the twenty-ninth of 1912, he was the only child of wealthy parents Catrina and Winnifred Berger. Catrina, an overly-large woman, suffered from bipolar schizophrenia, and physically abused him and his father on a regular basis. Young Karl, not understanding the reasons for the punishment, grew to despise both his mother for the abuse and his weakling father for not protecting him. Post-World War I Munich also aided in his character development, exposing him to daily doses of anti-Semitic rants by those who blamed the Jewish people for "all that was wrong" with Germany; an idea that was prevalent throughout the country at the time. With his mother successfully passing on to him the character traits of an abuser, and his home environment nurturing his complete hatred of Jewish people and those he considered weaker than himself, he became the product of his time: the quintessential Nazi, completely devoid of empathy.

Once in the Army he became an expert in hand-to-hand combat, and perfected a truly appalling method of murder that also gave him the euphoric feeling of total power over the life and death of another human being. This technique involved first beating his hapless victim, then placing them in headlock and breaking their neck. At the very moment he took their life he experienced this thrilling feeling, which temporarily satisfied his addictive craving to kill.

He committed this act on over one hundred innocent inmates at several of the Sachsenhausen concentration camps, allowing them the "privilege" of fighting him for their "freedom." After witnessing these fights first-hand and noticing how much pleasure he took by inflicting pain on inmates he deemed "worthy of attention," many of his fellow-SS officers even chose to avoid him.

At a commanding six feet eight inches tall and weighing more than two-hundred and eighty pounds, he was an imposing and intimidating figure. Not portly or overweight, his heaviness and bulky size were due to his obsession with fitness and staying in peak physical condition. This passion gave him the build and appearance of a muscular weightlifting champion. He also sported pure blonde hair on his head which he kept perfectly trimmed in a crew-cut style, a feature that made him look like a role model of the Nazi's fanatical idea of a pure Aryan-Nordic "master race."

His most distinguishing characteristic, however, was not his tall height nor his large muscular frame, but instead was his unnaturally dark eyes. Due to some form of genetic mutation, the dark green pigment of his irises almost matched the coal-black color of his pupils. Interred inmates, upon whom he perpetrated the most vile and cruel acts, believed he either possessed no human soul whatsoever, or that he was literally a mortal instrument of pure evil.

And his dark ink-black eyes, which resembled those you might see in a wild animal, coupled with his pure blonde hair earned him the fitting nickname of "The White Wolf."

With his accomplishments well-documented and having friends like Albert Speer seated in the Nazi leadership hierarchy, he naturally became the number one choice to fill the recently-vacated position of Deputy Director of the Reich Research Council. As an added benefit, this illustrious appointment gave him the highest level of security credentials and allowed him to oversee the Third Reich's secret weapon development programs.

~ Now ~

After a long and uncomfortable pause, the Führer's attention returned to General Johann Rattenhuber, his personal bodyguard and officer in charge of security in the underground headquarters.

"Hans, there is still no sign of him?" Hitler asked, addressing the general by his nickname.

"None, my Führer. My men not only searched all sections of the bunker complex, but they also scoured the Chancellery and surrounding area. We cannot find him. The guards at all the entrances have informed me that no one has left the bunker in the last three hours."

"Did you search the Ünterbunker?"

"Yes, my Führer. After you told me of its existence, I conducted the search myself, and except for the two dead Jews there was no one down there."

"What about the laboratory?"

"Besides the filing cabinets, chalkboards and the emergency radio equipment you told me about, the laboratory was empty."

"What did you say?

Rattenhuber repeated his report.

"Get one of the electricians in here immediately!"

The general nodded to his security men and two of them quickly exited. A few moments later they returned with Emil Brandt, one of the bunker's two master electricians.

"Herr Brandt," Hitler asked, "what do you know of the power disruption that occurred earlier today? Could it have anything to do with General Berger's disappearance?"

"I know that the power outage was caused by an electrical surge, which blew out several of the main fuses," Brandt replied nervously. "Hentschel and I are still investigating what might've caused it. The last time I saw General Berger was around eleven o'clock, well before the power went out. He was closing the door of the safe in the ventilation room. I was about to accompany him down to the Ünterbunker when he ordered me to leave."

"Did he say or do anything that seemed strange to you?"

"Now that you mention it, there was one thing I found a bit odd."

"Tell me!"

"I asked the general if he would like me to test the voltage in the Ünterbunker to make sure that the bombing had not damaged the electrical connections. He got extremely upset with me and told me that *he* would test the voltage in the Ünterbunker. Before this, he had always ordered either myself, Hentschel or one of our assistants to do such tasks. Never himself, my Führer."

While Brandt talked, Hitler listened intently and paced back and forth. Suddenly he stopped and looked through the doorway into his study, where a portrait of Frederick the Great hung on the wall behind his desk. His eyes were wide, but vacant — staring at but not focused on the painting.

"So the veil is lifted," he said slowly, "and I finally see the truth."

After a few moments, Hitler returned his attention to the electrician.

"Herr Brandt, I need you to do one last thing for me."

"Yes, my Führer?"

He motioned him to come closer, and whispered in his ear so the others wouldn't hear.

"Later today, when I am gone, you must destroy the Ünterbunker and forever seal the entrance to the lower level. No one must ever find out about Operation Firebird, or any other information General Berger kept down there. Do you understand?'

Brandt nodded.

"And you must never breathe a word about the Ünterbunker ever again."

"Yes, my Führer."

After motioning Brandt to leave, Hitler addressed everyone.

"This meeting is adjourned."

The tired Nazi leader proceeded out of the conference room and into his study, with Eva following closely behind. When he reached the chair behind his desk he slowly sat down and looked up at her.

"He has betrayed me," he said. "It's all over now."

At approximately 3:30pm, after successfully testing a cyanide pill on his dog Blondi, Hitler gave another to Eva and kissed her goodbye. A few moments later, after seeing her collapse and lose consciousness, he took one for himself, opened the desk drawer and retrieved his luger pistol.

* * *

Less than an hour after Hitler's death, Emil Brandt made his way through the cloak room to the ventilation room, where he removed a bomb, a detonator and a cable from a storage cabinet. After uncoiling the two wires from the bomb, he retrieved a wadded-up bundle of wires protruding from a pipe in the access shaft. The other ends of these wires were connected to four pre-positioned explosives planted down below in the Ünterbunker.

Closing the lower level's access cover, he carefully placed the bomb on top of it and began connecting the wires of the five

17

explosives to one end of the cable. Once he was finished, he picked up the detonator and proceeded out into the conference room, unwinding the cable as he went and closing the two rooms' doors behind him. Lastly, he hooked up the cable to the detonator and pulled up and pushed down on the t-handle.

He lost his footing and fell down on the dirty cement floor as the concussion from the explosion rocked the underground headquarters. Coughing and squinting from the cauldron of dust that was permeating in the air, he picked up the detonator, gathered up what remained of the cable and tossed them into a nearby garbage bin. Satisfied he had carried out the Führer's command, he went back to his small room in the Vorbunker and collected his papers and a few personal belongings. It wouldn't be long before the Russian Army overran the complex, and he was prepared to surrender to them.

Sitting on his cot, Brandt thought back to the Führer's last order. He hadn't the slightest idea of what Operation Firebird was, or what General Berger was working on down in the Ünterbunker. He was never permitted into the lower level's laboratory, only the central room to wire the junction box. *No matter*, he thought to himself, *everything in the Ünterbunker was either destroyed by the explosion or pulverized by the cave in.*

He then thought about the stunned look that had appeared on Hitler's face when he'd made his report. Losing the war was a foregone conclusion days ago, but it was as if the Führer had just then, at that very moment, realized Germany had been defeated. It was an image that seemed surreal, and a fitting culmination to a day filled with strange events – events that Emil Brandt will be asked to recall again, many years from now, on the final day of his life.

* * *

Two days later, the last remaining Germans in the underground bunker surrendered, but in the weeks that followed, rumors swirled about some high-ranking Nazi officers who might have gotten away. As a result, searches began all over the world to apprehend these individuals, and eventually many of them were captured, put on trial, and either imprisoned or executed for their crimes against humanity.

Despite the massive search, SS Lieutenant General Karl Berger remained missing. One of the more brilliant (but sadistic) designers of the Nazi concentration camps, who possessed top-secret information about the Third Reich's advanced weapon technology, had somehow slipped through the fingers of law enforcement and successfully eluded the world-wide manhunt.

As the years marched on, and our revered "Greatest Generation" grew old and passed away, Karl Berger was almost forgotten. His name, which at one time sat atop the list of most-wanted war criminals, was eventually catalogued as "presumed dead," until it finally became nothing more than a minor (often-overlooked) footnote in the annals of World War II.

The Nazi's White Wolf had disappeared into history.

Part One:
The Visitor

Chapter One
The Mysterious Mr. Stevens

Sixty-Nine Years, Three Months and Five Days Later
Wednesday, 6 August 2014, 18:00hrs
Inside the *Wasatch Front Senior Citizen Center, Layton, Utah*

Fifteen people diagnosed with Parkinson's disease sat at the tables in the main assembly hall, each one in a different stage of the illness and experiencing their own unique set of symptoms. These symptoms extended along the entire spectrum of the debilitating brain ailment, and included those that were severely noticeable to ones that remained imperceptible. The ages and genders of the patients were also diverse, ranging from a man in his mid-forties to a woman in her early-eighties, which portrayed both the nondiscriminatory nature of the disease and the unfairness of life. Next to the patients sat their significant others, some of whom were now delegated to the role of caregiver for their loved one. In front of these brave patients and the heroes taking care of them was where my wife Madison and I found ourselves this early summer evening.

I thought about how much the group had grown from when we had our first meeting. At that time only seven people attended and I was beginning to think this support group idea was going to be a failure. But as the word spread, more and more people started coming out until we reached an all-time high of fifty people at our Christmas party last December.

THE DEVICE

I remembered the day a little over two-and-a-half years ago when I was diagnosed with Parkinson's disease, and subsequently came up with the idea of starting a support group.

~ Then ~

It was an unseasonably warm late-October day in northern Utah in 2011, and a day I shall never forget. The leaves on the trees had changed to their familiar yellow-orange color, signaling that fall was well underway and that winter was just around the corner. I'm sure if I'd paid closer attention, I'd have seen children playing in a nearby school yard, or perhaps a flock of birds as they flew by. Instead, I was completely oblivious to my surroundings because my mind was entirely preoccupied with the devastating news I had just received. In a relatively short period of time, my entire world changed when the physician inside the nearby building concluded his diagnosis with the simple pronouncement of two words: Parkinson's disease.

"Did he say I had Parkinson's disease?" I asked Madison, hoping I'd heard it wrong.

"Yes," she replied, with tears in her eyes, "he said it looked like you have it."

We sat in silence, too stunned and shocked to say anything. All we could do was cry.

In the span of one hour, my entire life had been altered. I suddenly found myself feeling old and insignificant, as if I were a footprint on a sandy beach destined to be washed away at the next high tide. Even though my beloved wife was with me and giving me all the support a loving spouse could possibly give, I felt helpless and afraid.

In the months that followed we read a lot about Parkinson's disease, and learned two tried and true methods of combating it: stay physically active and socially interactive.

With regards to staying physically active, I visited a physical therapist at the University of Utah who specialized in working with Parkinson's patients and added several exercises to my workout routine that I hoped would help me combat the disease.

As for remaining socially interactive, one healthcare advisor suggested Madison and I attend a Parkinson's support group meeting so that we could meet and converse with other people who have the disease. After a bit of research, I found there were a few support groups scattered throughout northern Utah. Of the two closest groups, one met at the University of Utah in Salt Lake City and the other in Ogden. Unfortunately, the one in Ogden had recently suspended their meetings due to the facilitator's advanced illness. The next closest support group met in Brigham City, which was more than forty miles north of where we lived.

Throughout the next few months, Madison and I talked many times about what a shame it was that there wasn't a Parkinson's support group closer, somewhere between Salt Lake City and Brigham City. With a disease such as this one which affects so many people, there had to be other patients living in our immediate area who would be interested in attending. During one of these conversations, the idea came up that we should start our own support group, and a few months later the Wasatch Front Parkinson's Support Group was born.

~ Now ~

As I gathered my notes and prepared to make a few announcements, I looked around and noticed him again, sitting in the farthest chair in the back of the assembly hall. This was the fourth time I had seen the thin man, and I was beginning to wonder who he was. Was he a Parkinson's patient? Was he a caregiver to a spouse who had the disease? Or maybe he was just an average senior citizen living nearby who was dropping in to see what was on the menu for tomorrow's lunch?

Every previous attempt I'd made to meet this man had been unsuccessful because he always left the hour-long meeting early. In addition, when I made my announcements at the start of the night, I always made it a point to remind the new people to write their address or email on a roster so that they can receive news about future meetings and upcoming events. For the last three months, however, there were no new entries on the list that would identify who this strange man might be.

Each time I noticed him, he was wearing the same attire: black slacks, white dress shirt, black tie and overcoat, black fedora hat and white sneakers. He appeared to be a little older than me, mid-to-late fifties, walked with a limp and used a cane. I suspected his limp was caused by him having Parkinson's disease, but I hadn't been able to get close enough to him to know for sure.

Two months ago I gave Madison the job of finding out who this man was and to persuade him to come up and introduce himself to the group. Since she is one of the most personable and friendly people I've ever known, I thought if anyone could make him feel welcome and get him talking, she could. Each time she approached him, however, he would suddenly leave the room. The first time, he quickly made his way down the long hallway toward the entrance door and ducked into the men's room. The next month, he hurriedly left the building altogether.

Since that happened, I concluded that this man must be extremely shy about coming to a support group, which I found to be the case with other Parkinson's sufferers, and decided to stop trying to initiate contact, hoping he would eventually feel comfortable enough to come forward on his own.

I had the most unsettling feeling that I'd seen this man before, but I couldn't place where or when. The more I searched my memory, the more I drew a blank on who he might be. I also began to suspect he'd been following me, but I just wasn't one-hundred percent sure. For example, last month I was selected as the 2014 honoree for the Pedal Away Parkinson's bike ride. We were about two miles into the course, winding through one of our town's older neighborhoods, when I thought I saw him standing in the shade of an oak tree. As we got closer, Madison said something which drew my attention away from the tree, and when I looked back he was gone.

A couple of weeks earlier, I experienced a similar situation while we were riding in a vehicle that was pulling the Pedal Away Parkinson's float in our town's Fourth of July parade. We were nearing the final turn of the parade route when I thought I saw him. Making the turn, however, I suddenly heard the familiar voices of our two grandkids shouting, and after a few brief moments of smiling and waving back to them, I turned back and found him gone.

Now here he was again, wearing the same attire and sitting in the same place as the previous three meetings: farthest away from Madison and me but closest to the exit door.

"Do you want me to go on another secret mission and see if I can find out who he is?" Madison asked.

I shook my head. "Hopefully, when he feels comfortable enough, he'll come up and talk to us."

Although I was displaying a calm demeanor in front of Madison, his continued appearances were starting to make me nervous.

An hour and thirty minutes later, after the last of the support group members had departed, Madison and I were finishing straightening up the assembly hall and gathering up the flyers and handouts I provide at the meetings. Except for Tiffany, the facility's caretaker who normally stays until we are gone, we were the only ones to my knowledge still in the building.

"I didn't see our mystery man leave," I said.

"Me neither," Madison replied. "I wonder what his story is and why he's so afraid of coming in and meeting everyone?"

"I don't know, but I'm not going to embarrass him. If he wants to be anti-social that's his business."

A few minutes later, after pulling our truck up to the entrance and loading everything, I felt the need to visit the restroom. While making my way back inside, I passed Tiffany.

"Did you forget something?" she asked.

"No, I just need to use the men's room."

"Okay, just make sure the door is closed and locked when you leave. I'm out of here."

"Will do, and thanks again for everything."

After going and washing up, I turned to the paper towel dispenser to wipe off my dripping hands and found myself suddenly face to face with the strange man! Normally I'm not that jumpy of a person, but his sudden and unexpected appearance scared me half to death. I hadn't heard the door open, nor had I heard him walk up to within three feet of me.

"I'm so sorry if I frightened you, Mr. d'Clare," he said, "that was not my intention."

"Oh, that's all right. Just give me a chance to catch my breath and change my underwear."

He laughed and extended his hand in friendship.

"My name is James Stevens, but you can call me Jim."

This was the first time I'd seen him this close, and I immediately noticed his eyes were a piercing color of blue, and his intense stare instantly commanded my attention. His face looked tired, but not from physical exhaustion or lack of sleep. Instead, his weary expression seemed to come from a profound worry or loss he carried with him, as if he'd been laden with the weight of the world on his shoulders for a very long time. Up close, he also appeared younger than I first thought, probably in his mid-forties to early fifties by my estimation.

The question of whether he had Parkinson's disease was immediately answered. His voice was soft, just above a whisper, and his left hand showed an unmistakable tremor. Another thing about his voice I found interesting was that he spoke in a very articulate and distinct manner, as if he wanted to convey his feelings or thoughts to me as clearly as possible. Although I had just met him and knew nothing of his background, I suspected he was a highly educated and intelligent man.

"Okay Jim," I replied, obliging him with the handshake, "nice to meet you."

"You're probably wondering why I chose this setting to formally introduce myself."

I smiled. "The thought had crossed my mind, especially since I don't usually meet new members of the support group late at night in the men's room of the senior center."

He laughed again. "As I said, it was not my intention to frighten you. My real purpose was to meet you alone and without interruption. You see, I'm a very private person, Mr. d'Clare, and I value my privacy as much as I do my money in the bank. That being said, I don't venture out of the house and into the public very often."

"Parkinson's can easily turn anyone into a recluse, especially if depression sets in."

"How true, but in my case I choose to be private due to my life's work, not because of the affliction we both share."

"And what is your life's work?"

"I'm a retired physics professor. I spend most of my time researching theories, working out equations, studying the interactions of energy and matter, things of that nature."

"Wow, that sounds pretty cool. Physics and math were my worst subjects in college, totally out of my element, but like anything else, if you get into it I bet it can be pretty interesting."

I knew in an instant that my assumption was correct, and that this man's knowledge and education level were well above mine.

"Don't let my chosen profession intimidate you, Mr. d'Clare," he said. "I'm sure that if I were to try to restore a 1949 Seeburg Select-o-matic 100A jukebox, I would be totally out of my element."

"You heard about my old jukebox? Who told you about that?" Now I was completely stunned.

"You'd be surprised what you hear in the back of the room during one of your support group meetings."

"I guess I would."

"I don't want to take up any more of your time, because by now your beautiful wife might be wondering if you're sick or incapacitated. But I did want to meet you and introduce myself, and as a token of my goodwill give you this little donation for the support group."

He handed me a fresh, crisp one-hundred-dollar bill.

"By the way, you certainly have done a wonderful thing here by starting this group and giving hope to others who share our affliction. Good night, Mr. d'Clare. I'll be in touch."

He turned and immediately exited the men's room.

"Oh, good night Jim and thank you," I stuttered, "thank you very, very much."

I stood there for a moment staring at the large bill before stuffing it in my pocket and proceeding back to our truck. When I climbed in, Madison asked me what took so long, jokingly wondering if the restroom was now unsafe for human habitation.

I smiled. "No, I got held up. Did you see him?"

"See who?"

"Our mystery man. He came into the restroom and scared the living you-know-what out of me. He left just before I did, so I thought you might've seen him come out the door."

"Really? I didn't see anyone come out but you, and I've been sitting here the whole time."

We both looked over the parking lot, then back to the front doors of the building.

"Did he say anything?"

"Yes, he said his name is Jim Stevens and that he's a retired physics professor. And just as I thought, he's got Parkinson's. He also praised us for starting the support group and then he gave me this."

I reached into my pocket and pulled out the one-hundred-dollar bill.

"He said it was a token of his goodwill."

"Oh my goodness. Did he say anything else?"

"Yes, he said a lot of things. He even knew about our old jukebox."

"He what?"

I relayed to her the main points of the conversation.

"That is really weird."

"No kidding. And I got the feeling that he knew even more about us than he let on."

She laughed. "Maybe if you hang out in the men's room more often we could raise enough money to afford that vacation I've been wanting to go on."

"No thank you," I said, trying to keep a straight face. "My heart couldn't take more scares like that one."

We both laughed as I pulled out of the parking lot.

As I drove home, I couldn't stop thinking about the strange restroom encounter with Mr. Stevens. How could he have known about our old jukebox? I didn't buy his story about overhearing it at one of the support group meetings. On the few occasions that I'd mentioned it to group members, I never used the term, "100A," nor had I called it "Select-o-matic."

I also wondered why he was so standoffish at the previous meetings, seemingly not wanting to engage with us or the group at all. He even went out of his way *not* to meet us, and ran away when Madison tried to get close to him. This entire episode left me with more questions than answers, and I wondered what other surprises were in store for us the next time we crossed paths with him.

* * *

THE DEVICE

I was unaware at the time that this strange man who called himself James Stevens carried with him an incredible secret. A secret that would not only cause Madison and I to question all we knew about science, physics and the known laws of the universe, but also offer me the unfathomable opportunity to find the cure for Parkinson's disease.

Chapter Two
The Luncheon

Ten Days Later
Saturday, 16 August 2014, 12:30hrs
Northbound along *Highway Eighty-Nine, East Layton, Utah*

A current of warm summer air blew a wave into the long and brittle wild grass along the side of the road, making it appear as if an invisible curtain was opening and allowing us to pass. Normally different shades of vibrant green, the trees and other shrubbery that adorned the Wasatch mountains were brownish-gray in color; a drab reminder of the abnormally-low amount of precipitation in northern Utah this year. With its flora either dead or starving for moisture, the mountains now resembled giant foreboding monoliths, unwelcoming those who happened to venture up into their austere regions.

As Madison and I traveled along the mountain highway, I secretly hoped that the bleak look of the landscape was not a foreboding omen of things to come.

~ Then ~

Three days ago we received an unusual invitation from Jim Stevens, delivered to our doorstep (oddly enough) by a local courier service. After producing two forms of photo identification and signing the receiving documents in three places, the carrier released a standard paper-sized manila envelope into my custody. Not knowing what the envelope contained or who might have sent it with such high security measures, I hastily grabbed a pair of scissors, trimmed off one end and removed a simple three-by-five index card.

On one side of the card was the address 211 Orchard Drive, Mountain Green, Utah, while the other side contained a short note to Madison and me. Both sides of the card had been handwritten, with the most perfect penmanship I'd ever seen. So perfect, I wondered if whoever wrote it had a doctorate degree in calligraphy. The note read:

> Dear Mr. & Mrs. d'Clare,
> I would very much like the pleasure of your company for lunch this Saturday afternoon, August the sixteenth, at 1:00pm at my residence.
> Very respectfully yours,
>
> Jim Stevens

"First the strange sightings and evasive getaways, then the restroom introduction and now lunch? That is weird." I said.

"No kidding," Madison replied, "and he invites us to his residence? Who calls their house a residence?"

I smiled. "Apparently he does. So what do you think? Do you want to go?"

"I don't have anything planned for Saturday, and besides, he didn't leave a number to call if we *couldn't* make it."

"Even though we don't really know him or what he might be up to?"

Madison nodded. "My intuition is telling me that he's harmless and means well."

"I get that, but there's something about him I can't quite put my finger on." I paused, trying to think of the right description for my feelings, but the words escaped me.

"He's probably just a lonely man with Parkinson's disease who wants to talk about his life."

"Maybe so," I replied, "but if he's another crooked real estate salesman who wants to sell us an opportunity that only comes around once in a lifetime..."

We both laughed, remembering when a friend of ours duped us into a free lunch, and we spent the afternoon listening to time-share advertisements.

~ Now ~

As we neared the Mountain Green exit, Madison and I played a guessing game as to what Mr. Stevens did for a living.

"What if he's a secret Russian agent sent here to spy on Parkinson's support group organizers?" Madison asked.

I laughed. "No, I think he looks more like a mortician who forgot his dress shoes. Wait, that's it! He's here to measure me for a casket!"

We both cracked up.

"Seriously, could he be a long lost d'Clare relative who wants to include us in his will?"

"No, he couldn't be from my side. The d'Clare family tree ended when my mom married my dad and they had me. Neither one had any brothers or sisters, nor any other relatives that I can remember."

"Could he have known or worked with your dad?"

"I really don't know. If dad knew him or worked with him, he never mentioned him to me."

"And he said he was a scientist?"

"No, a retired physics professor who spends most of his time on his life's work, studying the interactions of energy and matter."

"Wow, physics," she exclaimed. "I never had to take it in college."

"I did, and I never fully understood it. I think the only reason I got a passing grade is because the professor invoked the mercy rule on me."

"Well, I hope Mr. Stevens invokes the mercy rule on us if he sees that we don't understand what the heck he's talking about."

"Amen to that. I would hate to have to go through a remedial physics course, especially on such a hot Saturday afternoon."

A short time later, we arrived at the "residence" of Jim Stevens. When we received the invitation I had visions in my head of an old medieval castle, unkempt and overgrown with untrimmed trees, weeds and other encroaching vegetation. To my surprise the house was a new, eye-catching L-shaped rambler, and quite a bit larger than the others in the subdivision. In addition, I thought that the house was too big for Mr. Stevens to take care of by himself, assuming he lived alone.

We were met at the door by a middle-aged man and woman, who we took to be his personal servants. Each one wore the same attire, consisting of white short-sleeved polo shirts, black slacks and black dress shoes. The man spoke to us first.

"Good afternoon, Mr. d'Clare. I'm Roy and this is my wife Shelley."

I shook his hand. "Pleased to meet you, Roy. This is my wife Madison."

After exchanging more handshakes, they showed us in.

"Mr. Stevens will be with you shortly," Shelley said. "In the meantime, if you would please follow us into the dining room you can get started with lunch."

As they led us down a long hallway toward the rear of the house, I couldn't help but notice the bare rooms. There weren't any paintings or pictures on any of the walls, nor was there any furniture in the rooms we passed. It looked as if Mr. Stevens had just moved in, or was in the process of moving out.

When we reached the dining room we were astonished by the food that had been prepared. Arranged buffet-style, there were two different salads, two main dishes, and two desserts to choose from down each side of the room. On one side were Madison's favorites, consisting of tossed green salad, raisin and carrot salad, prime rib with horseradish sauce, chicken enchiladas with salsa, chocolate brownies and licorice-flavored ice cream. On the other side were my favorites, including Caesar salad, tapioca pudding with mandarin oranges, filet mignon with sautéed mushrooms, lobster tail with butter, strawberry cheesecake and chocolate ice cream.

After loading our plates with as much food as we could safely carry, we sat down at the formal-looking dining table and awaited the arrival of Mr. Stevens. We didn't want to start eating without him, but after some prodding from Roy and Shelley, we dug in. This amazing meal was nothing short of fantastic and I silently wondered how much money it must've cost our generous host.

Surveying the room as we ate, I noticed that the walls on the dining room were also bare of any pictures or paintings. The furniture comprised of two long tables on the sides, which contained the food, the dining room table where we sat, one extra chair across from us and one large sofa and an end table against the far wall. On top of the end table were three framed photographs, two of which were very small, while the other was about the size of a standard piece of paper. One of the smaller photos appeared to be a snapshot of a very old office. Although extremely faded, I could make out a desk and a chair, and a piece of machinery that resembled an old radio sitting on top of the desk. The second small photograph, oddly enough, looked like debris you'd see after a building was hit by a wrecking ball. The third and largest photograph was a group of ten soldiers wearing uniforms from the World War II era. As with the two smaller photos, it too was extremely faded around the edges.

After about five minutes, Mr. Stevens came in, walking in slowly with his cane and seating himself directly across from us at the table.

"Mr. and Mrs. d'Clare, I am so glad you could join me for lunch. And what a pleasure it is to meet you, Mrs. d'Clare. My name is James Stevens, but you can call me Jim."

He held out his hand in friendship.

"You can call me Madison," she replied, shaking his hand.

"And you can call me George," I said. "No need to be formal now."

He smiled. "Madison and George it is then. Do you like the food?"

"This is absolutely incredible. Our favorite meals right down to the dessert."

"I know. I spared no expense in wanting you to both feel welcome and comfortable in my home."

"Have you recently moved in?" Madison asked.

He shook his head. "This house is only temporary. I plan on moving out soon. I've secured a modest little room up at the university which will afford me the opportunity to live closer to my work."

"Weber State or Utah?"

"The University of Utah. Since I am a former professor, they've agreed to loan me one of their older, unused buildings for my research."

I decided to forgo any further chit-chat.

"So Jim, I was wondering, how is it that you know us so well that you had our favorite meals prepared? To the best of my knowledge, before seeing you at the support group meetings, we've never met."

He locked his penetrating blue eyes on me.

"Not formally George, but I've been keeping track of you both for some time now, ever since I found your contact information on the Parkinson's website."

"You've been keeping track of us? What for?"

"Bear with me. I don't mean to alarm you, but my explanation is a bit complicated. As I told you the other night, I'm a retired physics professor and spend most of my time studying the interactions of energy and matter. I also conduct a lot of research, and am currently looking for volunteers to help me with a research project. That's why I invited you here today, to see if you both would be interested in joining my team."

"So that's what this is all about? Research? Why didn't you say so in the first place? I've participated in quite a few Parkinson's research projects."

"Not to be rude," Madison said, interrupting, "but this all seems very weird to me. If you wanted George for a research project, why didn't you just ask? Why all this sneaking around? And why have you been keeping track of us?"

He broke his intense eyes away from me and locked them onto Madison.

"I don't think you are being rude at all, Madison. You certainly have a right to know."

He didn't seem offended in any way with her directness.

"To answer your questions, there are three reasons why I've been keeping track of you. First, I had to make sure that you both were honest, and after attending a couple of the meetings and seeing how much work you put into it, I determined you were sincere in your actions. Second, I had to make sure that George was physically able to participate in the research. Or to be more specific, I had to make sure that you, George, were still in the early-onset stage of the disease. And I must say, for a man of fifty-four you look to be in excellent physical shape."

"Thanks. I try to stay fit."

"Okay, what's the third reason?" Madison asked, bringing the conversation back on track.

"The research I am conducting is highly-sensitive, which means I must take great precautions and incorporate extreme security measures. Since both of you are former members of our nation's military and have held top-secret clearances, I believe you can appreciate that."

I looked at Madison, and could tell from her wide eyes that she was thinking the same thing I was: this guy has done his homework.

"I had to make sure that I could completely trust both of you," he continued, "and I believe that I can now."

As he spoke, his penetrating blue eyes moved back and forth between us.

"Is your research that sensitive?" I asked. "You're not killing animals or anything like that are you?"

He laughed. "Good heavens no, George. The research I am conducting is not so medieval, but for right now, let's just say it requires the utmost secrecy and security."

"So what exactly are you doing?"

"Before I answer that question, I first want to tell you more about myself so that you can decide whether you want to join my team. It shouldn't take very long."

I nodded to Madison and received an approving nod back.

"Sure. We've got nothing going on, but we would like to get back by six o'clock. Our grandson is playing in a soccer game and we don't want to miss it."

He smiled. "I'm sure we will conclude in plenty of time so that you won't miss a single minute. But before I begin, please help yourself to more food, and don't forget the desserts that Roy and Shelley prepared."

After filling two new plates, he implored us, "Oh please, come sit over here on the sofa. After a while those old dining room chairs get uncomfortable."

As we moved over to the sofa, Jim stood up and had Roy reposition his chair directly in front of where we were sitting. He then told Roy and Shelley that they could leave, but to be back by five-thirty to help him clean up. A few moments later, we heard a door close in the kitchen and a car drive off.

During this time, Jim obtained a dessert plate for himself and filled it with a brownie and a scoop of chocolate ice cream. As he shuffled over to sit down, I set my dessert plate on my lap and picked up the largest photograph on the end table.

"I see you've found my dad's old pictures," he said, "I haven't had a chance to pack them for the move."

"Which one is your dad?" Madison asked. "Or can I guess?"

He smiled. "Please guess."

"I can't really see the faces of the men on each side, because it's too faded," she said, pointing to the left and right edges, "but assuming you look like your father, I don't think he is any of the guys in the middle."

"That gives you a fifty-fifty chance," I said.

"I'm going to say he's the man on the left."

"Correct, Madison. He's the only officer in the picture."

I looked again at the photo, and except for his father, each of the other men wore enlisted stripes on their sleeves. The edge was so faded however, I couldn't tell his dad's rank.

"Was he a lieutenant or a captain?" I asked.

"When that picture was taken, he was a captain, Captain Henry Stevens. For a short time, he was the commanding officer of these men."

"Was this taken in World War II?"

"Correct, George. My dad is the central character of the story I am about to tell you. It is because of him I studied physics, became a college professor, and why both of you are here with me today."

Now intrigued, I sat back in the sofa and got comfortable, with Madison doing the same. Although part of the mystery had been solved when he told us he was conducting research, something about his soft and articulate voice told me he had only scratched the surface.

"For most of the war," he began, "my dad was assigned to the intelligence arm of the U.S. Army known as G-2. He possessed a unique gift which proved to be invaluable to them: a photographic memory. He didn't always have this ability. At Ogden High School, he was just an average student who could barely pass a geometry exam."

"So your father grew up in Ogden?" Madison asked.

"Oh yes, forgive me. His family lived directly across the street from the high school on Harrison Boulevard. As I said, he was an average teenager who earned average grades in school. The only thing remarkable about him was his ability to throw a baseball, and while attending Ogden High he developed into a very good pitcher. Then just before graduating, he was practicing with a few of his teammates and was struck in the head by a line drive. The accident left him unconscious for two days, but miraculously, and in a very short time, he fully recovered."

He paused to take a drink of water, and continued.

"From all outward indications, it appeared as if he'd recovered from the accident unscathed, but things had changed quite a bit for my dad; things that would forever alter the course of his life. For lack of a better way to describe it, a doorway inside his brain had opened, and he now had the ability to learn and remember things very quickly."

"What did the doctors say about it?" I asked.

"They were completely baffled. Oh, they ran several blood tests on him and even had him perform some motor skills tests, like the ones they do now with Parkinson's patients, but since this was the late nineteen thirties, medical advances such as MRIs and CT scans did not yet exist."

"So what happened next?" Madison asked. "I assume since he was an officer he went to college?"

"Oh yes. He enrolled in Weber State that fall after the accident, and his abilities blossomed. He soon found that, given time to briefly review a chapter out of a textbook, he could recite the entire chapter back verbatim without missing a single word. Not only had his ability to recall or remember things improved, but also his cognitive reasoning and his ability to understand what he was reading. His problem-solving ability also advanced far above what it was before the accident. Even his hearing and eyesight improved significantly."

"Did he remember things for very long, or was it only temporary?" I asked.

"His abilities were sustaining, meaning that years later he could still recall the same chapter or detail with precise clarity. In other words, he maintained *total recall*."

"Wow," Madison exclaimed. "I've heard of people having photographic memories before, but not to that extent."

"Neither had my dad and he researched the subject quite extensively."

I smiled. "I can just imagine how that helped him in college."

"Indeed it did, George. In the spring of 1941, he graduated in mathematics with a stellar 4.0 grade point average. Since Weber was just a junior college back then and dad wanted to further his education, he enrolled in a master's program at the University of Utah. Then in December, just before completing the first semester, our country was attacked by the Japanese and the war broke out. Like many other patriotic young men at the time, he joined the Army, and since he had a bachelor's degree he received a commission and became an officer.

"Once he was in the Army, his gift was immediately noticed by his superiors and he was sent to Fort Ritchie in Maryland. Once there, the psychologists gave him a rudimentary eidetic memory test, which was the official name for it. The results are still classified, but suffice to say he did extremely well on that test. So much so, he was sent to Fort Richie's intelligence and linguistics schools, where he learned to speak and read German and Russian, as well as the tried and true methods of interrogation and interpreting enemy information.

"To tell you how advanced his learning abilities had improved, just one of these linguistics courses normally took the average person six months to learn the basics of the dialect, and hold one's own in carrying on a conversation. My dad learned to read and write *both* languages in less than three months."

He stopped for a moment and took another drink.

"It really was remarkable, him going from an average teenager in high school to an A-student in college, then to graduating at the top of his class in officer training as well as two Army intelligence schools.

"He also met a black man by the name of Benjamin Washington, who became his lifelong friend. You see, there was a shortage of lodging at the time and dad volunteered to share his room with him, which was the first time the Army school allowed integrated housing. Big Ben, as dad called him, was a very large mountain of a man from the small southern town of Troy, Alabama, while dad was an average-sized run-of-the-mill guy from the northern state of Utah. Although they couldn't have been raised more differently, neither of them smoked nor did they drink anything harder than Grapette soda, which was very different from the lifestyles of the other men attending the school. That difference brought them together, and as I said, they formed a lifelong friendship. Big Ben even tagged my dad with his nickname Hank."

Madison and I smiled, encouraging him to elaborate.

"By sheer coincidence, Ben's father's first name was Henry, whose nickname was Hank. Then one day, while practicing hand-to-hand combat at the school, Big Ben accidentally hit dad a little too hard with a baton and knocked him out cold. While trying to revive him, he happened to call him Hank and the moniker stuck. From that day forward he was known as Lieutenant Hank, then later as Captain Hank.

"As for Big Ben, he was also a very sharp college graduate who joined the Army, received a commission and got sent to Fort Richie. But things were very different for him because of racial bigotry that was alive and well in the military back then. Although he graduated from the school second only to my dad, he was never given any overseas assignment and spent the entire war working in a warehouse at Fort Meade."

"That's terrible but not surprising," I said. "After all, look what happened to the Tuskegee Airmen. As much as they contributed to the war they were still discriminated against."

"True," he said solemnly, "the Army could have used Ben's talents in so many ways. Although he became very bitter, he stayed in long enough to retire as a major."

He paused and took another drink.

"My dad ended up calling on Big Ben several times to help him with a few things."

"Backing up for a second, you said the Army sent your dad to two schools. What was the second?"

"Camp Savage in Minnesota, where he learned to speak and write the Japanese language. By September of 1942, he was proficient in the languages of two of our enemies, Germany and Japan, one not-so-friendly ally, the Russians, and knew the intelligence game as well as anyone in the armed forces at that time. And he hadn't yet gone out into the field."

"I bet he was in high demand from the Army brass," Madison said.

He smiled. "That would be an understatement, because by this time everyone had heard of Hank Stevens, the lieutenant with the photographic memory."

"Where did the Army end up sending him?"

"He was first assigned to the Office of Strategic Services, or OSS, where he worked on a wide array of projects. Then in 1943 he deployed to Istanbul, Turkey. You see, Turkey was a neutral country in World War II, and as such, both the allies and the Nazi's carried out a great number of, how shall I say, *covert* intelligence operations there."

"So they were spying on each other." I said.

"Correct, George. My dad helped organize and train Nazi resistance groups in a project called Net-1. He also collected and memorized all kinds of intelligence and reported his findings to his superiors. For a while, the information Net-1 gathered was instrumental in helping the allies support the underground, but in late May of 1944, the entire Istanbul operation was cancelled."

"How come?" Madison asked.

"My dad discovered that a Nazi double-agent had infiltrated the information network and was feeding the OSS false information. Some of the resistance fighters in the underground ended up being captured and shot by the Gestapo. In any event, the Net-1 operation was considered too dangerous and was discontinued."

"So where'd he go next?"

"This is where things got really interesting," he said, leaning in. "After hearing about my dad's incredible gift, and that he'd discovered the Nazi double-agent in Turkey, a general by the name of Leslie Groves pushed the OSS to have him transferred to an intelligence team he'd put together that previous fall. General Groves was the director of the Manhattan Project. Perhaps you've heard of it?"

"I have," I said. "It was the secret project to develop the atomic bomb."

"Correct again, George, but General Groves didn't recruit my dad to work on the Manhattan Project, per se. Instead, he wanted him for a mission that fell under the umbrella of the Manhattan Project. The code name for the mission was Alsos."

"Alsos? Why that name?" Madison asked.

"Alsos is the Greek word for grove, so in a round-about way they named the mission after General Groves."

Madison and I both let out a long "Oh" as the meaning came to light.

"The Alsos Mission was created to investigate the German's nuclear projects and other secret Nazi weapon development programs. In July of 1944, my dad received orders to report to Colonel Boris Pash in Rome, who was the field commander of the Alsos mission. For the remainder of 1944 and much of 1945, he worked for Colonel Pash, accompanying him all over Italy, England, France, and finally into Germany. Much of the work involved translating documents, interrogating captured German scientists, and reporting his findings to either Colonel Pash or to a civilian scientist named Samuel Goudsmit."

"They had civilian guys on this mission?" I asked.

He nodded. "Of the two groups assigned, one was entirely made up of civilian scientists who wore military uniforms but no rank. In any event, by this time dad had been promoted to the rank of captain and had developed quite a reputation with the men."

"Because of his photographic memory?" Madison asked.

"Exactly. You see, dad was quite a personable fellow with a great sense of humor. During long and uneventful downtimes, his team members playfully tried to stump him on just about anything you can think of. And of course, like crap games that were popular with GIs at the time, wagers and bets ensued. For example, one time they asked him to come into their tent, survey the scene, leave, and then come back five minutes later and tell them what was different. After returning, my dad noticed twenty-seven things that were changed in the tent, even down to an eraser on the end of a pencil that one of the men had pulled out and put in his pocket. Needless to say, those who bet against him lost quite a bit of their paychecks.

"But I apologize. I'm straying from the main story. It was now late April of 1945. As the allied armies swept deeper into Germany, the Alsos mission team, following closely behind the front-line combat units, gathered and studied the captured Nazi intelligence. As for Germany's nuclear program, you wouldn't believe the things they found. For example, in a small town called

Celle, which was about seventy-five miles south of Hamburg, they found an experimental centrifuge."

"Excuse me," I interrupted, "what's a centrifuge?"

"A centrifuge is a machine that spins things. The large centrifuge that the team found was being used to separate uranium isotopes. In layman's terms, it was part of their experiments to try to develop a nuclear weapon."

"The Nazis were *that* close to building an atomic bomb?" Madison asked.

"Official reports that were later released to the public made light of the team's findings, but according to my dad they were *very* close. So much so, when the team received information that they were within reach of Werner Heisenberg's laboratory, Colonel Pash created a special covert task force to go behind enemy lines and capture it."

"Werner who?" Madison asked, beating me to the question.

"Werner Heisenberg. He was one of Germany's brilliant theoretical physicists, a Nobel Prize winner whom the allies suspected was working on building a bomb."

"I take it they were successful?"

"Yes, and on April twenty-third, Task Force A, as it was called, located the laboratory in a town called Haigerloch. Inside, they found a couple of rudimentary, cylinder-shaped nuclear reactors."

"That's scary to think the Nazi's were *that* close to making the bomb," Madison said.

"Indeed. They also had to keep this information out of the hands of the Russians."

"Did the team find anything else?"

"In the town of Tailfingen they interrogated a small group of captured German scientists, one of whom was dying from an infected gunshot wound. As the medics were trying to save him, dad tried to keep him talking, hoping he wouldn't lose consciousness and die. From this scientist, he uncovered a thread of information about one of the Nazi's other top-secret weapon programs called *Unternehmen Zunden Vogel*, or translated, Operation Firebird.

"After the scientist passed away, dad reported it to Colonel Pash, but because most of the information was obtained while the dying man was delirious, the colonel dismissed it as unreliable. Then a few days later, the team discovered a container in a sewage drain. Inside, they found Nazi documents pertaining to their nuclear program, as well as another small file with information on Operation Firebird; information that more or less corroborated the dead scientist's story."

"So where did that lead them?" Madison asked.

"Well, they couldn't immediately act on this intelligence because the war hadn't ended. Remember, except for the Task Force A incursion behind enemy lines to capture Werner Heisenberg's laboratory, the Alsos team was still following the advancing allied armies. Then on the thirtieth of April, Hitler killed himself in his bunker, and two days later the last of the German forces defending Berlin surrendered. Hearing the news that the Russians had taken Berlin, my dad and a small reconnaissance team, this time designated Task Force B, were airborne and on their way to investigate the secret Nazi weapon program known only as Operation Firebird."

"On the way to where?" Madison and I asked, in unison.

"Coincidentally, to the very place where Hitler committed suicide: his bunker in the heart of Berlin."

He took another drink and leaned in, his penetrating blue eyes alternating between us again.

"What my dad and his team discovered in that horrible place is why I invited you here today, and why I asked both of you to join me in my research."

THE DEVICE

Chapter Three
The Story (Part 1)

Sixty-Nine Years, Three Months and Seven Days Earlier
Thursday, 10 May 1945, 02:00hrs
Alsos **Mission – Task Force B Reconnaissance Team**
Inside the *Ünterbunker, Berlin*

The old oil lamps the men had found for make-shift lights flickered, and cast ghost-like shadows off the polished-steel walls in the secret lower level of Hitler's underground headquarters. Adding to the creepy atmosphere, was the low static sound from the receiver-transmitter on the desk in the central room, and the putrid odor of the decaying corpses at the bottom of the access shaft. It was as if the sounds and smells, in their own way, were emanating a warning to those who dared venture into this ominous place. Still, in the middle of this frightening and gruesome setting, taking a long drink of water from his Army-issued canteen, was Captain Henry "Hank" Stevens.

He'd been examining the mostly-charred German documents for the better part of an hour, and with each piece of paper he translated and put to memory, he'd become more enthralled with the information. What he had deciphered so far, from just a small sampling of the stacks of Nazi paperwork, was so captivating that he hadn't noticed how much time had passed. He was in the frame of mind which caused him to literally ignore anything and everything around him, and focus his entire attention on setting to memory what he was reading.

Thinking back to the trail of intelligence that had brought him and his team here, he silently wondered whether the dying German scientist's story was a delirious rant after all.

~ *Then* ~

Captain Hank and his covert team had entered Berlin one week ago, and joined in the revelry with the Russian soldiers encamped in the city; the same soldiers that were responsible for toppling the last remaining Nazi troops defending the German capitol. The captain and his nine men were not in Berlin to celebrate, but instead were on a highly-classified intelligence-gathering mission, hoping to gain access into the now-infamous Führerbunker, where Adolph Hitler had lived out his last one-hundred and five days before committing suicide.

In preparation for this assignment, Hank reviewed several documents and intelligence reports to become familiar with the entire bunker complex. He learned that in 1936, the old Reich Chancellery was renovated and an underground level added, which was then used as an air raid shelter. The German's called this level the *Vorbunker*, or forward bunker. In 1943, Hitler ordered a lower level to be added to the shelter, and upon completion it was named the *Führerbunker*, or leader's bunker. At the same time, and known only by a select few of the Nazi high command, Hitler ordered Albert Speer to construct an even deeper level to the complex, known as the *Ünterbunker,* or under bunker. In the event Berlin came under attack, and the *Vorbunker* and *Führerbunker* became compromised, this lower level was to be used as a secret retreat point for Hitler and his most-trusted officers.

This last bit of information came to Captain Hank from a dying German scientist the team had captured at Tailfingen. Before he died, while his mind drifted in and out of consciousness, he'd talked of the top-secret lower level in the bunker and how it now contained a laboratory where the Nazis conducted undisclosed weapons testing. This secret weapon system, he said, was based on papers that contained complex mathematical formulas and theories; documents that the Nazi's had stolen from world-renowned physicists and scientists, such as Albert Einstein and Niels Bohr. Other information, including wild and fragmented stories just too impossible to be believed, were subsequently dismissed and attributed to the man's delirium.

With his final breath, the scientist's last coherent words gained the undivided attention of Captain Hank, who was helping the medics that were trying to save his life. Gasping for air, the scientist left this world with a warning: *"Find Operation Firebird in the Ünterbunker's laboratory. Destroy Hitler's final plan, or the White Wolf will destroy us all!"*

After receiving Hank's report and hastily reviewing another file pertaining to Operation Firebird his men had recovered in a cesspool in Haigerloch, Colonel Boris Pash, the Alsos Mission's field commander, called a meeting at their Forward North Headquarters in Aachen, Germany, and assigned men to a newly-designated "Task Force B" reconnaissance team. Since the target area was under Russian control and the window of opportunity extremely short, Colonel Pash chose Captain Hank, with his incredibly fast memorization ability, to command the team. He also handpicked the other nine enlisted members based on their experience working on the previous "Task Force A" operation.

The colonel wanted to command the "B" team himself, but earlier that morning he'd received word that the brilliant German scientist, Werner Heisenberg, was spotted in Urfeld, a small town only fifty miles away. Since capturing Heisenberg was a top priority, the colonel, accompanied by six civilian members of the Alsos Mission and soldiers from the 36th Infantry Division, headed out toward Urfeld the morning of May the second.

Just before he'd left, Colonel Pash's orders to Captain Hank were simple.

"If Berlin falls while I'm gone, you and your team have the green light to go in. Major Fisher has already set up your airlift to the drop zone. Maybe with all the confusion and celebrating going on in the city, you'll be able to get in, conduct your investigation, and get out without too many Russians noticing what you're doing."

Hank nodded.

"You know the drill. Bring back anything of intelligence value you can get your hands on, but if the Russians get close or it gets too dangerous, just blow it up or set fire to it and get out of there."

"Yes, sir."

"I wish there were another senior officer available to go with you, myself included, but right now we're spread pretty thin."

"I understand, sir."

"You know," the colonel said quietly, "I don't have your ability to put everything to memory. In fact, sometimes I'd forget my head if it wasn't screwed on. What I'm trying to say is, I didn't get a chance to read the entire Firebird file so I'm going on what you've told me. If there is something down in that bunker, I know you'll make the right decision. Good luck, Hank."

"Good luck to you too, sir."

Although Hank smiled at his commanding officer using his nickname for the first time, he was nervous about the safety of the nine men now under his command. There was no telling how the Russians would react to them being in the eastern part of the city, or what they might find down in Hitler's underground headquarters.

Thirty minutes after Colonel Pash and his contingent had departed Aachen in pursuit of Werner Heisenberg, the team received word that the Russian Army had circled Berlin; the fall of Nazi Germany was imminent. Hearing the news, the men loaded their equipment on a deuce-and-a-half truck and headed for the makeshift airstrip that was set up in a farmer's field just outside the town. Then in the early morning of May the third, merely a few short hours after they received another message that the Battle for Berlin was over, Captain Hank and the Task Force B reconnaissance team parachuted into the outskirts of the city.

Looking like grizzled veterans exhausted from the fighting, but acting more like American tourists on a sight-seeing trip, they slowly made their way into the center of Berlin and set up camp in a building across the street from the Reich Chancellery. Since the captain and three of his team members spoke fluent Russian, the language barrier was eliminated, which allowed them to gain the trust of the occupying Russian soldiers. It also helped that they had a seemingly endless supply of American cigarettes and whiskey, which the Russians took as both bribes and signs of friendship.

On a few occasions, higher ranking Russian officers asked what they were doing in the eastern (Russian-held) district of the city. In an elaborate lie, Captain Hank explained that since December, when his unit participated in the Battle of the Bulge, his men had been involved in non-stop fighting all the way into Germany. The nine men under his command were all that remained of a company that once had over one-hundred-and-fifty soldiers. He'd promised them as soon as they made it to Berlin and the Germans surrendered (whichever happened first) he would grant them two full weeks of rest and relaxation, so they intended to hide out in the eastern district with their new Red Army friends as long as possible. He enforced the cover story by telling fantastic tales of bravery his men had showed in battle, and cemented the lies with the free whiskey and cigarettes. So far, the Russians had bought it all; hook, line and sinker.

After four days of drinking, yelling, and participating in other revelry with the Russian troops, the team gained access to the old Reich Chancellery palace and the newer, more-modern Reich Chancellery building. At one time, these two huge structures were the location of Nazi Germany's central government, but now (after sustaining heavy damage from the allied bombs and Russian mortar shells that had dropped on them a week ago) each of the buildings stood mostly vacant. As the team members walked around inside the two buildings, looking amazed at the architecture and what was left of the furnishings, they became familiar with the interior design as well as the many possible hiding places and exit routes they could use later.

By Monday, May the seventh, the men had completely scoured the remains of the Chancellery buildings and located the entrance to the underground bunker. Surprisingly, they found the entry guarded by only two young Russian troops. Captain Hank then ordered Sergeant Phillips, the ranking noncommissioned officer on the team, to send a coded radio transmission to the Alsos headquarters, informing them that they were in place and to send in the deuce-and-a-half; a large cargo truck equipped with a special false bottom under the bed for captured intelligence. This vehicle would serve as the team's mode of transportation out of the city.

The morning after Phillips sent the message, the truck arrived at their location. Manning the truck were two Alsos mission team members, who had been commanded by their superiors to act *extremely put out* for having to come to Berlin to pick up their "vacationing" Army buddies – a show the Russians were sure not to miss. Again, the two men used bribes of American cigarettes and whiskey to gain access past several of the Russian checkpoints.

The incursion into the bunker was originally planned for later that evening, but Captain Hank received word that the Russians were going to pronounce Wednesday "Victory Day," and delayed the next step of the mission twenty-four hours. He thought this announcement would result in more revelry, and that his team would have the best chance of secretly breaching the bunker the night of the celebration.

On Thursday, May the tenth, a few minutes before one o'clock in the morning (and after promising the young Russian guards they would share any souvenirs they found) the captain and his men entered Hitler's underground bunker.

Following a quick search of the Vorbunker, which produced nothing, they immediately descended the connecting stairway. A few moments later, after passing through a hall and two reinforced steel doors, they arrived in the main corridor of the Führerbunker.

The first thing the men noticed was how bad the place smelled. Captain Hank, seeing a few of his men getting nauseous from the overpowering stench, ordered everyone to cover their mouths and noses with handkerchiefs. With everyone's faces covered, the team now resembled cowboys out of the old west conducting a bank robbery.

There were seventeen rooms in the Führerbunker, and the men turned each one of them upside down as they looked for a door or entryway that might lead down to a lower level. The only interesting passage they found was an emergency exit at the far end of the conference room, which contained a vertical shaft leading up to the garden of the Chancellery. As far as finding an entry to a lower level, the team came up empty. Just as Captain Hank was ready to call off the search and get his men out, however, Sergeant Atkins, the explosives expert on the team, reported finding something.

The last door on the left side of the main conference room, farthest from where they had entered, opened into a cloak room. On the far wall was another door that opened into a ventilation room. This second door, made of metal, was hard to open due to warps in its three hinges. The room was roughly ten feet square, and the inside was in complete shambles; rocks, plaster and other debris covered the floor. The rear wall, at one time finished, was now open to the bare rock. There was also a rather large safe buried in the debris, its door open and its contents empty.

When the team first searched this room, it looked as if the damage was caused by the allied bombing campaign; concussions from the impacts above ground resulting in this collateral damage below. Sergeant Atkins, however, had found the real cause.

"No doubt about it, sir," Atkins said, "someone deliberately set a bomb off in here. I found some wires and a detonator thrown into a garbage can out there." He pointed his flashlight out towards the main conference room. "From the looks of the damage, it was a pretty big explosive."

Hank and several of the other men shined their flashlights around the wreckage.

"It looks like the bomb was placed directly in the center of the room," Atkins continued. "If you look at the marks from the explosion on the left wall," he pointed his flashlight towards the discoloration, "and on the right," he moved the flashlight's beam over to the other side, "we can trace them down to their point of origin, which is right here."

"Anything else?" Hank asked.

"Just this." He pulled the remains of a chain hoist out of the debris and shined his flashlight on a wooden beam that was overhead. "It looks like it was mounted to those eyelets."

"Let's get these rocks cleared out of here," Hank ordered.

After moving out much of the stones and other debris, they uncovered a sharply-cut five-foot square opening in the center of the floor, and a few other large metal pieces. These pieces appeared to be what was left of a hatch that had once covered the access point. As the team crowded around and shined their flashlights down into the opening, Captain Hank knelt to take a closer look; studying each crack between the stones that blocked the way.

"I see a hand rail and a ladder rung, and if we can get some more of these rocks out of here we'll be able to get in."

After moving most of the rubble out into the cloak room, the men managed to clear away enough of a gap to gain passage over to the ladder. Sergeant Phillips, the smallest man on the team, volunteered to squeeze through the opening and go down first.

As soon as Phillips reached the bottom, cuss words filled the space.

"What is it?" Hank yelled, trying not to laugh at the sergeant's inventive expletives.

"Oh…" Phillips began, and he was suddenly overcome with coughing, hacking and what sounded like vomiting.

Serious now, Captain Hank entered the opening, and upon reaching the ladder shined his flashlight down. Just below him was a vertical shaft approximately twenty feet deep. Miraculously, the ladder was still intact and the pathway down was mostly clear of debris. It helped that the ladder was installed with an arched metal safety cage, like those found on the outside of a city water tower, which held the rocks away from the ladder rungs. At the bottom of the shaft, there was a pile of strange looking debris. Opposite the ladder, Phillips was doubled over near a door at the base of the wall.

Hank hurried down to the landing below. As soon as he had joined Phillips, he knew immediately that they'd found the source of the foul-smelling odor: the strange looking debris was actually two dead bodies laying on top of each other. Setting the scene to memory, he took note that the two dead men weren't dressed in normal German uniforms, but instead wore white laboratory smocks with the letters "RFR" stamped on the front pocket.

With his stomach also getting weak, Hank yelled up access shaft and ordered Sergeant Atkins, Sergeant Southerland and Private Jenkins to come down, and the remaining men to stay up top at the shaft entrance. A few minutes later, after the three men had joined him and Sergeant Phillips on the landing, Hank issued his orders.

"Southerland, Jenkins," he said, "stay here and check those bodies. See if you can find out who they were or if they have anything on them. Phillips, Atkins, you're with me. Weapons ready."

The two sergeants immediately switched the safeties off on their submachine guns and acknowledged Hank with a nod.

"When we go in, fan out and be careful. There may be booby traps or a couple of Nazi's who don't know the war is over."

THE DEVICE

Sergeant Phillips slowly opened the door and the three men stepped into the secret lower level of Hitler's bunker.

They entered a room that resembled an office, complete with a couch, chair and desk. On top of the desk sat a large suitcase-sized radio receiver-transmitter, which Hank recognized as one of the German Army's "Torn.Fu" models; still on and picking up a faint static sound. There was a door on each side of the room, and after receiving a decisive nod from Hank, they immediately proceeded through the left one. Inside, they found living quarters, including several cots and footlockers in the near area, and an open bathroom with a toilet and a shower at the far end.

Proceeding back through the central room to the other door, they found it opened into a larger room, roughly forty feet square. Unlike the other two rooms, this one had sustained quite a bit of damage, with the wall farthest from the entrance door partially caved in. This larger room resembled a college chemistry laboratory, complete with polished-steel plates covering the floor, walls and ceiling. The furnishings included kitchen-type counters, two rolling chalkboards and several tipped-over filing cabinets. Two of these cabinets were smashed and split open, and stacks of papers had spilled out onto the floor. Many of the documents were charred and partially burned, but the wet floor had prevented some of them from being destroyed altogether. The chalkboards looked as if they were once filled with writing, but had been hastily erased. Hank could still, however, make out some of the German lettering around the fringes of the board, parts of which looked like mathematical equations, but contained symbols he was unfamiliar with.

The area of the room farthest from the entrance door, where most of the damage had occurred, had three steps leading up to a higher platform or stage of some kind. It was impossible to tell what this area of the room was used for, because it was now covered with boulders, rocks and other debris. Strangely, there were also a set of small railroad tracks fastened to the floor on each side of the platform, and a single track attached to the center of the ceiling. The sets of tracks protruded out from the rubble toward the center of the room. Buffer stops, like the ones placed at the end of standard railroad tracks, were positioned directly in the center of the protruding track ends. Unlike the common metal spring ones found in railroad yards, these were made of heavy rubber.

After fifteen minutes of searching each of the rooms thoroughly, Atkins reported finding three unexploded bombs. Walking out of the polished-steel room to take a closer look, Hank found that the fearless sergeant had removed them from wherever they were planted, and had placed them on the top of the desk next to the receiver-transmitter.

"Looks like the whole level was wired, sir, but only two of the bombs went off" Atkins said. "The one in the room above, and the other against the far wall in there." He pointed back into the room the captain had just exited.

Hank took his handkerchief off and smiled.

"I'm assuming these are safe now, Sergeant?"

Atkins casually picked up one of the bombs.

"As safe as any bomb can be when its igniter fuse is soaking wet. As you can see, they were all wrapped in cloth rags, which soaked up this seeping groundwater like a sponge. If they'd stayed dry and all the charges had gone off, we wouldn't be standing here because this level wouldn't be here anymore."

Hank shined his flashlight on the bomb Atkins was holding and back to the other two on the desk.

"For the record, where were they planted?"

Atkins pointed his flashlight over the exit leading to the access shaft.

"One was on the ceiling over that door where we came in, and the other two were against that main support beam." He moved the light over to the spot.

"Anything else, Sergeant?"

"I don't know if this is important or not, sir."

"Try me."

61

"Well sir, these are very sophisticated explosives with a lot of firepower. By sophisticated, I mean they could be set off by either connecting them directly to a detonator, like these were to the one I found upstairs, or by a timer."

He showed Hank the small box with the clock face taped to one end of the bomb.

"The two they planted in here on that main support beam would've been more than enough to bring the entire ceiling down in all three rooms," he continued, "but why would the Nazi's go to all the trouble of digging this place out, and place all these high-powered explosives down here to blow it all up, when there's nothing down here *to* blow up?"

"Good question," Hank replied, pondering the scenario.

Phillips reported next, informing Hank that Sergeant Southerland and Private Jenkins had finished searching the two dead bodies, and found papers identifying them as civilian scientists assigned to the "RFR." From the intelligence he'd previously gathered, Captain Hank knew the letters referred to the "*Reichsforschungsrat*," or Reich Research Council, which was the entity in charge of the Nazi's weapon development programs.

"What were their names?" Hank asked.

"Jakob Eddleman and Abraham Kaufmann," Phillips said, handing him the papers. "And I know my German is a little rusty sir, but doesn't Juden mean Jewish?"

Hank took the papers from the sergeant and examined them. *Now that is strange*, he thought, *Jewish guys down here dressed as laboratory assistants? It didn't make sense.* After examining them for a few moments and putting them to memory, he re-folded the papers and stuffed them into his breast pocket.

So far, the information provided by the dying German scientist and the other documents they'd found in the sewer were true; there was an Ünterbunker and what appeared to be a laboratory. But what were the Nazi's up to? And as Atkins pointed out, why did they try to blow it all up when there appeared to be nothing of value down here at all?

Walking back into the larger room, Hank stopped and picked up a bundled file of papers off the floor which happened to be laying on a dry section, and slapped it against his leg to knock off the small rocks and dust. Shining his flashlight on the cover page, it read, *Unternehmen Zunden Vogel*, or in English, Operation Firebird. There was also a large red-lettered stamp across the top stating, *STRENG-GEHEIM*, German for TOP-SECRET. This immediately got his attention, and after translating a few of the pages he ordered his men out of the room and to stand by.

~ Now ~

Close to an hour later, which to Captain Hank seemed like only a few minutes, Phillips suddenly appeared and startled him. He was so engrossed with this latest bit of information that he hadn't heard the sergeant come in.

"Sir, the team is still standing by, awaiting your orders." From his nervous tone, Hank could tell the sergeant was growing impatient with the long delay.

"Good. We'll get started immediately," he said.

"In getting out of here, sir? This place gives me the creeps."

"No, in getting these papers and files gathered up. We're taking them with us."

As quick as Hank was at setting things to memory, there simply wasn't enough time to translate and review the large number of documents in the room.

"Find something interesting, sir?"

When he saw the perplexed look on Phillips' face, Hank could tell the sergeant couldn't understand the German writing or the complicated mathematical equations. *Good,* he thought, *the less anyone knows about this, the better.* He'd already decided a half-hour ago that the information he'd uncovered would require the utmost secrecy and security. At the same time, he needed to downplay what he found to his men (something he hated to do) so as not to draw any attention to it.

"Maybe, maybe not," Hank said, finally replying to Phillips' question. "That's for the brains above my pay grade to decide. But just in case, we'd better get this stuff out of here, and I want photos of all the rooms."

"Yes, sir. I'll get the men in here right away."

"Private Jenkins is carrying the extra duffel bags, so we can use them for the papers, but have Sergeant Atkins and Sergeant Southerland bring in those footlockers that were in the far room. I'd like to take what's left of that equipment back there."

He picked up his flashlight and shined it on the area of the room that had sustained the most damage. Amid the rubble and debris was a jumbled web of electrical wires protruding from conduits split open from the explosion. The other ends of the conduits were connected to different-sized metal boxes. These boxes contained switches and dials, and resembled control panels in an electrical power station. There was also some very odd-looking debris, circular in shape but broken in pieces now.

Walking over to take a closer look, Phillips knelt and picked up one of the arc-shaped pieces, which instantly snapped against his wristwatch.

"What is it, sir? Some kind of heavy-duty magnet?"

"Between you and me, and this goes no farther you understand."

Phillips nodded.

"It just might be," Hank hesitated to draw in the sergeant's attention and add drama to the lie, "the remains of an elaborate Nazi coding machine."

Phillips' eyes grew wider.

"Like I said, it *might* be, but I'm not one-hundred percent sure without an in-depth analysis. That's why we need to get what's left of it out of here, along with all of these papers."

"Yes, sir."

"And Sergeant?"

"Sir?"

Hank's penetrating blue eyes locked on him.

"Utmost discretion, you understand?"

"Yes, sir."

Captain Hank's eyes followed Phillips as he left the room, then panned back over to the heap of exposed wires and conduits that were mixed in with the rubble. Thinking about what he had set to memory so far, he wondered whether a sinister Nazi plot of unbelievable proportions had been perpetrated here? Or perhaps the bomb had put an end to such a plot? In either case, without a detailed analysis of the rest of the documents and the wrecked equipment, he just couldn't be sure one way or the other.

As his attention returned to the paper he was translating before Phillips had interrupted him, he suddenly had the strangest feeling he was being watched. A cold chill ran through his body and he looked around the polished-steel room again. Seeing nothing, he retreated in the direction of Phillips.

* * *

In all, Captain Hank and his team removed four completely stuffed duffel bags of papers, as well as three wooden footlockers containing the wrecked parts. It took the team almost an hour to gather the documents and stuff them into the duffel bags, sift the parts out of the rubble and pack them in the footlockers, and maneuver them all up the access ladder past the fallen rocks.

As soon as the last member of the team had departed to the level above, Hank blew out one of the oil lamps, and using the second quickly went through each of the rooms one last time to set them to memory. Surveying the room that looked like a laboratory, he once again experienced the same uneasy and uncomfortable feeling; almost as if someone were studying him from a secret window or vantage point that he couldn't see. Instead of simply dismissing it as he had a while ago, he decided to investigate.

Walking back to the area of the room that had sustained the most damage, he slowly moved the oil lamp back and forth in front of him, peering into the rubble to see if he could identify the source of his heightened awareness. Noticing nothing different, he turned and made his way back out to the central room and again attributed the strange feeling to the prolonged length of time he'd spent down in this eerie underground catacomb.

The last image he memorized before exiting the level was the desk in the central room, upon which sat the three bombs Atkins had found, and the Torn.Fu receiver-transmitter, still on and picking up the same faint static sound. Closing the exit door behind him, he took the few short steps to the ladder leading to the floor above and looked upon the two dead men. Blowing out the oil lamp and setting it on the ground, he placed his foot on the first ladder rung and climbed out.

Once he reached the Führerbunker level, Hank's first thought was to get his men and the intelligence out of there as soon as possible, but he soon realized that if something in the information made it necessary for them to return, he needed to figure out a way to hide the lower level's opening from the Russians. Remembering a drain in the floor of the cloak room next door, he walked in and looked it over again. This drain, which was four metal rods set a few inches apart and imbedded in a square piece of concrete, looked to be the same size as the access opening in the ventilation room. After taking a few moments to mentally compare both images, he knew for certain.

"What do you think, sir?" Phillips asked.

"I think we need to cover the opening in there with this, if we can get it out," Hank said, outlining the piece of cement with his finger. "Let's just say we don't want the Russians to find that lower level."

"What if we just have Atkins blow it up?"

66

"What if we find something in the intel and need to come back?"

"Never mind, sir. Forget I even mentioned it."

Phillips walked out to the main hallway where the rest of the team was waiting and ordered Sergeant Atkins and Private Jenkins, the two stockiest men on the team, to drop the duffel bags and go back into the cloak room.

After Captain Hank told them what he had in mind, they knelt along each side of the piece of cement, and gripping the metal rods in the center, pulled up on the heavy-looking slab – the piece instantly popped out of the floor.

"So where do you want it?" Atkins asked, in an exaggerated deep voice.

With all the men laughing, Hank and Phillips helped them move the piece into the ventilation room and set it into place.

Phillips grinned. "Someday, sir, you've got to tell me how you knew it would fit without a tape measure."

Hank smiled back. "If I told you, I'd have to kill you."

Following Hank's lead, the men kicked some of the rocks that were still in the room over the piece, and once finished, they repeated this procedure in the cloak room with the rubble they'd previously removed. Two minutes later, after filling in the hole in the cloak room, Hank topped it off with the metal pieces that were the lower level's access cover. The cloak room now appeared as if an underground steam pipe had backed-up and exploded.

Now satisfied with the appearance of both rooms, Captain Hank joined the men in the outside conference room.

"Sergeant Phillips, let's get out of here."

"My thoughts exactly, sir. How about we just go out the easy way?" He pointed to the emergency exit.

"No, the guards may alert their superiors if they think we're still down here, so we've got to show them we're all out."

"Yes, sir."

"Put the intel out there. When we get out I'll distract the guards, then you and the men can come back down through the garden and get it."

"You heard the captain," Phillips said, addressing the men, "let's get a move on."

After taking the footlockers and duffel bags out the emergency exit, the team reassembled in the main conference room and quickly made their way back to the Vorbunker. Just as the men emerged from the bunker's main entrance, the two young Russian guards were in their faces; yelling at them for taking so long. Captain Hank then presented them with a German luger pistol, a Nazi dagger, and a couple of small swastika-laden flags that the team had secretly brought along for bribery purposes, and the troops were suddenly delighted. In their native tongue, Hank engaged the men in a lengthy conversation while his team retrieved the duffel bags and footlockers from the emergency exit's stairwell.

A short time later, with the deuce-and-a-half loaded and the cargo concealed, Captain Hank ordered Sergeant Phillips to send another coded radio message to the Alsos headquarters, informing them that Task Force B was leaving Berlin. He cautioned the men that when they got back, they were to use "utmost discretion" when talking about their incursion with the other members of the Alsos team. Each man, in turn, nodded their acknowledgement of the code words meaning: keep your mouths shut.

Because of the Russian Victory Day celebration, more than half of the checkpoints the men encountered bringing the truck into the city were now abandoned. Hank assumed correctly that the revelry would take its toll on their occupying forces, and for most of the slow drive out the men saw Red Army troops asleep alongside the main road, some still clutching empty bottles of vodka or other alcoholic beverages. Twenty minutes later, after disbursing a few more bribes at the last Russian checkpoint, the truck carrying the Task Force B reconnaissance team and the recovered Nazi intelligence was out of the city.

As their truck drove away, Hank thought, *the easy part is over. Now how am I going to keep this stuff away from everyone at HQ long enough to put it to memory and see if what I suspect is true?* The answer presented itself seven hours later that morning, at almost the moment they arrived back at Aachen.

As they pulled into the headquarters area off the main road, there was an area cordoned off with signs designating the section restricted. Several lower-ranked enlisted men were busy packing material or putting wooden crates together. Hank remembered that the crates were being used to send the captured German intelligence to the Alsos mission's main staging base in Paris, then shipped back to the Army's G-2 intelligence section at Fort Meade, Maryland.

He ordered the driver to pull over and the men to unload the three footlockers. As soon as they were done, he told them to go on ahead and check in at the command post, and to put the four duffel bags in his quarters. After that, they could go get chow and some much-needed shut-eye.

Once the men were gone, he hurriedly pulled a small pad of paper from his breast pocket and scribbled three notes, placing one in each of the footlockers. The notes read, "Big Ben, hold for me. Thanks, Hank." At the bottom of each of the notes, he numbered them (1 of 3, 2 of 3, and 3 of 3, respectively) so that his friend would know there were a total of three boxes in the shipment.

He instructed the highest ranking enlisted man to nail the footlockers closed and secure them to a single pallet. Once the footlockers were secure, he instructed the man stenciling the shipping information to make an extra stencil and add it under the last line of the destination address. Now the only difference between the pallet containing the footlockers and the rest of the outgoing cargo was a bold, "ATTN: CPT B. Ben Washington" under the G-2 address of Fort Meade. After finishing, he took the stencil from the enlisted man, telling him that he would hang on to it in the event other things needed to be shipped to Captain Washington.

With this pallet mixed in with the other ones, Hank hoped that no one would notice the slight difference in the shipping label, at least until it reached Fort Meade. Even if the pallet were to be misrouted or end up somewhere else, the contents inside the footlockers would easily be mistaken for junky old radio parts, magnets and wads of twisted wires.

Hank walked leisurely up the dirt road toward the old country inn, which was being used as the Alsos forward headquarters command post. Most of the trucks, jeeps and other equipment that had rolled out the day his recon team had left for Berlin were still gone. Except for occasional laughs from a few of his Task Force B members smoking nearby, the area was quiet; a far cry from the hub of activity it was one week ago when Colonel Pash left in pursuit of Werner Heisenberg.

Entering the inn's lobby, Hank immediately noticed Sergeant Phillips talking to Second Lieutenant Steven Jeffries, one of the newer officers on the Alsos team.

"Am I glad to see you, sir," Jefferies said.

"What's going on, LT? Where is everyone?"

"Gone," Phillips interjected.

"That's right sir," Jeffries said, "as I was telling the sergeant, everyone has packed up and left for Frankfurt, and the brass have gone to brief the upper-brass in Paris."

"I take it that Colonel Pash is in Paris then?"

"Yes, sir. The day you guys left for Berlin, Colonel Pash and six of those civilian guys captured Werner Heisenberg in Urfeld. Got him right in his house!"

"Was there any resistance?" Hank asked, reaching over the counter and retrieving a pen to sign the duty log.

"When they got to the town on Tuesday, they got shot at a couple of times by some snipers, but thankfully no one got hurt. Then the strangest thing happened."

"Wait till you hear this," Phillips said.

Hank looked up from the counter.

"The seven hundred Germans who were defending Urfeld surrendered to Colonel Pash. Seven hundred Germans surrendering to only seven men, can you believe it?"

Hank smiled. "I thought the colonel had guys from the 36th with him?"

"He did, but on their way to Urfeld they got called to go fight some German holdouts in Bergheim, so Colonel Pash had Major Fisher call in the 3rd Battalion to help. I think he said they were from the 142nd Infantry. Anyway, the next day the guys from the 3rd Battalion showed up and took the seven hundred Germans into custody, and Colonel Pash and the six civilians went ahead and captured Heisenberg and a few other German scientists."

"Sounds like the colonel had his hands full there for a while," Phillips said, still smiling.

Hank nodded. "I take it Major Fisher is with the colonel in Paris then?"

"Yes, sir, along with Mr. Goudsmit."

"So who's in charge here?"

"I am, well, I mean you are now, sir. Colonel Pash took all the other officers to Paris with him. He left me in charge, at least until you got back. He left orders that if you found anything in Berlin that was earth-shattering, or if you needed to get a hold of him right away, he could be reached at the Paris HQ. If you didn't find anything, then you and the men could rest for a few days, and he would meet us back here on Tuesday or Wednesday, depending on how many meetings he has to go to."

Perfect, Hank thought, *the time off will give me four, possibly five days to review the documents.*

Jefferies smiled. "Did you find anything interesting?"

"I haven't had a chance to look at it."

"It looked like the men brought in a lot of papers."

"Utmost discretion, Lieutenant, utmost discretion."

"Yes, sir," Jeffries replied sadly.

After he finished signing in, Hank turned away and immediately smelled the food coming from the small dining room.

"Is the kitchen open?" he asked.

"I think the men can answer that, sir," Phillips said.

Leading Captain Hank down the inn's main hallway, they soon heard the familiar voices and laughs of the men who were on the recon team, and entering the dining area, Hank saw they were already digging into plates filled with food.

"Care to join us, sir?" Atkins asked, his mouth stuffed.

Hank smiled. "I believe I will."

After enjoying a big lunch, a lot of laughs and a group photo with the men, Hank stopped off at the command post and told Lieutenant Jeffries he had some entries to make in the log book, and if he wanted he could take a break for a few minutes. The lieutenant gladly accepted the offer, and hurriedly left through the inn's front door.

With Jefferies out of the way and the rest of the lobby empty, Hank quickly pulled a box out from under the front counter. On the outside of the box were the hand-written words "Col. P's Reports." Opening the four folded flaps, he found several bundles of files, each one containing statements and information on the areas throughout Germany where the Alsos mission had recovered intelligence. He withdrew the thin file that was titled "Operation Firebird," then re-folded the four flaps and placed the box back under the counter.

Looking around the desk, he discovered a few copies of the May eighth edition of the Stars and Stripes newspaper, whose front-page headline boldly read "Nazis Quit." Grabbing one of the copies, he folded it around the file to conceal it until he got to his room, and placed it aside. Picking up the log book, he made the required journal entries regarding the Task Force B incursion into Berlin – that all the men had returned safe and sound. Once Lieutenant Jefferies returned, he turned the command post back over to him, picked up the paper containing the file, and made his way up the flight of stairs to his room.

* * *

A short time later, after freshening up with a warm shave, shower and change of clothes, Captain Hank began setting the German papers to memory, starting with the small bundled file titled "Operation Firebird." Although he had already memorized this file, he wanted to review it again just to make sure he hadn't missed anything in the dimly lit laboratory of the Ünterbunker. As soon as he was finished, he closed the file and sat it on the floor next to the four duffel bags. Realizing that he had a laborious job ahead of him, he stood up and stretched, then walked over to the window. Looking up Aachen's main road toward the restricted area where he'd dropped off the three footlockers, he couldn't help thinking about the extent and possible consequences if what he'd discovered turned out to be true.

And if true, who could he trust with this information?

Chapter Four
The Late Meeting

Sixty-Nine Years, Three Months and Twenty-One Days Later
Saturday, 30 August 2014, 18:00hrs
Inside the *Roof Restaurant, Salt Lake City, Utah*

Large windows stretched from floor to ceiling across the west side of the dining room, making the high-end Salt Lake eatery resemble the observation deck of a giant airborne spacecraft. Outside and just below the windows sat the majestic Latter-Day Saint Temple, its spires pointing skyward as they glistened in the early-evening sun. Across the horizon behind the temple was a vast array of brilliant rust-colored clouds, whose glowing color provided a stunning backdrop and made the picturesque scene resemble a classical artist's painting. The view from this vantage point seemed to be the ideal setting for our second meeting with Jim Stevens.

As we sat at a corner table, eagerly awaiting the arrival of our strange new friend, I thought back to the events that had brought us here, and couldn't wait to hear the rest the story.

~ Then ~

Two weeks ago at his home in Mountain Green, Madison and I had sat captivated by the tale Jim told us about his father developing a photographic memory from a baseball accident, and a few years later becoming an intelligence officer in World War II. But before he'd finished telling us about what his dad had found in the secret lower level of Hitler's bunker (and how it pertained to Parkinson's research) he checked a message on his vibrating cell phone, became extremely nervous and abruptly asked us to leave.

No matter how much we assured him we were all right missing our grandson's game, and that we wanted to hear the rest of the story, our coaxing couldn't sway him, so Madison and I thanked him for the wonderful meal and we departed somewhat disappointed. Before we drove off, however, we exchanged phone numbers and promised that when we got together again, *we* would treat *him* to dinner.

For the next ten days, Madison and I couldn't stop talking about the incredible lunch, Mr. Stevens, and the story he'd told us about his dad Captain Hank. On one such conversation, we were sitting at our kitchen table enjoying a late breakfast.

"So what could his dad have found in Hitler's bunker that would even remotely pertain to Parkinson's research?" I asked.

"Don't ask me," Madison replied, shrugging her shoulders, "I'm as much in the dark as you are."

"He said the dying man told Hank that the Ünterbunker's laboratory contained documents full of mathematical theories and formulas. I remember reading a book about the Holocaust in high school, and how some of the Nazi scientists performed sadistic experiments on live inmates at the concentration camps. So maybe, in a twisted sort of way, they found a new drug or medical treatment for Parkinson's?"

She shook her head. "No, I don't think so. These were evil men bent on taking over the world. To me, it sounds like they discovered some new kind of weapon. Or wait a minute." She stared at me for a moment, before continuing, "Maybe it does have something to do with medical stuff. Remember, he said that before the team was sent to the bunker, they found a centrifuge that was used to spin those uranium thingamajigs?"

"Isotopes," I said, filling in the word for her.

"That's right, isotopes. I don't know how you remembered that."

I smiled. "Me neither. But let's say, for the sake of argument, that here was Joe Nazi scientist, spinning his uranium isotopes and doing whatever a Nazi scientist does while trying to make an A-bomb for Hitler. Suddenly, he unwittingly stumbles on to a medical breakthrough that can help people with Parkinson's. From what I know, uranium is radioactive, and doctors today use radioactivity to fight cancer."

"But since Jim *has* Parkinson's, don't you think if his dad found something like that, he would've used it on himself by now?"

"Maybe he has, but for some reason or another it hasn't worked, so he needs to try it out on another person like me."

"In a way that makes sense, but who knows?"

"Well I know one thing. This has been kept out of the newspapers since the war. When I searched the internet the other day, I couldn't find any information about a secret lower level being found in Hitler's bunker."

"Did it say anything about what the Russians *did* find down there? Anything that might give us a clue?"

"No, except for the furniture and a portrait of Frederick the Great the place was pretty much cleaned out. It also said before they surrendered the bunker, the Nazi's burned everything, including documents, files, and even the corpses of Hitler, his wife Eva and their dog Blondi."

"Now that's a great visual I wanted with my pancakes."

We both laughed.

In the ensuing days, as much as we speculated as to what Captain Hank and his team had found in the Ünterbunker and what it had to do with Parkinson's research, the more puzzled we were. It wasn't as if we were obsessing over the story, but the mystery was just too compelling to ignore.

In subsequent talks with Madison throughout the week, we found ourselves focusing more and more on Jim himself. One night we had a conversation about him while laying in bed.

"Do you think we are the first people he's told this story to?" Madison asked.

"Considering how strange he's acted since we first met him, if I were to bet on it I'd say yes."

"You know, the way he talked was so descriptive, it's almost like he was there; like *he* was Captain Hank."

"That thought crossed my mind too, but it would be impossible."

"How so?"

"Roughly how old would you say he is?"

"Early to mid-fifties."

"And how old am I?"

"Fifty-four."

"Case closed."

She laughed. "All right, Mr. Smarty-pants, maybe he's older but has had some plastic surgery."

"That would have to be some plastic surgery. Hey, maybe I can find out who his dermatologist is, just in case you might want to…"

She stopped me with a playful slap.

After Madison fell asleep, the feelings of foreboding that I encountered while driving to the luncheon returned and kept me awake for some time. I felt as though we were slowly being drawn into something that was much more complicated than just a Parkinson's research project.

The next morning, which marked the tenth day since our luncheon in Mountain Green, we both received text messages on our phones from Mr. Stevens. The short note read:

Dear Madison/George,
I am available for dinner this coming Saturday night.

Your choice of where/what time.
v/r
Jim

Madison and I talked it over, and we both agreed that we should treat Jim to a restaurant that was comparable to the fantastic lunch he'd provided us at his home. Having recently dined at the Roof Restaurant, and finding it to be a fantastic buffet, Madison and I scheduled our dinner with him there, and I sent him the reply:

> Hi Jim,
> This Saturday, 6:00pm at the Roof Restaurant.
> 15 E. South Temple, 10th floor of the J. Smith building, Salt Lake City.
> Madison and I look forward to seeing you there.
> George

A short time later he replied that he would be able to attend, and the stage was set for our second meeting.

~ Now ~

As we sat in the corner table at the picturesque restaurant, Madison and I again started playing our little guessing game, albeit a lot more seriously this time.

"What if his research involves you taking an experimental drug?" she asked. "Would you do it?"

"I don't know. I guess it would depend on the information he provides us of what the drug is supposed to do."

"Would you check with your doctor first before you took it?"

"Of course I would."

"I just don't want you taking something that runs the risk of counteracting the medications you're on now."

"I'll make a point to check with the doctor before I take anything."

"There could be unforeseen side effects. Remember what we heard at the symposium? They said the long-term use of Parkinson drugs could result in dyskinesia. If Jim introduces another unknown drug into the mix, who knows what that'll do to you. You might develop side effects…"

"Okay, okay," I interrupted, "you're getting yourself all worked up about something that might not even happen. Let's first wait and see what the research is all about before we make any snap judgments. If it is new medication, I'll tell him that I should first check with the doctor. Okay?"

"It's just that I love you," she said, wiping tears from her eyes, "and I don't want anything to happen to you."

I hugged her and gave her a kiss on the cheek.

"It'll be all right. I've done these research studies before and I really don't think this will be any different."

"But those studies were conducted by PhD students who just wanted you to do some balancing exercises, not by some strange man with a Nazi potion."

It was obvious that the longer we waited, the more worried Madison was becoming.

"I grant you that he is weird, but we'll be together the whole time. Remember, he said he wanted *both* of us to join his team, not just me, and he hasn't mentioned anything about experimental drugs, only research."

"I guess you're right. Maybe I'm just overreacting."

Glancing at my watch, I noticed that more than a half an hour had passed.

"Its six-thirty. He'd better get here soon, I'm hungry."

Just then, we heard the familiar tones coming from our phones, telling us we'd received a text message.

Dear Madison/George,

Please accept my sincere apologies.

I have been unavoidably detained.

Please go ahead and enjoy your wonderful dinner.

I will be in touch soon.

v/r

Jim

Madison was instantly irritated.

"See what I mean? This guy just gets weirder and weirder."

"How disappointing. I wonder if he's got some phobia about being out in public."

"Who knows?"

After a long pause, I heard my stomach growl.

"Shall we eat?"

Throughout the meal, Madison and I carried on with small talk but refrained from talking any more about Jim Stevens. We had reached a saturation point on the subject, and (reading each other's minds) silently agreed not to talk about him for the remainder of the dinner.

After we'd finished off two full plates of food from the Roof's incredible buffet, and an additional plate containing small portions of no less than three very tasty sweets from their dessert table, we were stuffed.

I signaled to the waitress for our bill, but she informed us that there would be no check this evening.

"Your friend, Mr. Stevens, already took care of it," she said. "He wanted me to tell you that he was sorry for being unavoidably detained."

Madison and I looked at each other dumbstruck. As much as we appreciated his gratitude, we didn't want him to pay for our meal. We'd hoped this dinner would somehow repay his generosity and answer our many questions. Needless to say, our frustration level was at an all-time high when we left Salt Lake City and headed north towards home.

* * *

No sooner had we reached our house and got inside to greet our two Shih-Tzu dogs, our phone rang.

"Hello George, Jim here."

"Hi Jim."

I silently motioned for Madison to come listen.

"Please again accept my sincere apology for missing our dinner appointment. But since I am here now on your front doorstep, perhaps you could let me in so that I can explain myself?"

A few moments later he was in our front room, fending off our playful puppies. Along with his cane, he carried with him a thick three-ring binder.

"Please sit down," Madison said, "and let me take your book."

"I'd like to hold it, if you don't mind," he replied, and instead handed her his cane.

Sitting down in our recliner, he suddenly found himself flanked by our hounds, who love to cuddle with anyone who sits there.

"Shih-Tzu's are such even tempered dogs, don't you think?" he asked, alternately petting them.

Madison smiled. "Yeah, they're pretty good pooches."

As we sat down on our couch, Jim removed his old-style fedora hat and set it on the floor. We immediately noticed he had a horrible bruise on the left side of his head.

"Oh my goodness Jim, what did you do to your face?" Madison asked.

"I'm afraid that Roy and I got into a little car accident earlier this evening. A driver decided much too late that he needed to turn, and Roy and I happened to be in his way. Unfortunately, our car

82

went off the road and we ended up a little bumped and bruised. That is why I was unavoidably detained and didn't make it to our dinner engagement. We were stranded, waiting for a tow truck and trying to arrange a rental car. Again, I apologize for standing you up."

"Don't you worry about that," she replied, "dinners can be rescheduled. The most important thing is that you are all right."

"I'll live, for a little while longer anyway."

"And as for dinner, we thought tonight was going to be *our* treat."

He smiled. "Once I realized that I wasn't going to make it, it was the least I could do."

"Well, thank you. You didn't have to do that."

"Yes, thank you," I said, "but what about Roy? Is he okay?"

"He's doing well. Like me, he was a bit shaken up, but he'll be all right."

"Can we get you anything?" Madison asked.

"If it's not too much trouble, maybe some water?"

"I'm on it," I said, and quickly retrieved a cold bottle from the fridge.

He unscrewed the cap of the water bottle, and took a small drink.

"If you both wouldn't mind staying up a little while longer, I would like to continue telling you the story I started two weeks ago."

"We'd love to hear it," Madison replied, "that is, if you're sure you are all right."

"Oh, I assure you I am quite well."

After screwing the cap back on the water bottle and setting it on the stand next to the recliner, he rested his hands on the large binder on his lap.

"As I was telling you, my dad found something in the secret lower level of Hitler's bunker that was so unbelievably powerful, he wasn't sure he could trust our country with it."

"Just to put our minds at ease," I interrupted, "it doesn't have anything to do with experimental drugs, does it?"

"Heavens no, George," he said with a laugh. "I can see your minds have been working overtime since our last meeting. What my dad found, which relates to Parkinson's research, will take a bit of time to explain, but rest assured my research does not involve you taking any experimental medication. But before I tell you *exactly* what he found, I first need to explain a few things so that you won't think I am crazy and belong in a padded room."

Madison and I both laughed at his description, while also hanging on his next words.

"For now, let's just say that what my dad and his team retrieved from the damaged section of the underground laboratory could best be described as the remains of support equipment, which at one time was connected to a machine. This equipment provided the machine with electricity, much like an auxiliary power unit provides electricity to parked aircraft.

"This machine, which my dad simply referred to as *the device*, was missing when the reconnaissance team entered the bunker and found the secret lower level. From the papers he gathered and set to memory, my dad learned that the device was the product of some of the most brilliant scientific minds who'd ever lived. By brilliant, I mean foremost experts in their respective fields of physics and mathematics, who either knowingly or unwittingly played a part in creating the device."

"Which scientists?" I asked. "Anyone famous we might know?"

"Albert Einstein for one. He is probably the most famous. Other names directly or indirectly connected to the project, which you've probably never heard of, were Niels Bohr, Walter Bothe, and Otto Stern, just to name a few."

"Wait a minute. I thought Einstein was on our side."

"He was, as was Niels Bohr. You see, Einstein was born in Germany and Bohr in Denmark, but both also happened to be Jewish."

Madison and I nodded, acknowledging the point.

"When the Germans started their German physics movement in the early 1930's, they labeled the work of Einstein, Bohr, and others as *Jewish Physics* and did their best to discredit them. But Einstein had already won the Nobel Prize in 1921 for his work in theoretical physics, so their attempts to discredit him were mostly in vain."

"What about the other guy? Bohr was it?" Madison asked.

"Niels Bohr won the Nobel Prize in physics in 1922 for his unparalleled understanding of the structure of the atom. The Nazi's had a hard time discrediting him, too. He founded the Institute of Theoretical Physics in Copenhagen, which is now named after him. From the mid 1920's to 1943, Bohr's institute was the central meeting place for physicists from all around the world. As a matter of record, some of the fundamental disciplines of atomic physics and quantum physics were developed there.

Somewhat embarrassed by my lack of knowledge, I said, "I've heard that expression, quantum physics, before, but I haven't the foggiest idea of what it means."

"Quantum physics is the study of the behavior of matter and energy at the microscopic or atomic level. *Quantum* simply refers to how much, and in this instance how much means very, very small."

To emphasize his point, he held up his hand and placed his thumb and forefinger almost together, but not quite touching. I nodded out of respect for his simple explanation, but knew that the subject was much more complicated than that.

"All the discoveries that were made in physics back then were due to brilliant people like Einstein, Bohr, and many others who dedicated years of their lives to studying it. These discoveries, in turn, led to more notoriety and more great minds wanting to study it. Physics became the twentieth century's exciting new science, and at Bohr's institute in Copenhagen these people got the chance to work with, or be mentored by, some of the world's foremost physicists of the day.

"Then in 1943, with Denmark occupied by the Nazi's, Bohr received a tip from an informer that the Gestapo was going to arrest him because he was Jewish. He quickly fled the country, and shortly afterward the Germans seized his institute and everything inside, including some of his personal notes and complex hypothetical formulas that he had informally discussed with colleagues."

"What about Einstein? Did he flee the Nazi's too?" Madison asked.

"When Hitler came to power in 1933, Einstein happened to be in the United States. He tried to return to Germany once, but on a ship heading for Belgium he received word that the Nazis had seized his house and boat. As with Bohr, his personal notes and manuscripts of unproven scientific formulas were confiscated and sent to the Reich Research Council."

"I'm sorry I keep interrupting," I said, "but may I ask another question?"

"Oh certainly, George. I know this is all new to both of you, so please feel free to interrupt me and ask me anything."

"Thanks, just a point of clarification. You said the device was the product of these men. I take it then that Einstein and Bohr were two of the scientists who, how did you say it, *unwittingly* played a part in making the device?"

He smiled. "Correct. These men revolutionized the science of physics. At the time of their discoveries, they had no idea that their theories, informal or otherwise, were going to be used for anything other than peaceful purposes and the advancement of knowledge for all mankind. But eventually, like many other things that happened back then, it didn't take long for the Nazis to exploit these discoveries to their own advantage. When you think about it, it was absurd. Here the Nazis were, preaching anti-Semitic rants against Jewish physics, but behind the scenes were using the knowledge they'd stolen from them."

"That's horrible but not surprising, at least from what I've read of the Nazis."

"What about the other scientific experts you mentioned? I take it they were Nazis?" Madison asked.

"Not all of them. Some were willing participants who simply wanted to further the science of physics, while others were blackmailed or forced into working on the project."

"Blackmailed? How so?"

"In 1943, the war was going very badly for the Nazis. The harsh winter had stalled their advance into the Soviet Union and the German Army was driven back. They believed, however, that they were still going to defeat the Russians but it was just going to take more time. The Reich Research Council then recalled more than four thousand of their scientists and technicians from their front-line combat units, in hopes of developing new weapons so that they could win the war."

"Four thousand? There were that many?" I asked.

"Oh, yes. The German operation to attack Russia employed over four million troops."

"Wow!" Madison exclaimed. "I had no idea they had that big of an army."

"That was just on the German operation to conquer the Soviet Union. At the time, they were also fighting the United States and the British on an entirely different front."

He paused for a moment and took a drink of water.

"The scientists and technicians they called back were given a choice to either work on special weapon projects or return to fighting on the Russian front. Those who chose special projects were disbursed throughout Germany, where they worked on many different weapon development programs. For example, some were sent to Peenemunde, which was on an island in the Baltic Sea, to work on their V-2 rocket program. Others were sent to assist

Werner Heisenberg and other members of what the Germans called the *Uranverein*, or Uranium Club, in developing an atomic bomb."

"With all the scientists and technicians they had working on it, it's a wonder they *didn't* develop the A-bomb first," Madison said.

"Agreed. But as scary as that sounds, my dad uncovered something even more frightening. He learned that seventy of the brightest scientists and technicians were handpicked to work on a special top-secret project for the Reich Research Council, and were ordered to report to Oranienburg, which was about twenty-two miles north of Berlin. Oranienburg was the place where the Nazis built one of their first concentration camps. Then in 1939, as the war progressed, the inmates were disbursed to several of the nearby Sachsenhausen camps and the buildings at Oranienburg were converted into weapon research facilities. When the scientists and technicians arrived, they were sequestered and went to work on a highly-classified project, code named Operation Firebird."

"Who handpicked these scientists?"

"They were selected by a lieutenant general of the Waffen-SS by the name of Karl Berger, who was not only brilliant, but was also, for lack of a better term, quite sadistic. You see, Berger was the Deputy Director of the Reich Research Council, which oversaw the Nazi's top-secret weapon development programs."

"I've never heard of this guy, and I've read quite a few books about the war," I said.

"Most people haven't. You'd have to dig deep into the history books to find any mention of the White Wolf, as he was called."

"So the Firebird operation that this General Berger oversaw was separate from the guys trying to build the bomb, this Uranium Club?"

He smiled an all-knowing smile. "Sort of. The Firebird project operated separately from the Uranium Club, at least on paper, but while it was operating General Berger borrowed scientists from the Uranium Club to help work out problems with the development of the device. For the first ten months of its existence, the Firebird project was nothing more than a think tank. Technicians assigned to it gathered all the information they could about physics theories, mathematical calculations, electricity, magnetism, gravity, and any other subject even remotely related to Einstein's two relativity theories. As this information became available, these scientists studied it, worked out problems and conducted experiments. They even got their hands on two extremely brilliant Jewish scientists that Niels Bohr unsuccessfully tried to smuggle out of the country, and forced them to work on the project."

"Who were they, or rather, what were their specialties?" Madison asked.

"Jakob Eddleman and Abraham Kaufmann. Eddleman specialized in electromagnetism, and Kaufmann was a foremost expert in thermodynamics, which is the study of temperature and its relationship to energy, heat and radiation. At one time, both were students of Einstein, Bohr and even Nicola Tesla, and had gone on to make important discoveries of their own."

"Those names ring a bell," I said.

"They should. They were the two bodies that my dad and his team found in the Ünterbunker. You see, General Berger received word that the Gestapo had captured Eddleman, Kaufmann and their families, and had them all brought to the Oranienburg facility. Once there, he threatened that if they didn't assist him with the Firebird project he would kill them, starting with their wives and children. Naturally, they capitulated. They were so brilliant that Berger brought them to Berlin with him when the Firebird operation got moved."

"That is so terrible," Madison said, "but wait a second. You said Einstein's *two* theories. I thought there was only *one* theory of relativity?"

THE DEVICE

"Einstein developed his Special Theory of Relativity in 1905 and his General Theory of Relativity in 1915," Jim replied, sounding like a professor. "As I mentioned earlier, much of the information the Nazis used in their research was stolen. Taken separately, the information was a collection of known physics equations, mathematical formulas or unproven hypothetical theories. But combined, and studied by some very smart people in a think tank for almost a year, the Firebird team made some very significant discoveries; advances that took the known science of physics to, as young people say today, the next level."

"From what you've said, I take it that these new discoveries eventually led them to building this device?"

He smiled. "Correct, Madison. There were actually three devices. They sent the first, a non-working prototype, to Werner Heisenberg's laboratory in Haigerloch."

"Isn't that where you said the Alsos team found a couple of nuclear reactors?" I asked.

"Yes, but with one exception. At first, they both *appeared* to be rudimentary nuclear reactors, but one of them was actually the Firebird prototype."

"What happened to that one?"

"The Alsos team blew it up. Colonel Pash, believing they were both nuclear reactors, ordered Heisenberg's laboratory to be destroyed before the Russians could get their hands on it."

"So that left the other two." Madison said.

"Yes. It was now the middle of March of 1945, and Hitler ordered the device that was nearest completion, Firebird One, to be moved to the bunker in Berlin and down into the secret lower level."

"But if Oranienburg was the center of the Nazi's nuclear program, why did they move it?"

"Two reasons. First, with the war going badly and the Russians closing in, Hitler wanted the device close to him in the event General Berger got it working. That way, if he lost the war he could activate it. Since he originally had the Ünterbunker

constructed as a secret retreat point, the largest room only needed a few modifications to house the device and its support equipment. Secondly, the Germans received word that we were close to finding out about their operation in Oranienburg."

"Had we?" I asked.

"Yes, and since the Oranienburg area was going to fall into the Russian zone of occupation after the war, Colonel Pash recommended to General Groves that we take out the facility, which our 8th Army Air Force did on March the fifteenth. And when they destroyed the think tank at Oranienburg, they destroyed the third device that was under construction, as well as the seventy scientists working on the Firebird operation."

"Wow." Madison exclaimed. "So what did your dad do when he found out about all of this?"

"Normally, intelligence this sensitive was collected and shipped back to the G-2 section of the Army Intelligence Corps at Fort Meade. My dad, however, was so frightened about what he'd uncovered, he took extreme measures so that no one, not even our own government, would ever find out about it."

"What do you mean by *took extreme measures*?"

"Quite simply, he set everything to memory and destroyed the information."

Like he did at his house in Mountain Green, Jim leaned forward, and his penetrating blue eyes alternated between Madison and me.

"He also started an exhaustive mental review of the information, to see if what he had discovered was true, and whether the Nazis had actually activated the Firebird device."

Chapter Five
The Story (Part 2)

Sixty-Nine Years, One Month and Fourteen Days Earlier
Tuesday, 17 July 1945, 11:45hrs
Alsos **Mission Debriefing**
Inside the *Pentagon, Washington, DC*

The burned-out bulbs in the overhead lights combined with the cigarette smoke hanging in the air, giving the tobacco-stained white walls and ceiling of the military briefing room a drab and weary appearance. Adding to the dim ambiance was a faded picture of the recently deceased President Roosevelt, hanging crooked and alone in the center of the longest wall, and an artificial tree in the far corner, its leaves dusty and full of cobwebs. The mundane furniture that adorned the room included eight dated wooden chairs around a matching eight-foot long by four-foot wide table, each one carrying their own unique set of scratches and chips from countless meetings convened throughout the war. Sitting quietly next to each other at one end of the table were Colonel Boris Pash and Captain Henry "Hank" Stevens, both perspiring heavily from the verbal assault they'd just received from their commanding officer, Major General Leslie Groves.

Normally, official reporting of intelligence operations took place immediately following the mission, or at least a couple of weeks after the mission's end. This debriefing, however, had been postponed for almost two months because of scheduling conflicts. General Groves, who was overseeing the military's atomic bomb development operation known as "The Manhattan Project," was a very busy man.

When the meeting first began, the general seemed quite pleased with Colonel Pash, and told him how impressed he was with both the information the Alsos mission had collected throughout Germany and the large number of Nazi scientists that were captured along the way. As far as that was concerned, the mission was a complete success. But when the subject of the Task Force B reconnaissance operation to Hitler's bunker came up, and the team had recovered essentially nothing, both the colonel and the captain endured a ten-minute brow-beating that would've made a seasoned sailor blush.

Colonel Pash, the man who had authorized the Task Force B incursion, received the most severe scolding. Even though the colonel had a separate budget for personnel and support supplies, General Groves let him know (in no uncertain terms) that staging such an operation was too risky, unnecessary and a complete waste of manpower and resources. In addition, the intelligence that initiated the reconnaissance operation was, in his estimation, unreliable.

Captain Hank didn't escape a tongue-lashing either, as the general reminded him no less than three times that although he possessed incredibly fast memorization skills, he lacked the field experience to command such a task force, especially on a mission into the heart of Russian-occupied Berlin one day after the German surrender. The general stopped short of reprimanding both men, and instead administered his official oral admonishment – the military phrase for a good chewing-out.

The briefing went from bad-to-worse when one of the general's aides interrupted the meeting to report that the aircraft carrying twenty-five members of the Alsos team from Paris to Manila (which happened to be the same plane Colonel Pash and

Captain Hank had disembarked earlier to come to Washington) reported having engine problems and didn't make its scheduled landing. Search planes combing the aircraft's incoming flight path reported finding floating wreckage approximately twenty miles off the Philippine coastline, with no apparent survivors.

Hearing the news, and knowing that both men needed some time to grieve for their men, General Groves ordered the two officers to turn in their official report as soon as possible and abruptly adjourned the meeting.

Once they were alone, Colonel Pash turned to Captain Hank.

"That could've gone better," he said.

Hank nodded in agreement but remained quiet, his mind preoccupied with the news of the tragedy. Of the twenty-five Alsos troops onboard the flight to Manila, nine were members of the Task Force B reconnaissance team he'd commanded two months ago. The week they were with each other in Berlin, he'd developed a close, personal friendship with the men, especially Sergeant Phillips and Sergeant Atkins, the two he'd relied on the most to keep what he'd discovered in Hitler's bunker a secret. It was hard for Hank to believe that now, in the blink of an eye, he would never see them again.

"Is there anything you want me to add to the report, before I turn it in?" the colonel asked.

Hank took the thin stapled stack of papers, silently checked off the main points and signed it.

"No, I think this sums it up. If the Nazi's were up to something down there, we'd have found it."

Colonel Pash took the papers and endorsed the report with his own signature.

* * *

Later that evening, Hank sat on his bed in the temporary lodging quarters thinking about the men who were lost and reflecting on the Task Force B operation. Since making the decision to hide and destroy the information, he'd debated with himself repeatedly on whether it was the right thing to do. He knew keeping it from his superiors broke every rule he'd learned in intelligence school, and that it was a crime punishable by court martial. If someone found out about it and reported him, he could find himself in Leavenworth.

Rationalizing, he told himself that he wasn't hiding the intelligence for personal gain nor was he going to try to profit from it. Instead, he was suppressing knowledge that (in his estimation) transcended Army rules and regulations and was simply too dangerous to disclose.

With his incredible photographic memory, he returned to the images in his mind and reviewed the steps he'd taken to destroy the Nazi paperwork. He believed he'd covered all the bases in destroying the papers his team had recovered, and changing the trail of information that initiated the Task Force B operation.

One point, however, stood out above all others: with the accident happening in the Philippines, he was now the only man who knew that the Nazi 's secret Firebird operation existed, and that his recon team had recovered a veritable treasure trove of intelligence related to the operation.

~ Then ~

Two months ago, after returning from Berlin to the Alsos Forward North Headquarters in Aachen, Germany, Captain Hank began an in-depth analysis of the papers his team had recovered. It ended up taking him a full five days to translate and memorize all the documents that were stuffed in the four bulging duffel bags. Although he could have completed it much sooner, he wanted to make sure he didn't miss a single detail. In that respect, even casual marks or minor handwritten notes on the back of the pages didn't escape his in-depth examination and memorization.

After a while his method became routine. First, he would memorize a small stack of paperwork and set it aside in a separate bundle, and when he went down to the inn's dining room to get something to eat, he would offer a break to the person manning the command post. As soon as they were gone, he would throw the bundle of papers into the fireplace of the main lobby. For the most part, no one took notice of him stoking the fire or what he was using to keep the fire burning. On one occasion, Lieutenant Jeffries commented that the fireplace always seemed to be roaring after he relieved him, but Hank told the young officer he'd caught a cold and just couldn't shake the chill. The ruse of not feeling well also worked with the on-going analysis and memorization of the Nazi documents, which allowed Hank to spend much of the five days alone in his room.

The majority of the information contained results of experiments conducted in a secret year-long research and development project at Oranienburg, Germany, that the Nazi's called "Operation Firebird." It helped that Hank had a Bachelor's Degree in mathematics, but his knowledge of physics was elementary compared to what was in the papers. To understand it, he had to mentally recall the introductory physics class he'd attended seven years ago to re-build his education base. Thankfully, the images of his text book were as crystal clear as the day he'd first put it to memory.

Hank learned that the Oranienburg facility was the central depository where the Germans compiled a vast library of scientific information. This material originated from discoveries made by some of the world's greatest theoretical physicists and scientists, and the list read like a "who's who" of famous Nobel Prize winners. Although some of this information was well-known and available to the public (such as Einstein's special and general theories of relativity) most of the collection had been stolen in the Nazi's raids to rid Germany of "Jewish Physics" and was unknown to the world's scientific community.

THE DEVICE

Based on Einstein's theories and Niels Bohr's scientific discoveries regarding the structure of the atom, the Firebird plan borrowed from (or expanded on) studies of matter and motion by using energy, force and momentum. Combined, all these theories eventually enabled the Oranienburg scientists to build a mechanism that literally did the impossible: the Firebird device.

It was late in the afternoon on Tuesday, May the fifteenth, when Hank suddenly came to the realization that he knew and understood everything about Operation Firebird. Even though a few pieces of information were missing (undoubtedly on the erased chalkboards in the Ünterbunker) his photographic memory and increased cognitive learning abilities enabled him to put the missing pieces together in his mind like a child's jigsaw puzzle. He now knew every aspect of the unthinkable Nazi plan, how it evolved, and how the Nazis had tested the new technology.

Hank also discovered that the Oranienburg facility had constructed three devices, one being a non-working prototype that was sent to Werner Heisenberg's laboratory in Haigerloch. Hank remembered seeing the large rudimentary nuclear reactor in Heisenberg's lab very briefly, and noticed that there was a second one (much smaller) in a shipping crate. Since the second one somewhat resembled the larger one, Colonel Pash believed it was a prototype. The only mistake the colonel had made was assuming it was a prototype for the nuclear reactor, *not* the secret Firebird device. In any event, Hank didn't get the chance to inspect it because he was sent out with a search team to look for more intelligence in the surrounding area, and by the time he returned to Heisenberg's laboratory, Sergeant Atkins and his team of explosive experts had already blown it up.

In another file, Hank learned that the working model of the device, named "Firebird One," was moved (along with the historical journals and test results) to the Ünterbunker around the tenth of March. This file also contained the original order signed by Adolph Hitler himself.

After he finished reviewing all the documents, Hank slowly closed the last folder. The final set of papers made him sick to his stomach, and he quickly made his way to the small water closet that was across the hall from his room. The folder contained elaborate and detailed descriptions of horrible experiments carried out on prisoners taken from the Sachsenhausen concentration camp to measure the effects of the emissions from the device. In most cases, these innocent victims died in mortal agony.

Those who happened to live through them, however, were allowed to participate in a ritualistic hand-to-hand fight for their freedom with the Nazi commander in charge of the project: a young SS lieutenant general named Karl Berger. Hank found this information on more than twenty papers contained in the folder outlining these so-called "freedom" fights. There was even a scorecard titled, "Prisoners Worthy of Attention," listing the names of the inmates who'd died at General Berger's hands.

As for Berger, Hank remembered his name from other intelligence that was seized by the Alsos mission in connection to both the Nazi's large-scale extermination plan against the Jewish people, and their secret weapon development programs.

Returning to his room, Hank picked up the small bundled file of papers off the floor, which happened to be the same file that got his attention in the Ünterbunker. As he went to add it to the stack set aside for disposal, a piece of paper dropped from the back; having obviously been stuck there. Picking it up and turning it over, he found it to be a photograph of a very big and muscular Nazi officer shaking hands with Adolph Hitler, while a few more officers looked on in the background. Remembering the ornate German uniform insignias from intelligence school, he saw the man was Waffen-SS with the rank of lieutenant general, and immediately realized he was looking at a photograph of General Berger, the leader of the Firebird operation.

Seeing what the general looked like for the first time *and* that he was shaking hands with Hitler, Hank was somewhat captivated with the haunting photograph. Recalling what this man did to the Sachsenhausen inmates, Berger's picture suddenly took on an entirely new persona – more evil in appearance. After committing it to memory, he started to add it to the stack of papers he was going to burn in the fireplace, then thinking he might need it someday, changed his mind and threw it on the bed.

When Hank finished burning all the papers in the duffel bags, he turned his attention to revising the two Firebird reports in Colonel Pash's file. First, he hastily prepared a revised transcript of what the dying scientist told him at Tailfingen; carefully omitting some of the references and making it sound as if the man was completely delirious. Secondly, he removed two other papers that were found in the sewage drain in Haigerloch. When he made his nightly visit down to the inn's café, he returned the file to the colonel's box of official documents and disposed of the remaining papers in the fireplace.

Returning to his room, Hank prepared his official report to Colonel Pash, summating the Task Force B incursion, and that the team had recovered four duffel bags full of documents having "no intrinsic intelligence value." He also included in the report that the team had recovered a small amount of electrical equipment, but were found to be nothing more than spare parts for the communication system of the bunker. These parts, along with the documents, were disposed of in a nearby landfill.

Colonel Pash returned to the Alsos Forward North Headquarters on Thursday, May the seventeenth. Late in the afternoon, he met with Captain Hank in the inn's café and read his report.

"Looks like we might be in for a chewing-out," Pash said.

"Maybe so, Colonel, but with the intelligence we had at the time, I still think it was a good idea we investigated."

"I agree, but I'm not so sure General Groves will agree.

Hank nodded.

"I probably don't need to ask this, but you're sure the documents you found were of no intelligence value?"

"Positive, sir. At first, I thought we'd found a Nazi coding machine, like the Enigma, but after examining the boxes of wrecked equipment and the papers, most of it was nothing more than spare radio parts and copies of supply requisitions for the bunker."

"Why do you think they went to the extreme of building the lower level in the bunker in the first place?"

"I believe Hitler was going to try to hide down there, hoping he could somehow escape the Russians."

"I guess we can speculate all day what they were up to, but sometimes we win, sometimes we lose. General Groves may not like it, but that's just the way it is. Oh by the way, did you get the word we're moving out to Frankfurt tomorrow?"

"Yes, sir, but why Frankfurt?"

"Even though the Germans have surrendered and the war over here is over, I was told in Paris that our mission hasn't changed. We are to carry on as before until we're ordered to Japan."

"I understand, sir."

"By the way, how are you doing? Lieutenant Jeffries tells me you've been sick, and I must say you don't look very well."

"I'll be okay, sir. I just have a cold that I can't seem to shake."

"All right, but if you get worse and need to take some time off, let me know and I'll see if I can get someone to take you to the dispensary in Paris."

"Thank you, sir."

* * *

Throughout the next two months, the Alsos team investigated numerous other leads with regards to the German's nuclear program. At one point, after many hours of meetings and exchanging information with the commander of the Russian's 8th

Guards Army, General Vasily Chuikov, Colonel Pash and a small group of civilian scientists were allowed access into the (now highly-secured) Russian-held district of Berlin. These investigations uncovered no new information regarding either the Nazi's nuclear weapon program or the Firebird operation.

In mid-July, the Alsos Mission received new orders: they were to proceed to the Philippines, join the combat units assigned to General MacArthur's Operation Downfall, and continue the Alsos mission into Japan. Just before taking off on the flight to Manila, Colonel Pash and Captain Hank were informed that General Groves wanted to see them both at the Pentagon as soon as possible, and they'd disembarked the doomed aircraft.

~ Now ~

With the briefing in the Pentagon over, Captain Hank sat alone in his temporary lodging quarters – eyes closed and deep in thought. After debating with himself on whether he did the right thing in destroying the intelligence, he mentally reviewed the plethora of documents he'd set to memory. In doing so, he connected the trail of information again and again to verify and validate the complex mathematical formulas and physics theories, and with each mental examination he reached the same conclusion: *The Firebird device the Nazi's conceived in the Oranienburg think tank was both scientifically plausible and technologically achievable!*

After a while, he turned his attention to another related piece of information he'd heard Colonel Pash say about the 8th Air Force's bombing of Oranienburg. The aerial surveillance team that had flown over the area the morning after the attack reported the buildings and entire surrounding area were completely destroyed. This meant that none of the remaining Firebird scientists who had worked on the year-long project had survived the bombing. In addition, the third device (which was under construction at the time)

102

as well as any other remaining documents regarding the secret operation were also destroyed in the air raid.

Hank then reviewed the images in his mind of the wrecked equipment that he and his men had recovered from the damaged section of the Ünterbunker's laboratory. Although he needed time to inspect these pieces more thoroughly, he knew the fragments were only those of the field accelerator and the support equipment that was used to provide power to the device, *not* the actual main structure of the device itself. That left only two possible explanations: either someone had dismantled and removed it from the Ünterbunker, or it was missing because someone had activated it.

Bringing his thoughts back to the papers, he carefully reviewed the timeline. The most recent test results of the device were dated the morning of April the thirtieth, the same day Hitler committed suicide. The Russian Army had surrounded Berlin by then, and the Germans surrendered on May the second. If tests were still being conducted on the thirtieth of April, it seemed highly unlikely that there was enough time for the Nazis to dismantle the main structure of the device in one day and move it out of the bunker to another undisclosed location. Even if they had moved it out, with the Russians surrounding the city where could they go with it? That left Hank with the only other possible explanation.

The last bit of information he mentally reviewed was the list of personnel that General Chuikov provided to Colonel Pash. This list contained the names of the people the Russian Army captured at the bunker the day of the surrender, and included General Hans Krebs, Chief of the Nazi General's Staff, General Helmuth Weidling, the last commander of the Berlin Defense Area, and General Johann Rattenhuber, the officer in charge of Hitler's personal bodyguard team. *Not* on this list was the name of the person who'd annotated the final test results of the device on the morning of April the thirtieth: SS Lieutenant General Karl Berger, the leader of the Firebird operation.

The understanding of what this all added up to hit Captain Hank's consciousness like a thunderbolt: *General Berger escaped by activating the Firebird device!*

He slowly stood up and walked over to the small room's wash basin, and after filling his cupped hands, splashed his face with the cold and refreshing water. After drying himself with a towel, he looked into the large mirror on the wall above the sink. He thought about all the circumstances that had converged to bring him to this defining point in his life. He now knew, without a doubt, everything that had happened to him (the baseball accident and the resulting increased mental abilities) was for this reason. He also understood, with crystal clarity, what he needed to do. Since he alone had the physics theories, mathematical formulas, and engineering designs of the Nazi device memorized, he must use this knowledge to find Karl Berger and stop him, before he implements the second phase of the Nazi's inconceivable Firebird plan.

After studying the situation for some time, he reasoned that his chances for success were slim, and hinged on whether he could gather the necessary materials and secretly build a device of his own. Knowing that it had taken the Firebird scientists almost a year to conceive and construct the device (with an unlimited budget and manpower reserve) Hank also knew that if he had any chance of building it, he simply couldn't do it alone – he was going to need some help.

Walking out into the hallway, he made his way down the stairs to the main office of the lodging facility. Finding an empty phone booth, he went in and sat down, dropped a dime in the payphone's slot and dialed the operator.

"I'd like to make a person-to-person call please to Captain Benjamin Washington, United States Army, Fort Meade, Maryland."

* * *

The next afternoon, after receiving permission from Colonel Pash to take leave, Hank boarded a northbound military bus that made daily runs to several of the surrounding Army installations. Throughout the hour-long ride from the Pentagon to Fort Meade, he wondered to himself whether he was doing the right thing involving Big Ben. He knew for certain he could confide in his friend, but with the story he had to tell now, would Ben believe him?

He arrived at Fort Meade just past fifteen-hundred hours, and made his way to the nearest shuttlebus stop. Fort Meade hadn't changed much since he'd last seen it, and just like last time, the heat was sweltering. Thankfully, there was a large oak tree with plenty of shade next to the bus stop, which made the short wait somewhat tolerable.

As he looked around at the familiar buildings, he was struck with a profound sense of guilt. The Army had taught him that it was every intelligence officer's duty to report all enemy information. The instructors had drilled that basic tenet into his brain throughout the course, and on his very first field command he'd broken that fundamental principle by destroying all the evidence of the Nazi's Firebird operation. As the bus pulled up and he climbed aboard, his mind returned to the danger the device posed, and he dismissed his guilty thoughts.

A short time later, the bus dropped him off in the shipping and receiving area of Fort Meade, where most of the buildings were large warehouses. Alive with activity, trucks of every size were either backing up to receiving docks or lined up departing the installation, an ongoing reminder that the country was still at war with the Japanese.

Looking ahead, he located building number five, where Big Ben was to meet him, and he proceeded down a narrow sidewalk that ran adjacent to the busy gravel roadway. After passing two long warehouses, he heard Ben's familiar baritone voice in the distance, barking out orders like a drill instructor. Hank couldn't help but smile when he heard the customary follow-up to one of his tirades, which was a loud and long belly laugh that could clear the cobwebs out of one's ears if they were standing too close.

Once he made it to the building, he walked up the cement stairs to the loading dock and found his friend kneeling in front of ten young enlisted soldiers, instructing them in the proper use of the Army regulation pallet jack. Ben was just as big and muscular as he remembered him, if not bigger. Silently, Hank snuck up on the group and hid behind two of the taller trainees.

When his friend had finished his explanation, and asked the men if they had any questions, Hank couldn't help it.

"Yeah," he blurted out in a squeaky voice, "why do we have to know all this crap?"

"Who said that?" Ben yelled, and quickly stood and began scanning the now-laughing group of troops. As soon as he saw Hank, trying in vain to stay behind the tall men, he let out a salvo of laughs that shook the rafters of the old warehouse.

"Gentlemen," he said, grinning from ear-to-ear, "allow me to introduce you to one of the smartest intelligence officers Ogden, Utah ever produced. Come to think of it, I think he's the *only* officer Ogden, Utah ever produced."

The trainees burst out laughing again.

"Men, say hello to my good friend just back from the war, Captain Hank Stevens!" He led the group in giving Hank a round of applause before embracing him in a giant bear hug.

"Big Ben," Hank said, struggling to get a breath, "you haven't changed a bit."

An hour later the two men left the warehouse and went to a nearby parking lot, where Ben climbed into a stripped-down Army jeep with no doors or top cover.

"Get in," he said.

"Is this yours?"

Ben laughed. "Let's just say it's mine to use because the captain in charge of inspecting intel shipments in warehouse number five needs his transportation."

Hank smiled and climbed in. "What do you do in the winter?"

"You know me. I win a few favors with some people in the motor pool."

"Oh, so you're still taking guys at craps."

"Is it my fault they don't know how to roll the dice? And since the Army, in their infinite wisdom, has seen fit to stick me in a warehouse for the duration of the war, I may as well make the best of it."

He hit the accelerator, and soon they were speeding down the gravel road toward the main area of the base.

"So how've you been?" Hank asked.

"I've had a few setbacks," Ben answered solemnly, "but I'm all right now."

"How's Amy?"

He hesitated a few moments before answering.

"She's gone."

"Really? Is that one of the setbacks you mentioned?"

"You could say that. She died a year and a half ago giving birth to my son."

"Oh Ben, I'm so sorry. I didn't know."

"It's okay, man. You couldn't have known, being over in Germany, fighting the war and all."

Hank felt a tremendous sense of sadness for his friend. He remembered Ben's adoration of Amy. Losing her must have been devastating.

"What about your son? How's he doing?"

"As good as any eighteen-month-old baby can be, and getting bigger every day. In fact, you're about to meet him. We're headed over to the base nursery right now to pick him up."

"I can't wait."

"So tell me, why did you send me those three footlockers full of junk all the way from Germany?"

"You got them then?"

"Yeah, I got them. One of the new guys, Private Dixon, rolled the pallet off the truck right in front of my commander in the middle of our annual inspection and asked me where I wanted him to put it."

"Oh no."

"Well, I was almost ready to tell him where he could put it, if you know what I mean, when I saw the address marked Captain B. Ben Washington, and since you're the only person I know overseas who calls me Big Ben, I had a strong hunch that the pallet load of footlockers came from you."

Hank smiled. "So what *did* you do?"

"Well, since there wasn't a packing slip attached to it, my commander thought it was a phony scenario, and that the inspectors were testing us to see if we would follow protocol for packages arriving without the required paperwork."

"Does that happen a lot? Getting things in without paperwork?"

"Man, you wouldn't believe how much stuff comes in here. Sometimes we don't even know which field unit sent it or what country it came in from."

"Really?"

Ben nodded. "The Army just doesn't have a standardized process, and the war just complicates things. I've been to some high-level meetings where bird colonels got chewed out because some top-secret intelligence got lost in transit somewhere."

"Do you go to a lot of these high-level meetings?"

"Two or three times a month, and you wouldn't believe some of the things I hear that are going on in this man's Army."

"What about the footlockers?"

"Since my commander is new and just got transferred in, I assured him that I'd take care of them. Then after I got him out of my hair, I had Private Dixon take the pallet to one of our empty storerooms and stash it. A few days later, after everyone had gone home for the weekend, I went down to the storeroom and opened them up, thinking my old friend Hank had sent me some German lugers or Nazi flags. Instead, I find nothing but junk."

"Are they still there?"

"Yeah, they're still there."

"They're safe then?"

"Of course they're safe. They're the safest three footlockers of junk in this man's Army."

"Good. I'm glad they got here."

The jeep rolled to a stop in front of the base nursery, whereupon Ben turned to Hank.

"So what gives?"

"Let's get your son and go have some dinner. This is going to take some time to explain."

A few minutes later, one of the nursery attendants brought Ben's son out to the lobby and Ben effortlessly scooped him up.

"How's my boy doing?"

"He had a good day, Captain," the attendant replied, "and I just changed him so he's all ready to go."

"Thanks, I appreciate it."

Ben turned and walked over to where Hank was standing.

"There's someone I'd like you to meet, little man. This is my friend, Captain Hank Stevens. Hank, meet my son Ben Junior, or as I like to call him, J.R."

Hank smiled. "Hello there, J.R. I hope you don't grow up to be like your daddy."

The baby suddenly giggled as if he understood the joke, and both men burst out laughing.

"See? He knows what I'm talking about."

Both men and J.R. continued to laugh and giggle all the way out the door.

* * *

After finishing dinner, Hank cleared the empty Chinese food boxes and silverware from the table, while Ben took J.R. into a corner bedroom and started singing lullabies.

A few minutes later, Ben tip-toed back into the kitchen, and whispering, asked Hank if he wanted another Grapette.

"Sure," Hank whispered back, "but I've got to ask you, what was that awful caterwauling I heard just a minute ago?"

"You don't like my singing?"

Hank smiled. "Oh, that's what it was."

"Man, you just don't appreciate a great singing voice when you hear one. Let's go out on the porch so that we don't wake the little man. Besides, this part of the house is just too hot in the summer."

"At least you get to live in base housing for free while you're stationed here."

"Yeah, I can't complain too much."

They sat down and took turns popping the tops off their sodas with a bottle opener.

"You have a beautiful son, Ben," Hank said.

"Thanks, man. He's all I have left of Amy, and I'm going to make sure he grows up right and stays out of trouble. That's the promise I made to her before she died, and I intend to keep it."

"Well I, for one, am sure you'll keep that promise."

"What about you, man? How did the war go? Did you see any action?"

"Not really. For the most part, the unit I was assigned to just followed the guys on the front lines, looking for enemy intel after they'd cleared the towns."

Ben grinned. "Sounds like the perfect assignment."

"It was for a time, but my priorities have changed."

"How so?"

"I plan on leaving the Army."

"What?"

"You heard me."

110

"You can't leave the Army, because in case you haven't heard, there's still a war going on."

"I don't mean *right now*. As soon as we defeat the Japanese and the Army has a draw-down, I'm getting out."

"What makes you so sure there is going to be a draw-down?"

"It's a matter of record that after every major war the Army cuts back its personnel, and when they do I'm resigning my commission."

"Don't tell me something's finally gotten to you? What happened to the Hank who said he was going to be a lifer and stay in until he made general?"

"Like I said, my priorities have changed."

"What happened? Did you screw something up?"

"No."

"Did an officer chew you out for something?"

Hank shook his head.

Ben grinned again. "Is it a girl?"

"You're way off base."

"So tell me, what would cause my good buddy, Captain Hank Stevens from Ogden, Utah, the one with the photographic memory, to leave this man's Army?"

"Before I answer that, I want to ask you something."

"All right, shoot."

"And I'm asking you this as a friend and not as a fellow Army officer."

"Okay," Ben replied, dragging the word out slowly.

"Let's suppose that you went out on a mission, and found..."

"Impossible. The Army doesn't send black captains out on intelligence missions."

"I know my friend and I'm sorry about that, but for the sake of argument, let's say this time your commander is color blind and he sends you out."

"Okay, for you I'll suspend my disbelief."

"Say you're on this mission and you uncover something so unbelievably dangerous that you are actually afraid of reporting it to the Army, or to anyone else for that matter. Oh, and let's say that no one else knows about this but you. What would you do?"

Ben thought about it for a moment.

"I guess it would depend. How dangerous are we talking?"

"*Very* dangerous."

"The first rule of an intelligence officer is to report all enemy information," he replied, quoting the Army regulation.

"But I'm talking about something so incredibly threatening that it could literally destroy the world as we know it."

"Man, you're starting to scare me,"

"That's not my intention. I just want to know what you would do if you came across something that dangerous."

"Well, officially, as an intelligence officer in this man's Army, it would be my duty to report it. Unofficially, and just between you and me, if I came across something that dangerous and I was the only one who knew about it, I would try to blow it up or get rid of it. Then I'd report that I hadn't found a damn thing."

The men sat quietly for the next few minutes, sipping their sodas.

"I need your help, my friend," Hank said, finally ending the long silence, "and right now you're the only person in the world I can completely trust."

"I feel the same way about you, my man."

"Good, because I need you to suspend your disbelief a little while longer and trust that what I'm about to tell you is the God's-honest truth."

"Why's that?"

"Because quite simply, you're not going to believe what I found."

* * *

The next morning, the two men sat in the kitchen with Ben feeding J.R. in a highchair. The only sounds breaking up the morning silence were the toddler's occasional garbled baby talk and slapping of hands on the table.

"You know," Ben said, "I didn't sleep a wink last night thinking about what you told me."

"I can honestly say that I haven't slept well since I figured all of this out either."

"You said that as soon as the war is over and the Army has the draw down, you're going to get out. So what are you going to do?"

"I'm going after him."

"And just how do you think you are going to do that?"

"I've got a plan, but I need some time to carry it out. As much as I love wearing this uniform, I'm sorry to say that the Army is not part of my plan. I simply cannot be tied down by changing duty assignments, deployments, training exercises and endless inspections."

"Okay, knowing you like I do, when you say you've got a plan, you've got a plan. So where do I fit in? What do you want me to do?"

"Stay in the Army."

"Stay in the Army? How can I be of any help to you stuck in a warehouse inspecting intel shipments?"

Hank leaned in. "Believe it or not, a lot. After I leave the Army, I'll need someone to be my eyes and ears on the inside. You said yourself that you hear a lot of things at those high-level meetings."

"True."

"And the fact that you're able to accept undocumented shipping might come in handy someday."

"I see where you're going, but are you sure you want to do this?"

"I've thought about it a lot, ever since I put the pieces of information together. But as you know, I've always believed that things happen for a reason."

Ben nodded.

"I now believe that the baseball accident that gave me the photographic memory was for this reason, and from here on out my sole mission in life is to find and stop this evil man. So will you help me?"

Ben scooped up J.R. and held him close.

"Yeah man, I'll help you. From what you've told me no one is safe from this guy, not even my little man here. And I swear, as long as I'm standing upright and with a heartbeat, no one is going to hurt my little boy."

* * *

Two days later, back at his temporary lodging quarters near the Pentagon, Captain Hank laid awake in bed putting things in perspective. In the last sixty days, he'd discovered, set to memory, and disposed of the most advanced (as well as dangerous) scientific information man had ever conceived. The only other person who possessed this knowledge was the same individual who'd either experimented on or cold-bloodedly murdered more than a hundred inmates taken from the Sachsenhausen concentration camps: SS Lieutenant General Karl Berger.

After deciphering the papers and realizing the incredible threat the device posed to the world, Hank had dedicated himself to the mission of finding and stopping General Berger. He understood that by accepting this undertaking, he was also putting his personal safety at risk, and that he was now on a path leading in only one direction: to an inevitable confrontation with the man who had spearheaded the Firebird operation, and perhaps the most evil and malicious person to ever wear the Nazi uniform

The cold chill Captain Hank had felt in the Ünterbunker returned, and to stave off the shivers he pulled the sheet and blanket up close to his neck. Unable to sleep, he stared at the ceiling and thought about what he needed to do to build the device. With Big Ben's help, it was still going to be a monumental task, and even if he is able to build it and get it to work, where would he go to find the Nazi's White Wolf?

Chapter Six
The Hit-And-Run

Sixty-Nine Years, One Month and Seventeen Days Later
Saturday, 6 September 2014, 23:45hrs
Inside *Station Park, Farmington, Utah*

Even though the sun and its afterglow had disappeared from the western sky more than an hour ago, the temperature still hovered above the ninety-degree mark. Helping the night stay warm were the black asphalt streets and cement walkways radiating heat from the day's blistering sun, and the lack of a significant breeze which stifled the muggy air. The only sounds were the automatic sprinklers hissing in the pots of hanging flowers and the chirping of male crickets as they stridulated their wings in hopes of attracting females. It was here, strolling arm-in-arm down one of the walkways of the newly completed open-air shopping mall, where Madison and I found ourselves this hot summer evening.

Normally we were in bed by nine o'clock, but this night was different. Having endured an eventful and depressing week, we'd decided to catch a late movie at the Station Park cinema in hopes that it would take our minds off these recent events. The show, titled "The Edge of Tomorrow," starred Tom Cruise as a futuristic soldier caught in a time warp, who endlessly replays his own death in a battle against invading aliens. Normally I'm not much of a Tom Cruise fan, but this film was very good and it ended up being the perfect ending to our evening out, as well as an eerie omen of things to come.

It had been seven days since our late-night meeting with Jim Stevens, the mysterious man with the incredible story, and I knew deep inside it wouldn't be our last.

~ Then ~

The previous Saturday night, after standing us up at the Roof Restaurant, Jim suddenly appeared at our house and continued to tell us the story about his dad, Captain Hank, and how he'd memorized and destroyed all the documents his reconnaissance team had recovered from the secret lower level in Hitler's underground bunker. These documents contained a storehouse of scientific information regarding a Nazi operation, code named Firebird.

He also told us in detail how the Nazi's sequestered seventy scientists for almost a year in a research and development facility in Oranienburg, Germany. As a result, they'd created a mechanism that his dad simply referred to as "the device." In addition, his dad figured out that a brutal SS lieutenant general by the name of Karl Berger, the leader of the Firebird operation, had activated the device to perpetuate his escape from the bunker. It was Madison who asked Jim the most important question of all, and it took him a long time to finally answer it.

"You still haven't told us what this device was or what it did. Up until a short time ago, I thought it was a bomb, but then you told us your dad figured out that General Berger escaped by activating it. So what exactly was it?"

"I apologize, Madison, but I first wanted to give you as much background information as I could so that you wouldn't think I was mad or that I had somehow lost my mind. The device was essentially a mechanism that transported a person to another place."

I immediately thought of the small sets of railroad tracks his dad had found protruding out of the pile of rubble.

"Did the railroad tracks lead to a secret way out?" I asked.

"No, George. The back wall of the laboratory was solid rock. There was no other opening."

"Then how on earth did he get out?"

He smiled. "In the area where the Ünterbunker's laboratory was damaged, my dad found a raised area that looked like a platform or stage. When the device's main structure was there, it was mounted in the center of this platform. As you remembered George, there were two sets of small railroad tracks on the floor of each side of this platform, as well as a single track on the ceiling directly overhead, centered between the two on the floor. These tracks were used to support the outer part of the device called the *field accelerator*. This accelerator was arc-shaped, like a giant horseshoe, and when turned on it traveled back and forth along these tracks at a very high rate of speed. Or in other words, *around* the device's main structure. When it reached the end of the tracks, there were thick rubber bumper stops mounted on the ends that would bounce it back in the other direction."

"So what exactly did this field accelerator do?" Madison asked.

"It was used to generate a high-intensity magnetic field around the device's main structure, which the Firebird scientists found affected the forces of gravity around it. This main structure was made from cobalt metal alloy, which Werner Heisenberg discovered is one of the few natural elements whose magnetic poles are aligned at the atomic level. This alignment makes the alloy extremely susceptible to the forces of magnetism. When they initiated the accelerator around this material, the effect caused the magnetic forces to increase exponentially."

"What was this main structure? Or rather, what was it used for?"

THE DEVICE

"The main structure was cylindrical in shape. Imbedded in its fuselage walls were a set of eighty small motors. Each of these *exciter-motors*, as they were called, powered a tiny electromagnet, which aided the propagation of the magnetic field. As for the inside of the fuselage, it was used in the same fashion as the cockpit of a modern-day fighter aircraft: to carry the pilot of the device. Instead of moving, however, the main structure remained stationary. With that in mind, think of a flight simulator."

We nodded.

"A very well-known physics test known as the Stern-Gerlach Experiment was reversed from a particle shooting *through* a magnetic field, to the field being created *around* the particle. In this case, and on a much larger scale, the particle was the device's main structure."

"In other words, around the cockpit."

"Correct, Madison. As the speed of the accelerator increased, so did the magnetic field around the main structure, until it finally reached what is known as the *magnetic moment*."

Getting lost, I asked him to explain.

"In simplest terms, the magnetic moment is the point where the magnetic forces of both the accelerator and the main structure attract to each other. Think of it this way: say you're holding two magnets, one in each hand, with the north pole pointing up on one and the south pole pointing up on the other. As you move them towards each other, you'll reach a point where they will attract and snap together. That exact point of attraction is the magnetic moment. The same could be said if you were holding them with both north poles pointing up, in which case the magnetic poles would be alike. As you bring them together now, they reach a magnetic moment where the forces will start to resist each other.

"But again, on a much, much larger scale, the momentum that was built up by the device's field accelerator, coupled with on-board electromagnets, caused the magnetic forces of both the accelerator and the main structure to merge into one big powerful magnetic field. And as I mentioned before, this also influenced the forces of gravity holding the main structure in place, whereby it would *distort* the gravitational field around it. Once these combined forces were at their peak, the pilot of the device would change the polarity of the on-board electromagnets, and the main structure would immediately deflect away to another place."

"What place?" Madison and I asked in unison.

"To answer your question, first think about what, exactly, the science of physics actually is."

He paused for a moment.

"Physics is the study of matter and how it moves through space and time by energy, momentum or force. Einstein proved in his theories of relativity that gravity influences how matter moves in space. Space, as everyone knows, has the three dimensions of length, width and height, and all three are affected by the forces of gravity. Einstein also proved that there is a fundamental link between these three dimensions and the fourth dimension, which is time. Now as far as time is concerned, it too can be affected by the forces of gravity. For example, time passes more slowly for objects inside a different gravitational field, or if gravity is distorted in some way."

"Which is what happened when they turned on this field accelerator and the exciter-motors," I said.

He smiled. "Correct, George. The Firebird scientists achieved what is still thought of today as being impossible: they'd penetrated the boundary layer between our three-dimensional world and the fourth dimension."

Madison beat me to the question.

"Jim, correct me if I'm wrong, but it sounds as if you are telling us that the Firebird device was some sort of time machine?"

"As unbelievable as it may sound, Madison, that's *exactly* what it was."

Madison and I looked at each other.

"I know it sounds impossible, but it's true. The device could actually transport a human being into the fourth dimension."

"I'm not saying I don't believe you," I said, "but couldn't there be another explanation? Couldn't the device have done something different or have been used for something else?"

Jim's penetrating blue eyes locked onto me.

"No. My dad recounted his steps repeatedly to verify the trail of information, and to ensure that the physics theories and the related mathematical formulas were valid. That trail ended up leading him to the most advanced scientific knowledge on the face of this earth!"

Again, Madison and I looked at each other.

"Okay, for the sake of argument let's say that the Nazi's did develop this device so that they could go into the fourth dimension," Madison said. "What were they going to do? Go back in time and change history so they could win the war?"

"At first that was the plan, but they found that the device wouldn't work that way. Apart from a few exceptions, it could only propel the pilot into the future and return to the time it had left, not the time *before* it had left. To go back any further would break the *law of causality*."

I asked him to explain.

"You probably know the law of causality by its simpler name: the law of cause and effect. It's one of the fundamental laws of physics which states that all events are caused by prior events. Think of it like a loaded gun. If you pull the trigger it will cause the gun to fire. The gun firing is the effect that is caused by you pulling the trigger. The cause *must precede* the effect, because the cause is responsible *for* the effect. You can't un-pull the trigger after you've fired the gun."

"That makes sense."

"Like I said, the law of causality is one of the fundamental laws of physics. As far as the device was concerned, the Nazi's couldn't go back and change the decisions they'd made that caused them to lose the war because they were already living in the effects of those decisions. I'll admit, it does get complicated when you think about it from that perspective."

"But if the Firebird device could take its pilot into the future, wouldn't returning to the point in time it left *break* the law of causality?" Madison asked.

"No, and this is where it gets real interesting. The deflection propelled the main structure of the device into an aperture or tunnel. Scientists today call it a *closed time-like curve*. This aperture allowed, for a short time, the device to return to its starting point."

"Why only a short time?"

"Because as the old saying goes, for every action there is an equal and opposite reaction. When the deflection happened and the main structure entered the aperture, the forces of nature that were disturbed when it opened immediately started to push back and try to close it. And although the exciter-motors and electromagnets in the device's main structure were very powerful, they could only hold the aperture open for a short period of time."

"Was that one of the exceptions you mentioned?" I asked.

"Yes, and there are a few others, one of which directly relates to this area of discussion. Bear with me for a moment, because it too is a bit complicated."

We nodded.

"The point in time that the pilot returned to was found to be directly proportionate or equal to the time the pilot spent in the future. For example, say you got into the device and activated it at 12:00 pm on Monday, went forward in time to Tuesday, and after spending one hour in the future returned to Monday. The earliest time you could return to would be 1:00 pm on Monday; the hour you spent in the future was equal to the time the device returned you to *after* you left. This was a phenomenon my dad called *equivalent elapsed time displacement.* But as I mentioned before, if you stayed too long in the future you would never be able to get back because the aperture would've closed behind you when nature righted itself."

"How long could you stay in the future and still get back safely to your own time before the aperture closed?" Madison asked.

"Three hours and fourteen minutes, give or take a few milliseconds. And that number was found to be constant in all tests of the device."

"Why so?"

"As simple as I can explain it, think of the aperture as having a circular entrance. The time it took to close and nature to right itself was found to be an exact exponent of the milliseconds of time it took for the device to open it. This number happens to equal the product of a multiple of Pi."

"Pi? That rings a bell," I said.

He smiled. "You're remembering your junior high school mathematics, George."

"Only the word, not what it was."

"Pi, whose first three numbers are 3.14, is the never-ending mathematical calculation of the ratio of a circle's circumference to its diameter. Not to bore you with how deep this math goes, let me just say that when the calculation is made and converted to milliseconds of time, reduced down it equals approximately three hours and fourteen minutes."

"This is incredible."

"But what would prevent, say Pilot A from going into the future and Pilot B from boarding the device and returning to the past?" Madison asked.

"As incredible as it may sound, the device itself. Or perhaps I should put it another way. The scenario you described was attempted three times by the Firebird scientists. Each time, the device malfunctioned and the aperture closed, which prevented the second pilot from returning to the past. Eddleman and Kaufmann believed it had something to do with the alignment of the atoms, but no one really knows for sure."

"The alignment of the atoms?"

"As I mentioned before, the device was constructed out of cobalt, whose magnetic poles are aligned at the atomic level. The two scientists speculated that when they activated the device and the forces of the field accelerator and the main structure merged at the magnetic moment, it temporarily aligned *all* the atoms, to include the pilot of the device. The majority of all these atoms still needed to be in alignment for the pilot to return to his starting time. If they weren't, the device would malfunction."

"Which is what happened when Pilot B boarded the device and tried to return in place of Pilot A."

"Exactly, Madison. But again, this was only a theory."

"So if the Nazi's couldn't go back and change the past, then what were they intending to do once they made it to the future?" I asked.

"Originally, the Firebird plan was called *Unternehmen Stechuhr,* or Operation Time Clock, and consisted of two phases. The first phase called for the development of a device capable of traveling into the fourth dimension. The second phase was to go back into the past and change the course of history so they could win the war. Upon completing the first phase, however, they found that the second phase was impossible to achieve; they couldn't break the fundamental law of causality."

"So where did that leave them?"

"With the war going badly and the device not being able to go backward in time, it forced them to revise the plan and rename it *Unternehmen Zunden Vogel,* or Operation Firebird."

"Why is that so important? Wasn't it just a bold code name?"

"No. In this case it was an important clue as to what the revised plan was all about. Think about the word *Firebird.*"

Madison and I looked at each other, shrugged, and looked back at him.

"In Greek mythology, *Firebird* was another name for *Phoenix.*"

"The bird that died and rose up from its ashes," Madison said.

He smiled. "Precisely. The Firebird operation called for several devices to be built, and for Hitler and a few of his high-ranking officers to escape into the future. Once there, they planned to rebuild their army and fascist dictatorship into a Fourth Reich."

"I take it then, that General Berger threw a monkey wrench into that plan?" I asked.

He nodded. "From the intelligence he memorized and the circumstantial evidence that later became known, here's what my dad believed happened."

Now completely captivated with the story, Madison and I leaned in.

"In early March of 1945, Hitler ordered General Berger to move the device that was nearest to completion, Firebird One, to the Ünterbunker. When he received the order, Berger knew that if he got it working, Hitler would take it, escape into the future, and leave everyone else behind. Remember, the general was not only sadistic but also quite brilliant.

"My dad believed that Hitler underestimated the general, and by this time the Firebird project had become Berger's obsession. Knowing the potential of the device and what a powerful weapon it could be, he wasn't going to let the Führer or anyone else take it away from him. Not only that, Berger knew that if he could get the device to work, it was his way out. And as I told you earlier, when my dad figured all of this out and realized that the main structure was missing from the Ünterbunker, he subsequently made it his life's mission to find General Berger, but unfortunately was unsuccessful."

"This story just seems too impossible to believe."

126

He nodded. "When my dad first told it to me, I didn't believe it either."

"You said time passed more slowly for objects inside a gravitational field or if gravity is distorted, which is what happened to this main structure?" Madison asked.

"Correct, but from the pilot's perspective, the time outside the field was moving very fast."

"How fast could the device travel, or I mean slow down time for the pilot?"

"That depended on how much electrical current the pilot applied to the exciter-motors powering the electromagnets, which in turn increased the strength of the magnetic field. At one-third power, which was just enough to keep the main structure in the fourth dimension, one second of time for the pilot inside the device equated to one minute of real time outside the field of the device. If the pilot moved the throttle forward and added more current, the time passing outside increased exponentially, as would, conversely, the slowing down of time for the pilot."

Madison and I looked at each other again.

"I apologize for throwing all of this at you at once. I understand that it is very difficult to comprehend, but since it is now well past two-o'clock in the morning, and any further talk will simply tire you more and add to your skepticism, I should go."

I looked at my watch, not believing it was that late.

"Before I do, I would like to leave you with this book."

He patted the three-ring binder on his lap and handed it to me.

"All I ask is that you keep it in a secure hiding place."

"What's in it?" I asked.

"It's my dad's diary, written in his own hand. Although it contains much of what I've already told you, you'll be able to understand the story better than I can recount with my fading memory. Look through it when you are rested. Once you finish it you'll understand why I'm so overly-cautious in not wanting this information to fall into the wrong hands. That said, do you have a place you could hide it, and I don't mean in obvious places like a safe or filing cabinet."

"I've got an idea," Madison said. "I saw this in an old movie once. I think it was Casablanca."

She stood up and proceeded to clear the family pictures off the top of our upright piano. When she opened the lid, I handed her the binder and she placed it on an inside shelf where the piano's wires were the shortest.

"An ideal place," Jim said, "just like Bogey hiding the secret papers from the Nazi's in Sam's piano. How fitting, considering what the diary contains."

After closing the lid, we returned the photos to their previous spots, while Jim retrieved his hat and cane and made his way to the front door.

"But you still haven't told us what all of this has to do with Parkinson's research?" Madison asked.

He stopped and turned. "As I mentioned before, I decided to confide in both of you because I believe you are sincere in your desire to help people who suffer with this affliction, and because you both have a personal stake in the research I am planning to conduct."

"Which is?"

"Quite simply, Madison, I'm offering you a spot on my research team. George, I'm offering you the chance of a lifetime: to go into the future and bring back the cure for Parkinson's disease."

I was completely stunned.

"You've built a device?" I asked.

He hesitated before answering.

"I'll be in touch. Good night to you both."

* * *

The next morning, Madison and I had the first of many discussions regarding the fantastic story Jim had told us, the first of which occurred while we were eating breakfast outside on our patio.

"What do you think?" Madison asked.

"I don't know what to think. Either someone is playing an elaborate joke on us, or our strange new friend has quite an active imagination."

"You don't believe any of it then?"

"I didn't say that. I think many parts are probably true. As for the device being a time machine? Well, let's just say there must be another explanation."

"Like what?"

"I don't know, but I'm not ready to take a leap of faith and believe wholeheartedly that the device could actually transport a person into the fourth dimension." As I spoke, I motioned my middle and index fingers on both hands into quotation marks.

"What do you think?"

"I think I'd like to look at his dad's diary," Madison said.

A few moments later, she returned to the table with the large three-ring binder.

Opening it, we found half the papers were extremely complicated mathematical formulas, all written in the same perfect penmanship as his invitation. The second part of the binder was the diary (also perfectly handwritten) categorized by year and separated by tabs. We also found an unmarked key card inside the back pocket of the binder, like those given to guests in modern hotels.

What drew our attention the most was a plastic sheet protector after the last page, which contained an old black and white photograph. Roughly eight inches wide by ten inches high, this worn and faded picture showed Adolph Hitler shaking hands with a Nazi officer, while several other German soldiers looked on with broad smiles on their faces. The man gripping Hitler's hand looked like a giant in comparison to the Nazi dictator; at least twice as large in stature and a good head and shoulders taller. His neck seemed overly big, which reminded me of modern-day football players when they are introduced on television before the game. Adding to his immense size was the tightly-stretched shirt of his uniform, which displayed his well-developed upper-body and muscular physique.

At first glance, I thought his face bore a striking resemblance to an old movie star, whose face I could see in my mind but whose name I couldn't remember. He was a handsome man, with chiseled features many women would find attractive and many men would be envious of. Even though his uniform hat shaded most of his face from the sun, I could still see that there was something hauntingly captivating about his large eyes, which appeared to jump out of the shadow and grab my attention. Still another facial feature that stood out was his closed-mouth smile, which at first looked to be genuine, but upon closer examination seemed Cheshire cat-like – more menacing in appearance.

On the back of the picture, again in perfect penmanship, was the inscription, *"Only known photograph of SS Lt. Gen. Karl Berger."* Madison quickly turned it back over and we looked again at the picture, which now took on a more ominous appearance. His large muscular build, eerie-looking dark eyes, and threatening false smile seemed to emit an aura of evil.

"So that's the White Wolf," Madison said.

"Look at how much bigger he was than Hitler," I whispered.

"He reminds me of one of those huge wrestlers you see on TV."

After a few moments, Madison finally broke away from the captivating photograph and turned the pages back to the first section.

"George, look at this."

The open pages contained the longest math problem I'd ever seen, and it went on for eight more pages. Not only was the problem long, it also contained elaborate symbols and figures. What they stood for, I hadn't a clue.

"It looks pretty close to the same writing that was on the invitation he sent us," I said. "Do you think perfect penmanship runs in his family?"

"Jim did say his dad wrote it, but he must've transcribed some of it."

"I agree. And get a load of that math problem. I'd rather decipher ancient hieroglyphics than to try to tackle that one."

"No kidding. Where's a math professor when you need one?"

"It's too bad we don't know someone who could tell us whether this is advanced scientific calculations or whether it's really just a bunch of meaningless mumbo jumbo. Then we'd know if Jim was telling us the truth, or if he's off his rocker."

After slowly looking through all the pages of the enormous math problem, Madison stopped and looked across our back yard.

"Wait a minute. Remember that friend of yours who we saw at my work's Christmas party last year? He told us he left the Aircraft Division right around the same time you retired."

My mind drew a blank.

"He said he'd landed a new job as an engineer in the Space Division, remember? He was dating Elaine, the gal I worked with last year."

I simply stared back at her, wondering if I was having a forgetful Parkinson moment.

"He was the nerdy bald guy with the black horn-rimmed glasses. You said he re-wired the amplifier in the old jukebox."

The recollection suddenly dawned on me.

"Oh, you mean Gary Tomkins."

"Yeah, that's the guy. Do you think he could tell us what this means?"

"Maybe. His specialty was electrical theory, but now that you mention it I think he had a degree in math. Be forewarned, he's a little strange."

"That's what Elaine said, and why they're not dating anymore."

"When we were on the same repair crew we became good friends. After I got to know him, I found he was almost like a savant; not very good with social skills, but a genius in other areas. I remember one time I bought an old radio from an antique store in Salt Lake and told him about it. He asked me what the make and model was, and of course I couldn't tell him."

She smiled.

"That night I took the back cover off the radio, found the little identification tag and copied down the make and model number. The next day at work when I showed it to Gary, he proceeded to tell me, right off the top of his head mind you, what year the radio was made and the part numbers of the tubes that went in it. When I got home that night and checked the tubes, he was one-hundred percent right. And to top it off, that radio was manufactured in 1937!"

"Are you kidding me?"

I laughed. "I swear I'm not making this up. Like I said, he was a very strange guy, but as far as aircraft electricians go there was no one on the repair line who matched his knowledge. Can he tell us what this problem means? I don't know."

"I say we give him a try."

She opened the three-ring binder and removed the huge math problem, and after retrieving an orange manila envelope from our filing cabinet, placed the papers in it.

"Okay, it's all set. I'll see if I can look him up when I go back to work."

* * *

When Madison got home on Tuesday afternoon, she couldn't wait to tell me about her meeting with Gary. She came rushing into the house waiving the manila envelope.

"You're not going to believe what Gary said about this math problem!"

"Oh? What'd he say?"

"First, it took me forever to find out where he's working now because the employee roster is so out of date. When I finally found his number and got ahold of him, I told him we had a very complicated math problem for him to look at, and if he could tell us what it meant we would treat him to dinner. Then you know what he did?"

I shook my head.

"He hung up on me."

I laughed. "Really?"

"Yes, really. Then about five minutes later he shows up at my office all panting and out of breath."

"He always ran everywhere when he got excited, just like a little kid running after an ice cream truck. What happened next?"

"I made him promise to keep what I showed him confidential."

"Good thinking. I would've never thought of that."

"Then you know what he asked me?"

I smiled. "He probably wanted to know if we were doing something illegal."

She laughed. "Yes! How did you know?"

"He used to ask everybody that. He's such a character. It's nice to know he hasn't changed. So what did he say about the math problem?"

"At first he got real excited and kept asking me where we found it. All I said was, at this point we're not at liberty to say."

"Oh, that was good too."

She smiled. "After studying it for a few minutes, he told me he thought it had something to do with Einstein's theories of relativity, but he needed to borrow my computer to check a few things out."

"Did you let him?" I already knew her answer.

"Of course I did, but I didn't know he was going to stay on it for an hour and a half!"

"An hour and a half?"

"Yes," she said, sounding annoyed. "If he looked up one thing about math, he looked up a dozen more about physics then back to math again. I got the feeling that if I hadn't finally stopped him, he'd still be there at my desk trying to figure it out."

"That's Gary. If he couldn't fix something on the jet he'd stay well past the end of his shift troubleshooting the problem. Did he figure out any of it? Anything at all?"

"Part of it, but he still couldn't definitely tell me what the equation meant or what it was trying to prove. He said if it had something to do with electricity he could've told me immediately, but since he hadn't had a physics class in over twenty years it was going to take him some time. So I copied a page of the problem and let him take it, which excited him to no end."

I smiled. "What part *did* he figure out?"

"Just before he left, he said it had something to do with Einstein's Field Equations."

"Einstein's what?"

"Field Equations."

She pulled the papers out of the envelope and set them on the counter.

"So what are Einstein's Field Equations? Did he say?"

"Before he totally lost me, he said to understand it a person had to know a lot about physics, calculus, differential geometry, and multi-linear algebra, whatever the heck that is. And even though Einstein's Field Equations look like one big complicated math problem, they're really sixteen separate equations in one. They show how mass, energy and momentum determine the curvature of space-time."

All I could do was stare at Madison with my deer-in-the-headlights look, whereupon she pulled another piece of paper out of her purse.

"Don't worry, I wrote it down. How else was I going to remember this stuff?"

After a moment, she found the place she was looking for.

"Here it is. He said way back when Einstein put forth his theories of relativity, he figured out that there are three spatial dimensions, which are length, width and height, and that there is one temporal dimension, which is time. Putting them all together, Einstein called it space-time, or as it is known today, the space-time continuum."

"That sounds like what Jim told us."

"I thought so too. From what Gary remembered, exact solutions to Einstein's Field Equations are extremely rare. To figure them out, a person must make assumptions and show what they *don't* equal or prove, so that they can determine what they *probably* equal or prove. That's why most of the solutions are only approximations."

"It's no wonder people like me hate math so much."

"I know, it's way deep for me too, but in the case of *this* problem, Gary said it looked like someone had figured out an *exact solution* to one of the field equations."

Astonished, I picked up the first page to take a closer look.

"Oh, there's more. He also found on the internet that theoretical physicists and research scientists take the approximate solutions of these equations and plug them into other geometric formulas and math problems, normally when they conduct studies on the things I mentioned before; mass, energy and momentum. They also use the equations to study gravitational waves. Speaking of which, you'll never guess what came up on the internet when he searched for gravitational waves."

"What?"

"One of the definitions said that gravitational waves were, and I quote, ripples or distortions in the space-time continuum."

"Are you kidding me? Let me see that." I took her page of notes and quickly read it.

"You know what this means, don't you?"

"Yes. It means that our mysterious new friend is an expert in math and physics."

She slapped me lightly. "No, it means Jim is telling us the truth."

"I don't know," I said, pondering her comment. "I just don't know."

* * *

On Wednesday morning, Madison and I got into a heated argument about Jim's story. I was sitting at the kitchen table reading the morning newspaper while she was getting ready for work.

"Aren't you even going to look at it?" she asked, referring to the diary.

"Probably not."

"Why not? Don't you want to know what happened to his dad after he memorized the information?"

"I've given this a lot of thought, and I just think this whole thing sounds utterly preposterous."

"You heard what Gary said about the equation."

"Yes, but what are we talking about here? Time travel? The Nazi's making a time machine? When you take a step back and think about it, it really sounds crazy."

"I know, but don't you think we should at least make sure before we write him off as a crackpot?"

"And how do we do that? He hasn't offered us one shred of proof."

"Oh yes he has. The diary."

"Okay, let's talk about the diary."

I rose to my feet and made my way over to the piano. After clearing the photos, I opened the lid and removed the binder.

"You know, anyone could fill up a book with huge math problems and a fictional story, and say that everything in it really happened."

"So you're saying Jim made this whole thing up?"

Ignoring her question, I set the binder down on the kitchen table and retrieved Jim's dinner invitation from under a magnet on the fridge.

"He told us that the writing in the diary was in his dad's own handwriting, right?" I asked.

"Right."

"Don't you find it odd that his dad's handwriting is perfect, and looks identical to the invitation he sent us?"

She merely looked at me, not answering.

"And look at that clean paper. You're telling me that paper is over sixty years old?"

"I'll admit some things are a bit strange, but I still think we should give him the benefit of the doubt and read it with an open mind."

"I thought you were the one who said he keeps getting weirder and weirder?"

"I never said that."

"Really? I swear I heard you say that when we were waiting for him at the Roof Restaurant."

She smiled. "Well, maybe I did say that, but that was before we talked to him."

"Okay, if I have time I'll look it over."

"If you have time? You're retired!"

"I said I'd look at it and I will."

"Thank you. I appreciate it, and I know Jim will appreciate it too."

After Madison left for work, I poured a fresh cup of coffee and began examining the diary. I felt as if the fantastic story Jim had told us was a figment of his imagination, or at the very least, from a man with too much time on his hands. I also thought he could be suffering from another dreaded relative of Parkinson's disease called Lewy-Body dementia, which can cause hallucinations and visual misperceptions. Thinking along those lines, it made perfect sense, and was a more plausible explanation than the Nazi's building a time machine.

Just as I began skimming through the diary, the phone rang. It was Madison.

"Guess what?"

"You got a raise?"

"Gary figured out the field equation!"

"Really?"

"He left me a phone message at one forty-five this morning. He said he stayed on his computer all night until he finally got it."

"Did he say anything else?"

"Just that he would be in around noon, and after he goes to his office and checks in, he'll be down. I was thinking, if you'd like to take me to lunch, say around eleven, when we get back you could come with me to my office and hear what he has to say."

Thinking it would be nice to catch up with him and see how he was doing, I accepted. "Okay," I said, "that sounds like a plan. I'll see you at eleven. I love you."

"I love you too."

I closed the binder and returned it to the hiding place in the piano, thinking that I'd wait to see what Gary says before wasting any more time reading it.

Five hours later, after Madison and I ate lunch at a nearby restaurant, we made our way back to her office. While waiting for Gary to arrive, she logged into her computer to check her email messages, while I checked the candy dish her co-workers keep stocked with chocolates.

Suddenly, Madison let out a gasp.

"Oh no. George, look at this."

I popped a chocolate chunk in my mouth.

"What is it?"

"Look at this. It just can't be."

The title of the email message was, "One of our own," which normally meant that someone who either worked at the base or who had retired from the base had died. The message read:

"The Space Division is saddened to report that Gary Tomkins, one of the division's lead electrical engineers, passed away this morning in his North Ogden home from an apparent suicide. Funeral arrangements will be forthcoming."

Madison scrolled down and we saw a photo of Gary accepting an award he'd received the previous year. His bald head and black horn-rimmed glasses, coupled with the plastic pen holder in the front pocket of his dress shirt, made him look like the role model nerd; exactly how I remembered him when I'd worked with him all those years ago.

I was too stunned to speak.

"I can't believe it," Madison said. "He didn't seem like a guy who'd kill himself."

I briefly thought of the field equation that we might never know the answer to, but the memories of the fun times I'd had working with Gary suddenly pushed the thought aside. Seeing my eyes water, Madison stood up and embraced me.

"I'm sorry, George."

Reaching behind her, I grabbed a tissue from the box on her desk and wiped my eyes.

"I'm okay. It's just, he helped me a lot when I first got hired on. I can't help but feel for the guy. I know I said he was a little weird and kind of on the savant-side, but I meant it in all respect, meaning he was so smart."

"I know you did. You don't have to explain."

"I guess you just never know what people are thinking anymore."

"I guess you don't."

* * *

On Saturday morning, Madison and I attended a "Celebration of Life" in honor of Gary at a nearby funeral home, which turned into somewhat of a reunion with many of my former co-workers from the aircraft hangar. We reminisced about happier times, when we'd worked on the old F-4 Phantom jets that used to come in to the huge depot maintenance facility. We also laughed about some of the pranks we'd pulled off on Gary, as well as some of the ones he'd pulled off on us.

I got to meet Gary's mom and dad, who were quite elderly and still in a state of shock over his passing. I told them that he was one of the smartest people I'd ever known, and that I was proud to call him my friend. I knew it was no solace for losing their son, but I felt it was important to let them know that I appreciated all the help he gave me when we worked together on the same crew.

Madison also got to visit Elaine, her friend who'd briefly dated Gary. While they talked, I made my way around the room, visiting other former coworkers I hadn't seen in many years. I also overheard one of them, Steve Wilson, talking about Gary's death. Steve had a little brother who was a deputy sheriff in Weber County, who also happened to be the first to respond to Gary's house when the 9-1-1 call came in.

Apparently, a boy who lived next door had hit a baseball into Gary's backyard. After knocking on his door and getting no response, the boy decided to go around the house to see if the gate was open. Looking in a basement window, he saw Gary's body and ran home and told his parents.

When Steve's brother arrived at the scene, he found Gary had apparently hung himself from an open ceiling rafter at the top of the stairs. The rope he'd used had broken, and his body had tumbled all the way down to the basement floor. He also mentioned that there seemed to be a lot of blunt-force trauma on Gary's body, and at first it looked as if someone had beat him up. The detectives, however, subsequently determined the cause of the bruising and other injuries had occurred from the fall down the stairs, and the coroner ruled Gary's death a suicide – specifically from a broken neck.

* * *

When Madison and I got home that afternoon, we were exhausted. Just as we were getting ready to take a well-needed nap, our cell phones rang. When we opened them, we found a new text message from Jim Stevens, which read:

> Dear George & Madison,
> I would very much like to talk to you both as soon as possible.
> This is extremely urgent!
> Let me know what day/time will work best for you.
> Very respectfully yours,
> Jim Stevens

Great, I thought, *just what I don't need right now.*

"What do we tell him?" Madison asked.

"How about four weeks from next Thursday?"

"George, he says it's urgent."

"And I have an urgent need for some sleep right now. It was a long morning."

"George?"

"Okay, but not today. Please?"

"Reply and tell him we're having a date night, and are going to a late movie at Station Park. We'll meet with him tomorrow, all right?"

"What time?"

"Noon is good with me."

I typed in the response and sent it off. Almost immediately, we heard another ring tone and received another message, which read, "Noon at my house in Mountain Green will be fine."

"*Now* can we take that nap?"

She blew me a kiss and mouthed the words, "I love you."

A few minutes later, we were laying in bed with our puppies between us.

"You know, George, we really could make it a date night tonight and go get something to eat over at Station Park."

I smiled, "And afterward go catch a late movie."

"Why didn't I think of that?"

We laughed.

~ Now ~

As Madison and I walked along the dimly-lit sidewalks of Station Park, she spoke about Gary.

"So why do you think he decided to kill himself? He didn't seem depressed."

"I guess we'll never know. I knew quite a few guys in the hangar who committed suicide while I worked there. One was a good friend I played volleyball with every day at lunch. I never thought he'd commit suicide either."

"What do you think Gary found out about the math problem?"

"Search me. Even if we did know, it's probably so far over our heads we wouldn't be able to understand it."

We stepped out from the sidewalk to cross the street.

"But it does make you wonder, doesn't it?" she asked.

"Yes, but…"

Before I could finish my thought, we heard a voice yelling behind us.

"George! Madison! Please wait! I need to talk to you both right now!"

We stopped half way through the crosswalk, and turning, saw Jim Stevens frantically trying to catch up with us. With no hat and his cane wildly flailing as he tried to run, he appeared to be having a full-blown panic attack. Once he caught up with us he started to say something, but I couldn't make out his words due to his heavy labored breathing.

"Take it easy Jim, what's the matter?" I asked.

Madison and I moved to both sides of him, and tried to steady him as best we could. In his agitated state, however, his Parkinson's symptoms were on full overload and it was difficult for us to get a firm grip on his arms due to the pronounced tremors.

Suddenly, out of the corner of my eye, I noticed a vehicle coming towards us. At first glance, I thought my new bifocal contact lenses were playing tricks on me, as they had done many times since I'd bought them. This time I did a double take, and realized there was indeed a large black SUV bearing down on us from behind – without headlights and going at a high rate of speed.

Since they were facing the opposite direction, Madison and Jim couldn't see the oncoming threat. In addition, a passing commuter train with its loud locomotive engine and whistle was masking the sound of the SUV's roaring engine. If it hadn't been for the faint reflection that was cast off the car's hood from a nearby streetlight, I'd have missed it altogether.

Because Madison was more towards the center of the street and stood the greatest chance of being hit, I quickly let go of Jim, grabbed her arm and jerked her out of the way. When I did, she lost the hold she had on Jim's other arm. Her sudden and unexpected break away from him caused her to crash into me, which resulted in our feet getting tangled and both of us falling to the ground. As the SUV raced by, I heard a sickening thud and thought for a moment that my beloved Madison had been hit. When I regained my senses, I stood and found her unhurt.

143

THE DEVICE

Jim, however, was a different story. His body had apparently taken the full force of the impact, and he was laying fifteen feet away from us in a crumpled heap against one of the ornate lampposts.

While Madison retrieved her phone to call 9-1-1, I ran over to him, and as I knelt down he turned himself over to face me.

"Take it easy, Jim. Don't try to move."

"Are you all right, George? What about Madison?"

"We're both okay. She's on the phone right now calling the paramedics."

"Oh, thank goodness. If something had happened to either of you, I would've never forgiven myself."

There was a trickle of blood coming from his mouth, and I was sure this meant he'd sustained some very serious internal injuries.

"I'm sorry George, truly sorry that I put you and your beautiful wife in danger. If it wasn't for my declining health, due to this insufferable condition we both share, I wouldn't have involved either of you."

"You don't have to be sorry about any…"

"No, you don't understand," he interrupted, "with my declining physical condition, I could no longer pilot the device. I thought that if I brought in a man like you, who had the disease in the early-onset stage, you could use the device to bring back the cure. Then after I regained my health, I would be able to complete the mission."

"The mission? What mission?"

"The mission I dedicated my life to over sixty years ago, to find a very evil man," he gasped, "but I'm afraid he found me first."

He looked around for a moment, as if he couldn't see me.

"Jim! Stay with me!"

His eyes appeared to refocus and he motioned me to come closer, and I put my head down so that my ear was right next to his mouth.

"Look in the diary. The key is there. Use the device to find the cure. Once you find the cure, complete the mission. Promise me that you'll complete the mission!"

As he gasped for the next breath of air, he started to cough up blood. I looked up at Madison, who shook her head in frustration at not being able to get the call through.

"I promise, Jim, I promise," I said, trying to comfort him, "but you've got to stay with me. The paramedics are coming!"

Miraculously, he suddenly had some last-second strength, and he grabbed me by the collar and locked his piercing blue eyes on me.

"In case you haven't already guessed, my name is Henry Stevens, but you can call me Captain Hank."

I looked at him for a moment, stunned at the revelation, then his eyes went vacant and his grip on my collar relaxed.

After a few moments, I slowly rose to my feet and walked over to Madison.

"He's gone," I said.

She dropped her cell phone and buried her face in my chest. When I embraced her, our tears began to flow. We'd not only been close to losing each other, we'd also lost the sudden friendship of this strange man named Jim Stevens. Although he had only visited our lives for a short time, there was no denying that he'd had a profound effect on us.

His dying words and the admission of his true identity gave me feelings of guilt and remorse for not believing him. As much as I'd doubted him before, I knew now deep in my heart that the incredible story he'd told us about the device was the truth.

As I looked back at his broken and motionless body, it seemed as if his sudden violent death was not meant to be; like an historic anomaly at this point in time. It also felt like Madison and I had just witnessed the passing of the last true hero of the Greatest Generation; the final casualty of a conflict that had begun more than seventy years ago. Even though all the battles were over and the famous participants had died, the war hadn't really ended. Instead, it had lasted longer than anyone could've ever imagined, and had now claimed the life of Captain Henry Stevens.

* * *

In his mission to find the missing Nazi war criminal, Captain Hank had paid the ultimate price. His death left Madison and I with heavy hearts and a countless number of unanswered questions. In the days that followed we would find the answers to those questions, eventually revealing themselves from both an unexpected source, and in the perfectly-handwritten pages of the diary he left behind. These answers would not only tell us the rest of the story about the device, but they would also serve as a catalyst in cementing my resolve to fulfill the promise I'd made to him before he died.

What Madison and I didn't know at the time (but would quickly realize) was that the mostly-tranquil life we'd enjoyed before meeting Captain Hank was over, and that the individuals responsible for killing him were already plotting their moves against us. We would soon find ourselves trapped in a very deep abyss without an escape route, blocked by one of the most predatory of all creatures – the White Wolf.

Chapter Seven
The Interrogation

Two Days Later
Monday, 8 September 2014, 06:00hrs
Inside the *Weber County Jail, Ogden, Utah*

Three pieces of furniture adorning the eight-foot square room included two thinly-padded metal chairs, containing many scratches, and a cheap veneer-covered desk, its corners broken and worn. Except for one large framed one-way mirror, used to observe the proceedings from next door, the satin-white walls were devoid of any color or décor. A lone light fixture hanging from the center of the ceiling contained a set of eight extra-large bulbs, which not only over-illuminated the small space but also drove the temperature up to well over one-hundred degrees. On top of this fixture sat a five-bladed fan, intentionally left off to prevent the air from circulating. The high-intensity lighting and hot stuffy atmosphere were tools being used to create stress and anxiety, with the end goal of eliciting information. It was here in this uncomfortably hot questioning room, where I found myself this early fall morning.

Across the table from me sat a red-haired man with a walrus mustache. As he questioned me, I felt utter contempt for him. When we'd first met, he'd identified himself only as "Agent O'Leary," but finding out he was a seasoned veteran in the medieval methods of interrogating a prisoner (using threats and intimidation) I had secretly nicknamed him "Master Inquisitor." I'd stopped answering his barrage of redundant questions over half an hour ago, and in retaliation he'd ratcheted up the warnings and possible consequences that would befall me if I didn't tell him everything I knew about Mr. James Stevens.

My right arm and leg were visibly trembling, but not from the abuse. Instead, they shook from having been denied my Parkinson's medication, and now the dopamine-starved neurons in the left side of my brain were sending sputtering signals to the right side of my body. To the casual observer (as well as the Master Inquisitor) it must have appeared as if I was quaking from fright. In addition, ever since I'd been diagnosed with the disease my symptoms had blossomed whenever I encountered a high amount of emotional stress – and this was definitely one of those times.

As much as I hated the tremors and the other symptoms associated with Parkinson's, it paled in comparison to how much I despised the limping man with the Irish accent who was sitting in front of me. My hatred stemmed from the way he treated Madison and me when he'd taken us into custody. At that time, when I'd questioned our arrest, he walked over to me in a very calm and calculated manner and sucker-punched me in the stomach. When Madison tried to help me, he backhanded her across the face, and the ring he was wearing opened an inch-long gash on her right cheek. Even if it meant a beating at the hands of this bully, I promised myself that someday I would return the favor of the backhand he'd so easily given to Madison, as well as the punch he'd delivered to me.

His entire appearance, from the western boots on his feet to the ill-fitting cowboy hat on his head, added to my loathing of this country and western piece of work. I even found myself hating popular country songs, which he continually whistled throughout my entire interrogation.

As I sat there not saying a word, I thought back to the hit-and-run that had killed Captain Hank, and the ensuing circumstances that resulted in Madison and I being arrested and taken to the Weber County Jail. To say it had been an eventful forty-eight hours would be an understatement.

~ Then ~

Following the hit-and-run, Madison retrieved her phone and called 9-1-1 while I thought about what we were going to say to the authorities. After quickly explaining who she was, where we were and what the emergency was all about, she walked over to me.

"Oh George, what are we going to do?"

"We tell them the truth. That a black SUV came down the street going too fast and hit this man. From the erratic way they were swerving, the driver must've been drunk."

"Do you really believe that?"

"Of course I don't, but until we can figure out something else that's what we'll say."

"Should we tell them who he was or how we knew him?"

"I think the less we say the better. As far as anyone is concerned, we knew Jim Stevens from the Parkinson's support group. We ran into him on our way out of the movie and the accident happened. That's all we know. If we say anything else it might open up an entirely new can of worms."

She nodded in agreement.

The paramedics showed up about the same time as the police, and after checking Captain Hank's vital signs and finding no pulse they pronounced him dead at the scene. While this was going on, the two police officers took our statements. Madison and I told them the story we'd agreed on, and that we knew "James Stevens" from the support group. A short time later they loaded Captain Hank's body into the ambulance and the police released us to go home. Before we left, however, I retrieved his cane from the curb where he'd dropped it; if for nothing else, just to remind me of him.

THE DEVICE

On the slow and quiet ride back to our house, Madison stared blankly out the window while I remained frustrated at my inability to formulate a plan of what to do.

It was twenty minutes past two o'clock in the morning when we finally got home. Exhausted, we made our way up to the bedroom, and a short time later were nestled in bed with our puppies. As tired as I felt, my sleep was restless for the remainder of the night.

Late the next morning, I was sitting at our kitchen counter sipping a cup of coffee while looking through Captain Hank's three-ring binder. It was hard to imagine that the complicated math equations were the keys to unlocking a doorway into the fourth dimension and traveling through time. I found myself taking extra precautions (turning the pages ever so slowly) so as not to accidentally tear this holy grail of scientific information.

About five minutes into my examination, Madison came down the stairs and sat down beside me.

"What time did you get up?" she asked.

"A little while ago. I wasn't sleeping well."

Before she could reply, our front doorbell rang. I immediately closed the binder and returned it to the piano. Once we'd finished resetting the photos on top, I peeked through the closed window blinds. Instead of finding someone on the porch, there was a brochure on the stair railing secured with a rubber band.

"Another salesman," I said, "he left something outside."

"On a Sunday?" she asked.

I shrugged my shoulders and opened the door to retrieve the brochure. I saw it wasn't one person who'd left it, but instead a very well-dressed couple making their way down the sidewalk to our next-door neighbor's house.

"Oh yeah, there they are. At least these two are trying to make an impression, all dressed up I mean."

"What are they selling?"

Looking at the brochure, I found it to be an advertisement for solar panels.

"Free energy, but only after you invest in their product."

Madison glanced at the brochure and placed it on a pile of newspapers destined for the recycle bin, then stuck her head out the door to see the couple.

"Wow," she exclaimed, "they do look nice."

"I bet the suit that guy is wearing cost him a pretty penny."

"Oh George, I don't know why but they just reminded me of Jim, or I mean Captain Hank. Do you think his family knows he's dead?"

"I wouldn't think so, since the name we gave to the police wasn't his real name."

"We've got to do something. What if he had a wife and kids? We've got to let them know."

"I know. I wish he would have told us something…"

"Hey, wait a second," she interrupted. "I know who'd know. Roy and Shelley."

"How about we go get some lunch then go up to Mountain Green and see if they're there."

She smiled and kissed me on the cheek. "I like that plan. I'll go take a shower."

* * *

At two o'clock in the afternoon we arrived at Captain Hanks's house in Mountain Green. There was a car parked along the side of the home which I recognized from the day of the luncheon.

"We might be in luck. Isn't that their car?" I asked.

"It looks like the same one to me."

When we reached the front door, Madison pushed the doorbell, but we didn't hear a ring.

"It must be out of order," I said.

When I tried knocking, the door immediately opened.

151

"Roy? Shelley?" I yelled.

No response.

Madison yelled their names a few more times, and still not hearing a reply, stepped inside and proceeded down the long hallway towards the rear of the house. I looked around outside for a moment, and not noticing anything out of the ordinary, hurriedly followed her inside.

She was about fifteen feet ahead of me when she reached the end of the hall. Turning to go in to the dining room, she suddenly stopped and stood motionless.

"What is it?"

She started to say something but couldn't get the words out, then raised her arm and pointed to something in the room. I also noticed she was trembling and had a look of sheer terror on her face. As I hurried my pace and got closer, her knees began to buckle. As soon as I reached her, I grabbed her arms to steady her and said her name a few more times to keep her from passing out. The combination of me holding her and yelling her name worked, and she suddenly came to her senses.

While still holding her arms, I turned around to face the dining room to see what had caused her to almost faint. The scene before me not only chilled me to the bone, but also made me realize we were up against a truly evil man.

Shelley and Roy were laying side by side in the center of the dining room table. From their unblinking vacant eyes, sorrowfully staring off into nothingness, I knew immediately they were dead.

I walked Madison over a dining room chair that was still upright and sat her down. After making sure she was all right, I turned and approached the table to have a closer look at Captain Hank's personal assistants.

The first thing that stood out in my mind was that they were both beaten very badly, so much so that their faces were almost unrecognizable. I quickly looked away from the macabre sight and focused my attention on the rest of the room.

152

It was hard for me to believe that this was the same place where we'd enjoyed the extraordinary meal a few days ago. Most of the dining room chairs were tipped over or broken, as was the end table the photographs had been on. There were also holes of various sizes punched into the surrounding walls, indicating that someone or something had impacted against them with a great deal of force. In addition, a great amount blood spatter lined the floor, furniture and walls.

When I returned my attention to Madison, she looked up at me and began to cry.

"George, what have we gotten ourselves into?"

"We'd better get out of here," I whispered. "Whoever did this might still be around."

"Shouldn't we report it?"

"When we get outside we'll call 9-1-1."

Helping her to her feet, we made our way back down the long hallway and to the front door. The instant we stepped out onto the front porch I heard guns being drawn and the clicks of safeties being taken off. A booming deep voice with a pronounced Irish accent followed.

"This is Agent O'Leary of the FBI. Hold it right there!"

Madison and I froze in our tracks.

The group of agents consisted of five men and one woman. Most were wearing black. One wore western attire.

"Don't shoot," I yelled, "we just found two people murdered."

"Shut up and raise your hands! You two are under arrest!"

As Madison and I slowly raised our hands, Agent O'Leary limped forward and ordered the others to put us in handcuffs. When I protested our arrest, Agent O'Leary administered his surprise punch to my stomach and backhanded Madison across her face.

* * *

THE DEVICE

Once we reached the Weber County Jail the agents immediately commandeered the place, barking orders at the minimally-staffed weekend duty officers as if they were drill sergeants yelling at new recruits. Madison and I were separated, whereupon they placed me in a holding cell inside the men's section. When I last saw her, she was being escorted towards the women's area of the jail by the lone female agent in the group. Since the laceration on her face was still bleeding quite heavily, I silently prayed they were taking her to get some medical attention.

I waited several hours before two of the men who arrested us finally came back and took me to an interrogation room. After another long wait, Agent O'Leary came in, whereupon I resolved to tell him only the barest of details of how we came to be in Captain Hank's house.

He was in a highly-agitated state when he first walked through the door. In seconds, he'd harshly picked me up and shoved me back down onto a different metal chair than the one I'd been sitting in. As he placed restraints on my wrists, he calmed himself somewhat and began cheerily whistling a country song to himself; as if what he was doing was pleasing him. Once he had my wrists secure, he bound my legs to the bottom of the chair with a wide leather strap, tightening it until I was completely immobile.

When I'd first set eyes on Agent O'Leary at the house in Mountain Green, I thought he was nothing more than a redneck stooge who took his orders from higher-ups. When the questioning began, however, I realized that he was no dummy at all. Instead, he was a very skilled expert in the art of interrogation, and his bullying methods of threats and intimidation were just two of the many tools he used to practice his craft.

His main area of inquiry was about Jim Stevens, how we knew him and whether he'd given us any information. He didn't ask very many questions about Shelley or Roy, but instead concentrated squarely on what I knew of the man who'd died in the hit-and-run the night before.

The methods he employed to question me seemed right out of a detective's handbook, and followed the same pattern throughout. He'd start by asking me one set of related questions, then switch the subject to another set of questions unrelated to the first. As the session continued, he went back to the first line of questioning, re-phrasing the same questions differently to trip me up on some minor detail. Whenever he did cross me up on something, or thought that I'd contradicted myself, he would pounce on it with another set of questions, all of which were followed by a barrage of insults and threats to the point of absurdity. This scenario played out repeatedly throughout the next several hours.

As the questioning continued, the thin pad on the seat I was sitting on became so uncomfortable that I had to keep shifting my weight to stop the cramps. To top things off, my bladder was ready to burst, but my numerous requests to use a restroom were repeatedly denied. My discomfort coupled with my worsening Parkinson's symptoms seemed to bring delight to O'Leary, emboldening him to continue his incessant threats and non-stop cross-examination.

I also noticed throughout the entire grilling that he was a very shrewd observer, employing the "Reid Technique," which I'd learned in the military – a method of watching body language to detect whether a person is lying. Unfortunately for him, my prominent Parkinson's tremors masked some of these non-verbal signals, and allowed me to get away with not telling him everything I knew.

Another tried-and-true approach he used was the good-cop/bad-cop routine. Approximately four hours into the interrogation, in the middle of asking me another set of redundant questions, he checked his watch and abruptly stood and left the room. A few minutes later another agent came in. This second man was the polar opposite of Agent O'Leary: short, thin and frail.

In a pleasant voice, he identified himself as Agent Crosby and asked if he could be of any assistance.

"Of course you can," I said, matching his condescending tone with my own, "you could take me to my wife, give me back my Parkinson's medications and let us go."

He smiled. "I'll make that happen if you tell Agent O'Leary what he wants to know."

"I've already told him everything I know!" I yelled.

"If you're not going to cooperate, I can't help you. I've seen him get very physical with people who make him mad. So if you know what's good for you, you'd better talk."

Agent O'Leary must've seen enough from behind the one-way mirror, because he suddenly came bursting back into the room and dismissed Agent Crosby in a blink. A few moments later, after again calming himself, he sat down across from me and the questioning continued.

~ *Now* ~

I was at a point where I was not going to say another word, and I silently promised myself that no matter what tactics he used I was going to sit there in utter silence.

In turn, O'Leary ramped up the threats and began physically abusing me. He began by grabbing and twisting my shirt collar until I was choking and administered several slaps to my face, all while demanding answers to his questions. When I still refused to say anything, he delivered a hard punch to my left eye followed by another punch to my stomach.

After enduring a few more blows to my face, stomach and ribcage, my bladder couldn't hold back any more and it let loose like a tidal wave. Seeing my accident, he grinned and laughed, as if he'd achieved some great milestone in embarrassing me.

The abuse finally ended when Agent Crosby returned and whispered something in his ear and they both exited the room, leaving me alone to ponder what was going to happen next.

Doing a quick self-assessment, I realized that at least two of my ribs were either broken or badly bruised. My left eye was completely swollen shut and there was a cut on my eyebrow above it, dripping blood down my cheek and neck. My stomach was also hurting, and each time I took a breath the throbbing intensified.

Approximately fifteen minutes later, two uniformed deputies came in and removed my restraints, and after helping me to my feet they led me out into the hallway. Looking around, I found it odd that I didn't see Agent O'Leary or any of the other agents who'd arrested us.

As the deputies escorted me down the hall, one of them commented, "I don't know what you did, but you sure know how to make the feds mad."

Thinking this might be another tactic employed by the Master Inquisitor, I remained silent.

When we reached the front of the building, I found Madison sitting in a waiting room, her hair disheveled and looking exhausted. When she stood and turned to face me, the sight of the large bandage taped to her right cheek immediately brought tears to my eyes.

"What have you animals done to my husband!" she screamed.

"It wasn't us lady, it was the feds," one of the deputies said.

We embraced, and I held her for as long as my trembling body could before I finally collapsed into a nearby chair.

Just then, another uniformed officer came into the waiting room and motioned the other two deputies to leave. He was a big man, both tall and muscular, and was carrying a cold compressor pack.

"I'm Deputy Sherriff Robert Alvarez," he said, handing the pack to Madison.

Taking it from him, Madison placed the compression gently on my swollen eye.

"Did you beat up my husband?"

"No ma'am. I just came on duty a few minutes ago. The night shift told me you were brought in yesterday afternoon by the FBI. Since the agents were gone before I got here, and they didn't tell any of my guys what you were arrested for, if you don't mind me asking, what did you do?"

Ignoring him, she turned back to me.

"What can I get you, George?"

"My PD meds and a shot of whiskey," I said, barely managing to get the words out, "not necessarily in that order."

"Where's your pill box?"

"I don't know. They took it from me."

"My husband has Parkinson's disease," Madison said, addressing the officer. "Do you think you could find his pillbox so that he can take his meds? It's a little green plastic box about this big." She showed him the approximate size with her fingers.

He left without saying a word then returned a few moments later with my pillbox and a bottle of water. He also had my wallet, keys and Madison's purse.

"I've called an ambulance to take you to Ogden Regional."

"Oh thank you very much, how considerate," Madison replied sarcastically.

"Look, I don't know why the FBI brought you here and I don't like being kept in the dark, especially when it involves this facility. So is there anything you'd like to tell me?"

"No! We just want to get out of here!"

A few minutes later the ambulance arrived, and with much needed assistance from Madison I managed to get back on my feet.

When the big deputy moved to try to help, she stopped him with a shout.

"Don't you touch him!"

"All right," he said, backing away, "but I'm still going to follow you up to the hospital. When they see both of you they'll want to report it."

"Report it? What do you mean?"

"Whenever they suspect domestic abuse, they're required by law to report it. I'll take care of it."

Madison begrudgingly nodded, and we proceeded out of the waiting room and into the front lobby.

As we slowly made our way out of the building, I glanced back at the digital clock that was hanging on the wall above the reception desk. It was half past six on Monday morning.

Madison and I had been detained for more than sixteen hours, seven of which I'd spent in an interrogation room at the mercy of the Master Inquisitor.

* * *

As the ambulance transported us to the hospital, Madison was still fuming.

"If it's the last thing I ever do I'm going to have the badge of that smirking, limping, red-headed, Irish son of a..."

"Madison!" I yelled, interrupting her with all the strength I could muster.

She stopped her rant in mid-sentence and looked at me.

"We can't do anything."

"What do you mean we can't do anything? Of course we can. All we have to do is call the FBI and find out how to file a complaint."

"No, you don't understand. While I was being questioned I realized that Agent O'Leary and the rest of his group weren't FBI agents."

"Then how did they gain access to the jail and order those deputies around like they did?"

"Forged credentials more than likely."

"How could you tell? Did one of them let something slip?"

"You could say they all did." I motioned her closer so that the two men in front wouldn't hear. "I didn't think of it until later," I whispered. "When we were taken into custody they didn't read us our rights. That's the first thing a police officer is supposed to do when they arrest someone."

"With everything that's happened, I forgot," she whispered back.

"But that wasn't the clincher. When O'Leary questioned me, he wasn't interested in the murders of Shelley or Roy at all. Instead, his entire line of questioning always returned to the same two things. First, what exactly did Jim Stevens talk to us about, and second, whether or not Jim gave us anything,"

Her eyes grew large as the realization came to her.

"They're after the diary."

"Exactly. I just hope that by the time we get home our house isn't completely torn apart."

* * *

While the emergency room doctor treated me for my injuries, Deputy Alvarez kept a watchful eye on us. True to his word, he informed the attending physician and nurse that the injuries we sustained were not from domestic abuse, but instead were from an assault by persons unknown.

Once the deputy stepped out and we were alone in the treatment room, I learned from Madison what happened to her after they took her to the women's section of the jail. Apparently, Agent O'Leary planned to interrogate her too, but his plans were thwarted by an unexpected development.

"I'd been waiting in the holding cell for I don't know how long," Madison began, "then Agent Denney came back to get me."

"Agent Denney?"

"She was the female with O'Leary. At least that's what she called herself."

I nodded.

"Anyway, when Agent Denney came back to get me, she told me O'Leary wanted to ask me a few questions."

"They didn't take you to a doctor to have that cut looked at?" I asked.

"I'm getting to that," she said, patting my hand. "When we reached the interrogation room, we were met by the graveyard shift supervisor who'd just come on duty. Her name was Deputy Crystal Rivers, and guess what?"

"What?"

She grinned. "She was large and in charge."

Even though I was hurting, the connotation that Madison and I frequently used whenever we meet someone with a strong personality still made me laugh.

"Not an overly big woman, but when she entered the scene there was no doubt who was in command. She first demanded to know what was going on in *her* jail. While Agent Denney tried to explain, Rivers saw the cut on my cheek, crossed her arms and shook her head like this."

Madison mimicked the move, making me hurt again from laughter.

"When Denney explained that her superior, Agent O'Leary, wanted to question me about two murders, Deputy Rivers told her in no uncertain terms that she was going to first contact the jail's physician and have him treat the cut on my cheek. Then afterward, *she* would be the one to decide if there was going to be any questioning."

"So what did Agent Denny do?"

"She got right on her phone and called Agent O'Leary, and when he showed up you talk about a fight."

"They actually fought?"

"Not literally, but it almost came to that. It was easily the biggest shouting match I've ever seen. As much as O'Leary got in her face and tried to order her around, Deputy Rivers got into his. I'll tell you one thing, that red-headed Irishman had met his match. As much as he tried to bully her or pull rank on her, the more she dug in her heels. His face got so red I thought he was going to have a stroke."

"Oh, I would've loved to have seen that. So what finally happened?"

"O'Leary left and the doctor came in and sewed up my cheek. When I told them how I'd gotten the cut, and that Agent O'Leary had backhanded me, Deputy Rivers made a few phone calls. From then on, she didn't leave my side."

"Well thank goodness for Deputy Rivers. Did O'Leary come back?"

"Yes. He showed back up a while later with Denney and the four other agents who arrested us. Deputy Rivers must've thought something like this was going to happen, because she alerted three other deputies. When O'Leary and his people tried to take me into their custody, he suddenly found himself up against four deputies and the doctor."

"The doctor?"

She smiled. "Yes, even he joined in. All of them formed this wall around me and it got pretty scary. For a minute, I thought they were going to draw their guns on each other."

"What happened next?"

"After about twenty minutes, O'Leary stormed off taking his people with him."

"That explains why he was so mad."

"What do you mean?"

"When he came in to question me, he was already ticked off about something. It must have been because of Deputy Rivers."

"Oh George, I didn't think he would take it out on you. I'm so sorry." Tears welled up in her eyes.

"You don't have to be sorry. It's not your fault. I'm just glad Deputy Rivers was there to stop O'Leary from working on you like he did me."

"She was so awesome. You know, she stayed by my side until she got off shift and waited with me until just before the deputies brought you out."

A voice from the door suddenly startled us.

"She is one of a kind."

It was Deputy Alvarez.

"How long have you been there?" Madison asked, irritated.

"Long enough to know that if Deputy Rivers was involved in a standoff with FBI agents in the women's section of the jail last night, and these same agents were the ones who assaulted both of you, I'm opening an investigation. Now will you please tell me what is going on and why you were brought in last night?"

I could tell Madison was about to tell the deputy what he could do with his investigation, and I stopped her with a pat on the back of her hand. There was something about his authoritative deep voice and professional demeanor that told me we could trust him. But for now (until we knew him better) I decided to only tell him *part* of the story.

"Sit down, Deputy," I said, "this is going to take some time."

We recounted the events of the last two days, starting with the hit-and-run at Farmington Station Park on Saturday night.

* * *

When Deputy Alvarez stepped out of the treatment room again, I sat quietly with Madison and thought about how I'd struggled to protect her throughout this whole ordeal. As much as I hated to admit it, a fifty-four-year-old man with Parkinson's disease was no match for O'Leary and his well-armed squad of phony FBI agents. It made me realize how vulnerable we were, and if we stood any chance of fulfilling the promise I made to Captain Hank we certainly couldn't do it by ourselves – we needed some help.

As often happens in life, help arrives at a time or a place you least expect it, and in the days that followed assistance would come to us from four individuals. Two of these people, Deputy Alvarez and Deputy Rivers, helped us because of their positions in the Weber County Sherriff's Office. The other two happened to be sibling twins, who came to our aid for more personal reasons. Their names were Ethan and Evelynn Washington, whose grandfather was Major Benjamin Washington, the best friend of Captain Hank.

Chapter Eight
The Twins

Six Hours Later
Monday, 8 September 2014, 15:15hrs
Inside the *d'Clare Home, Layton, Utah*

The crystal clear late afternoon sky and the sun's bright rays made the spectacular view of the Wasatch mountain range look like a photograph out of a Utah travel brochure. In the foreground stood several abundantly blossomed rose bushes, alive with bees gathering pollen, and two rows of petunias, thriving with small butterflies darting off their petals. Completing the picture, between the mountains and the flowers, were several couples dressed in shorts and t-shirts pushing their baby carriages along the sidewalk. As I sat on the edge of the bed taking in the summer sights outside our bedroom window, I was struck at how peaceful and serene everything looked; the polar opposite of what Madison and I had experienced a few hours ago.

Feeling groggy from the pain pills I'd received at the hospital and the lack of sleep the night before, I sat for several minutes allowing my head to clear. Noticing my right arm and leg trembling, I rose to my feet and retrieved my Parkinson's medications and a glass of water. The instant I stood up, the aching of my injuries returned in full force, and after quickly taking the dose I sat back down almost out of breath.

While waiting for the waves of pain and tremors to dissipate, my thoughts returned to the events that had transpired earlier. Even though the sun shined brightly outside, I felt an invisible cloud hovering over our house, darkening the otherwise picturesque day.

~ Then ~

Five hours ago, Madison and I were in the back seat of Deputy Alvarez's police cruiser, making our way south through Weber canyon toward our home. Throughout the twenty-minute ride from the hospital, I silently prayed we wouldn't find our house in complete shambles or (worse) our little dogs hurt or killed. As far as that was concerned, if they'd trashed our house it could be repaired, but if they'd harmed our defenseless pets the damage would be irreparable. When I thought of how Hank, Shelley and Roy had lost their lives, I knew we were dealing with heartless individuals who had no qualms about taking a life, be it human or otherwise.

I also worried about Captain Hank's diary. When Madison had first suggested using the piano as a hiding place, I thought it was the perfect spot and that no one would ever think to look there, but the closer we got to our house, the more I thought the place was too obvious.

When we finally got home and opened the garage door, we found our wall cabinets open and their contents scattered around on the floor. Our second vehicle's doors were also open, and the contents of the glove box were on the passenger seat.

Seeing our garage in such disarray, Deputy Alvarez ordered us to remain there, and after withdrawing his firearm he cautiously entered our home. As soon as he'd gone inside, Madison moved close to me.

"What are we going to do if the diary is gone?" she asked, whispering.

"I don't know," I whispered back, "but I'm glad he's here."

"Do you think we should've told him about it?"

"No, that would've just led to more questions. Before we tell him anything I want to be one-hundred percent sure we can trust him."

"And how do you propose to do that?"

I smiled. "Again, I don't know. I'm kind of making this up as we go along."

A few minutes later, Deputy Alvarez emerged from the house carrying both of our Shih-Tzu puppies; alive and well with their tails wagging.

"I found these two in the basement. Do they belong to you?" he asked.

"They sure do," Madison said.

When we took our dogs from the deputy, their tongues immediately went to work on our faces.

"Your house is clear, but it looks like your upstairs and kitchen were ransacked. I can only assume it was the same people who took you into custody last night and brought you to the jail. Now I know I'm repeating myself, but are you sure you don't know what they were after?"

"Like I told you at the hospital, all O'Leary wanted to know is what Mr. Stevens told us when we were with him, and if he gave us anything," I said.

He looked at Madison, who simply shrugged her shoulders.

"If you think of anything or remember something, let me know. You've got my number."

We nodded.

"Are you two going to be all right?"

His concern seemed genuine.

"We'll be okay," Madison said.

"Just to be on the safe side, I'm going to request a patrol car from Davis County make regular passes outside your house for the next couple of days. Oh, and could I get the keys to your vehicle?"

Suddenly remembering he was going to arrange to bring our truck back from Mountain Green, I dug into my pocket and handed him the keys.

Madison and I stayed in the garage waving goodbye until his car disappeared around the corner, after which we ran into the house and made our way straight to the piano. Quickly removing the photos and opening the lid, we found the diary still there. Breathing a sigh of relief, I took it out and brought it over to the kitchen table, where we conducted a quick inspection. Once we were satisfied nothing had been disturbed, we turned our attention to the rest of the house.

Just as Deputy Alvarez told us, our upstairs and kitchen had been turned upside down: the cabinets and dressers were all open and their contents strewn about on the floor. Our front room, lower family room and basement, however, appeared to be untouched, which made me think that something must've happened that interrupted the search.

Proceeding back to the front room, we sat down on the sofa and I painfully placed an arm around Madison. I thought for a moment that this invasion of our privacy might be the last straw in breaking her down, but I couldn't have been more wrong.

"If it's the last thing we ever do," she said, "we're going to get these people."

~ *Now* ~

Fully-cognizant from my marathon nap, I made my way to the top of the stairs and found Madison in the kitchen straightening things up. Because we'd been so exhausted when we got home, we'd hardly said a word to each other since discovering the diary was still in its hiding place.

As I took a step the stair creaked, and upon seeing me she put a finger to her lips, signaling me not to say anything.

I mouthed the word "What?" and she walked over to the kitchen table, picked up a pen and a pad of paper, and started writing. Once she was finished she held it up for me to read.

"The house might be bugged, so don't talk about the diary!"

I nodded. "Boy did I conk out."

"You're telling me. I could hear you snoring all the way down here."

She pointed across the table at the solar panel brochure that had been left on our front door the previous morning. I hadn't bothered opening it, and I remembered she'd placed it on a stack of newspapers I was going to throw in the recycle bin. It was laying open now, and there was a small yellow sticky note on the inside, which read:

G/M,

Your house is being watched.
Be careful what you say – bugs.
We'll make contact soon.
Friends of Cpt. Hank

I immediately searched my memory to see if we might've said anything that would tip off the location of the diary. Taking her pen, I hastily scribbled, *"I can't remember if we talked about the diary, so I don't think the piano is safe anymore."*

She took the pen and wrote back, *"So where should we hide it?"*

Retrieving the diary from the piano, I looked at it for a few moments and had an idea. When we'd remodeled our kitchen, the kick panel on the bottom of the dishwasher hadn't stayed fastened. I'd subsequently had to use Velcro stickers to keep it in place. Bending down, I removed the panel and slid the binder in, and it missed the water connections by less than an inch. After replacing the panel, I stood and gave the thumbs up signal to Madison.

"I think I'll go take a shower." I said. "When I'm done, how about we go get something to eat?"

"I could call for a pizza. Canadian bacon and pineapple?"

Knowing that was my favorite, I gave her a quick kiss on the cheek.

"Sounds like a plan."

I took a lengthy shower in hopes that it would soothe the aches and pains in my ribcage and abdomen. The hot water was somewhat refreshing, but exiting the shower and taking a deep breath, my sore ribs and stomach instantly reminded me again of the interrogation. While silently cursing O'Leary, I gingerly got dressed, and after putting a new bandage on the cut above my right eye, proceeded to the kitchen.

"Are you hungry? Madison asked.

"It's here already?"

She smiled. "The pizza guy showed up a few minutes ago."

After eating the delicious pizza, Madison cleared the table while I emptied the garbage. Lifting out the heaping bag, I proceeded down the stairs and out through the door leading into the garage. Pushing the button to open the large door, I made my way past our vehicle and waited momentarily for it to fully-open. As soon as it was up all the way, I found myself face-to-face with the couple who had dropped off the solar panel brochure.

They were both tall and appeared to be extremely physically fit; the woman slender, and the man of a more muscular build. They were dressed in the same black business attire I saw them in yesterday, and each carried black bags; his being a hard briefcase type and hers resembling those that college students carry laptop computers in. From their clean-cut and professional appearance alone, they could've easily passed as representatives of a major corporation. From their similar facial resemblance, I surmised they were brother and sister, perhaps even twins.

"Hello, sir," the man said, friendly and salesman-like, "my name is Ethan and this is my sister Evelynn. We were wondering if we might have a moment of your time?"

With my sibling deduction confirmed, I smiled to myself.

"Sure, just give me a second."

"Certainly, George."

Seeing me struggle to get the heavy garbage bag in the dumpster, he offered to do it for me, and after depositing the bag he returned to Evelynn's side.

"Thanks, I appreciate it," I said, and shook both their hands. "I'm curious. Are you two twins?"

"Yes," Evelynn said.

"We were born on New Year's Day, 1983," Ethan added.

"Please come on in. Sorry about the mess, we're in the middle of cleaning."

Evelynn smiled. "We won't judge. We promise."

I led them inside and up the short flight of stairs.

"Honey, we've got company."

"Who is it?"

"Ethan and Evelynn..." I stopped when I realized I didn't know their last name.

"Smith," Ethan said, reaching out his hand. "Ethan and Evelynn Smith. Nice to meet you Mrs. d'Clare, or may we call you Madison?"

I took note that he knew our first names, and wondered if they worked for O'Leary.

Madison nodded and shook their hands. "Could I get you something to drink? A bottle of water or a soda?" she asked.

"I'll take a bottle of water," Evelynn said.

"Make that two," Ethan echoed.

I offered them seats on the sofa in our front room, and when they sat down our playful dogs immediately jumped on their laps.

"Hey girls, get down."

171

"They're all right, George," Evelynn said, petting our smaller dog. "My brother and I love animals. What are their names?"

"You're holding Ginger and Ethan has Spice."

Evelynn smiled. "Ginger and Spice, how nice."

We all laughed at the rhyming quip, which never seemed to grow old.

Madison brought in the bottles of water, and after a few more moments of fawning over our pets Ethan cleared his throat and spoke first.

"I see you found the brochure we left the other day."

"Yes, we were just looking it over," I said.

He held a finger up to his mouth, signaling us to be quiet, and pointed to Evelynn.

"Great. If you've got a few minutes, we'd like to tell you more about our product and how we can make your home work for you."

While he was talking, Evelynn opened the bag she was carrying and took out a pad of paper and a pen.

"We're friends of Capt. Hank," she wrote. *"We haven't heard from him. Do you know where he is?"*

Madison took the pen from her. *"He was killed Saturday night."*

Tears immediately came to Evelynn's eyes. Ethan, also visibly shaken, cleared his throat a few times and continued to talk about the solar panels.

"Here's some information on the packages we are currently offering, and the potential money you could save on your monthly utility bill."

As he was talking, he retrieved a pen for himself from inside his jacket.

"We saw you taken into custody," he wrote. *"Did they do this to you?"* He motioned to my face and to the cut on Madison's cheek.

172

Madison and I nodded.

"We'll check your house for bugs, but we can't stay. Things are too hot here."

After he finished writing he continued talking about the solar panels, not missing a beat with his long and drawn-out sales pitch. While he was talking, Evelynn opened her bag and removed a small box that resembled a transistor radio, but with a digital display. She also took out a small roll of masking tape and handed it to Madison. When she did, I noticed tears running down her face.

"Do you have some tissues?" she asked. "My allergies are acting up again."

"In the bathroom at the top of the stairs," Madison said. "Let me show you where it is."

They both headed upstairs and a few moments later Evelynn emerged from the bathroom holding the little box, and proceeded slowly down the hallway towards our bedroom; keeping a watchful eye on the digital display. Madison (following closely behind) carried the roll of tape, apparently to be used to mark the location of the bugs.

"I don't know if I can make a large investment right now," I said, addressing Ethan. While I was talking, I retrieved the pen and the pad of paper.

"Who are you?" I wrote.

"Oh, absolutely no pressure George, but if you do see a package that you think you can afford or have questions about, let me know. Now here's the brochure on our Gold Star Plan, and you can see here what is included."

He took the pen and pad and hastily scribbled, *"Our real name is Washington."* Then he retrieved his wallet and showed me his Maryland driver's license. Returning to the paper, he wrote, *"Our parents and grandfather were friends of Captain Hank. Did he mention us?"*

I shook my head. "What do the other plans offer?"

"Here's our Silver Star Plan, and finally the basic Bronze Star Plan. Look them over for a few minutes, and let me know what you think."

"*You have to trust us,*" he wrote, underlining it several times and adding three exclamation marks. "*We got in late Saturday. Capt. Hank was to pick us up at the airport, but didn't show. What happened?*"

I studied his face for a moment, and thinking he was sincere motioned for the pad of paper.

"*A black SUV ran him down. We couldn't see the driver.*"

Just then the ladies came back down the stairs, and after checking the front room, kitchen and dining room, Evelynn motioned to Madison for a piece of tape. Handing her a small piece, she placed it on the ceramic centerpiece on our kitchen table, after which they proceeded downstairs to the family room.

While this was going on, Ethan wrote another quick note.

"*Is the diary safe?*"

I nodded.

"*Good! Keep it hidden.*"

When the women returned a few minutes later, Evelynn held up her hand, signaling the number four, and mouthed the words: kitchen, bedroom, front room and family room.

Ethan immediately went back to writing.

"*Tell us that you'll think about buying the product and we'll leave. We'll call in a couple of days when the heat dies down. If you get in trouble, call us.*" He added their cell phone numbers.

"Thanks for the information," I said. "Let Madison and I talk it over. If we decide to invest in your solar panels we'll give you a call."

"Certainly, but keep in mind we can only offer the Gold Star Plan at the discounted rate until the end of the month."

Seeing us nod, Evelynn took the pad of paper.

"*Still be careful of what you say...our bug finder is not the best.*"

174

Madison took the pad from her.

"How can we trust you?" She underlined the question several times, and handed the pad back to her.

"Because we're on the same side, and we need each other's help to finish Capt. Hank's mission."

We looked over at Ethan, who simply nodded and placed the bug finder back in its box.

After wishing us a good day, they hastily exited out the front door.

* * *

That night, after removing the bug from our bedroom, Madison and I laid awake in bed whispering about the twins' visit.

"Do you think we can trust them?" I asked.

"I think so."

"What convinced you?"

"Did you see their expressions when I wrote that Captain Hank was killed?"

I nodded. "That was a telling sign, especially when Evelynn burst into tears."

"What do you think?"

"I'm not sure. O'Leary is a crafty guy. I wouldn't put it past him to hire two people to impersonate someone Captain Hank might've known just so he can get his hands on the diary. On the other hand, Ethan did show me his Maryland driver's license, which is where Fort Meade is and where Captain Hank met with Ben Washington."

She nodded. "And Evelynn wrote that we needed each other's help if we are to finish Captain Hank's *mission*." She emphasized the word using her fingers as quotation marks.

"Yes. That's exactly how Hank referred to it when he was dying. So let's just say I'm cautiously optimistic they're on our side."

175

THE DEVICE

We talked until Madison started to fall asleep, at which point I kissed her good night and turned off the light. I laid awake a while longer, thinking about the twins and hoping Madison and I could trust them.

We wouldn't find out (for certain) that the twins were on our side until we finished reading the perfectly hand-written diary Captain Hank had left with us, detailing the events that transpired after he decided to leave the Army and build the unimaginable device. In the heart-wrenching story that followed, we learned that Hank's mission to find and stop the Nazi's White Wolf had cost the lives of two people: the parents of Ethan and Evelynn Washington.

Part Two:
The Divulgence

Chapter Nine
The Diary

Seventeen Hours Later
Tuesday, 9 September 2014, 12:30hrs
Southbound along *Main Street, Layton, Utah*

A multi-car accident in a construction zone clogged Interstate 15 for several miles in both directions, bringing traffic to a screeching halt. The only vehicles moving were a plethora of emergency response vehicles, their sirens blaring and lights flashing as they sped towards the scene. With the long delay, impatient drivers were either exiting the overly-congested freeway or taking different routes altogether. Unfortunately, the large volume of motorists choosing these strategies overwhelmed Main Street (which ran adjacent) and effectively reduced its speed down to a slow crawl. It was amid this bumper-to-bumper traffic where Madison and I found ourselves this early afternoon, and where we noticed again that we were being followed.

We had just picked up our lunch at a local fast-food restaurant and were on our way home when Madison noticed a large black SUV in the rear-view mirror. It looked like the same one that had followed us when we'd left our house, and like before it stayed at a discreet distance behind us.

Because of my sore ribcage and swollen eye, I had reluctantly given up my chivalrous driving duties to Madison, which now left me free to try to identify the driver of the vehicle. When I finally got a clear view, however, its tinted front windshield made it impossible for me to see inside. With no way to identify who was following us, I turned back around and silently reviewed the steps Madison and I had taken to copy Captain Hank's diary.

~ Then ~

Earlier that day, we'd cleaned our house from top to bottom, and swept the house again with the bug detector. This time we conducted a slower and more thorough search, and included the garage, our SUV, and even our storage shed in the back yard. We found two more hidden bugs: one in our vehicle under the dashboard, and a second in our living room underneath the radio. That brought the total to six, and the way the detector was working, which was sporadic at best, we believed there were more.

To bring us some peace of mind that we weren't being listened to, and at the same time trick whoever was listening into thinking we hadn't found them, I cranked up our old jukebox and filled the house with oldies music. As an added measure, we carried on fake conversations and used the pads of paper to write notes like before, and destroyed the used sheets in our paper shredder after each conversation.

In the event O'Leary and his people came to our house and demanded the diary at gunpoint, Madison and I decided to make a copy of it. The only thing we could think of was to scan all the pages of the binder into our computer, and transfer the electronic file over to a portable flash drive. That way, we would be able to hide it or carry it around easier. This presented us with the problem of how to scan the documents into the computer without O'Leary and his people hearing it.

After exchanging a few written messages with Madison, we came up with a plan on how we could mask the scanner's sounds. I took one of the jukebox's remote speakers up to the top of the stairs and pointed it towards the den. With Rod Stewart's "Maggie May" blaring out of the speaker, I knew that if we kept the music going it would drown out the sounds of the scanner.

Copying the diary's information onto a flash drive also presented us with another problem: if we were apprehended and searched again, O'Leary and his people were certain to find it. As small and differently shaped as flash drives are, anyone with even a novice background in computers can easily identify them. Fortunately, I remembered Madison had recently attended a cosmetology convention, and when they drew for door prizes she'd won a unique flash drive: one that could be worn as a barrette.

When she first showed it to me, it reminded me of the gaudy jewelry women used to wear in nineteenth-century photographs. It was somewhat large, flowery-shaped, and decorated with dozens of tiny colored sequins. Detaching the flower from the snapping hair clasp revealed the hidden flash drive. If Madison didn't mind wearing a barrette that made her look like a spinster from the gilded age, I thought this flash drive would be the perfect place to hide the electronic copy of the diary.

I wrote a short note explaining what I had in mind and we started scanning the pages of Captain Hank's binder, which took us the better part of an hour to accomplish. Once we had all the pages scanned, we split the contents into two separate electronic files; placing the math and physics equations in one titled "Formulas," and the journal part in the other titled "Diary." That way we wouldn't have to sift through all the pages of equations every time we wanted to read it.

After separating the files, Madison picked up a pen and a pad of paper.

"Should we scan the photo?"

I nodded. Taking the pen from her, I wrote, *"We may need to give it to Deputy Alvarez."*

"He'll never believe the story about the device."

"No, but he might believe Capt. Hank discovered the whereabouts of a Nazi war criminal."

She smiled and drew a happy face on the paper.

After scanning in the picture and copying all three files into the barrette flash drive, I placed the thick binder back in is hiding place below the dishwasher.

A short time later, when we pulled out of our driveway to go get some lunch, Madison noticed there was a black SUV following us.

~ Now ~

As soon as we were back at our house, I walked out of the garage and glanced up and down the street a few times. Not seeing any sign of the black SUV, I shrugged at Madison and we proceeded inside. Since both of us were eagerly anticipating reading Captain Hank's diary, we soon forgot about the black SUV.

After greeting our puppies, Madison lowered the blinds on all the windows and re-checked the locked doors, while I retrieved the diary from underneath the dishwasher and brought it down into our family room. We realized that if we played the jukebox too much to mask what we were doing, it might arouse the suspicions of O'Leary and his people, so we turned on the television to a national news channel and periodically made comments about the various stories.

For the remainder of the afternoon and well into the evening, Madison and I read the captivating and perfectly hand-written journal of Captain Hank. He'd made it his life's mission to find SS Lieutenant General Karl Berger, who'd disappeared at the end of the war. For the ensuing search, he'd spent literally years learning the skills and gathering the materials necessary to build the device. As fascinating as the first part of the story was when he'd told it to us, the second part was just as mesmerizing.

The first entry contained a one-hundred and twenty-seven-page summary of what had occurred between early 1946, when Hank resigned his commission and left the Army, up to July of 1991. This introductory portion was also divided up into smaller titled sections.

The following passages are condensed from those sections:

The Problem of Money for the Mission

In the spring of 1946, after resigning my commission, I returned to Maryland and accepted a position as a physics professor at St. Andes University, which is located close to Fort Meade. With a starting salary of over six-thousand dollars a year, I felt the job would provide me a steady income that was more than enough to pay my living expenses.

As for extra money to build the device, I decided to invest in the stock market. Having no previous experience, I visited several nearby libraries and memorized volumes of business publications. Once I'd identified the safest stocks with the highest potential yields, I visited a brokerage house and purchased shares using the money I'd saved from being in the Army. In a relatively short amount of time, I'd amassed a substantial amount of capital, and used it for obtaining or manufacturing the parts I needed for the device.

Big Ben, always looking for an opportunity to make money, took notice of my green thumb in the stock market and asked if I would teach him. Throughout the time we were building the device, I mentored him on how it all worked, and in no time at all he was on a first name basis with my stock broker, and was buying and selling stocks like a Wall Street tycoon. The stock market eventually made Ben and I independently wealthy, and we would never worry about money again.

Back to School

In the fall of 1946 I settled into my new position as a physics professor, and after becoming comfortable with my class schedule and teaching routine I enrolled in several nighttime courses at a local vocational school. Throughout the next year, while teaching at the university during the day and attending the occupational courses at night, I became proficient at welding and machining metal. I also became an expert on using a wide variety of tools and lathes – all geared toward fabricating the parts I needed to build the device.

My Best Friend, Benjamin Washington, and his son, J.R.

One of the few people I shared the secret of the device with was my dear friend, Big Ben Washington. True to his word, he remained in the Army for many years after the war. Behind the scenes, he provided me with information and much-needed assistance in my plan to build the device. Time and again he proved himself to be the perfect assistant, in that he grasped what was at stake in our endeavor, as well as brought to my attention any information that might be pertinent or material that might be of any use.

I also developed quite a bond with Ben's son J.R., and took time off from building the device to play games with the little boy whenever he accompanied his father to the warehouse.

Worth mentioning is the reason Ben continued to refer to me with my old rank and nickname combination, even though I was no longer a member of the armed forces. On one occasion, he explained to me that he would always refer to me in that manner because of "The Poem." I immediately harkened back to the days we roomed together at Fort Meade's intelligence school, when I volunteered to recite Walt Whitman's ode to Abraham Lincoln, "Oh Captain, My Captain," to our graduating class. As an admirer of President Lincoln, Ben had read the stirring and emotional tribute before, but hearing me recite it aloud at the ceremony moved him to tears. After he explained this to me, I accepted the title as a term of endearment.

Much to my regret, subsequent events prevented me from thanking Ben and J.R. personally for their friendship, as well as the assistance they gave to me on the mission. I now look upon this as a complete travesty on my part, and something that will haunt me for the rest of my life.

Our Headquarters

In early 1947, we were searching for a garage or warehouse near the Fort Meade area where we could set up our base of operations. Big Ben learned from a co-worker that Fort Meade had recently instituted a "Community Partnership Program," which included opportunities for local businesses to lease some of their facilities, including a select few of their industrial buildings. My friend obtained a list of warehouses that were available and we selected a cinderblock building, Warehouse 1373. The location of this building had several advantages: it sat apart from the others in the warehouse area, it was near the base's old train depot, and it was somewhat secluded by a grove of trees on one side and a utility power substation on the other.

To save money I planned on living at the site, and the interior of this building worked perfectly into that plan. Three months prior it had been renovated, and the front was now equipped with drinking water, restrooms and a small shower. There were also two small rooms that were previously used as break rooms and a foreman's office, which I could use as my kitchen and bedroom. As an added safety measure, there were two sets of emergency lights that stayed on all the time inside each end of the building.

When it came time to complete the lease paperwork, Big Ben worked a deal with Fort Meade's contracting office which would allow me to rent Warehouse 1373 for the next sixty years, provided I kept paying the monthly rental fee of thirty-seven dollars and fifty-five cents! How he managed to pull this off I hadn't a clue, but I suspected it was because he'd started dating a woman named Elizabeth who worked as a secretary for the base's Director of Contracting. In any event, we now had a good-sized building that we could use for a very long time.

DRMO

One of Big Ben's duties entailed inspecting outgoing items at Fort Meade's Defense Revitalization and Marketing Office, or DRMO. Once a month, this office conducted public auctions to dispose of outdated surplus government supplies and equipment. Before these items went to auction, however, they were required to be inspected by military intelligence personnel to ensure that they did not contain anything that could be considered "sensitive." This placed Ben in a perfect position to target some of the tools and machinery we could use in manufacturing the device, and acquire them at a price that was well below market value. In less than eight months, Warehouse 1373 took on the appearance of an industrial machinist's factory.

The Room for the Device

We built a wall separating the front half of the warehouse (where we stockpiled the tools and machinery) from the rear where we planned to assemble the device. Like the laboratory in the Ünterbunker, we lined the rear section with sheets of polished steel. This was necessary because of something I found in several mental reviews of the Nazi information, and pertained to something General Berger had discovered.

Although he was the most cold-blooded and ruthless person I'd ever read about, Berger was also a brilliant scientist in his own right. In one of his more-notable moments of insight, he surmised that if the laboratory was lined with polished-steel plates, it would amplify the magnetic forces generated by the device's exciter-motors and field accelerator. After he ordered the walls of the

186

Ünterbunker's laboratory to be lined with the metal and the device was tested, his hypothesis was proven correct.

Throughout the fall of 1947 and into the summer of 1948, Big Ben and I spent several hours each evening cutting, mounting and polishing the metal sheets, until we had completely covered the walls and ceiling of the rear section of the warehouse. Finishing, I couldn't help but notice how the back of the building now eerily resembled the Ünterbunker's laboratory.

The Railroad Tracks

In a few of our "midnight requisitions," Ben and I acquired the necessary rails needed for the device's field accelerator to travel on. In this undertaking, we located some excess railing behind one of the maintenance buildings near Fort Meade's old train depot. We also "borrowed" five small railroad wheels, two mechanical lever assemblies, and numerous other parts for the carriage the field accelerator was to be mounted on.

Our Stinky Little Friend

It was well past twenty-three hundred hours (eleven o'clock in the evening) when Big Ben and I set out on our fifth and final incursion to the railroad yard. After one of our previous trips, Ben mentioned that he'd spotted a buffer stop through one of the maintenance building's broken windows. "Buffer stops" are energy-absorbing assemblies that are placed at the end of rails to prevent a loose train car from going past the end of the track. I remembered seeing some smaller ones made of rubber attached to the ends of the tracks in the Ünterbunker, and wanted to set a standard one to memory to compare the two. Entering the building, we found the buffer stop partially concealed by a tarp. When Ben pulled the tarp away, we were suddenly overcome with a foul-smelling odor and knew immediately we had disturbed the dwelling of a very large and not-too-friendly skunk!

187

Attempting to escape our predicament, we tripped over each other and fell to the ground. To make matters worse, we were making so much noise we unwittingly alerted a pair of military policemen who were patrolling the train depot. To avoid being arrested and having to explain ourselves, we had to remain silently crouched down in the maintenance building with the stinky skunk for almost an hour before the MP's finally went away. Although it wasn't funny at the time, and required several tomato juice baths to completely kill the smell, Big Ben and I later laughed until our sides hurt whenever we talked about it.

Acquiring the Cobalt

One night at dinner, Big Ben wanted me to explain to him why cobalt was so important to the project. I recalled the intelligence I'd put to memory and relayed to him the significance of the metal, and how it all related to magnetism.

The Firebird scientists had studied the discoveries of one of their own countrymen, the Nobel Prize-winning physicist Werner Heisenberg, who found that cobalt (at the atomic level) had magnetic poles that were aligned. This alignment made the alloy extremely susceptible to the forces of magnetism. This attraction, in turn, allowed the cobalt-based main structure of the device to become susceptible to the magnetic forces generated by both its on-board electromagnets and the field accelerator. In addition, cobalt has advantages of being both high-strength and wear-resistant, which were two additional reasons why the Firebird scientists chose the material for the project.

A week after hearing my explanation, Ben arrived at the warehouse and excitedly told me of a meeting he'd attended earlier that day, where he learned that the Defense Department had placed a high level of importance in stockpiling their supply of cobalt, and had found two sources from where to obtain it, the largest being on the side of a mountain in the state of Idaho. As for the other source, the government had recently found cobalt in the "slag" or waste material of smelted copper.

After hearing this, I immediately asked him if he would like to take some leave, and with his new wife Elizabeth and J.R., accompany me on a trip to Utah. Dumbfounded, he asked, "I thought we were looking for cobalt?" to which I replied, "We are. My brother Robert works at Kennecott." After keeping him hanging for a few more seconds, I informed him that although Utah was small it did have a few distinct landmarks, one of which was Kennecott, the largest open-pit copper mine in the world.

The Trip West

In August of 1948 we arrived in my hometown of Ogden, where I showed my friend and his young family all around the various sights and attractions of northern Utah. Since both Ben and Elizabeth were originally from the south and hadn't traveled west of St. Louis, Missouri or Memphis, Tennessee, respectively, what impressed them the most were the stretch of mountains along the city's east side. In that regard, they'd never seen such a breathtaking sight before.

I knew how much Big Ben loved to fish, so one day I took him and his son up Ogden Canyon to try their luck at the recently-completed Pine View Dam Reservoir. Although we ended up not getting a bite, I could tell Ben and J.R. were overjoyed with the experience, and we repeated it as often as we could for the remainder of the trip.

While we were fishing, my mother Nora took Elizabeth on shopping trips around the city, and even ventured over to Rainbow Gardens a couple of times for a swim. Since my father had passed away some years ago, and my brother Robert had recently moved to Magna to be closer to his job at Kennecott, my mother had developed the empty-nest blues. She was therefore overjoyed to have Elizabeth visiting, and it gave her the perfect excuse to go shopping.

THE DEVICE

Early in the week, Big Ben and I traveled out to Magna (which is located roughly fifty miles southwest of Ogden) and met with Robert. My brother immediately endeared himself to Ben when he made a joke at my expense, and for the next hour I had to listen to them re-hash almost every embarrassing moment that had ever happened to me; both in my childhood and at the Army's intelligence school.

When the talk eventually turned to the reason for our visit, Robert informed us that his friend Simon was meeting us at the plant later that afternoon with information on how we could buy the cobalt. When we made the short trip up to Simon's office, which was located on the edge of the huge open-pit copper mine, Big Ben could only look on in amazement at the massive man-made crater and its seemingly endless spiral of railroad tracks leading down to the bottom.

At the meeting, Simon casually mentioned that it was too bad we didn't work for a recycling company, because Kennecott sold scraps to recyclers at a much lower rate than the going market price. We informed Simon we were planning to use the cobalt to make high-strength drill bits and corrosion-resistant tooling. All we needed to get our new business venture off the ground were pieces of the alloy until we were established. By the end of the afternoon, we had purchased the first load of cobalt for the device.

During the next two years I made six cross-country trips to Kennecott, where I picked through the tons of excess cobalt scraps in the milling yard and selected the pieces to use for the device. Due to his Army commitments, Big Ben was not able to accompany me on every trip to Utah, but when he did we had the time of our lives and further established our bond of friendship that was as strong as I had with Robert.

Building the Device's Main Structure

From the spring of 1949 through late October of 1950, I worked tirelessly at nights and throughout each weekend forming

190

and shaping the cobalt scraps, until the web-like framework of the main structure took form. Cylindrical in shape, the outer hull was ten feet in length by five feet in diameter, while the inner wall was eight inches shorter in both directions. The cowlings (skin) on the outer hull needed to be made to come off so that I could subsequently install the exciter-motors and their corresponding electromagnets. In addition, a small hinged door with latches needed to be manufactured with an arc and fitted into the access opening of the cockpit. This tube-like configuration made milling and bending the cobalt alloy challenging, cumbersome and time-consuming to say the least.

Although Big Ben assisted me when he could, his family obligations and Army duties made his participation in the project occur less frequently. This had a detrimental effect on me, and I became completely obsessed with completing the device; so much so, I became somewhat of a social outcast. Upon achieving a certain milestone, I would tell myself to take a break, but then plunge headfirst into the next phase of the construction. Building the device had started to take a mental and physical toll on me.

Lana

Big Ben noticed the change that had come over me and put Elizabeth to the task of finding me a female companion. For a short time, each dinner invitation I accepted from them included a blind date with a different girl who worked with Elizabeth. Although many of these dates ended up being disasters, the one where I met Lana had a happy ending.

Lana worked at Fort Meade as a civilian secretary and had been recently transferred to the contracting office where Elizabeth worked. When Big Ben and Elizabeth introduced me to her, I was smitten. I also thought that this beautiful brunette woman, with the dark-brown eyes and the movie-star-like looks, was completely out of my league. To my surprise and delight, we had similar personalities and interests, and subsequently started dating on a regular basis. In a relatively short amount of time we fell deeply in love with each other, and on several occasions talked about getting married.

As much as I loved Lana and wanted to spend the rest of my life with her, I simply couldn't bring myself to tell her about the secret I'd uncovered in Hitler's bunker, or about the unbelievable device I was constructing in the Fort Meade warehouse. In that regard, I didn't think it would be fair to her if I couldn't completely devote myself to our relationship and possible marriage, when I'd already committed myself to the mission of finding and stopping General Berger. I also speculated that if I was to throw caution to the wind and marry her anyway, and my haphazard plan turned out to be successful, the ensuing confrontation with Berger might result in her getting hurt or killed, and I simply couldn't allow that to happen.

In the end, my relationship was destined to end prematurely and I would forever regret losing this wonderful woman because of my shortsightedness and my obsession with the device.

Building the Field Accelerator

After mentally reviewing the intelligence from Hitler's bunker regarding the device's field accelerator, I surmised that Jakob Eddleman (one of the Firebird scientists whose body we found in the Ünterbunker) was not only an expert on electromagnetism, but he was also a genius. Reversing the design of the Stern-Gerlach Experiment was as simplistic as it was brilliant, and proved to be one of the greatest (though covert) milestones in the science of physics. How he'd come up with this idea while his family was being held at gunpoint by General Berger is beyond my comprehension.

Following Eddleman's lead, I went to work on trying to locate a very large piece of soft iron. On one of my nights out with Lana, casual talk led her to telling me about a recent meeting she'd attended at the Maryland office of the Pennsylvania Steel Company,

192

which was located merely thirty miles away from Fort Meade at Sparrow Point. This meeting included a tour of the massive ship-building facility, where she'd been shown how they forged gigantic iron pieces that later became the keels of naval ships. The next available day Ben and I had off during the week, we paid a visit to Sparrow Point, met with a sales representative and ordered the part. Six weeks later, the piece of soft iron was delivered to Big Ben in the Fort Meade receiving dock, and shortly thereafter we had it tucked away in Warehouse 1373's workshop.

Next came the redundant task of winding the wire around the large piece of metal, which (when energized with electricity) transformed the inert soft iron into a giant pulsating electromagnet. It helped that I had pieces of the Nazi's field accelerator in the three footlockers my team had retrieved from the Ünterbunker, which allowed me the luxury of seeing exactly what gauge of wire was used, and copying the amount of thickness of the windings. As slow as this process was, it later paid dividends: I never had a problem with the field accelerator generating the needed amount of power for the deflection.

Once I finished winding the wire around the iron, Big Ben helped me anchor and align the two sets of railroad tracks on the floor at each side of the platform, as well as the one fastened to the center I-beam in the ceiling. In that regard, each pair of tracks on the sides needed to be perfectly positioned at the same exact distance from the center so that the accelerator could travel back and forth at its incredible speed without binding. Once the railroad tracks were aligned, we used a pulley to mount the wheeled carriage to the tracks, then mounted the accelerator to the carriage. Eight high-speed motors, taken from discarded clothes washers we'd purchased at the DRMO yard, were then used to power the carriage's wheels.

On Christmas Eve of 1950, we completed the device's giant horseshoe-shaped field accelerator.

Acquiring the Exciter-Motors

With the field accelerator finished, I focused my attention on the small oddly-shaped exciter-motors for the device's main structure. To do this, I again recalled and studied the intelligence my team had recovered from the Ünterbunker. In addition to the field accelerator, these small alternating current induction motors (placed at diametrically congruent positions in the fuselage) were needed for the successful operation of the device.

In operation, these motors supplied electrical current to a corresponding miniature electro-magnet, which magnetized (or "excited") the cobalt alloy of the main structure. What fascinated me the most about the exciter-motors (even more than the fact that they were heat-resistant and self-generating above a 66.67% threshold) was the puzzle of how they were developed. At the center of this mystery was the man who invented them, and unfortunately was the second man my reconnaissance team and I found dead in the Ünterbunker: Abraham Kaufmann.

In reviewing the intelligence, I learned that Kaufmann, in his younger years, studied electrical theory under Nicola Tesla, the man who patented the A/C induction motor. Kaufmann was also an expert in thermodynamics, which is a discipline of physics that deals with how heat, temperature and other variables relate to the production of energy. I also surmised that Kaufmann was the intellectual equal to Tesla, being that he also had a hand in designing the highly-complex magnetic power distribution network which sat in the cockpit underneath the seat. In that regard, I believe even Tesla would've been dazzled by the array of threaded wires, polarity-reversing switches, and mercury-enhanced vacuum tube triodes which made up the network.

After mentally examining Kaufmann's exciter-motor schematics several times, I am still at a loss as to how he came to invent them. Like his colleague Eddleman, what added to my amazement was that he managed to develop them while under the stress of his wife and children being held hostage by General

Berger. I can only speculate that to protect his family, he desperately threw every outlandish idea he could think of into the project and somehow happened upon the right answer.

I now had the enormous task of fabricating eighty of the small exciter-motors and their corresponding electro-magnets, as well as three-hundred and twenty L-shaped cobalt brackets to use for mounting them. My burden was somewhat lifted when I learned of a manufacturer in the state of New York who could supply us with the motors.

It happened over dinner one night with Lana, Big Ben, Elizabeth and J.R., when the women took notice of the dermatitis that had broken out on my hands. (I found out later this was a common allergic reaction to cobalt exposure.) This led them to directly asking us what we were working on in the warehouse.

After dramatically making the girls swear to secrecy, which somewhat lightened the mood, I informed them that while on active duty, I'd uncovered a piece of Nazi intelligence that had to do with the Messerschmitt ME 262 (the first operational jet fighter) that the Luftwaffe had developed at the end of the war. This technology, I explained, could propel a jet past the speed of sound and would (very likely) be in high demand in the future. Therefore, we were constructing a new super-sonic aircraft for our military, and the structure we were building in the warehouse was a prototype of the cockpit. If successful, our new Air Force might want to buy the design and manufacture them, and if that were to happen Ben and I could make a fortune.

By laying on some complicated electrical jargon, I had the girls convinced that the field accelerator and the polished metal lining the room were necessary to conduct the tests. Cementing the lie was the fact that the girls knew all about my photographic memory and thought both me and Big Ben to be quite brainy.

I felt profoundly guilty for telling Lana and Elizabeth the lie, especially after seeing how wide-eyed and giddy they became after hearing the story. Shortly afterward, they were asking us how they could assist us with the project. I jokingly mentioned that if they knew an electrical manufacturer who could make eighty small A/C induction motors, it would help us out immensely. To my surprise, Elizabeth told me of one who might be able to do it: Faraday Manufacturing in Albany, New York. Two weeks later, the four of us took a road trip to visit this company and we found that they could indeed manufacture the motors to my specifications. This time, it was Big Ben and I who sat astonished as we watched Elizabeth and Lana use their contracting skills to negotiate the price of the motors, to include free shipping.

With the exciter-motors on the way, my attention turned to the small electro-magnets that the motors supplied power to. From early 1951 to the summer of 1952, Fort Meade Warehouse Number 1373 became a production facility for both the tiny electro-magnets and the cobalt brackets to hold them in place.

The Cobalt Windows and the Vacuum Tube Triodes

Throughout the time I was constructing the small electro-magnets and brackets for the device's main structure, I procured the last major parts for the device: the cobalt windows and vacuum tube triodes. At first, I thought both would present me with the greatest problem, but as it turned out they were the easiest and the cheapest to obtain.

As for the windows, it may not have been a necessity to look out of the device while piloting it, but it would offer me a measure of safety. Theoretically, if I were to reenter real time after an earthquake or some other occurrence, and a large piece of debris happened to have moved into the same stationary plane I was occupying, the device would immediately merge with the debris at the sub-atomic level and kill me instantly. (A sobering thought of how dangerous the device could be for its pilot.)

The triodes, however, were a different story: they were necessary for the successful operation of the device. At the time, triodes were common glass amplification tubes used in radios and

196

televisions, but the ones for the device needed to be constructed with mercury vapor inside the glass. The Firebird scientists found that this enhancement prolonged the life of the charged electrons inside and prevented the triode from losing energy.

In mid-December of 1951, I was on a semester break from the college when I happened upon a source for both the windows and the triodes while looking through a Popular Mechanics magazine. It was an advertisement for radio tubes that were manufactured at the Glass Works in Corning, New York, which happened to be located roughly two-hundred and sixty miles north of Fort Meade.

Since Ben and his family were gone on an early Christmas vacation to Alabama, and Lana was tied up at her job all week, I paid a visit to the Glass Works company and ordered the needed parts. Two weeks later Big Ben received them, and I now had the final structural pieces and electrical components I needed to finish the device.

Completing the Device

In August of 1952, I finished building the small dual-wound electro-magnets and cobalt brackets, and immediately went to work on wiring the magnetic power distribution network, which was located on the floor of the cockpit under the seat. Since each row of ten miniature exciter-motors and corresponding magnets in the hull needed to be wired in series (one continuous loop) this became a tedious and time-consuming task. After all the wires were finally routed to the cockpit, I had the intricate job of installing the polarity-reversing switches and mounts for the triodes, which I obtained from several television and radio supply stores.

That fall, Big Ben and I managed to procure or build the remaining parts for the cockpit, which included a main power switch, a polarity-reversing switch, the front and right-hand consoles, a throttle, a small interior light, and a cover over the power system that would also serve as a seat. After finishing the cockpit, we tapped into the utility power station next to the warehouse, which gave us the electrical power we needed to activate the device.

The last part installed in the cockpit, which essentially completed the construction, was something that touched me more than words can say. It was the last week of October, and I happened to be on a short mid-semester break from the university. I had just gotten out of bed and walked into the polished-steel room, when I noticed the device's hatch was closed. There was a large decorative bow and ribbon taped to the outside of it. Wondering if this might be one of Big Ben's practical jokes, I decided to take the bait and quickly unlatched and opened the hatch. To my amazement I found a perfectly tailored padded cushion and matching adjustable headrest, which fit on the cover of the power system like a glove. Adding to my astonishment was the fact that the entire assembly looked to be fashioned from an antique barber chair, complete with ornate gold tassels hanging from the edges of the seat cushion. Tears came to my eyes as I realized that Ben and the girls must have worked on this without my knowledge for a very long time.

Suddenly, a loud shout of "Surprise!" filled the room, and I was swarmed upon by Lana, Big Ben, Elizabeth and J.R. At first I was dumbfounded, but then I remembered it was October the thirtieth. In my obsessive preoccupation with completing the device, I'd completely forgotten it was my birthday. All of us then enjoyed an impromptu party, complete with cake and ice cream for breakfast, in celebration of my turning thirty-two years old.

My birthday on that chilly October day was the first of two milestones I reached in the span of twenty-four hours. The second occurred (appropriately enough) on a day set aside for remembering the dead and is synonymous with the sights and sounds of the macabre.

On Halloween night of 1952, the device was complete.

A Clock and a Calendar

Big Ben's son J.R. unknowingly gave me an idea of how I could tell how much time was passing outside the field of the device while I was traveling in the fourth dimension.

I'd dropped over to their house for lunch, and while enjoying a toasted-cheese sandwich and a bowl of tomato soup I noticed the calendar on their wall was still showing the month of October. Except for the last day of the month, all the days had large "X's" through them, which meant that J.R. (who had calendar duty) had forgotten to mark off the day and hadn't changed the month from October to November.

After lunch, Ben and I immediately went to the post exchange and found a fairly-large Julian date wall calendar, a glass picture frame for it to fit in, several black grease pencils and a large wall clock. I selected the Julian calendar for the simple reason that it counted all the days of the year consecutively (without starting over each month) which eliminated the need to remove it from the picture frame. By the end of the day, we had the clock and framed calendar mounted on the wall underneath the emergency light in the polished room, which was also clearly visible to me through the device's front window. I asked Ben to drop by each day I was gone and cross off the day using a grease pencil. Since my pursuit of General Berger may take years, I told him not to forget to update the year of the calendar every New Year's Day.

Synchronizing the Device

The final step before testing the device was to synchronize the power of the two main components: the field accelerator and the main structure. Even though this sounded quite easy, it was the hardest step to accomplish and was critical to making the deflection possible and the device to operate correctly. In studying the Firebird intelligence, once again I found that Eddleman and Kaufmann made another significant contribution to the project when they figured out the mathematical formula of how to measure the forces of gravity (or "gravitational waves") around a stationary object, which essentially solved one of the greatest problems of modern-day physics.

This discovery led them to figure out another formula of how to manipulate the forces of magnetism to affect those gravitational waves. These equations told the scientists how much electrical current was needed to achieve the magnetic moment, and where they needed to set the power levels to stop the device in the future, hold the time aperture open, and reverse the polarity to bring the pilot back to the present – all of which needed to be calculated with consideration given to the time-varying magnetic and gravitational fields.

After recalling the formulas and spending several hours synchronizing the power system, the device was operational.

The Plan

While building the device, I gave a great deal of thought as to how to test it (and if successful) search for General Berger in the vast expanse of the future. I decided to fashion my pursuit the same way I planned to test it: in stages. The first stage was to go forward in time one day and return. If it worked, I would move to stage two and go into the future a week and return. The third stage would carry me forward a month, with the final testing stage being the six-month mark. Once I was satisfied that the device worked properly, I would conduct my search in the same manner and go forward in time a year, five years, ten years, etc., and return each time to report what I had found to Big Ben.

In reviewing the Firebird intelligence, I learned that General Berger possessed a ruthless disregard for human life, and (reading between the lines) an insatiable appetite for power. I surmised that if he was going to start a future Fourth Reich, as the original Firebird plan called for, there was a good chance that the United States would again be involved in a world war. I highly suspected I would encounter this scenario at some point in the future. Being armed with the device, Berger could easily gain certain knowledge of the future and manipulate key events to his liking. In my estimation, this was the most dangerous aspect of the device and the reason I chose to keep it from my reconnaissance team, Colonel Pash and General Groves.

I also decided with each successive stage of the search, when I reentered real time in the future (and if Big Ben wasn't around) I would immediately make my way to Fort Meade's Medal of Honor Memorial Library and quickly check the newspapers to see if there was any mention of a war, a new Nazi uprising, or any other event that might give me a clue as to General Berger's whereabouts. Once I finished my review at the library, I would make my way back to the warehouse, activate the device and return to the present. I concluded that I could easily accomplish these steps within the three hours and fourteen-minutes time limit, and well-before the time aperture closed and nature righted itself.

I talked over my plan with Big Ben and discussed different scenarios that might occur once I departed into the fourth dimension. I also emphasized to him the importance of secrecy. In that regard, we decided no matter what happened we wouldn't tell Lana or Elizabeth until the mission was over. I felt if we told them the truth, they would think my undertaking too dangerous and stop me from the search.

Testing the Device

On Sunday, November the second of 1952, we ran our first test, and much to my delight the device worked perfectly. I got into the device at ten o'clock in the morning, and had Ben apply electricity to the device's main structure. Once the exciter-motors energized to roughly seventy percent of their potential power, they became self-sustaining. After waiting a few moments for the current to stabilize, I signaled Ben through the cockpit window to turn off the power to the main structure and to turn on the field accelerator. Seconds later, the horseshoe-shaped part slowly started to move down the railroad tracks, and reaching the end, immediately bounced back in the opposite direction. With each pass, the accelerator's speed increased until it became a blur. Once the field surrounding the accelerator and main structure reached magnetic moment, and the forces merged into one, I threw the polarity-reversing switch in the cockpit.

At first it felt as if nothing happened, then the gravitational forces pressed my body against the seat and (strangely enough) my ears popped. When I looked out the window, I could see Big Ben walking very fast in front of the device, and the minute hand of the clock racing around the numbers. The throttle, which controlled the power to the exciter-motors, was only at the one-third mark above the idle position, meaning that the device was traveling at the slowest rate possible short of coming out of the time aperture. I eased the throttle forward, and the hour hand of the wall clock started spinning around faster; the minute and second hands rotating so fast they were invisible. When the time reached six o'clock the next morning, I eased the throttles back into the one-quarter position, which brought the device out of the fourth dimension, but didn't close the aperture. After waiting exactly one minute, I eased the throttle forward and threw the polarity-reversing switch again. Looking out the window now, I could see everything that had previously happened, but in reverse; the hour hand in the clock was spinning counterclockwise and Ben was pacing backwards. The device slowed and stopped on its own merely a few seconds past the minute I'd left.

Climbing out of the device, I was a bit lightheaded and had developed a slight headache. My ears were also ringing, but only enough to cause minor irritation. Big Ben helped me out of the room and into the workshop, where we both sat down and talked about what had happened. I explained to him that from my point of view, everything going on outside of the device appeared to be moving in fast-motion. He told me that from his point of view, when the deflection occurred the entire main structure glowed bright blue and

202

hummed before disappearing in a blinding flash of light. When I came back and reentered real time, the sequence was reversed.

Throughout the next week and a half, Ben and I succeeded in repeating the first test several times as well as the next three stages, where I went into the future a week, a month, and finally six months and returned safely. I also became aware of a phenomenon that occurred whenever I went into the future which I called, *"equivalent elapsed time displacement."* In simplest terms, I found that the time I spent in the future was equal to the time I was returned to in the present *after* I'd left.

With the testing stages successfully completed, my attention turned towards the mission, and the reason I'd built the device in the first place: to find General Berger in the future and stop him.

The night before the search, the girls must have sensed that we had reached a milestone on our "cockpit" project when I treated Lana, Ben, Elizabeth and J.R. to a steak dinner at Fort Meade's Officer's Club. It was one of the merriest times I'd ever spent with the people I loved the most.

Later that evening, Lana and I had a long discussion about our relationship, and whether we were going to get married. I assured her several times that I was madly in love with her, but the time for marriage just didn't seem right. I first wanted to be sure the project was going to pan out, so that when we did get married she would be well-taken care of financially.

Merely a few short hours after the incredible dinner with Ben, J.R. and the girls, on a day I will always remember, my life would change drastically. The subsequent events would leave me fractured physically and emotionally, and lead me to question my long-held belief that everything happens for a reason. The day was Tuesday, November the eleventh of 1952, when I activated the device and began my search for the Nazi's White Wolf.

* * *

THE DEVICE

Except for one last sorrowful paragraph, this marked the end of the first part of Captain Hank's diary. So far, the story of how he'd built the device was both informative and touching. As Madison and I continued reading, however, his story took an abrupt turn. Not even his fantastic photographic memory (which could recall something as complicated as the power system of the Firebird device) nor his increased cognitive abilities (which enabled him to learn things at a highly-accelerated rate) could figure out a way to change the outcome of the devastating events that happened to him.

Word for word, the final paragraph of the first part of his diary read as follows:

"Much to my regret, I found out later that the triodes I'd purchased at the Corning Glass Works had a slight (but significant) manufacturing flaw. Nearly invisible to the naked eye, this tiny imperfection consisted of a minute air pocket in the glass, whose thin membrane (when heated for an extended period) was destined to rupture. This resulted in a leak in the electron-sustaining mercury vapor trapped inside and eventually caused a catastrophic failure of the triodes. In my haste to get the device running and pursue General Berger, I'd neglected to test the triodes before installing them into the device's power distribution network. That mistake would cost me dearly, and I would never see my beloved Lana, or my best friend Ben and his wife Elizabeth, ever again."

With tears in our eyes, Madison turned the page.

Chapter Ten
The Story (Part 3)

Twenty-Three Years and Two Months Earlier
Wednesday, 10 July 1991, 04:15hrs
Inside *Warehouse 1373, Fort Meade Army Base, Maryland*

The stagnant smoke hanging in the air carried with it the pungent scent of arced electrical equipment and burned wire insulation, giving the polished-steel room the distinct aroma of ozone. In addition to the stale and smelly air, the dimly-lit lights in the ceiling and thick dust on the floor combined to produce an old and haunting ambiance, while at the same time denoting their unkemptness from years of neglect. The only things that appeared new and shiny were the trail of recent footsteps, having disturbed the dust, and the cylinder-shaped main structure of the device, now back from its journey in the fourth dimension. Amid this lonely and depressing setting, sitting on the floor with his head in his hands, was Captain Henry "Hank" Stevens.

As hard as his mind searched for a cause of why the device had malfunctioned, the more he came to the realization that he had no answer. Not helping matters was the incredible headache, dizziness and ringing in his ears, which were the same side effects he'd felt during the testing stages the previous week, but much harsher this time. He also felt a slight tremor in the pinky finger of his left hand, which he attributed to his abrupt reentry back into real time.

With the pain throbbing in his brain, he mentally re-traced his steps several times in hopes of finding a hidden clue that would tell him where he'd made the mistake while constructing the device. In each examination, however, he couldn't pinpoint the cause of what went wrong or why the electrical current in the exciter-motors had suddenly surged and failed. All he knew for certain was that the damage to the device's power system was irreparable, and three hours and fifteen minutes had elapsed since his return.

Captain Hank was now trapped in the future, with no way to get back to his own time.

He looked up again at the calendar on the wall, and saw that Big Ben was still marking off the days and changing the number of the year. As the cold harsh reality of his situation began to sink in, tears came to his eyes and he reached into his back pocket for a handkerchief to dry them.

A short time later, after his headache had somewhat subsided, his thoughts returned to the happenings of that morning and the subsequent event that had marooned him almost forty years in the future.

~ Then ~

For Captain Hank, earlier that day was Tuesday, November the eleventh of 1952. Big Ben and J.R. had shown up at the warehouse, like they always did, with four doughnuts from a nearby bakery. Ben normally consumed two, gave one to J.R., and offered one to Hank. Even though he was busy preparing the device for the first stage of the mission, he'd taken time out to enjoy the treat and a cup of coffee with his friend and young son.

When Ben departed to take J.R. to the nursery, Hank packed every spare part and tool he could think of in the small forward console of the cockpit, including the four extra triodes for the

206

magnetic power distribution network. As for the triodes, he concluded that if something were to happen in the future and one of them burned out, he could keep the power on, remove the seat and cover, and quickly replace it.

Once Big Ben returned to the warehouse, Hank instructed him what to do in the event he *didn't* return within the three-hour and fourteen-minute time window: wait patiently, mark the days off on the calendar, and continue to make the monthly rental payments on the warehouse. Above all, he was to make sure the stationary plane (the area where the main structure was mounted to the platform) remained clear of debris.

As far as money was concerned, Hank had already added Ben to his bank accounts and his investment account at the brokerage firm. This allowed his friend access to his money to pay the rent for the building, and gave him the rights to buy and sell his stocks.

With the instructions gone over thoroughly and the financial arrangements taken care of, both men shook hands and Big Ben wished him luck and a speedy return. As a parting gift, Ben gave Hank a brand-new .45 caliber pistol that was exactly like the firearm he was issued in the Army. Although Hank had planned to carry a gun for his eventual confrontation with General Berger, he was so absorbed with building the device that he'd completely forgotten about it.

After shaking hands again, Hank climbed into the cockpit and latched the door while Ben took his place next to the electrical service panel. As soon as he received the signal of thumbs up from Hank, Ben applied power to the main structure of the device. A few moments later, after receiving another signal from Hank, he turned off the power to the main structure and turned on the field accelerator.

Just as it had performed throughout the testing stages the previous week, the accelerator's speed slowly increased back and forth along the railroad tracks until attaining an almost-supersonic

207

rate of speed. Upon achieving the magnetic moment, a low hum emitted from the generated field and the main structure started glowing a bright shade of blue. After a final thumbs-up signal between the two men, Captain Hank activated the polarity-reversing switch inside the cockpit and entered the fourth dimension.

At first, everything seemed to be working as before, but when Hank eased the throttle forward to increase the power of the exciter-motors, something happened that was very different from the test runs. He suddenly heard several popping sounds, as if someone had lit a string of firecrackers underneath him. The entire cockpit began to shake and he was thrown back into the seat. Realizing there was a power surge in the electrical system, he pulled back on the throttle, but it was unresponsive. After another series of loud pops and forceful vibrations, the entire electrical system died.

A feeling of lightheadedness, followed by an almost-incapacitating headache and ringing in his ears overwhelmed Hank's consciousness, and he held his head in his hands trying to stave off the pain.

He suddenly smelled something burning, and fearing the device was on fire he quickly unlatched the door and jumped out of the cockpit. Except for the small emergency lights above the clock and calendar, the main lights in the room were out, so he hurried over to the switch next to the door. Turning the lights on, he found a ring of smoke emanating from inside the device's cockpit.

He ran back and quickly unpinned the flashlight from the forward wall, then retrieved a screwdriver from the front console. A few minutes later, after removing all the screws, he pulled out the ornate seat and uncovered the power distribution network. A feeling of utter hopelessness came over him when the beam of his flashlight met with the mass of smoldering wires, burned out switches and broken vacuum tube triodes – the network was a total loss.

Since the malfunction had happened so quickly after he'd entered the aperture, he thought that he couldn't have traveled very far into the future, but after checking the calendar on the wall, he discovered that the last date marked off was July the ninth of 1991. After quickly doing the math, he concluded that the power surge had shot him forward in time approximately thirty-nine years and seven months from the day he'd left.

For the next three hours, he searched his memory for anything that would tell him what might have caused the breakdown and subsequent failure of the device's power system. In doing so, he recalled all the information he had found in the Ünterbunker having to do with the testing of the Nazi's Firebird device. Reviewing his own device's test results and mentally comparing the two, he found they were essentially same: each device had performed almost identical to its counterpart during the testing stages.

With the three-hour and fourteen-minute time window running out, he thought for a moment that he might be able to jury-rig the network and get the power back on, but realized that even if he could re-start the device, it wouldn't matter – the exciter-motors supplying power to the electromagnets were what kept the aperture open. When the device malfunctioned, the aperture closed and nature had righted itself. He was now forever trapped in the future, with no way to get back to his own time.

Out of options, he sat on the cold, dusty floor of the polished-steel room wondering what awaited him outside the warehouse.

~ Now ~

U. S. Army Lieutenant Colonel Benjamin Washington Jr. (J.R. to his family) started the jeep he and his dad had restored, and headed down to the shipping and receiving area of the base. For more than two-and-a-half years, prior to going to work, he went through the morning ritual of stopping by Warehouse 1373 and marking a large black "X" on the calendar in the polished-steel room. He knew the importance of this little chore, because his dad (before he died) had told him the incredible story of what happened to his best friend, Captain Hank.

At the time, J.R. was on leave from his duty station at Fort Ord, California, and after hearing the story he pushed for (and received) a transfer to Fort Meade. Then just before the accident, which turned out to be the last time his dad had spoken to him, he promised to stop by the warehouse every morning and mark off the day on the calendar.

Yesterday, however, things changed drastically when he received a certified letter from the base's contracting office notifying him that they were terminating the long-standing contract to lease the warehouse. He now faced the problem of what to do with all the tools and equipment that were in the building, not to mention the giant field accelerator that was still mounted on the carriage in the polished-steel room. In addition, the termination was scheduled to take effect July thirty-first, leaving him only twenty-one days to clear out the building. As if that weren't enough, his Army unit was due a visit from the inspector general, and his commander had assigned him as the project officer for the inspection. With all these things happening at once, J.R. was glad he was retiring at the end of the year.

He thought of Captain Hank. After all this time, he highly suspected his dad's best friend was dead. If he happened to still be alive and traveling in the fourth dimension, he now had less than three weeks to return to real time. If he didn't, he ran the risk of having the stationary plane blocked by the new building construction.

After parking in front of the warehouse, he got out of the jeep and looked up at the old building. For some reason, it seemed more dilapidated today than usual; almost as if it had finally outlived its usefulness.

Unlocking the front door and going in, he immediately noticed the illumination from under the door at the far end of the shop, which meant that the lights were on in the polished-steel room. At first, he thought he might've left them on the day before, but he remembered he'd been running late for a meeting with his commander and had hurriedly made the daily annotation *without* turning them on.

He grabbed a large hammer from on top of the nearest work bench, crept over to the door and placed his ear against it. After waiting a few moments and hearing nothing, he slowly opened the door and peeked inside.

For the first time in more than thirty-nine years, J.R. saw his dad's best friend, Captain Hank. He was sitting in the middle of the floor, and from the way he was holding his head in his hands appeared to be in pain. Behind Hank, just as he remembered it, was the large cylinder-shaped main structure of the device.

He immediately dropped the hammer and ran over to him.

"Captain Hank, are you all right?" he asked.

"Ben?"

Seeing Hank's face, J.R. immediately thought of his dad and stepmom.

"No, I'm Ben's son J.R."

"J.R.?"

"That's right."

He noticed Hank's eyes were red and tears were streaming down his face.

"Are you injured?"

"No, just a bad headache, dizziness and some ringing in my ears."

"Can I get you anything? Aspirin, water, maybe something to eat?"

"Sure, but first I would very much like to talk to your dad and tell him what happened."

J.R. hesitated a moment, and his eyes watered.

"I hate to be the one to tell you this, but my dad passed away."

THE DEVICE

J.R. embraced him and the thoughts of the accident came flooding back, as if the terrible event had happened only yesterday.

* * *

One hour later, Hank sat at a table in the far corner of Fort Meade's officer's club, sipping a large cup of coffee. Still upset from the news of Big Ben, he hadn't touched his plate of food nor said hardly a word since the two men had arrived at the club.

J.R., returning to the table, sat down across from him.

"My commander is okay with me taking off, so we've got all day to catch up."

"Thanks J.R., I appreciate that."

"I think the weirdest thing about all this is that I am now older than you."

Hank smiled, but his thoughts were still on Big Ben, and more importantly, the woman he loved.

"What happened to Lana and your dad?"

"Lana eventually retired and moved away from Fort Meade. My mom used to get letters from her from time to time, telling her how she was doing. She never married, and from what my mom said never got over losing you. It was about four years ago that we received a letter from her sister, who she was living with, that contained her obituary. It didn't state the cause of her death."

"Oh my," Hank said, hardly getting the words out.

"My dad saved it for you, along with a few other things he thought were important. I'll get them for you later when we go over to my house."

Hank nodded, staring blankly at his coffee.

"As for my dad, it happened a little more than two-and-a-half years ago on Christmas Eve of 1988. It was late in the evening, and he and mom were heading into Fort Meade in the middle of a bad snowstorm. At the intersection outside the main gate, a drunk driver ran the red light. My dad was killed on impact, but mom lived until the next morning."

"Elizabeth is gone too?"

J.R. nodded. "She was driving because dad was too sick."

"Sick from what?"

"He basically had everything that affects people when they get old; prostate cancer, heart disease, Parkinson's disease, beginning stages of Alzheimer's, you name it."

Hank stared off into space, his eyes watering again.

"I talked to my mom in the hospital before she passed, and she said that they were on their way to the warehouse."

"To the warehouse? Why on earth would they venture out on Christmas Eve in a bad snowstorm to come to the warehouse?"

"She said dad saw something on TV."

"TV?"

"Television."

Remembering the fledgling medium, Hank nodded for J.R. to continue.

"She said he insisted that she take him to the warehouse so he could get a message to you."

"To me? Do you know what the message was about?"

J.R. shook his head. "My poor mom thought that since he hadn't seen you in over thirty years he was having an episode of dementia. To calm him down, she took him there. That's when they got into the accident."

Thinking that Big Ben and his wife had been killed trying to get a message to him made Hank feel even worse.

"I don't know what to say, except that I am so sorry. It's all my fault."

"Your fault? How could it be your fault? You were gone."

"If I hadn't built that infernal device, none of this would have happened and they would still be alive."

"Look, dad told me all about the mission and what the device could do. The way I see it, you had to try."

213

"I appreciate your kind words, but it doesn't alter the fact that your mom and dad are gone because of me."

The men sat in silence for a few moments, before J.R. finally asked Hank what happened, after which he recounted the events and how the device had malfunctioned.

"And to think," Hank concluded, "all of this, from building the device to coming here, was completely unnecessary."

"Unnecessary? How can you say that? As far as I'm concerned, you had the greatest of intentions going after General Berger."

"No, you don't understand. It came to me just before you found me at the warehouse. As I was sitting there, I thought about your father and how fortunate I was to have such a wonderful friend. At the time, I believed he was still alive because the calendar on the wall was still being marked off. I noticed a few of the polished-steel plates had fallen out of the ceiling but weren't in the room, which told me he was still making sure the stationary plane was clear for my reentry. I don't know why I didn't think of it before, but I suddenly recalled the images of the Ünterbunker's laboratory. The explosion that occurred prior to my team and I going in had caused a partial cave-in. The debris field, where we retrieved the pieces of the field accelerator, was covering over half of the raised platform."

J.R. nodded.

"If General Berger attempts to reenter real time now, he would immediately merge with that debris field and die. That being said, he's trapped in the fourth dimension."

"Couldn't he wait it out, and reenter real time when it's clear?"

"Sure, but who's going to clear it for him? Nobody knows about any of this, or that there was a secret lower level in the bunker where this took place. All the scientists who were involved in the Firebird project are dead. Although the device's exciter-motors are self-sustaining, the triodes will fail at some point, and when the power system finally does go out, General Berger will die upon reentering real time. So you see, my entire plan of building the device to pursue him into the future, which eventually led to your parent's deaths, was completely unnecessary."

"I still believe you should've gone after him," J.R. replied, "and my parents' deaths were by no means your fault."

Oblivious to what J.R. was telling him, Captain Hank buried his head in his hands.

The mission he should've never started to begin with was over.

* * *

Later that day, Captain Hank sat on the couch in the front room of J.R.'s home replaying the events in his mind. He still felt responsible for causing the chain of events which led to Big Ben and Elizabeth dying in the car accident, and after hearing what J.R. said about Lana, he concluded that he was the root cause of her death too. If he had only stopped to think about General Berger's situation more closely, and not been so obsessed about building the device and going after him, none of this would have ever happened.

Just then, J.R. came in and handed him a fresh cup of coffee, and sat down on the opposite end of the couch. With both men now composed, they reminisced about old times, and as the conversation progressed, Hank found out a lot about his friend's son and why he'd chosen a career in the Army.

He learned that Big Ben was quite strict with J.R. while growing up, and always made sure he did his homework before doing anything else with his friends. Whenever J.R. did struggle with a class, his dad would immediately get him a tutor so that he didn't fall behind his classmates, and follow up with his teachers to see how he was progressing.

In high school, Big Ben took a different approach to motivating him to get good grades: bribery. Captain Hank smiled as

J.R. told him how his dad used to say, "If you want to succeed in life, and not become a damn bum on a street corner begging for money, you need a college education, and to get into college you need good grades." He then offered him a rather large amount of money for every above average grade he earned.

When Hank asked why he'd decided on the United States Military Academy at West Point (instead of one of the civilian colleges nearby) J.R. told him that it all boiled down to three reasons. First, he'd developed a strong sense of patriotism while studying history in high school, and he had always admired his dad for being a member of the military. Second, he was interested in fixing up old cars, and had helped his dad restore his old Army jeep. Therefore, if he served twenty years in the military and retired, he would have a steady income for the rest of his life to pursue this hobby; perhaps even open a shop of his own. The third reason he decided to join the Army was because of Elizabeth and Captain Hank.

Surprised, Hank asked him how he could have had any influence on his decision, to which J.R. replied, "Several of my friends in high school turned out to be flakes, and became addicted to drugs and alcohol. At the time, I was in the mindset of just wanting to get away and meet new people who weren't losers. Since dad met both my stepmom and you during his Army service, I started thinking that I could do the same by joining the Army."

Captain Hank felt truly touched with the compliment, and could only admire J.R. for making a life-changing decision at such a young age.

J.R. told him that he ended up graduating in the top five percent of his class, and went on to have a successful career in the Army. For the next half-hour, he caught Hank up on all the wars and military operations the United States had been involved in while he was away. Although it didn't matter now, J.R had also kept a watchful eye on the news and world events, paying special attention to modern-day neo-Nazi groups.

After the conversation ended J.R. excused himself, then returned a moment later with a large manila envelope. Thumbing through its contents, Hank found Lana's obituary paper-clipped to three others: one for Big Ben and Elizabeth, one for his mother Nora and the last for his brother Robert. Overcome with grief, Hank reached in his pocket for his handkerchief to dry his eyes.

The door leading from the garage into the kitchen suddenly opened and snapped Hank out of thinking about his loved ones. A few seconds later two children and a woman entered the home, at which point Hank rose to his feet. The woman was tall, thin, and roughly thirty-five years of age, in Hank's estimation. From the close facial resemblance, the children appeared to be twins.

"Valerie, kids," J.R. said, "I'd like you meet an old friend of grandpa's, Henry Stevens." Turning to Hank, he continued, "This is my wife Valerie, and our two brats Ethan and Evelynn."

"Nice to meet you, Valerie," Hank said, extending a hand.

After the brief handshake, his attention turned to the children.

"And nice to meet you two. Tell me, how old are you?"

"Eight and a half," Ethan answered.

"But I was born first," Evelynn blurted out.

"You were not!" Ethan said, at which point the sibling argument escalated.

"That's enough," J.R. ordered. "Captain Hank doesn't want to hear you fight about who was born first."

"Captain Hank?" Ethan asked.

"That's the nickname grandpa gave to Mr. Stevens."

"You knew our grandpa, Captain Hank?" Evelynn asked.

Hank smiled. "I sure did. He was my best friend."

"Really?" Ethan asked. "Grandpa was your best friend?"

"He really was. Big Ben and I served together in the Army."

"Wow," both children replied, in unison.

"Could you excuse us, Mr. Stevens?" Valerie asked. "I need to talk to J.R. for a just a minute."

"Oh certainly, Mrs. Washington. Would you like me to step out?"

"No, no, that won't be necessary. We'll just be a minute. In the meantime, could I get you something to drink?"

"Sure, I'll take a Grapette if you've got one."

"Excuse me?"

"A Grapette?"

"Um," she said, looking around.

"All we have is orange soda or root beer," Evelynn said.

"Then I'll have a root beer."

"That's my favorite," Ethan said proudly. "Would you like a hot pocket?

"A what?"

"A hot pocket. I can make you one in the microwave in ninety seconds."

"A micro what?"

"No hot pockets," J.R. said sternly. "We're going out to a restaurant tonight and eat real food."

A few moments later Valerie had J.R. cornered in the bedroom, with the door ajar just enough to keep an eye on her husband's guest.

"All right tell me the truth," she whispered, "who is he?"

"I did tell you the truth."

"The man in there can't be much older than thirty. There's no way he served with your dad in the Army."

"Look, it's a long story, but trust me when I say that he is who he claims to be and he did serve with dad during the war."

"But how can that be?"

"Like I said, it's a long story. When we have more time I'll tell you all about it, but right now he's my guest and I'd like to take him out to eat with us. In case you couldn't tell, he's been through a lot today."

"Is that why he looks like he's been crying?"

218

"Yes. I told him about the accident, and he just finished reading the other obituaries dad left for him.

"Other obituaries?"

"His mom, his brother, and his old girlfriend he was going to marry."

"Oh my goodness. So where's he been? How come he didn't know what happened to all of them?"

"He's been away for a very long time. I'll explain later after the kids go to bed."

Valerie studied the face of her husband for a few more moments.

"All right, I'll make nice."

* * *

After returning from dinner, the twins sat on the sofa begging Captain Hank to tell more stories about their grandpa. Having already exhausted his supply of yarns from intelligence school, as well as a few more from the time he and Big Ben were building the device, Hank capped off the evening by telling them the story about the skunk they'd uncovered in the railroad maintenance building.

"I remember that," J.R. added, "Grandpa and Hank stunk to high heaven for about a week."

Ethan and Evelynn filled the room with laughter, until Valerie reminded them that they had school the next morning. Amid many protests, they wished Captain Hank good night and made their way to their bedrooms, with Valerie following closely behind.

As soon as she was out of earshot, J.R leaned forward and whispered to Hank.

"Valerie thinks we're both lying to her about who you are."

"Can she be trusted to keep the secret?" Hank asked, whispering too.

"Yes, if you tell her first that it is a secret. I know that sounds strange, but believe me it's important."

Before Hank could ask why, Valerie came back into the room and sat down next to J.R.

Hank, noticing J.R.'s slight nod urging him on, started the conversation.

"Thank you for the wonderful evening, Valerie."

"Well, thank you for putting up with the twins."

"They are very delightful children."

"Oh, they're a delight all right," J.R. interjected, "a double-handful of delight."

Hank smiled. "I was happy to hear that J.R. followed his father's career, and he tells me that you work for the Army too, but in a civilian capacity?"

"That's right. I work in the legal office."

"She helps the detectives catch and prosecute the bad guys," J.R. added.

"A worthy profession. I suppose you have a high security clearance then?"

"Yes, why do you ask?"

Hank leaned forward in his seat and locked his penetrating blue eyes on her.

"I suppose you're wondering how a man my age could've served with J.R.'s father during World War II?"

"Now that you mention it, I am a bit curious."

"Before I tell you, I need you to promise me that what I am about to say stays in this room."

"You can't tell anyone about this Val," J.R. said. "Not a soul."

"Okay," she replied, dragging the word out. "I promise not to breathe a word about this to anyone."

"Thank you," Hank said. "I know it's a bit melodramatic, but after you hear the story you'll know why it's a necessity. I don't know if J.R. told you, but just before I graduated from high school, I was playing baseball and got hit in the head by a line drive. The accident left me with certain abilities that are, for lack of a better way to describe them, truly amazing."

"What kind of abilities?

"Quite simply, I can memorize and learn things rather quickly."

"He's got a photographic memory," J.R. added, "and his eyesight, hearing and problem-solving abilities are far better than a regular person's."

"Really?" she asked.

Hank nodded.

For the next two hours, Hank told her the story of how he'd recovered and memorized the Nazi intelligence, built the device, and how he ended up stranded more than thirty-nine years in the future. At first, from the way she raised her eyebrows and kept looking over at J.R., he could tell that Valerie was having a hard time believing him. As the tale progressed, and with J.R. adding in things from his memories, she became completely captivated with the story. Before she would accept it wholeheartedly, however, she first wanted to see the device, whereupon J.R. offered to stay with the kids while she drove Hank back to the warehouse.

When Hank opened the door to the polished-steel room and had Valerie follow him inside, the moment she laid eyes on the device she dropped her purse and car keys, and stood motionless for several seconds completely mesmerized. Finally tearing her eyes away, she turned to Hank.

"So it's all true? You actually time-traveled here from the past?"

Hank nodded. "As hard as it is to believe, it's all true."

* * *

Waking the next morning from a restless sleep, Hank made a pot of coffee and poured himself a hot steamy cup. Although not

221

completely gone, the headache, dizziness and ringing in his ears had subsided to a tolerable level, which enabled him to review the letters J.R. had told him about, and the contents of the manila envelope Big Ben had left for him.

The first two letters were statements from his bank and the brokerage firm, where he and Ben invested in the stock market. J.R. told him that several years ago, when his dad revealed to him the secret of the device, he added him to their accounts. After all these years, the savings and stock values had grown to astronomical proportions, and looking at the balances now, it was hard for Hank to comprehend that he and J.R. were multi-millionaires.

The third letter Hank reviewed was the one J.R. received a few days ago from Fort Meade's contracting office. After reading it, he realized he needed to disassemble the device and move everything out as soon as possible. As to where to move it, J.R. suggested using one of the storage companies near the base. Having never heard of these types of businesses before, J.R. explained them to him, whereupon Hank put finding a storage site and renting a garage at the top of his priority list.

After reviewing the letters, he placed them to the side and dumped out the contents of the manila envelope on the work table. Once again with watery eyes, he read the obituaries, his heavy heart filling again with regret for leaving his loved ones in the past. He reverently placed the obituaries to the side with the letters and began looking over the other things Ben had saved for him, which consisted of a page torn out of a magazine and a copy of Fort Meade's "SoundOff," the base's weekly newspaper.

The torn-out page was from a publication titled, "Military Historian," dated January 1979, which contained a full-page story about the death of Samuel Goudsmit, the civilian scientist on the Alsos mission. Along with his many scholarly achievements, the article also mentioned that he was originally from the Netherlands (of Dutch-Jewish descent) and that he'd lost his parents in the Holocaust. Since Mr. Goudsmit had spent most of his time with the other civilians on the mission or with Colonel Pash in high-level meetings, Hank never knew this about him. In addition, the article said he wrote a book titled "Alsos" in 1947, but since Hank had been so pre-occupied with building the device, he'd never heard of it before. He made a mental note to go to Fort Meade's library at his earliest opportunity to see if they had a copy of it.

Setting the clipping aside, he picked up the SoundOff newspaper, which was dated Friday, January the twenty-fourth of 1986. Thumbing through it, the weekly publication appeared to be nothing more than a modern-day version of other base newspapers he was familiar with, but when he turned to the last page the article Big Ben had left for him immediately grabbed his attention.

The story was titled *"Bunker Electrician Recalls Hitler's Final Day,"* and was a re-cap from a talk given earlier that week at Fort Meade's museum as part of their on-going series of historical lectures. Now spellbound, Hank read the account of Emil Brandt, one of the Führerbunker's master electricians who was stationed inside the underground headquarters in April of 1945, and was one of the last people to see Adolph Hitler alive. Up until this point, Hank didn't know there was a second electrician working in the bunker.

Thinking back, he remembered Brandt's name from the list the Russian General provided to Colonel Pash, which contained the names of the Germans who were captured at the bunker the day of the surrender. Without any rank or title before Brandt's name, Hank had concluded that he must've been one of Hitler's aides. The electrician he remembered on the list was Johannes Hentschel, and was identified as such with the Russian word "elektrik" annotated next to his name.

Studying the mental image of the list more closely, Hank suddenly realized why Brandt's name hadn't been given the same annotation. Brandt's name was at the bottom of the page underneath Hentschel's, and there was a space before Hentschel's name which set their two names apart from the others. From a different

223

perspective, he could now see that the Russian annotation was referring to *both* men – not just Hentschel.

The article, which highlighted the main points from Brandt's speech, described how the electrician had attended the final staff meeting of the German high command the day Hitler committed suicide. When the last of the Nazis finally surrendered the bunker, Brandt was taken into custody by the Red Army and imprisoned for almost a year. After his release, he was reunited with his childhood sweetheart, whom he later married. In 1955, the couple and their young son immigrated to the United States, where he started a small electrical business in upstate New York. Brandt was quoted in the article as saying, "Although I worked in the Führerbunker, I never considered myself a Nazi. I was just trying to earn enough money to feed myself. And as far as Hitler was concerned, I hated and feared the tyrant."

The last thing the article mentioned was that his co-worker, Johannes Hentschel, was also captured by the Red Army when the Nazi's surrendered, but was not released until 1949. He subsequently died in 1982, leaving Brandt as the last known living person who'd worked on the maintenance staff in the bunker. Going strong at eighty-seven years of age, he lived with his son in Buffalo and still ran the family's electrical business.

Hank immediately concluded that Brandt must have known about the device, due to the simple fact that it required a great amount of electricity to activate it. Even if he didn't know about it or was just an assistant to Hentschel, he still would've been in a position to observe what happened when General Berger disappeared with it. And since the story said Brandt attended the last staff meeting before Hitler died, that scenario was a distinct possibility.

Hank knew that no matter what information Brandt possessed, it couldn't alter his present situation. Still, he felt he needed to talk to him. Since Brandt had made the speech five years ago, he would now be ninety-two, so the chances of him still being alive were rather slim. But if Brandt was still living, perhaps he might be able to answer a few of the remaining questions Hank had about the events that had taken place in the bunker.

When J.R. stopped by to take him to lunch, Hank told him about Brandt and asked if he'd like to accompany him on a short trip up to Buffalo to question him. J.R. jumped at the chance to go on the fact-finding investigation with Hank, and immediately called Valerie to make sure she was all right with him leaving for most of the weekend.

* * *

When J.R. arrived to pick Hank up early Saturday morning, Valerie was accompanying him.

"Is it okay if I come along?" she asked.

Hank smiled. "Of course it's okay, but we might be going on a wild goose chase. Brandt was quite old when he made the speech and might've passed away by now."

"Oh, he's alive," J.R. said, chuckling. "Val has already conducted her own investigation."

"What?"

"I found the telephone number to Brandt's electrical business," she said, "and called and posed as a reporter who wanted to interview him about the time he worked in the bunker."

"What did he say?"

"Unfortunately, I didn't get to talk to Brandt himself, but I did talk to his son Stefan. He told me his father is now institutionalized at the Niagara Nursing Home suffering from Alzheimer's disease. Although his dad would appreciate the visit, he thought it best I not disturb him."

Hank thought for a moment before replying.

"Like I said, this may be nothing more than a wild goose chase, so if you'd rather not go I can drive up by myself."

"Are you kidding? After what you told me the other night, and that we have an opportunity to talk to someone who was there? I wouldn't miss this for the world."

"What about what his son said? I mean, if Brandt is as sick as he says they might not let us in to see him."

Valerie smiled confidently. "I already have it worked out. You are his long-lost grandson from Germany who wants to pay him a visit."

"Okay, but what about the twins?"

"Oh, they're taken care of too," J.R. said. "Our neighbors, the Seymour's, have agreed to watch them."

"Their two kids and ours are best friends," Valerie added, "so we're all set to go."

J.R. smiled. "And besides, you can't drive."

"I most certainly can."

"Oh no you can't. Because if I were to guess, I'd say your driver's license expired over thirty years ago, and we can't have a senior citizen, such as yourself, endangering our nation's highways."

They all cracked up laughing, at which point Hank noticed how much J.R.'s booming laugh resembled Big Ben's.

"You know, you're just like your dad! Just like your dad!"

During the long drive to Buffalo, they told Hank about their plans, which included J.R.'s impending retirement from the Army. Having joined almost twenty-nine years ago, he'd originally planned to stay in until he'd made full-bird colonel. The massive inheritance his father left him had changed his mind, and he now saw no further need to remain in the military. He planned on using some of the inheritance money to finally open the automobile restoration shop he and Big Ben had always dreamed of. Valerie, on the other hand, loved her job and planned to stay working for the foreseeable future.

When the conversation turned to what Hank's plans were, he told them he hadn't had time to think about it. J.R. asked if he

226

would be interested in joining him in his business venture, and with the mission being over Hank eagerly accepted. By the time they reached Buffalo, they'd agreed on a full partnership as well as a name for the new business: "Ben & Hank's Classic Car Shop."

* * *

Later that afternoon, the three arrived at the Niagara Nursing Home. Before going inside, they agreed on their plan of having Hank pose as Brandt's grandson and speak only in German, while Valerie and J.R. would act as long-time friends.

Entering the rather run-down care facility, Valerie walked over to the receptionist.

"We're here to visit Mr. Emil Brandt."

The heavy-set woman, whose nametag read, "Joy," thumbed through a clipboard.

"Says here that only Mr. Brandt's family can see him."

"We're friends of the family, and this is his grandson Frederick."

"Guten tag," Hank said.

"Can he speak any English?" Joy asked.

"Hardly a word. He just got in from Germany, and because of the storm he couldn't get a hold of his dad. He wanted to visit his ill grandfather, so he called us and…"

"Okay, sister, okay. I get the picture. Sign in here."

After Valerie added their names to the list, Captain Hank's being "Frederick Brandt," Joy showed them in and directed them to the south wing, Room 13.

When they reached the room, they found the door slightly ajar and the inside lights on, but set to dim. A curtain was half-drawn across the front section of the room, and there was a heart monitor on a wheeled stand next to the bed. The only sounds were the cyclical beeps from the monitor, the rain pelting the window, and the long rattling breaths of the patient in the bed.

First to walk in, Captain Hank looked upon the still and motionless old man who was laying there. His arms were down at his sides, bent at the elbows, and the fingers of his hands were interlocked across his stomach. He had very pronounced wrinkles on his sunken face, and his skin, ashen in color, almost matched his unkempt gray hair and beard. Although his eyes were open and he appeared to be awake, his vacant stare betrayed the fact that he was losing his battle with Alzheimer's disease.

Emil Brandt was at death's door, and Hank hoped they hadn't arrived too late.

He pulled up the nearest chair and sat down close to the edge of the bed. Valerie and J.R., doing the same, took their seats on both sides of him.

"Mr. Brandt? Emil Brandt?" Hank asked.

No response.

"Mr. Brandt, can you hear me?"

He suddenly stirred and looked over.

"Who are you?" he asked, with a pronounced German accent.

"Friends of your son Stefan. We've come to visit you."

"You know Stefan? He is such a good boy."

"Mr. Brandt, we'd like to ask you about the Ünterbunker."

"The Ünterbunker?"

"Yes, the Ünterbunker."

"I was told never to speak of the Ünterbunker."

"It's all right, Emil," Valerie said calmly. "You can tell us."

"You are a very pretty woman, Miss." He coughed several times, trying unsuccessfully to clear his throat.

"Valerie, and thank you for the compliment. We'd like you to tell us about the Ünterbunker."

"I cannot tell you anything about the Ünterbunker, because it is not there anymore. I blew it up."

This first piece of information almost caused Hank to jump out of his seat with excitement, but he held his demeanor in check so that Valerie could continue to work her magic.

"Why did you blow up the Ünterbunker?"

"Because the Führer ordered me to. He was very upset with the general."

"General Berger?"

"Yes. We could not find him, and the Führer was so distraught he ordered me to blow it up."

"Have you ever heard of Operation Firebird?" Hank asked.

Brandt nodded. "That is why the Führer ordered me to blow up the Ünterbunker, to keep the Firebird information away from the Russians." Looking back to Valerie, he repeated, "You are a very pretty woman, Miss."

He was now laboring to breathe and his wheezing was becoming more pronounced.

"Valerie, and thank you very much. Now tell us Emil, what do you know about Operation Firebird?"

He smiled an all-knowing smile. "I do not know anything about it, but I *pretended* that I did."

"Why did you have to pretend?" J.R. asked.

"So that I wouldn't be shot. Since I was the one who hooked up the electricity to the Ünterbunker, the Führer thought I might know why the power went out."

"There was a power outage?" Hank asked. He could hardly believe he was getting such detailed information.

"Yes. Around noon, an electrical surge blew out several of the main fuses and all the power went out. That is when General Berger went missing. Then a few hours later at the staff meeting, the Führer asked me if I thought the two incidents were related."

Hank leaned in. "What did you tell him?"

"I told him I saw General Berger at eleven o'clock, closing the door of the safe in the ventilation room. I wanted to help him test the power in the Ünterbunker, but he got mad at me and ordered me to leave."

"What did Hitler say to that?"

"The Führer ordered me to destroy the Ünterbunker, and that no one was to ever learn the secret of Operation Firebird or any other information General Berger had down there. That's when I pretended I knew what it was, so that I wouldn't be shot."

He started to say something else but began coughing again, whereupon Hank leaned back and waited patiently until he was done.

"Did you ever go into the Ünterbunker's laboratory?"

"No, I was only allowed in the central room to wire the junction box."

"But if you were kept out of the laboratory, who planted the bombs?"

"Hentschel told me the Gestapo planted them." He coughed again, and looked at Valerie. "Do you know my friend Hentschel? He is such a good man, and I haven't heard from him in a very long time."

"I don't know him," she replied, "that is why we want to know what he told you about the bombs."

Brandt nodded. "Hentschel told me that the Führer ordered the Gestapo to plant the bombs, and that they were to be used if the Russians got into the bunker. He even showed me how to wire them in the ventilation room. Wasn't my friend nice for taking the time to show me what to do?"

As he started to say something else, he went into yet another coughing spell, more violent this time. Hank held up his hand, signaling Valerie and J.R. to hold their questions and give Brandt a moment. When the coughing fit finally subsided, Hank leaned in again.

"Is there anything else that you remember, Emil? Anything at all?"

"I thought the Führer was acting strange."

"You mean he was ranting and raving?"

"No, everyone was used to his tantrums. I mean later, after I told him about seeing General Berger in the ventilation room. He acted sad, as if he'd lost all hope. It was only a short time later, after he ordered me to destroy the Ünterbunker, when we heard the shot and he was dead."

As he saw the blank stare start to return to Brandt's face, Hank tapped him on the shoulder.

"May I ask you one more question Emil?"

"Who are you?"

"We're friends of Stefan, and we'd like to ask you one more question about the Ünterbunker."

He nodded.

"What was in the safe in the ventilation room?"

Brandt thought for a moment and suddenly began to cry.

"I don't want to think about that."

"It's all right, Emil," Valerie said, again using her calm and soothing voice. "You can tell us. We're friends of Stefan. What was in the safe in the ventilation room?"

"Gold and silver. Many bars of gold and silver. I think General Berger stole them and put them in his brief case, but I don't want to think about them."

"Why don't you want to think about the bars of gold and silver, Emil?"

"Because of the fillings."

"The fillings?" Valerie looked at J.R., then over to Hank. "What does he mean?"

Knowing what Brandt was alluding to, Hank tried to quickly think of another question but it was too late.

"Yes, the fillings," Brandt said, still crying and gasping for air. "I overheard General Berger one time, laughing about the inmates he'd murdered. After he killed them, he pulled out their teeth with pliers to get their fillings. I try not to think about how

THE DEVICE

many fillings were melted down to make all those bars of gold and silver."

Valerie immediately started to cry, whereupon J.R. quickly escorted her out of the room.

As soon as they were gone, Brandt looked at Hank.

"Do you know what happened to General Berger and all the bars of gold and silver? We looked for a long time and could not find him."

"He's dead," Hank replied, patting his hand. "You killed him in the Ünterbunker when you blew it up."

Brandt's sobbing suddenly stopped, and his eyes grew wide with astonishment.

"*I* killed him?" he asked.

"Yes, Emil. You killed the White Wolf."

He smiled and looked around, as if he wanted to share the news.

"I killed the White Wolf," he said, repeating it several times.

Then the smile on his face was replaced with a look of confusion, and the vacant stare of dementia once again fell upon his eyes. He laid back down, as if to take a well-needed nap, and a few moments later his labored breathing slowed to a stop. The sudden warning sound of the heart monitor disturbed the serene moment, and a nurse came in and checked his vital signs. A simple shake of her head told Hank that the electrician's life had ended, at which point she silenced the alarm and turned off the machine.

Standing up, Hank said a little prayer over Brandt's now-motionless body and silently thanked him for answering his questions. He rejoined J.R. and Valerie in the hall, and the three quietly exited the nursing home.

Emil Brandt, having divulged the last secrets of Hitler's underground bunker, passed into the next world believing he was a hero.

* * *

When they began the long and somber drive back to Fort Meade, the heavy rainfall had started to let up. Valerie, sitting alone in the back seat, laid her head back and closed her eyes. Hank, sitting in the front next to J.R., stared at the dark road ahead, mentally reviewing the information Brandt had told them.

"You know," J.R. said, speaking low, "when I studied history and World War II, the stories of the Nazi atrocities were just that, stories in a book. But now, after hearing about it first-hand from someone who was there, it's hard to believe they were that cruel. And to think, all of this happened in your time. I mean, not that long ago."

"That's why I went after General Berger to begin with. Could you imagine someone like that armed with a weapon as powerful as the device? But thanks to Brandt, we don't have to worry about him anymore."

"Amen to that. Did he answer all of your questions?"

Hank nodded. "Up until today, I didn't know who set off the explosives or that the power went out. It all makes sense now. Would you like to hear what I think happened?"

"Sure."

Hank paused for a moment to organize his thoughts before beginning.

"It was on or around March tenth of 1945. Hitler, knowing the war was lost, ordered General Berger to move the nearly-completed model of the device, Firebird One, from the Oranienburg think tank to the Ünterbunker. For the next twenty days the general tested it, and by threatening to kill the families of the two Jewish scientists, Eddleman and Kaufmann, got it fully operational. Then on April thirtieth, he murdered the scientists and stole the gold and silver from the safe in the ventilation room. Brandt must've caught him in the act."

"Which is why he got mad at him and ordered him to leave."

"Exactly. Then around noon, Berger activated the device and escaped into the future. I can only speculate that the Russian mortar shells and allied bombing campaign had caused some degree of damage to the electrical system in the bunker, because when he activated the device this time the power went out."

J.R. nodded.

"When Brandt and Hentschel finally got the electricity back on, Berger was nowhere to be found, at which point Hitler ordered everyone to search for him. Then right around three o'clock, Hitler called his generals together in what would be his final staff meeting. When he learns that Berger still hasn't been found, he has Brandt brought in for questioning."

"That's when he asks him if the two incidents, Berger's disappearance and the power outage, were related."

"Right. By this time, Hitler has probably learned that the main structure of the device is gone, and when he hears Brandt's report of General Berger closing the safe in the ventilation room, he realizes he's been double-crossed and orders Brandt to destroy the Ünterbunker. With no way out, the device gone and the Russians closing in, Hitler chooses his only alternative: suicide."

"Wow," Valerie said, startling the two men.

"I thought you were sleeping?" J.R. asked.

"Are you kidding? After hearing Brandt's story?"

"It was pretty graphic" Hank said. "I guess I should've warned you."

"Oh, I'll be all right. I just wasn't expecting it. But I do have a question."

Hank turned to face her.

"Do you think Hitler distrusted General Berger all along? I mean, since he had the Gestapo plant the bombs, maybe he thought Berger would double-cross him."

"I don't think so. From everything I've read, up until that point Berger was one of Hitler's most trusted generals. He completely believed in the Nazi cause. Remember when Brandt said

Hitler acted sad, as if he'd lost all hope? That tells me Berger's double-cross came as a complete surprise and disappointment to him. As for the bombs, I think it was just as Brandt said. Hitler had the Gestapo plant them to keep the Firebird information away from the Russians."

"But if Berger believed in what the Nazi's were doing, why do you think he turned on him?"

"Knowing what we do now, I think Berger got caught up in the power of the device and what he could do with it if he got it working. That and the self-preservation factor."

"He wanted to save his own skin," J.R. interjected.

"Yes, because by that time the Russian Army had surrounded Berlin, and he was as trapped in the bunker as Hitler was. If the Russians were to get their hands on the Nazi's White Wolf, with his record of murder and torture they would've surely executed him."

"Well I, for one, am glad that Brandt remembered those details," Valerie said. "Hopefully, we can put all of this behind us now."

"I wish I could," Hank said sadly. "If I'd only thought more about the explosion and cave-in, and how Berger is trapped in the Ünterbunker, then your parents would still be alive."

"I know it's no consolation, but we'd be honored if you spent the rest of your life with us in our time."

Hank smiled and thanked her, knowing he really didn't have any other choice.

* * *

Once they returned from Buffalo, Valerie volunteered to tackle the problem of getting Hank new identification. On Monday, she called the Social Security Administration and asked how to get a new card, then the Maryland Department of Motor Vehicles to see how to obtain a new driver's license. After learning that both agencies required an official birth certificate, she decided the easiest thing to do was to forge a new one. She later had lunch with J.R. and Hank, and they discussed what information they should include on it.

Since Hank was thirty-two years old (in real time) they decided he go forward with the first name "James," his birth date of October the thirtieth of 1960, and his mom and dad listed as Lana and Henry Stevens. As for the rest of the information, Hank provided Valerie a copy of his original birth certificate that he still had with his Army discharge paperwork. Later that afternoon she forged the new document and mailed a copy to the Social Security Administration requesting a new card.

The days he spent waiting for the card to arrive, Hank rented an apartment that was two miles from Fort Meade's main entry gate, and a large garage at the Oriole Self-Storage business. He got into the routine of jogging to the base in the morning, then spending the rest of the day at the warehouse boxing things up. Later in the day, when J.R. came by after getting off work, the two men would pack the jeep full of the boxes and take them over to the storage garage.

Eight days later, when Hank's new social security card came in the mail, J.R. drove him over to the Department of Motor Vehicles to get his new driver's license. It took Hank five minutes to fill out the forms and take the written exam, then less than half an hour to complete the driving portion of the test using J.R.'s jeep. Since it hadn't taken long for them to obtain the new driver's license, the men immediately went to the brokerage firm, where J.R. had Hank's new persona of "James Stevens" added to the stockholder account. A short time later, they made another stop at the bank to do essentially the same thing with the savings and checking accounts.

With Valerie busy helping the twins with a science project, J.R. suggested to Hank that they go look for a new vehicle for him. Although he tried to steer him towards a sports car, Hank opted for a truck. Since he still had a lot of things left to move out of the warehouse, he felt it was the practical choice. The two men then investigated several local dealerships until Hank finally decided on a truck with an automatic transmission – a feature he found utterly fascinating.

On Monday, July twenty-second, Hank was back at the warehouse, packing up the main structure of the device. At first, he contemplated scrapping it and taking the many loads of cobalt-metal parts to a nearby salvage yard. After giving it some thought, however, he decided to save it so that someday (when he found another place) he could re-construct it to find out exactly what had gone wrong with the power system. Right now, however, his priority was to get everything moved out of the warehouse.

Late that afternoon, J.R. showed up with some good news. Some friends he knew at the motor pool owed him a favor, and they had agreed to come over Friday with a forklift and a large truck and help move the heavier parts and machinery, to include the huge horseshoe-shaped field accelerator. If everything went as planned, they should be finished vacating the warehouse the next weekend.

Delighted with the news and needing to take a break, Hank suggested they go to the store and get some food and soda for a barbeque. J.R. immediately accepted, on the condition that Hank allow him to drive his new truck.

Just as they were making their way out of the warehouse area, Hank noticed one of the base's directional signs. At the bottom of this sign was an arrow pointing the way to the Medal of Honor Memorial Library. Remembering the article about Mr. Goudsmit, Hank asked if they could first stop at the library.

"Sure," J.R. said, "we've got plenty of time. It's Valerie's turn to pick up the twins, and they won't be home for another hour. Is there a book you want to check out?"

"Yes. Remember that article your dad left for me about the civilian scientist on the Alsos Mission?"

"Yeah. Samuel Goldsmith, wasn't it?"

Hank smiled. "Samuel Goudsmit. Anyway, the article said he wrote a book about the mission and I want to see if they have it."

"Let's go."

A few minutes later, the men were at the front desk of the library. As they waited for the attendant, Hank looked around. Things were much different here than at Weber State College, the most noticeable being the strange looking machines that were on some of the desks.

"May I help you, sir?" a woman asked.

Turning around, Hank found himself face-to-face with a very attractive blonde woman. She was wearing an expensive-looking black skirt and white top, which highlighted her tall and slender figure. On the front left side of her shirt was an identification badge with the name "Stacy" handwritten in.

"What?" Hank answered.

"May I help you?"

"Oh yes, I was wondering if you had the book Alsos by Samuel Goudsmit?"

"Alsos?"

"Yes, Miss, or I mean Ma'am. That's correct. Alsos."

"Can you spell the author's name for me?"

"Samuel, S, A, or, I mean Goudsmit." Hank spelled it out for her.

"Give me a moment?"

"Certainly."

When she disappeared into the back room, J.R. moved in close to Hank.

"Samuel. S. A. M."

Hank smiled. "Shut up."

Just then, Stacy reappeared.

"You're in luck, mister…"

"Stevens, Hank, or I mean Jim Stevens. My friends call me Hank and this is my friend J.R."

She nodded to J.R. and returned her attention to him.

"The book you want, Mr. Stevens, can be found in the History Section over there." She pointed to his right. "They're alphabetized by the author's last name."

"Thank you."

As they walked off towards the area she'd directed them to, J.R. once again started spelling out the word Samuel, and got another grin from Hank.

"Man, she's hot," J.R. said.

"What do you mean?"

"Good looking. Beautiful. You know."

Hank smiled again. "She sure is."

"You ought to ask her out."

"No, I'm still trying to get over Lana. Besides, she's probably married."

"I didn't see a ring on her finger."

"Let's just say I'm not quite ready for that, okay?"

"Okay man, but it's your loss."

Hank couldn't believe how much J.R. reminded him of Big Ben.

After retrieving the book they returned to the front desk, then Stacy assisted Hank in filling out a short form and prepared his new library card.

"Is there anything else I can do for you today, Mr. Stevens?"

"Yes. Could you tell me what those strange-looking machines are over there?" He pointed to the desks he noticed when he came in.

"The microfiche readers?"

"Is that what they're called?"

"Where have you been? Those old readers have been here for years."

"What do they do?"

Stacy looked over at J.R.

"He doesn't get out much," J.R. said, chuckling.

239

"They're used to look up information," she said, addressing Hank again. "Mostly newspaper and magazine articles."

"Really?"

She smiled. "Yes, really. Do you see those cards with the little slides in them?"

Hank nodded.

"All the information is stored on those little slides. The reader is used to light up and enlarge the slide."

"How far back does your inventory of cards go?"

"Some go way back."

"To 1988?"

"Oh, way before 1988."

Hank looked at J.R. "Could we stay for a few more minutes? I want to see if I can find something."

"Sure," J.R. replied, checking his watch. "We still have plenty of time."

A few moments later, Hank and J.R. were seated at two of the desks, with Stacy showing Hank how to use the microfiche reader.

"Is there any particular publication you're interested in, Mr. Stevens?"

"No, just the national newspapers from 1988."

She walked over to a large cabinet, which Hank thought resembled a standard card catalog, and retrieved a stack of cards.

"Here's the 1988 cards we have from many of the major newspapers; the New York Times, Chicago Tribune, and the Miami Herald, to name a few."

"That should be good."

Is there any particular day in 1988 you're looking for?"

"Christmas, or the day after."

"Are you wondering what my dad might've seen on the TV?" J.R. asked.

"Yes. I'm thinking if he saw something on television on Christmas Eve, it might've made the papers the next day."

"December's cards are normally in the back of the stacks," Stacy explained, "but sometimes the college kids don't put them back in order. Do you know what you're looking for?"

"Not really," Hank confessed.

She looked at J.R.

"Long story short," J.R. said, "Hank's been out of the country for a long time. My parents saw something on the television on Christmas Eve of 1988, and were on their way to send him a telegram about it when they got killed in a car accident."

"Oh, my goodness. I'm sorry for your loss."

Stacy joined the two men, and soon all three were searching through stacks of microfiche cards. In trying to identify the story she read the headlines aloud, while Hank and J.R. (remaining silent) reviewed their own sets of cards.

"Investigators continue to comb over Lockerbie crash site of Pan Am Flight 103." After hearing no response, she continued, "Parliament of Europe envisions growth. Yugoslav Envoy perishes in car accident."

After reading off a few more, she stopped and sighed.

"Can't you give me even a hint as to what we are looking for?"

"We'll know it when we see it," Hank said, not taking his eyes off the display.

J.R. concurred with a nod, also not looking away.

"Brazilian Union Leader Chico Mendes is murdered," she continued. "Simon Wiesenthal Center's traveling Holocaust exhibition, *Courage to Remember,* begins cross-county tour."

Both men immediately leaned over to look at the article.

"Close," Hank said, setting it to memory, "but I think it's something else."

"I feel like we're looking for a needle in a haystack, I don't see anything else on this slide, unless you're interested in construction workers getting blown up while digging near Hitler's bunker in Berlin."

"That's it!" Hank and J.R. yelled, jumping out of their seats with excitement.

Stacy, having already pulled the glass out to remove the slide, pushed it back in and quickly found the article. With Hank kneeling on her left and J.R. on her right, she joined them in reading the story.

The article, titled, "Explosion at Hitler's Infamous Bunker Site Kills Two Construction Workers, One Missing," read as follows:

> Berlin - A powerful explosion at the site of Adolph Hitler's infamous bunker has claimed the lives of two construction workers, while one remains missing. A spokesman for Greater Berlin Construction Consultants, Oskar Schmitt, said in a statement, "It first appeared as if the men might have accidentally hit a pocket of natural gas, but now we believe it was an unexploded bomb from World War II." The men, whose names are being withheld pending notification of their families, were digging at the site late Friday night when the explosion occurred.
>
> These fatalities represent the latest chapter of the ongoing saga of the much-maligned Help Now Housing Project. When the announcement of the massive apartment complex was made early last year, and that Greater Berlin Construction (an independent

company) had won the contract, union organizers protested the decision. The ensuing boycott of companies supplying building materials resulted in construction being delayed for over eight months. A settlement was reached three months ago when Greater Berlin bowed to pressure from the city, and agreed to employ fifty union workers with full wages and benefits.

Two weeks ago, the project made the news yet again when work crews uncovered some sections of Hitler's bunker still intact. Since that time, the construction company had been allowing historians limited access to study and photograph the site. With the accident occurring last evening, however, Greater Berlin has permanently closed the area due to safety concerns. After the investigation is complete, the company plans on sealing or filling in the remaining areas of the bunker uncovered during the construction.

Adolph Hitler lived in the bunker during the final 105 days of his life, before committing suicide on the 30th of April, 1945. Both the new and old Reich Chancellery buildings, which sat atop the bunker, were demolished by the occupying Russian Army in 1947. Then in 1959, the East

German government set off a series of explosives at the site to completely remove all traces of the bunker. The area remained abandoned and undeveloped until three months ago, when construction for the Help Now project began.

"What's the date of the article?" Hank asked.

She moved the slide up.

"December twenty-fifth, 1988."

"Since the explosion happened late Friday night, it would've been on the TV Saturday," J.R. said. "It has to be the same story dad saw."

Hank, deep in thought, stared off into the distance and nodded slightly. After a few moments, he returned his attention to Stacy.

"Thank you, Miss, you've been a great help."

Hank stood and motioned to J.R. that they were leaving.

"Oh, you're welcome," Stacy said, "If you need to look up anything else, come see me."

As soon they were outside and out of earshot of other patrons, they discussed the article.

"What do you think?" J.R. asked.

"I don't know what to think."

"Didn't you say the explosives guy on your team found three unexploded bombs?"

"Yes. Sergeant Atkins placed them on the desk in the central room. They were soaking wet from the ground water, which was why they hadn't gone off. That was the last place I saw them, still sitting on that desk."

"Well if you ask me, after all those years they must've dried out. Then late 1988 comes along, the construction crew starts digging around, and boom."

Hank nodded.

"And everyone knows that explosives become more unstable as time goes on."

He nodded again.

"Or maybe one of the bombs the government set off at the site in 1959 was a dud, and the construction workers accidentally hit it and set it off."

"I've got to go back."

"Go back? To the library?"

"No, back to Berlin."

"What?"

"Everything points to one of the scenarios you described, but either way I have to see for myself."

"How are you going to do that? There's probably nothing even left of the bunker."

"They said that they were going to seal some of the areas."

"They also said they were going to fill them in."

"True, but if part of it is still there and I can find a way into the ventilation room, I'll be able to tell immediately if those bombs were the ones that killed the construction workers."

"How so?"

"The desk was right inside the entry door at the bottom of the access shaft. Sergeant Atkins told me that the bombs had a lot of firepower. If the construction caused those bombs to go off, then the access shaft will be destroyed and I won't even be able to get down to the Ünterbunker."

"That's a lot of ifs, man."

"True, but if the shaft is still there and the bombs are still on the desk, we'll know that the bomb that killed the construction workers was either a dud the government planted in 1959, or just as the man in the article said, an unexploded one from the war."

"But what if you find the shaft intact *and* the bombs gone?"

"Then we've got ourselves a mystery or a worst-case scenario."

"What do you mean?"

"We won't really know what happened, which opens up other possibilities."

"Such as?"

"Either the construction workers found them and were trying to make off with them when they exploded, or General Berger got out and exploded the bombs to hide his tracks."

J.R. nodded. "That would be a worst-case scenario."

"Whichever the case may be, I have to know for sure."

"Let me come with you. Together we can…"

"No," Hank interrupted, "you really don't need to. I'll be in and out in less than a day. And besides, you've got that inspection coming up."

"Okay," J.R. acknowledged sadly. "So when did you want to go?"

"Immediately."

"Slow down. Before you go anywhere overseas you've got to get a passport."

"Oh, I didn't think of that."

"Let's talk to Val and see what she says. Maybe she knows a workaround."

A short time later, J.R. and Hank were explaining to Valerie what they had uncovered at the library, and that Hank wanted to go back to Berlin.

"You're sure?" Valerie asked. "I mean, it seems like such a long shot that you'd even find a way in."

Hank locked his penetrating blue eyes on her.

"I have to know that he didn't get out."

"All right, come with me to work in the morning. After I take care of a couple of things we'll go over to the transportation office and walk the paperwork through."

"Thank you. I know it's a lot to ask."

"We'll call you when we get there," she said, addressing J.R., "and if you're not tied up with the inspection, maybe you could meet us."

"What for?"

"We may need your rank muscle."

J.R. smiled. "I'll be there."

* * *

It took them less than an hour the next morning to walk the required paperwork through Fort Meade's transportation office and have the passport issued. At first, Hank thought their next stop would be the Baltimore airport to purchase a ticket from one of the commercial airlines. J.R., however, suggested that they first check to see if there were any military flights going overseas. In what could only be described as a stroke of luck, there was a flight scheduled to depart the next morning for Ramstein Air Base, Germany, and there was one seat still available.

Citing a seldom-used exception to the rule that prohibits civilians from flying on military aircraft, and using the ruse that Hank was a veteran and had a loved one gravely ill in Germany, J.R. convinced the young private working the reservations desk that they should allow Hank on the flight. J.R.'s large build and lieutenant colonel rank helped and somewhat hindered the plan; the private was completely intimidated, and could only utter "Yes, sir" repeatedly as he scrambled to confirm Hank's reservation.

Walking out of the transportation office, Hank thought of one last minor detail regarding the warehouse.

"I don't anticipate being gone for more than a couple of days, so could you call your friends at the motor pool and re-schedule the forklift and truck to next Monday?"

"Not a problem," J.R. replied. "There's still plenty of time for us to get the warehouse cleared out by Wednesday."

"For the sake of argument," Valerie said, "say you get in and find evidence that Berger got out. What'll we do?"

"If he got out, then he's had over two-and-a-half years to go into hiding and create another identity for himself. If that has happened then he could be living anywhere, and since it is now almost forty years later, not even his next-door neighbor would know who he really is. That said, I got an idea from something I read at the library."

Hank turned to J.R.

"Remember that story Stacy found about the Simon Wiesenthal Center's traveling Holocaust exhibition?"

"Yeah, but I didn't read it."

"Who is Simon Wiesenthal?" Valerie asked.

"He's a Jewish man that survived the Holocaust who is famous for hunting down former Nazis. The article said that the Wiesenthal Center had offices all around the world and that their headquarters is in Los Angeles. They conduct investigations and work with law enforcement agencies to track down war criminals."

"Are you thinking of contacting them?" J.R. asked.

Hank nodded. "It's a place to start. Hopefully we can enlist their help, but first I'll need *your* help."

"Anything," J.R. and Valerie answered, in unison.

"I'll prepare a letter to the Wiesenthal Center and tell them that Berger is still alive, and was last seen on Christmas Eve of 1988, in Berlin at the bunker site."

"They'll want to come and ask you a lot of questions," Valerie said.

"I'll make it an anonymous letter."

"But won't they think it's a crank, since the information is two-and-a-half years old?" J.R. asked.

"I don't think so," Hank replied, confidently.

"What makes you so sure?" Valerie asked.

"They'll believe it if I provide them a copy of the only known photograph of General Berger."

"You've got his photograph?"

"Yes. In all those papers that my team recovered from the Ünterbunker, I found his photograph, and if you let me treat the two of you to lunch, maybe afterward we could go get it and use that copying machine in your office. Assuming, of course, that it can copy photographs?"

"Sure it can. Anything else?"

"Yes. I'll need the address to the Simon Wiesenthal Center in Los Angeles."

"That's easy. I'll just call information."

"Information?"

"In your time, I think they called it *operator assistance.*"

"Oh, okay," Hank said, as the meaning became clear. "I'll write the letter tonight and leave it in the false bottom of the grey tool box." He looked at J.R. "You know where."

J.R nodded.

"If I find that General Berger somehow got out of the Ünterbunker, I'll call and have you mail the letter. If not, we'll all be laughing about this in a couple of days when I get back."

* * *

Thirty-two hours later, Hank was standing in the central room of the Ünterbunker. On top of the desk, sitting alone and by itself, was the old Torn.Fu receiver-transmitter. The only trace that remained of the unexploded bombs were three impressions in the thickly-accumulated dust. Seeing that the bombs were gone, Hank's heart sank in his chest, but after thinking it through he concluded that just because the bombs were gone it didn't necessarily mean that General Berger had gotten out. The rational explanation was that the construction workers had found them, and they'd inadvertently exploded when they'd tried to make off with them.

Walking in to inspect the rest of the Ünterbunker, Hank recalled the images in his mind of the last time he was down here.

Except for the bombs and the door leading into the laboratory (which was now closed) everything looked the same. Opening the door, he found a wall of earth and rocks, among which were pieces of the polished-steel plating that had once lined the entire room.

After studying the rocky mound for a few minutes, he noticed there was a strange-looking piece of metal sticking out towards the ceiling, just beyond his reach. Climbing up to take a closer look, he found it was a scrap of cobalt like the one he and Big Ben had used to construct the main structure of the device.

He placed the flashlight under his arm, and after pulling and rocking the piece several times, managed to dislodge it. Climbing back down, he set it on the floor and examined it closely. The surface was smooth to the touch, and except for a small, sharply-cut round hole (roughly the size of a dessert plate) the edges were torn and jagged. From the scorch marks and blackened color, he could tell the piece had been damaged by an explosion. Turning it over, he found the other side was painted white, and what looked like the tip of a bird's talon.

The realization of what he was looking at hit him like a thunderbolt: *this was a section of the Nazi's Firebird device!*

Now deep in thought, he studied the sharply cut hole and thought back to the intelligence he'd memorized. The only area that showed a hole this size was the lower rear section of the fuselage, where the electrical power was connected to the main structure. Since the piece was mostly smooth, it meant that when the device reentered real time its stationary plane had been clear. If it hadn't been clear, it would have immediately merged with the debris field at the subatomic level, and would be intermixed with the rubble.

As improbable as it seemed, and as much as Hank wanted there to be another explanation, the evidence told him that General Berger had returned from the fourth dimension safely and was now living in this time. It also explained why the bombs were missing from the desk in the central room, and why there were blast marks on the piece of cobalt. Berger, he concluded, had used the bombs to blow up the device and hide all traces of his arrival.

The cold chill that Captain Hank had felt the first time he'd come down to the Ünterbunker returned, as did the tremor in his left pinkie finger; albeit a bit more pronounced this time. He knew now for certain that the worst of all possible scenarios had happened, and that his mission of finding and stopping General Berger was far from over.

On the ride back to his apartment from the Baltimore airport, Hank sat in the backseat of the yellow taxi with his eyes closed, trying to formulate a plan of what to do next. *Where in the entire world do I even begin to look for Berger? South America? The United States? Still in Germany?* The possibilities of where he might be and what identity he had assumed were endless, which made the probability of finding him even more remote. He resolved, however, to continue the mission and keep searching until he had exhausted all possibilities.

* * *

Captain Hank never imagined that a little more than two-and-a-half years ago, General Berger had asked himself the very same questions and was now on a mission of his own: to find the American Army officer who had ordered his men to steal the Firebird information.

The hunter had unknowingly become the hunted, and in the last thirty-one months the Nazi's White Wolf had tracked his prey to Warehouse 1373, at the Fort Meade Army Base in Maryland.

Chapter Eleven
The Escape

Two Years, Seven Months and Five Days Earlier
Friday, 23 December 1988, 21:30hrs
Inside the *Ünterbunker, Berlin*

A sudden flash of bright light and a low-pitched hum disturbed the ink-black stillness in the secret lower level of what was once Hitler's underground bunker. As the blinding illumination dimmed, a large cylindrical object faded into existence, glowing an ever-brighter shade of blue as it materialized. Once the last atomic molecule of the cobalt-metal vehicle completely reentered real time, the aperture it had emerged from closed and the magnetic force released its vice-like hold. With its mounting points destroyed long ago by the explosion and partial cave-in, and over half of the polished-steel floor underneath it now missing from the excavation, the cylinder immediately crashed into the rocky mud and slid several feet before coming to a standstill.

As the main structure's temperature cooled, symbols from the past, representing one of the darkest chapters in human history, became visible on the surface of the steaming fuselage. These ornamentations included the letters "RFR" inside a large round swastika on the front, and majestic bald eagles with fiery wings painted down each side. Above each of the paintings, scorched but still legible, were the cryptically-written German words, *"Zunden Vogel Einser."*

From one of the deepest corners of the fourth dimension, Firebird One had returned!

~ Then ~

Approximately forty minutes ago, a three-man construction crew equipped with heavy-duty crawler-crane and cable-suspended grab bucket were digging at the infamous bunker site, searching for a broken main water pipe. Earlier that day, the survey team told the men that the pipe, which once supplied fresh water to Hitler and his staff in the bunker, should be right around the fifty-meter mark. When the men excavated to that depth, however, the pipe was nowhere to be found. Under pressure to get the foundation footings of the new apartment building ready for Monday's cement pour, the workers had little recourse but to continue digging, even if it meant staying late on a Friday night before the holiday weekend.

The man operating the crane, Eric Müller, and his spotting partner, Fritz Lehmann, had worked jobs like this for more than fifteen years, and throughout that time had developed a close personal friendship. Both men were well-respected by their peers and had earned the reputation as Greater Berlin Construction's best crane-digging team. So when it came time to lay people off, due to the agreement the company was forced to make with the city and union over the Help Now Housing Project, Müller and Lehmann had been able to retain their employment.

Unfortunately, they were forced to work with another person who was a member of the union. This man received pay and benefits well above the rate they were earning, which created a great deal of animosity between them. Therefore, tensions had been running high ever since Thomas Fenton O'Malley, Local No. 104637, had been assigned to their digging team. Not helping matters was the communication barrier Müller and Lehmann had with O'Malley, who they found could barely speak the German language. Not only that, he was one of the laziest people they'd ever had the displeasure to work with.

Originally from one of the more poverty-stricken areas of Dublin, Ireland, O'Malley grew up on the streets. When he was ten years old, his single mother died from a drug overdose, and with no other relative to take care of him the state placed him in an inner-city orphanage. With his rather large build and bullying nature, he found he could intimidate the other children into doing what he told them to do or giving him what he wanted. *Why do anything,* he asked himself, *when I can get others to do it for me? And if I can't get them to do what I say, I'll use my fists and make them!*

This attitude stayed with him throughout his adolescent years and naturally led him to a life of crime, which over time escalated from petty theft and burglary to loan-sharking and drug-dealing. When he reached the age of twenty, he caught the attention of Sydney "Big Sid" Mcloughlin, the president of Dublin's teamsters union, who was actually the head of one of Ireland's more-powerful organized crime syndicates. For the next five years, O'Malley made his living as a union steward (the Irish underworld's title of a mob enforcer) who broke fingers and arms (and on occasion murdered) at the behest of Big Sid.

Things were going good for O'Malley until four months ago, when he was sent to collect a gambling debt from a man in Belfast. After he broke some fingers and received the payment, the man's wife attacked him with a cast-iron frying pan. If there was one thing he hated, it was a sniveling woman getting in the way of business, and he became so enraged he wrestled the pan away from her and used it to beat her to death. Since the husband could finger him, he killed him too.

Unfortunately for O'Malley, the couple he'd murdered were related to a prominent figure of Ireland's Taoiseach coalition government, who pressured local law enforcement to find out who was responsible. In turn, the syndicate started feeling the heat and many of its members were brought in for questioning. Because he liked O'Malley and didn't want to lose one of his best stewards, Big Sid contacted one of his associates in Germany, a man known only as "Steinmetz," who owed him a favor. He then ordered O'Malley to report to Steinmetz in Berlin, lay low, and try to keep himself out of trouble until the heat was off.

When O'Malley arrived in Germany, Steinmetz thought it best to hide the Irishman at a construction site, whereupon he sent him to join a handful of union workers picked up by the Greater Berlin Construction Company to work the Help Now Housing Project. The foreman in charge assigned O'Malley to the night shift, where he was to assist Müller and Lehmann (two men he immediately detested) with menial work meant for commoners (something he despised).

In the days that followed, O'Malley's attitude, combined with the large amount of money he was earning, resulted in him having several confrontations with Müller and Lehmann, one of which ended three nights ago with a physical altercation. Although he could handle himself quite well in a one-on-one fistfight, he wasn't counting on the two stout construction workers teaming up on him with lead pipes, and the fight ended rather quickly when Müller and Lehmann beat him to a bloody pulp.

Bruised, sore, and with no other recourse, O'Malley kept reporting to work, but resolved to do as little as possible until Big Sid called him back to Dublin. He also silently promised himself that one day he would return to Germany with a couple of his men and administer his own brand of justice to Müller and Lehmann.

Sitting on an oil drum smoking a cigarette, O'Malley watched Lehmann ride atop the crane's connecting hook until he disappeared into the pit. A few minutes later Müller pulled him out, and seeing Lehmann shake his head again, the Irishman knew it was going to be another long night.

He stood up and flipped his cigarette stub, and immediately reached in his jacket pocket to retrieve another. After lighting it, he sat back down and watched Müller maneuver the grab-bucket back down into the shaft and remove another load of muddy rocks and sediment.

Unbeknownst to the three men above, the additional excavation had caused a landslide at the bottom of the pit which brought down the rear wall of the Ünterbunker's polished-steel laboratory. When Müller subsequently pulled two more bucket loads of mud and rock out of the hole, he'd also unknowingly removed the remaining rubble and debris away from Firebird One's stationary plane.

~ *Now* ~

Lehmann, standing on the side of the crane and watching the hole, saw the flash of bright light and heard the crash, at which point he immediately signaled Müller to hold. Staring down into the darkness, the walls of the shaft suddenly became emblazoned with bright blue light. He couldn't see what was causing the strange illumination, however, because the grab bucket was blocking his line of sight down to the bottom. A few moments later the light went out, and the entire hole dimmed to black once again.

Thinking Müller might've inadvertently struck an electrical line that supplied power to Hitler's bunker, Lehmann yelled at O'Malley.

"Come here!"

"What do you want?" O'Malley snapped back.

"Get down in there."

"I'm busy right now!" he replied, mocking Lehmann's German accent.

Müller, who could speak English quite well, chimed in.

"You heard what he said. Grab your walkie-talkie and flashlight, and climb down on the bucket."

"Why should I?"

"Because Fritz needs a break and you've done nothing all night but smoke."

O'Malley started to protest, but seeing that Müller had once-again brandished his lead pipe, decided he'd better cooperate.

Begrudgingly, he snatched up his walkie-talkie and flashlight, stepped onto the connecting hook, and grabbed hold of the cable.

As soon as he was aboard, Müller harshly jerked up on the control lever, swung the bucket out over the center of the hole and released the cable, resulting in the entire assembly freefalling down the shaft. When the cable was out to the approximate length of its last decent, Müller sharply applied the hydraulic brake and the cable and bucket snapped to a halt.

O'Malley, who'd hung on for most of the ride, was finally thrown off when the cable suddenly stopped, and landed face-first in the muddy rocks at the bottom. He managed to hang on to the flashlight and walkie-talkie, and after taking a few moments to gather himself, pressed the button on the side of the radio and cursed up a storm.

The only reply was laughter from the men above, and when it finally died down Müller spoke.

"Quit acting like a *säugling* (German for "infant") and see if you can find the water pipe."

Turning on the flashlight, O'Malley found himself in front of an image of a bald eagle painted onto a large piece of curved metal. There was writing just above the eagle, but because it was in German he hadn't a clue what it said. Reaching out to touch the painting, he burned the tip of his right index finger when it made contact, and immediately pulled his hand back. Sticking his finger in his mouth to cool it, he spit several times when he realized that along with his finger he'd placed a large amount of mud on his tongue.

Shining the flashlight ahead of him, he cautiously walked down to the end of the metal object, looked around the corner, and surprisingly found the wall of the shaft opened into a large finished room. Except for several tipped-over filing cabinets and chalkboards, the room looked futuristic; polished and glistening.

After a few moments, his attention turned back to the metal object, and when he saw the large swastika on the end of the cylinder his blood ran cold. Turning to leave, he stopped when he saw what appeared to be an opening on the other side of the object. Creeping over and shining the light in, he found stacks of brick-sized bars of gold and silver.

"By all things that are holy," he said, aloud and to himself, "good fortune has finally shined a light on O'Malley."

Not believing what his eyes were seeing, he set the walkie-talkie on the ground, and trying to avoid being burned again, carefully reached through the opening. Picking up the nearest bar, the heavy gold almost slipped out of his muddy hand. As he looked at it closer, the light from his flashlight cast a golden reflection back into his now-staring eyes. *What luck! What riches*, he thought wildly to himself. *I'll be able to buy anything!* With his blood instantly warmed by gold and silver fever, his mind schemed on ways to keep the treasure away from the two men above.

He suddenly became aware of someone standing behind him. He'd had the same feeling when that idiot's wife in Belfast had snuck up on him and attacked him with the frying pan. Thinking Lehmann might've followed him down, he quickly thought of the best way to kill him. Gripping the gold bar as tightly as he could he turned around, but instead of the short, stocky construction worker, he found himself face-to-face with the biggest, most physically imposing man he'd ever seen. He was blonde with a short haircut and was dressed in a German uniform, complete with high black boots and large shoulder epaulettes. He couldn't see his entire face, however, because the large man had one of his palms pressed against his forehead, blocking the view. From the way his eyes were wincing, the giant man appeared to be in a great deal of pain.

The man's huge frame and rippling muscles immediately intimidated him, and he dropped the gold bar but somehow held on to the flashlight. Sensing danger, he started to back away, at which point the big man unbuckled the holster on his belt, pulled out a German luger pistol and pointed it at him.

"*Wer bist du?*" ("Who are you?") the man asked.

"I *nicht sprechen das deutsch,*" (I don't speak German) O'Malley stuttered, which was the extent of his foreign vocabulary.

"Englander?"

"No, I…I'm from Ireland."

"*Welches jähr haben wir?*"

When O'Malley didn't answer, the large man spoke in English.

"What year is this?"

"Year?" O'Malley hesitated, temporarily not knowing how to relpy to such a strange question.

The huge man suddenly kicked O'Malley's right knee, shattering his kneecap and almost breaking his leg backwards. The move was so unexpected that it took the Irishman completely by surprise.

Falling to the ground and screaming in agony, O'Malley tried to crawl away, but the large man (disregarding his own apparent pain) quickly moved in on him.

Grabbing the Irishman by the collar, he effortlessly picked him up and forced the muzzle of the luger into his mouth.

"I am General Karl Berger," he said, slowly and with authority. "When I ask you a question I expect an answer."

The flashlight, which had dropped, rolled to a stop and was now pointing back at the two men, illuminating the general's entire face.

Seeing the dark and souless eyes, O'Malley's blood ran cold again.

"Now," Berger said, forcing the muzzle deeper into his mouth, "are you going to tell me what I want to know?"

In a sea of pain, O'Malley managed to nod, while silently praying that the huge man wouldn't pull the trigger. After a few moments, Berger pulled the gun out.

"Tell me, what year is this?" he asked.

"1988."

Looking off into the distance, the general repeated the year, then turned his attention back to the Irishman.

"Who are you and what are you doing down here?"

"Tom...Tom O'Malley," he stuttered, "I'm on a...a construction crew. We're trying to find a broken water pipe."

Just then, the walkie-talkie came alive with Müller's voice.

"Did you find it?"

Berger dropped O'Malley and whirled around at the sound. After quickly locating the walkie-talkie, he picked it up and examined it. After a few moments, he returned his attention to the Irishman.

"How many more are with you?"

"Just two. Two more up top."

"I see," Berger said, and moved in on him again.

"Don't kill me, please don't kill me!"

"Why shouldn't I, Irishman? I have no use for a construction worker."

"I can help you. Do things for you."

He knelt and placed the barrel of the luger against O'Malley's head.

"How can you help me? You don't even know me."

"I'm not like the two up there. I work for other people. Very powerful people."

"What powerful people?"

"The mafia, the underworld."

"The *Unterwelt*? You are a murderer then?"

"I've...done a few jobs."

"What about the two above?"

"They're just idiots."

After a few moments, Berger moved to within inches of O'Malley's face.

"Very well, I will keep you alive under one condition."

"Anything! I'll do anything! Just don't kill me!"

"A man stole something from me and I want it back. Do you understand?"

O'Malley nodded.

"If you help me find him, I will make you rich beyond your wildest dreams. But I warn you, if you betray me…" He pressed the barrel harder against O'Malley's head. "I will most assuredly put a bullet in your brain. Do you understand?"

"I…I understand."

Berger smiled. "Good. Then I think those two men up above are worthy of attention."

"What do you want me to do?"

"Call one of them down here." He tossed him the walkie-talkie.

A few moments after making the call, Müller replied, "Fritz is coming down."

Hearing the crane engage, Berger dragged the Irishman a short distance into the polished-steel room and motioned him to be quiet.

As Lehmann neared the bottom of the pit, the lower part of the grab bucket collided with the Nazi device, at which point he radioed Müller to hold. Shining his flashlight down, he saw the top of the cylinder-shaped object with the faded German words painted down the side, and slid down off the side of the bucket to take a closer look.

With his eyes wide, but still in a great deal of pain, O'Malley watched the murder unfold. At first, he couldn't help but laugh at Lehmann, overjoyed that he'd gotten what was coming to him. Later, after seeing the savagery of the attack and the way the big man took pleasure in taking Lehmann's life by breaking his neck, it chilled him to the core.

When it was over, the Irishman realized he'd entered into an agreement with the devil, but if helping this giant of a man who called himself "General Berger" meant he could get his hands on some of those gold and silver bars, so be it. There were worse ways to make money, like working at a construction site.

Berger deposited Lehmann's dead body next to him, at which point O'Malley looked up.

"Who are you?" he asked.

Berger simply smiled at him, ignoring his question.

~ *Then* ~

From General Berger's perspective, earlier that day was Monday, April the thirtieth of 1945, and his escape was near-perfect. After documenting the final successful test results of Firebird One and murdering the two Jewish scientists, he'd climbed up the access ladder to the ventilation room to retrieve the gold and silver. While he was emptying out the safe, Emil Brandt happened into the room. He should have murdered the electrician then and there, but decided against it. Since his partner Hentschel was busy keeping the power going to the rest of the bunker, if something were to go wrong with the electricity in the Ünterbunker he might need Brandt to repair it. Instead of killing him, he screamed at the sniveling coward and sent him on his way.

At noon, after making his final preparations and loading the large briefcase full of gold and silver bars into the cockpit, he activated the device and entered the fourth dimension. Normally, operating the device required two people; one applying power to the main structure and field accelerator, and the pilot inside the cockpit reversing the polarity of the electro-magnets. But a few days ago, Hentschel had showed him the bombs the Gestapo planted, and educated him on how the dual-action igniter fuse worked; either with direct current, or with the timing delay. It took Berger less than fifteen minutes to cannibalize a couple of old alarm clocks and connect them to the switches providing power to the device, which allowed him to activate Firebird One by himself.

Merely a few short seconds after he had entered the time aperture and made his escape, he felt a strange rocking motion. Holding up a lantern to the front window, everything outside appeared to be the same, but when he turned around and shined the light out the rear, he saw that the window was now covered with rocks and dirt.

He slowed Firebird One's exciter-motors down to their minimum speed, carefully making sure he didn't reenter real time. Shining the light of the lantern out the window again, he realized that one of the bombs the Gestapo had planted must have exploded. Hitler had told him the bombs were to be used in the event the Russians overran the complex, but he never thought the Führer would actually give the order. After all, the device was the Third Reich's most-prized accomplishment.

Since the area in front of Firebird One still looked clear, he concluded that some of the explosives must not have detonated, otherwise the front window would also be covered. Remembering what the scientists had told him about reentering real time with the stationary plane blocked, he decided to go on into the future. Hopefully, an earthquake or some other type of natural disaster would eventually clear away the stationary plane for his reentry.

Before throttling-up, however, he noticed soldiers enter the Ünterbunker. Although they were moving real fast (due to the time differential) it appeared as if they were conducting a search. One man, obviously the commanding officer, ordered the other men out of the laboratory and began reading the Firebird files by himself. A short time later a man rejoined him, and then all the men were back in the laboratory; packing the Firebird files and what was left of the field accelerator into several duffel bags and foot lockers.

After the other men left with the information, Berger finally managed to get a glimpse of the officer who was giving the orders. He was holding a lantern, and walked up to the area directly outside of Firebird One's front window. Even though it was only for a fraction of a second, he managed to look in his eyes and memorize his face. Since he was an expert identifying uniforms worn by enemy soldiers, he also recognized the red square patch the man wore on his sleeve.

With the laboratory now dark once again, he thought about what he had just seen outside the window, and concluded that the entire appearance of these soldiers in the Ünterbunker didn't make sense. He remembered General Weidling, the commander of the Berlin Defense Area, specifically mentioning that the Russian Army had surrounded the city, but the men he'd just seen weren't Russian – the patch on the officer's sleeve proved that. In addition, the man in command was merely a company-grade officer, and in charge of three or maybe four men; undoubtedly a small detachment from a larger intelligence-gathering unit. And because the Red Army was more than likely occupying Berlin by now, he speculated that the operation these men were conducting must be covert, without the Russians even knowing about it.

Sitting back in the seat, he eased Firebird One's power throttle forward. He also swore to himself that if he ever escaped the fourth-dimension alive, he would find this officer and recover the plans of the Firebird operation.

A short while later, after untold years had passed outside the aperture, General Berger felt Firebird One shudder. Glancing out the rear window, he was astonished to find the stationary plane now clear, and he immediately flipped the polarity-reversing switch and reentered real time.

~ *Now* ~

Looking at the bomb he had in his hand, Berger saw that it was the same type as the one Hentschel had showed him. He could also see that the paper on the sticks of explosives were discolored and wrinkled, which told him they were wet at one time. He then remembered where the electrician said the Gestapo had planted them, and glancing over to the main support beam and the Ünterbunker's exit door, he found both places empty.

Remembering the fifth bomb in the ventilation room above suddenly reminded him of the normal way out of the Ünterbunker: the access shaft. He didn't know why he hadn't thought of it before, but suspected it was because his attention was thoroughly focused on what had happened in the Ünterbunker while he was in the fourth dimension. Also hindering his thoughts (to some extent) was the massive headache he was experiencing, which he'd learned from testing the device was an unavoidable side effect.

Returning his attention to the Ünterbunker's exit, he thought if the way was clear, he could simply murder the Irishman, take the bars of gold and silver, and be gone. He quickly opened the door and started up the ladder, but couldn't reach the top because rocks and other debris had fallen against the safety cage and narrowed the ladder passage, making it too small for him to squeeze through.

He now knew for certain that out of the five bombs the Gestapo had planted, only two had gone off; one at the top of the shaft and the other in the laboratory behind the device. The three bombs on the desk must have gotten wet and misfired. The soldiers searching the lower level, he concluded, must have found these three and placed them on the desk.

Satisfied that he now knew what had happened while he was trapped in the fourth dimension, he scooped the three bombs up in one arm and returned to the laboratory. Shining his light on the Irishman, he found him fumbling with the dead construction worker's trousers, trying to remove his wallet.

Seeing Berger return, O'Malley stopped what he was doing and looked up at him.

"We'll need some money, and he won't be needing it."

"You may continue."

After removing Lehmann's money and tossing the billfold aside, O'Malley picked up the walkie-talkie.

"Müller's been calling. He wants to know what's taking so long."

"Tell him it will be a few minutes."

After hearing O'Malley obey the order, Berger picked the Irishman up with his free arm, and effortlessly carried him over to the grab-bucket.

"Get in," he ordered.

O'Malley, still in a great deal of pain from his broken knee, took hold of the connecting hook, and after several tries managed to swing his injured leg up and over the edge.

While O'Malley was struggling to get aboard the grab-bucket, Berger made his way over to the access hatch of Firebird One. He set the bombs down and removed the large briefcase from the cockpit, and quickly refilled it with the gold and silver bars that had spilled out during the crash. After hauling the heavy case full of bars to the grab-bucket, he returned to the bombs, set the small timers to twenty-minutes and placed them inside the cockpit. Climbing into the grab bucket, he ordered O'Malley to call the man above and pull them out.

Ten minutes later, after murdering Müller, Berger threw the body into the pit then retrieved the gold and silver-laden briefcase from the grab bucket.

* * *

As the two men made their way out of Berlin, an explosion rocketed into the air. Even though they were now more than two miles away from the bunker, the blast of the bombs was still loud enough to startle O'Malley and cause him to jump in his seat. Berger, on the other hand, didn't move a muscle. Staring straight ahead, his mind was focused on the day's events and what he needed to do.

Although he hated blowing up Firebird One, he simply hadn't been able to think of any other alternative. The Ünterbunker was compromised by the construction crew, and the main structure was simply too large to pull out through the shaft. Since he was determined not to let anyone else find it, study it, and possibly steal the technology out of it, blowing it up was the right move to make.

In any event, all was not lost. He had returned from the fourth dimension without being killed on reentry, and escaped Hitler's bunker alive with the bars of gold and silver. Since it was now forty-three years later, no one would know him or even suspect who he really is. If by chance someone did recognize him, they would be very old now, and their belief that he (still a young man) was Nazi Germany's notorious General Berger would call their memories into question.

As for the Firebird technology, he had to recover it at all costs. The ability to temporarily go into the future and return to the present could not be ignored – it was the greatest power ever conceived by man! He could use it to create a new Fourth Reich, but this time defeat nation after nation by altering the course of battles *before* they happened. Finally, with the conquest complete and himself installed as the new Führer, he could rule the world!

It wasn't just ambition, it was also personal. The entire Firebird operation was *his* undertaking. *He* was the one who had pleaded with the Führer to commit more reichmarks to the project. *He* was the one who had talked Albert Speer into letting him handpick only the best and brightest German scientists returning from the front. *He* was the one who had threatened the Jewish scientist's families, until he had ripped the secret of fourth dimensional travel out of their puny little brains. Therefore, the Firebird technology was *his and his alone*, and he was determined to recover it regardless of how many people had to be murdered in the process.

As Berger thought back to the events that had transpired earlier in the Ünterbunker, he reviewed the clues he had to the man's identity – man who had stolen the Firebird information. His uniform and rank insignia told him he was a captain in the

American Army, and from the red patch he wore on his sleeve he knew he was assigned to a component of the Sixth Army Group. In 1945, this man had commanded a small intelligence team on a mission into Berlin and into the bunker. Since he saw him reading the Firebird files, this man knew the German language, and because the operation was carried out under the noses of the Red Army, the probability was high that this man also knew how to speak Russian. From the split-second glimpse of the man's face, he knew what he looked like, especially what they had in common: their unique eye color. Yes, this man's eyes were far from his dark green color, still, their deep sapphire pigment made them distinguishable nonetheless.

It wasn't much to go on, but at least he had a starting point, and with the Irishman's underworld connections and some well-placed bribes, he should be able to learn the man's identity and location. When he finally catches up with him and recovers the stolen Firebird documents, he was quite sure this American Army officer with the penetrating blue eyes will be worthy of his attention.

Free of the confines of the fourth-dimensional prison, the Nazi's White Wolf now had his sights set on finding Captain Henry "Hank" Stevens.

THE DEVICE

Chapter Twelve
The Assault

Twenty-Five Years, Eight Months and Nineteen Days Later
Wednesday, 10 September 2014, 11:45hrs
Inside the *Regional Medical Center, South Ogden, Utah*

The white box sitting atop the small-wheeled stand automatically monitored the vital signs of the patient, and displayed the data in different colors on an eight-inch square digital screen. As it picked up an additional reading from the deflating arm sleeve, the display changed to show the blood pressure numbers, and returned to the previous screen containing the cardiac and respiratory information. In the upper left-hand corner of the display, standing out because of their larger size and bold-white lettering, was the abbreviated name of the patient laying in the bed: "d'Clare, M." Having returned from the operating room, Madison was now resting comfortably and out of pain – a sharp contrast to what her condition had been just a few short hours ago.

As I sat in the recliner next to her bed, I silently blamed myself for her injury. I should've known that the people after Captain Hank's diary would stop at nothing to obtain it, and been better prepared for the attack of the previous evening. I was now in the middle of a situation I never thought I would find myself in, and could no longer live up to one of the vows I'd made to Madison when we'd gotten married: to protect her.

271

THE DEVICE

As I looked over at the foam-rubber sling strapped around her neck, which immobilized her arm and shoulder, I thought back to the events that had transpired in our home twelve hours ago, and our being assaulted once again by O'Leary and his group of phony FBI agents.

~ Then ~

Madison and I were roughly three-quarters of the way through reading Captain Hank's incredible diary, when I realized I was late taking my Parkinson medication. Like a silent but dependable alarm clock, if I neglect to take my little yellow pills my right arm will weaken and start to shake with tremors. This time, my symptoms were at a heightened state because of my prolonged preoccupation with the story in the diary.

After informing Madison that I needed to take a temporary break to retrieve a glass of water, I heard the chiming sound of my cell phone telling me I'd received a text. As Madison and I read the message, a cold chill ran down my spine:

> Top 'o the evening to you, Mr. d'Clare,
> Your old friend Agent O'Leary here.
> I'll be wanting that diary now, so if you would be so kind as to bring it out your front door we'll be on our way.

Madison instantly retrieved her phone from her purse and quickly found Deputy Alvarez's number in the list of contacts. While she waited for the call to go through, I hurriedly ran back up to the kitchen and placed the binder back in its hiding place under the dishwasher.

The second I got the diary re-concealed and the baseboard back in place, our front door burst open and in stormed O'Leary,

Crosby, Denney, and the three other men from the night of the interrogation. Our two Shi-Tzu puppies, not used to sudden intrusions into our home, cowered away from the intruders while also filling the house with the sounds of uncontrolled barking.

Looking around to find something to defend myself, I reached into the nearest utensil drawer and pulled out a large butcher knife. Although my Parkinson's symptoms were now quite evident in my right arm, I still managed to hold the knife out in front of me in a threatening manner with my steady left hand.

Madison, still waiting for the call to go through to Deputy Alvarez, tried to exit the house through the door leading to the garage, but she was too late. In an instant, Denney jumped down the entire flight of stairs, slammed the door closed and savagely slapped the cell phone from Madison's hand. In a moment that made me proud to be her husband, Madison connected a right cross to Denney's face, which completely startled the woman. In trying to follow up the surprising punch with a kick to Denny's stomach, however, Madison landed only a glancing blow, which resulted in her losing her balance and falling to the floor. Denney recovered quickly and was immediately on top of her, and after being joined by Crosby soon had Madison's right arm twisted around behind her back. Once Madison was subdued, Denney and Crosby walked her up the stairs to the scene of my standoff with O'Leary and the other men. Grinning, the Irishman limped over to Madison, and in one swift move took her away from them.

"Crosby, shoot those mutts!" O'Leary ordered.

"That might alert the neighbors," the frail-looking man replied.

While the Irishman thought for a moment, my heart was sinking in my chest.

"Then stick them in the basement," he said.

I breathed a sigh of relief.

After obeying the order, Crosby rejoined Denney at the top of the stairs and nodded to the Irishman.

O'Leary, still maintaining the restraining hold on Madison's right arm, shuffled her forward until they were both approximately three feet away from me.

"Mrs. d'Clare, you'd best tell that husband of yours to drop that knife he's holding and hand over the diary, or rest assured I'll break your shoulder."

I hesitated, not knowing if I should lunge the knife at him or drop my only means of self-defense.

"Don't give it to him!" Madison yelled in utter defiance.

O'Leary inched Madison's arm up her back. As the growing discomfort appeared on her face, I couldn't bear to watch it any longer and I dropped the knife on the kitchen counter.

"Okay!" I shouted. "Let her go and I'll give it to you!"

Two of the other men came around the counter and grabbed each of my arms, at which point O'Leary violently jerked up on Madison's arm until her shoulder popped. Screaming in agony, she crumpled to the floor.

"No!" I yelled, struggling to get free.

O'Leary stood over Madison for a few moments, glaring down at her before finally looking up at me.

"One day I'm going to kill you," I said.

He smiled. "You'd best get in line for that, Mr. d'Clare, but for right now I'll have that diary. Or would you like me to break your wife's other shoulder?"

Knowing he wasn't bluffing, I nodded in resignation.

"Let him go," he said, and the two men relaxed their grips on my arms.

Bending down to retrieve the diary from under the dishwasher, I became aware that someone else had entered the house. Since O'Leary and his people were all crowded into our kitchen watching me, they hadn't noticed this other person come in. I could see through my peripheral vision that the individual sneaking up on them was wearing a police uniform and holding a shotgun.

Not wanting to alert the Irishman or his people, my eyes remained locked on the grinning pompous face of O'Leary. Instead of retrieving the diary from its hiding place, I moved to my left and slid open the lowest kitchen drawer, which I knew contained only hand towels. The man who'd been restraining my left arm shoved me away and knelt to inspect the contents. Finding nothing, he looked up at O'Leary and shook his head.

Standing up straight, I summoned up my best fake Irish accent.

"Oh, will you look at that now. Looks like a wee little leprechaun made off with it."

The Irishman's hands began to shake and his face became a bright shade of red.

"All right Mr. d'Clare, have it your way!" He nodded to the two men beside me, who again took hold of my arms.

As he reached down to Madison, I heard the familiar voice of Deputy Alvarez.

"If you touch that woman you're a dead man!"

Looking past the now-frozen O'Leary and his startled group, I saw Alvarez had been joined by no less than seven other uniformed officers, all with their police revolvers drawn. One of these officers was a female, and from the description Madison had previously given me I concluded she must be Deputy Rivers. I could also see what seemed to be an almost constant stream of red flashing lights reflecting off the blinds in our front room window.

With his group now unexpectedly outnumbered, O'Leary was temporarily at a loss for words, but he quickly recovered.

"Top 'o the evening to you, officer. I'm Agent O'Leary of the FBI..."

"You've got two choices," Alvarez interrupted, "either you and your people drop your weapons in the next ten seconds, or I will order my deputies to open fire."

"You don't have any idea what you're getting yourself into."

"You've now got five seconds," Alvarez replied coldly. As he spoke, he slowly moved forward until the barrel of his shotgun was within three feet of the Irishman's face.

O'Leary nodded to his people, at which point they lowered their guns. Immediately, half of the deputies in the room holstered their weapons and converged on them. Deputy Rivers moved in on Denney, and after handcuffing her and handing her off to another deputy, knelt to check on Madison.

"You've just gotten yourself into a lot of trouble," O'Leary said.

"Not as much trouble as you're in," Alvarez countered. "Now turn around and place your hands behind your back."

When O'Leary refused to move, Alvarez delivered a strong blow with the butt of his shotgun to the side of the Irishman's head, instantly dropping him to the floor. The swift and unexpected move was such a surprise it caused me to jump back. Inside, however, I was teeming with glee over the fact that O'Leary had met his match as far as physical violence was concerned.

Moving the shotgun forward until the barrel was touching O'Leary's bleeding head, Alvarez reiterated his order.

"When I tell you to turn around and put your hands behind your back you'd better damn well do it. Do I make myself clear?"

Begrudgingly, the Irishman slowly stood up and turned around, offering no further resistance, at which point Alvarez stepped back and two other deputies moved in and restrained him.

After the other deputies escorted him out, I rushed to Madison. She was laying on the floor on her left side, with her right arm grotesquely bent behind her back. By the look on her face, I could tell she was in excruciating pain, which caused a river of tears to flow from my eyes.

"I'm so sorry, sweetheart. This is all my fault."

"Don't you... be sorry for... anything, George," she said, barely managing to get the words out. "This is not your fault."

"But if I had just given it to him to begin with..."

276

"He probably would have killed us both."

"I've called for an ambulance," Deputy Rivers said, placing her hand on my shoulder.

Not able to look up, I simply nodded.

"She's right, Mr. d'Clare," Deputy Alvarez offered, "there was really nothing you could've done against six armed assailants."

His comforting words didn't deter the fact that I was unable to protect my beloved wife.

When the ambulance arrived, we were taken to the Ogden Regional Medical Center where Madison was immediately admitted. Fifteen minutes later, a nurse and an orderly came in and wheeled her away, at which point I gathered her personal belongings in the book bag I'd brought along, and placed the barrette flash drive in a side pocket for safe keeping.

The procedure lasted almost ninety minutes, after which they wheeled her to a secure room in one of the long wings of the hospital. When the trauma physician came in to give me an update of her condition, he told me that the operation had gone better than expected. When he'd first examined her shoulder he thought he'd have to perform major surgery, but when he moved her arm back to its proper position it had popped back into the joint. Unfortunately, the x-rays showed she had sustained a torn labrum and rotator cuff, so he'd performed the (less-intrusive) arthroscopic procedure to repair them both.

After the doctor left, Deputy Alvarez came in to check on us. He informed me that he'd coordinated with the Davis County Sheriff's Office to have several officers patrol our neighborhood in case there were any more of O'Leary's people around that we weren't aware of. He put my mind at ease by telling me he'd re-secured our front door as best he could with a pair of two-by-fours he'd found on our patio. He also made sure that our two dogs had been given plenty of food and water, which I thought was quite thoughtful of him.

THE DEVICE

After Alvarez departed, Deputy Rivers stayed with Madison and I in the hospital room, remaining steadfastly alert for anything out of the ordinary and seemingly impervious to exhaustion.

~ Now ~

I was reviewing the events of the previous evening, trying to think if there was something I could have done to prevent the attack, when I fell asleep. The bright morning sun shining through the open blinds in the window hit my eyes and caused me to waken, at which point I looked around and noticed things were mostly the same as they'd been when I'd dozed off: Madison was still asleep and Deputy Rivers was reading a college textbook on calculus.

As I straightened up in the recliner, the door opened and Deputy Alvarez walked in. When he reached the edge of Madison's bed, he positioned the last remaining empty chair so that it faced me. Deputy Rivers, who was seated on my right side, leaned in to hear him.

"I've got some news, but I'm afraid it's not good. O'Leary and his people have been released."

"Released?" I almost screamed the word, but thankfully didn't wake Madison from her slumber. "How could they be – released?"

"Less than an hour ago, by Sanders himself."

"Who's Sanders?"

"The Davis County Sheriff."

"Why would he do that?"

"Because he's a pinhead who suffers from little-big man syndrome," Rivers interjected.

"I've got Johnston and Martineau tailing O'Leary," Alvarez continued, "so we should find out something soon."

"I don't understand. These men broke into our house, assaulted Madison, and now, less than twelve hours later they're released?"

I suddenly found myself in the crosshairs of Deputy Alvarez's penetrating stare.

"It might help if you told us what this is all about."

Turning to Deputy Rivers, I found her also staring me down.

"We can't help you or your wife unless you're honest with us," she said.

"George," Madison whispered, "tell them."

Standing up and moving past Deputy Alvarez, I went to her bedside.

"How are you feeling?"

"I'm okay. Did they fix my arm?"

I nodded. "The doctor said it popped right back in, but he did have to scope it to repair a few things."

"Oh, that's good."

"Can I get you anything?"

"Just a drink of water and maybe something for the pain."

I pressed the call button on her bed and a few minutes later a nurse arrived with a cup of ice water and some medication.

Once the four of us were alone again I sat back down, and after receiving an approving nod from Madison began telling the two deputies some of what we knew – carefully omitting the story about the device.

"What O'Leary and his people are after is a photograph that Mr. Stevens gave to us."

"The man who was killed in the hit-and-run at Station Park?" Alvarez asked.

"Yes. He told us that if anything ever happened to him we were to give it to the authorities."

Alvarez nodded to Rivers, who retrieved a pen and small pad of paper from the breast pocket of her uniform and started writing.

"Is that what you meant last night, when you told your wife you should've given it to them?"

I nodded, thinking nothing gets past this deputy.

"Why didn't you tell me about this before?"

"Because after our encounter at the jail we weren't sure who we could trust, or whether you were working with O'Leary."

"Fair enough. I guess if I were in your position I would've felt the same way. So what's in the photograph?"

"As unbelievable as this may sound, a Nazi war criminal."

Deputy Rivers stopped writing and looked up. "Seriously? A Nazi?"

"I told you it would sound unbelievable, but Mr. Stevens told us he'd uncovered the identity of a Nazi war criminal. The photograph he gave us is the only known picture of him."

Alvarez continued staring at me, as if he were studying me for any non-verbal sign that would tell him I was lying.

"Did he give you a name?" he finally asked.

"Yes. His name is Karl Berger. He was a lieutenant general in the SS who disappeared at the end of the war." As I was talking, Alvarez nodded to Rivers and she started writing again.

"Did Mr. Stevens tell you what name he might be using now?"

"No, but if I were to venture a guess, I'd say O'Leary and his people are either working for him or are connected to him in some way."

"How can that even be possible?" Rivers asked. "World War II ended in 1945. That would make this guy really old."

"Not as strange as you think," Alvarez said. "Every so often I read in the newspaper about some former Nazi being found." Returning his attention to me, he said, "I'll need to see that photograph."

"Do you have a laptop computer?"

"I've got one right here," Rivers said, and pulled it out of her briefcase.

After explaining how we'd scanned it, I retrieved the barrette flash drive out of my book bag and handed it to her.

As soon as she plugged it into the laptop, the flash drive's contents immediately came up, displaying the three files.

"What are the other two files?" Alvarez asked.

"The one titled *Diary* is Madison's personal diary."

"If you don't mind, I would appreciate it if you respected my privacy," Madison said. Even though she was still groggy, she'd caught on to what I was up to.

"What about the other one, titled *Formulas*?" he asked.

"Those are formulas from a physics class I started to take last year at Weber State. It was so hard I ended up dropping it. I don't care if you look at them."

After a moment's hesitation, Rivers bypassed the first two files and clicked open the third, titled *Berger Photo*. The haunting picture of the general shaking hands with Adolph Hitler instantly filled the screen.

"Wow!" Rivers exclaimed. "He's big *and* scary-looking."

Alvarez studied the photo for a few moments without saying a word, then asked Rivers to email him the picture.

"Sure thing, Bob."

"I'll send out an inquiry," he said, addressing me, "and see if anyone's ever heard of this guy."

After sending the message, she closed out the flash drive, unplugged it from her laptop computer and handed it back to me.

I breathed a sigh of relief. They hadn't opened or copied the other two files, and Captain Hank's earth-shattering secret was still safe and secure. Smiling to myself, I placed the barrette back in the side pocket of my book bag and zipped it closed.

* * *

The next morning, Madison felt well enough to go home and she was released from the hospital. Deputy Rivers, who had again spent the night in our room, offered us a ride back to our house.

As we made our way along the mountain road, I secretly wondered whether O'Leary and his people had returned to our home and continued their search for the diary. My concerns were soon put to rest when we turned the corner into our subdivision and I saw three patrol cars; one parked in our driveway and two others in the street alongside our front curb. Two uniformed officers and a shorter man in civilian clothes were talking to Deputy Alvarez. One of the officers, Randy Johnston, I recognized; he was a neighbor who lived across the street and a couple of doors down. Since he was only a casual acquaintance (a man who I'd seen in his yard a couple of times) I hadn't made the connection when Deputy Alvarez mentioned his name the day before.

When Madison and I got out of the vehicle, Alvarez told us we could go in, but asked Deputy Rivers if she could join him and the others for a few minutes.

As soon as Madison and I got into the house, we were immediately greeted by our adoring hounds. Madison, still groggy from her pain medication, gingerly made her way to the recliner in our front room. A few minutes later she was stretched back comfortably, flanked by our two canine companions and sound asleep.

After seeing her nod off, I made my way to the kitchen and removed the baseboard from under the dishwasher. Finding the diary still safe and secure, I re-concealed it and started to walk away. Thinking Deputy Alvarez might want to see the original photograph of General Berger, I quickly took it back out, removed the picture from the plastic sleeve, and placed the binder back down in its hiding place. Looking around to find a secondary hiding place for just the photograph, I settled on placing it in one of Madison's recipe books.

A few minutes later, I heard a knock on our garage door, and opening it discovered Deputy Alvarez, Deputy Rivers, and the short man in civilian clothes. The big deputy was holding a thick manila envelope and a smaller pocket notebook, while the other man carried with him a large three-ring binder, red in color.

"There've been some developments," Alvarez said. "May we come in?"

I nodded. "Just try to keep it down. Madison's asleep."

They followed me up the stairs and we gathered around our kitchen counter.

"First off," Alvarez said, "this is Albert Greenbaum. He's from the Los Angeles office of the Simon Wiesenthal Center. This is George d'Clare."

"Mr. Greenbaum," I said, shaking his outstretched hand. "Call me George."

He was a thin man, around forty years of age, with black curly hair and a bushy unkempt beard and moustache. The brown three-piece suit he was wearing was wrinkled and worn. as if he'd slept in it.

He smiled. "Call me Albert or Al. I'll answer to either one."

Deputy Alvarez, laying his envelope down, got right to business.

"When did you know your house was bugged?" he asked.

Knowing that he must've seen the bug detector the twins had left, I lied.

"Mr. Stevens warned us just before he died that the people who were protecting General Berger would stop at nothing to keep his identity a secret, including bugging our house, monitoring our phone calls and email messages, internet use, things like that. When we got home after he was killed, I couldn't sleep and started feeling paranoid. Looking around, I happened to find one in our front window sill. The next day, I went to that old electronic supply store on Ninth West in Salt Lake and bought the detector."

He nodded. "I noticed it when we were here the other night, so while you were in the hospital I had one of our deputies come over and sweep your entire house. He found a total of six bugs. Since he'd never seen bugs like this before, he took them to our forensic lab. Before I came over here, they informed me that those bugs were made in Europe, probably Ireland. Now is there anything else you can tell me about your conversation with Mr. Stevens?"

"No, nothing that really comes to mind."

He flipped through his notebook until he came to the page he was searching for.

"You told me you met Mr. Stevens at one of your Parkinson's support group meetings. When was that exactly?"

"I don't remember the exact month but it was right around the first of the summer, probably May."

"And you never saw him before that?"

"Never."

"And he told you he was from Maryland?"

"Yes, I believe he said Baltimore."

"That's what his driver's license says, but therein lies the problem."

"What problem?"

"After we talked at the hospital, I called Davis County to see where they were at on the hit-and-run investigation. They told me when they ran his prints through the FBI, they came back matching Mr. James Stevens of Baltimore, Maryland, born in 1960."

"Why is that a problem?"

"Because there was a second match to a Mr. Henry Stevens of Ogden, Utah."

"But I thought no two people could have the same fingerprints?"

"Up until yesterday, so did I. To be sure, I went down to the coroner's office and fingerprinted the body again myself, and when I ran them through the second time the results were the same."

"That's incredible. There must be some mistake."

"I thought so too, but the FBI just incorporated a new fingerprint database that is more accurate than the old one, and now includes all the records of military service members going back to 1905.

"Now as far as this Henry Stevens is concerned." He pulled a piece of paper out of the envelope and laid it on the counter. "I obtained a copy of his birth certificate from the Weber County

Recorder's office. As you can see, he was born at the old Saint Benedicts Hospital in Ogden in 1920."

He pointed to the annotations and referred to another page in his notebook.

"He graduated from Ogden High School in 1938, and earned a Mathematics degree from Weber State in 1941. That fall, he enrolled in classes at the University of Utah, but in December dropped out of all of them. Since that was the month Pearl Harbor was attacked, I assumed he'd joined the military. Checking that, I found he did, in fact, join the Army in mid-December and became an intelligence officer. For most of the war, he was assigned to the U.S. Sixth Army Group. Then in 1946 he resigned his commission.

"Since there were no other records of him in Utah, I checked the records in Maryland and found that in 1946 he was employed as a physics professor at St. Andes University near Fort Meade. In November of 1952, the school terminated his employment when he failed to show up for work. Other than that, I could find no other information on Henry Stevens after 1952. It's as if he'd just vanished off the face of the earth.

"Hitting a brick wall there, I started looking into your friend James Stevens and managed to obtain a copy of his birth certificate from the Social Security Administration." He pulled it out of the envelope and placed it on the counter next to the other one.

"Now, look at this Mr. d'Clare." He pointed to where Henry and Lana Stevens were listed as the parents.

"He was his son?" I asked.

"Look at it a little more closely. The place of birth says Saint Benedicts Hospital in Ogden, but the official stamp impression of where this birth certificate was recorded is Fort Meade, Maryland."

"How can that be?"

"It can't be because it's a forgery."

"A forgery? Who would forge a birth certificate?"

"I don't know, but as you can see most of the information on the two certificates are the same, which tells me that whoever forged James Stevens' birth certificate *knew* Henry Stevens. To make sure it was a forgery and not just a clerical error, I also checked the Weber County records and went as far as contacting the records offices in Maryland. There is no record of James Stevens being born in October of 1960, or in all of 1960 for that matter."

"What about Fort Meade itself? Could he have been born on the base?"

He shook his head. "The base is required by law to report all births to Anne Arundel County."

"So who is James Stevens?"

"According to his fingerprints he's Henry Stevens of Ogden, but that can't be, can it Mr. d'Clare?"

"No it can't. This is unbelievable. There must be a mistake."

"Unbelievable is an understatement. We now have a dead man in the morgue with a forged birth certificate who can't be much older than fifty or fifty-five years old, who's fingerprints match a man who was born in 1920. Now is there anything he might've said to you that can shed some light on all of this?"

"No, nothing that I haven't told you already."

From the way the two deputies and Mr. Greenbaum were staring me down I could tell they didn't believe me, and after a few uncomfortable moments Alvarez finally turned to another page in his notebook.

"Okay, let's talk about O'Leary and his people. When we first arrested them we ran their fingerprints too, but the inquiry came back without any wants or warrants, which is one of the reasons Sheriff Sanders released them. But I thought it was strange that this O'Leary character didn't have a criminal record so I called the FBI's headquarters in Quantico. When I got one of their computer support agents on the phone, she told me that their fingerprint database system is so new and has so many firewalls to prevent hacking that it's been slow to connect with computer systems of local law enforcement agencies. Since most of these problems were cleared up on her end, she offered to run the inquiry for me. After I emailed her the sets of prints of O'Leary and his people, she sent me this."

He reached back into the envelope and took out a small stack of papers bundled together with an elastic band, then pointed to the top sheet.

"O'Leary's real name is Thomas Fenton O'Malley, wanted in connection to numerous murders, robberies and thefts dating back to 1987. The woman calling herself Agent Denney is actually Danielle Marie Dennison. She's a computer expert who is wanted by Scotland Yard for a variety of cyber-crimes, including identity thefts, hacking into bank accounts, things of that nature. The man calling himself Crosby is actually Victor Robert Hope, an Irish-born theoretical physicist. He's a member of one of the splinter groups of the Irish Republican Army which is a known terrorist organization. He's wanted for trying to obtain enriched plutonium and cobalt on the black market. The three other men, William Slone, Alex Benoit and Lance Petri, are known associates of O'Malley, and wanted by Scotland Yard, Interpol, and about a dozen other European law enforcement agencies. All of them have one thing in common. They're all linked, one way or another, to an organized crime organization whose headquarters is in Dublin, Ireland. Now these are some very dangerous people to have after you. Did Mr. Stevens ever mention them?"

"No, but like I told you at the hospital, I'd bet money that O'Malley and his group are somehow connected to the Nazi war criminal, General Berger."

"Now don't take offense to what I'm about to say, but you and your wife seem to be just two ordinary people. Why would Mr. Stevens involve you in any of this business?"

"Madison and I are as much in the dark about this as you are. Like I told you the other night, Mr. Stevens said he was involved in some type of innovative Parkinson's research and wanted us to join his team. He chose us because he found out I had started the support group and that I was still in the early-onset stage of the disease. What that has to do with these people and why they were after him, we haven't a clue. I did get the feeling, however, that he was about to tell us but was afraid to."

"Afraid?"

"Yes, but not for himself. He was more concerned with our safety than his own. One of the last things he said to me before he died was that he was sorry for contacting us and putting our lives in danger."

He looked at me for a few moments, then removed the rubber band on the small stack of papers.

"One more interesting thing I found out about O'Malley. His print matched one that was taken by an arson investigator at the scene of a fire in 1991. You'll never guess where this fire happened."

"Where?"

"Fort Meade, Maryland."

"Really?"

"There's more," he said, flipping to another page in his notebook. "Before coming over here I managed to get in touch with the arson investigator, Fireman Clarence Russell, who's still working for the Maryland Fire Department. He remembered the fire because it was a high-profile case that involved the murders of two people, U.S. Army Lieutenant Colonel Benjamin Washington Jr. and his wife Valerie Washington."

Since I hadn't finished reading Captain Hank's diary, my heart sank.

"Fireman Russell said that in all the years he'd worked as an arson investigator, if he were to pick out one case that really bothered him because he hadn't been able to solve it, it was this case."

"Why so?"

"Because of the way the colonel and his wife were murdered. Both were beaten very badly and their necks were broken."

I instantly recognized the signature killing method of General Berger which Captain Hank had written about in his diary. It also must've been news to Albert, who immediately asked to see the report. Alvarez pulled it from the bundled stack and handed it to him, then waited a few moments to let him examine it.

"Fireman Russell pulled O'Malley's print off one of the work benches in the warehouse," he continued, "but since the fingerprinting system they had at the time wasn't linked to law enforcement agencies overseas, he wasn't able to identify who it belonged to. As for the fire, he firmly believes it was an attempt by the murderer (or murderers) to destroy the bodies and hide the evidence. As for the warehouse, it was scheduled to be demolished in August of 1991, but was still under lease when the fire occurred. You'll never guess who leased it."

Already knowing the answer, I didn't reply.

"Henry Stevens of Ogden, Utah. Now I ask you again, George, did James Stevens talk about any of this with you?"

"No, he never mentioned it."

He sighed, then turned to another page in his notebook.

"I did some checking and talked to an official at the State Department who knew something about Nazi war criminals. They referred me to the Simon Wiesenthal Center in Los Angeles, which is why Albert is here. He's very familiar with the case of General Berger and immediately flew up here to help with the investigation."

"May I see the photograph that Mr. Stevens left with you?" Albert asked.

"Sure." I quickly retrieved it from the recipe book and handed it to him.

He placed it on the counter, and after removing a pair of glasses from his vest pocket and putting them on, leaned over to examine the picture. A few moments later he turned it over and read Captain Hank's perfect handwriting, proclaiming the picture to be the only known photograph of General Berger.

"This is incredible," he said. "Absolutely incredible."

He opened the red three-ring binder he was carrying and placed it down on the counter next to the photograph. On the left side was a letter that matched Captain Hank's handwriting, and on the right an envelope that the letter had apparently been mailed in.

"This letter was sent to the Simon Wiesenthal Center from an anonymous source in 1991."

"Just a short time after the warehouse fire at Fort Meade," Alvarez added, pointing to the date stamp. "And the writing on the letter matches the writing on the back of the photograph."

"Attached to the letter was this," Albert said.

He turned the page, revealing a copy of the exact same photograph.

"It's the same picture," I said.

"Looks like it to me," Rivers echoed.

"What did Mr. Stevens tell you about the photograph?" Albert asked.

"Only that the man shaking hands with Hitler was SS Lieutenant General Karl Berger, a Nazi war criminal who had escaped at the end of the war."

He took his glasses off. "He wasn't just *a* Nazi war criminal, George. Next to Hitler, he was perhaps the most sadistic Nazi who ever lived. We'll never really know how many innocent people he tortured and murdered, but it numbered well into the hundreds."

He paused for a moment, letting his words sink in before continuing.

"Do you know how he used to do it? Torture and kill his victims? He would first conduct horrible experiments on them, and if they didn't die from the experiments he would stage phony fights, promising them their freedom if they could defeat him in hand-to-hand combat. During these fights, he would beat them unmercifully and break their necks."

"I don't know if you noticed or not, George" Alvarez said, "but that matches the description of the deaths of Lieutenant

Colonel Washington and his wife at Fort Meade, as well as Mr. and Mrs. Roy Harrison, whose bodies you and your wife found in Mr. Stevens' home in Mountain Green."

Before I could comment, there was a knock on the door leading out to our garage, and both deputies immediately unbuckled their holsters and drew out their weapons. Moving over to the stairs, Alvarez crept down to the lower landing and yelled through the closed door.

"What is it?"

"Bob, it's Martineau. I've got the photos."

Alvarez holstered his firearm, opened the door and took a manila envelope from the deputy. After exchanging a few words, he checked the contents of the envelope and paused for a moment before rejoining us in the kitchen.

Looking at Albert, Alvarez pointed to the picture of General Berger.

"When was this photograph taken?"

"It is believed to have been taken some time in 1944, when the general was assigned as Deputy Director of the Reich Research Council."

"Are you absolutely certain this is General Berger?"

"No question. We had over five different eyewitnesses sign affidavits. I have copies of them here." He flipped through the pages of his binder until he found the testimonials, then turned the binder around so we could see them.

Alvarez reached into the manila envelope.

"Then how do you explain these photographs that were taken less than twenty hours ago by Deputy Martineau at Farmington Station Park?"

A cold chill ran down my spine. The two pictures he placed down on the counter were undoubtedly of General Berger. In one of the photos he was standing next to O'Malley and appeared to be ticked off about whatever the Irishman was telling him. Several other members of his gang stood nearby, looking away from them;

like secret service agents protecting the President. I also noticed how big Berger was – at least head and shoulders taller than O'Malley.

The second photograph was a clearer and more close-up view, and the captured image was roughly the same angle as the old photograph Captain Hank had found. Appearing slightly older now, his hair was still short on the sides with a flat crew-cut style on the top. He was wearing slacks and a short-sleeved polo shirt, which enhanced the size of his huge biceps. The only thing not standing out was his dark eyes, which now seemed to be a normal shade of hazel.

"Wow," Deputy Rivers exclaimed, as she looked back and forth at the pictures.

Albert simply stared at the photos, not saying a word.

"It looks like him," I said.

When nobody said anything, I looked up and found myself once again in the crosshairs of Deputy Alvarez's intense stare.

"How is that possible, George?" he asked. "How could a missing Nazi war criminal, who would be well over a hundred years old today, *be* the man in these photographs?"

I didn't answer but my Parkinson's symptoms did, suddenly emerging in my right arm.

"Up till now I've given you some latitude due to the way you were falsely arrested and incarcerated at our jail, but my patience has run out. Either you tell us what you know or I'm going to pull our deputies off this investigation and let you deal with these people. And in case you need reminding that you're in over your head, take a look at your wife in there. Now for the last time, did Mr. Stevens say anything else to you?"

I looked over at Deputy Rivers and Albert who simply stared back at me. I remembered Madison telling me once that I was a very bad liar, and the glares I was receiving confirmed her statement.

Deputy Rivers, who had remained mostly silent while Deputy Alvarez explained what he had uncovered, finally spoke.

"Like I told you at the hospital George, we can't help you unless you're honest with us and tell us what you know."

"If you have any information," Albert added, "anything that could shed some light on how it is possible that this monster is still alive then for the sake of all those innocent victims you must tell us."

"You wouldn't believe me if I told you."

"Try me," Alvarez said.

I waited a few moments, trying to think of where to start, before finally replying.

"Okay, I'll tell you what Madison and I know, but I must have assurances that what I am about to say remains confidential." Remembering what Captain Hank had said to Big Ben, I added, "Because it involves something so dangerous it could literally destroy the world as we know it."

"Now don't get all dramatic on us George," Rivers replied sarcastically.

"He's not!" Madison shouted from the front room.

The four of us looked at each other and walked in to see her – she was now sitting upright.

"How do you feel?" I asked

Ignoring me, she stared down the two deputies and Albert Greenbaum with the most intense look I have ever seen on her face.

"Once you hear what this is really all about you'll know that my husband isn't over-exaggerating! If anything, he's *understating* just how dangerous this is, and if we take you into our confidence you'll need to keep a tight lid on it!"

"Okay, let's meet half way." Alvarez said. "I can't speak for Mr. Greenbaum, but as far as Deputy Rivers and I are concerned, if it helps us apprehend O'Malley and his people and whoever is behind them, whether it be the man in this photograph or whoever, we must have the freedom to use the information you have. Anything else, whatever story this James Stevens might've told you we'll keep confidential for now. Fair enough?"

THE DEVICE

Madison and I looked at each other, and after seeing her nod we both turned our attention to Albert Greenbaum.

"I know you don't know me," he said, looking back and forth at us, "but all I can do to gain your trust is to tell you that I have a history with this case that goes back more than twenty years. I was the man who found the letter in a pile of anonymous mail and brought it to the attention of my superiors. Since that time I've done quite a bit of research on General Berger, so I guess you could say I am a subject matter expert. I can also tell you that this letter and the photograph are the only solid clues as to General Berger's whereabouts that have ever been found. So in the spirit of working towards a common goal, which is to hopefully get to the bottom of this unbelievable mystery, I will agree to follow the decisions of the deputies."

After receiving another nod from Madison, I turned back to them.

"This is going to take some time. Could I get anyone a bottle of water?"

"Sure," Rivers said. Alvarez and Albert simply nodded.

"Could you bring me one too?" Madison asked.

After getting four cold bottles from the fridge and passing them out, I went back to the kitchen, removed the baseboard from underneath the dishwasher and retrieved Captain Hank's diary. Although I felt I could trust the two deputies, there was still a small part of me that remained suspicious, so before taking it in to show them I quickly removed the unmarked key card from the binder and slid it into my back pocket. After bringing it into the front room, I placed it down on our coffee table.

"As unbelievable as this may sound, the name of the man in the Davis County Morgue is really Henry Stevens, born at Saint Benedicts Hospital, October the thirtieth of 1920. The man Deputy Martineau photographed at Station Park yesterday is really SS Lieutenant General Karl Berger, the Nazi war criminal known as the White Wolf."

294

"How can this be possible?" Albert asked.

"Because of what Mr. Stevens, or as he was known by, Captain Hank, discovered on an intelligence mission at the end of World War II." I placed my hand on top of the binder. "*This* is what they are after."

With Albert and the two deputies listening intently, I proceeded to recount the incredible story Madison and I had read in Captain Hank's diary.

* * *

Two hours later, Madison and I finished explaining all we'd learned in the diary up to that point.

"So that's as far as you got when O'Malley stormed into your house?" Alvarez asked.

"Yes," I replied. "We didn't get a chance to read the rest of it. I barely managed to get it hidden again."

"If it weren't for the bodies in the morgue and the attacks upon you two, I'd say someone is pulling off an elaborate hoax."

"Are you saying you believe all this stuff, Bob?" Rivers asked.

"I'm not saying I believe the entire story, but it's not really a question of whether I believe it. The people who are after this diary believe it and are willing to do just about anything to get their hands on it." Turning his attention back to me, he asked, "Is there anything else you'd like to tell us?"

"I also think Berger is responsible for the death of our friend, Gary Tomkins."

"The suicide in North Ogden last week?"

"Yes. At his viewing, I heard how your man found him."

"I remember that," Rivers said, "I heard Wilson talking about it on the radio. He said he hung himself, but the rope broke and his body fell down the stairs."

"So why would he go after your friend?" Alvarez asked.

295

"When Mr. Stevens told us about all of this we were as skeptical as you are. To check out his story we decided to have Gary look at one of the problems."

"And how did you know him?"

"I worked with him many years ago, and thought if anyone could figure it out he could. In my opinion, he was the best electrician on the aircraft production line and one of the smartest people I've ever known." I turned the pages of the diary and showed them the math problem. "Early in the morning on the day he died, he left Madison a message that he had found out what this equation meant. Later that morning we learned he'd committed suicide."

"Did he say anything else?"

"Yes," Madison answered. "When I gave him a copy of the problem, he told me that it looked as if someone had found an exact solution to one of Einstein's Field Equations. He also said that physicists and scientists use the approximate solutions of these equations to study mass, energy, and gravitational waves, which are ripples or distortions in the space-time continuum."

From the way Deputy Rivers looked at Madison, with overly-large eyes and a look of astonishment, I could tell she was completely stunned at the news.

"But if Mr. Stevens had a photographic memory, why did he need to write any of this down? Why keep a diary at all?" Albert asked.

"I've given that some thought," I said, "and I think something happened to him, because in the short time we knew him I don't think he had that ability anymore. That's one of the questions I'm hoping is answered when we read the rest of the diary."

Just then we heard several knocks at our garage door. Deputy Alvarez and Rivers immediately stood up, unbuckled their holsters and drew their weapons. Like before, Alvarez slowly moved down the stairs and yelled through the closed door.

"What is it?"

"Bob, it's Johnston. We might have a situation out here."

"Stay with them," he ordered Rivers, and proceeded out the door.

I crowded into the recliner next to Madison, both of us holding our puppies in our laps. Deputy Rivers took up a position behind the counter in our kitchen, instructing Albert to move around behind her.

After a few anxious minutes the door opened.

"George, would you come down here a moment?" Alvarez asked.

I rose to my feet, handed Ginger off to Madison and made my way down the stairs. As soon as I entered the garage, I saw Ethan and Evelynn Washington handcuffed and on their knees in our front driveway. Deputy Johnston and another officer were standing next to them.

"Johnston noticed these two drive by several times," Alvarez said. "They say they are friends of yours. Do you know them?"

"Yes. Please let them go and have them come in. I think you'll want to hear what they have to say."

Alvarez's eyes widened, which told me he understood, and he ordered the other deputies to release them.

While their handcuffs were being taken off, Ethan and Evelynn looked up at me and I mouthed the words, "It's okay."

A few minutes later, after Alvarez praised Johnston and the other deputy for being vigilant, we were all back inside the house, gathered together in our front room.

"Deputies, Mr. Greenbaum," I said, "I'd like you to meet two people who have lost more in this story than we can ever imagine. This is Ethan and Evelynn Washington, whose parents were Lieutenant Colonel Benjamin and Valerie Washington of Fort Meade, Maryland."

* * *

It took Madison and I twenty minutes to convince the twins that the two deputies and Albert Greenbaum were there to help us. For a while I wasn't sure we were going to sway them, because they remained silent and refused to answer any of the deputy's questions. After telling them about the attack two nights ago, which resulted in Madison's shoulder being dislocated, and that Deputy Alvarez had taken them all into custody, I was finally able persuade them that the three were on our side.

Ethan, who was staring at the diary on the coffee table, was the first to speak.

"How much do they know?"

"We've told them roughly three-quarters of it," Madison said, "which is what George and I have read so far."

"You understand just how dangerous this information is and what would happen if it were to fall into the wrong hands?" Evelynn asked, her eyes alternating between them.

Alvarez repeated what he'd told Madison and me, promising to keep the information confidential, for now.

"Okay, but I want you to understand something. Our parents were murdered when we were only eight years old, and the men responsible have never been brought to justice." Tears ran down Evelynn's face, and she took a moment to compose herself before continuing. "And now, the only man who knew why they were killed and had dedicated his life to finding their murderer is dead."

Ethan gently put his arm around her.

"Why don't we all just sit down, take it easy for a few minutes, and have you tell us what you know," Deputy Rivers said.

"How about we start with the last section of Captain Hank's diary?" I asked. "If we have any questions, maybe you two can fill in the blanks?"

After receiving nods of approval from the twins, I opened the binder, found the page where Madison and I'd left off, and started reading it aloud.

* * *

For the next two hours we learned the heart-breaking details of what happened when Captain Hank returned to Fort Meade from Berlin and discovered the twins' parents had been murdered. Although their deaths would send him down a spiraling path towards self-destruction, he would eventually regain his faith that all things happen for a reason. That faith would also drive Hank forward in an unwavering determination to rebuild the device, and continue the mission of finding and stopping the Nazi's White Wolf.

Chapter Thirteen
The Story (Part 4)

Twenty-Three Years, One Month and Sixteen Days Earlier
Saturday, 27 July 1991, 15:20hrs
Inside the *Office of Colonel Lincoln Stillwater, Fort Meade, Maryland*

An impressive array of military recognition plaques and a colorful collection of Navajo Indian decorations adorned walls of the large and comfortable-looking office, quietly telling the story of the Native-American's illustrious career in the United States Army. The furniture, which included an oak desk, modern high-back chair and a brown leather sofa with six matching seats, all looked to be of the finest quality, which made the room appear more like a wealthy veteran's den than a place where government business is conducted. Sitting on the sofa, staring blankly at the floor, was Captain Henry "Hank" Stevens.

He knew now that the sadistic Nazi war criminal, General Berger, had somehow discovered his whereabouts and murdered his best friend's son and wife. As he tried to comprehend the shock, he watched the tall officer move over and sit down at his desk, and proceed to make several phone calls: the first to the duty officer in Fort Meade's Command Post, and the subsequent ones to the numbers he'd obtained from that officer.

THE DEVICE

While the colonel was busy calling people on the phone, Hank thought back to the events that occurred after the taxi had picked him up at the airport. His mission of finding and stopping General Berger had taken another turn for the worse, this time resulting in the deaths of J.R. and Valerie Washington.

~ Then ~

The connecting flights from Berlin back to Baltimore totaled more than twelve hours and involved numerous airlines. Although he tried to catch up on some well-needed shuteye during the last and longest leg of the flights, Hank's mind refused to wind down long enough for him to get any restful sleep. Keeping him awake, like a never-ending supply of caffeine being fed to his brain, were thoughts about what he'd uncovered in the Ünterbunker and where to begin his search for General Berger in this time period.

When he called J.R. from his hotel room in Berlin and told him that Berger had made it out alive, they'd talked briefly about what steps they could take to find him. J.R. told him he would talk to Valerie about possibly using this new invention they called the "World Wide Web" to track him down, but how they would do that Hank hadn't a clue. In any event, J.R. assured him that he would stop by the warehouse at his earliest opportunity, retrieve the letter from the false bottom of the gray toolbox, and mail it to the Simon Wiesenthal Center. At the very least, the letter and accompanying photograph should spark some type of investigation.

After landing in Baltimore and retrieving his luggage he hastily exited the airport. Since J.R. and Valerie had given him the ride to Fort Meade's flight terminal when he'd left for Berlin, he didn't want to bother them again and simply hailed a taxi to take him home. Sitting in the back seat of the yellow cab, he closed his eyes and speculated where General Berger might be.

Suddenly, the blaring sirens of several firetrucks approaching from behind broke his intense concentration, and

302

opening his eyes noticed his cab was pulling over. After a short delay to allow the emergency vehicles to pass, the heavy unkempt taxi driver, whose nametag read "Fred," shifted the cab back into gear and they proceeded on their way.

Reaching his apartment, he unpacked his suitcase and called J.R., and when he didn't answer he tried Valerie's number; leaving messages for both to call him. Hoping it would help him think more clearly, as well as cleanse him of the taxi driver's foul-smelling cigarette smoke, he decided to take a long, hot shower.

While toweling dry, his left pinkie finger trembled as if it were shivering from a non-existent cold breeze. *Strange*, he thought, *it's been doing that ever since I re-entered real time in the device. It must just be some sort of temporal side effect, like the headaches and ear-ringing, or something else that hasn't yet worked itself out in this time period.*

After getting dressed he tried to call J.R. and Valerie again, and when neither of them answered he decided to watch some television. The instant he picked up the remote control, which he thought was another fascinating invention, feelings of foreboding unexpectedly entered his mind, as if he were receiving a silent and ominous premonition that something was terribly wrong. Attributing it to his jet-lag and the constant thoughts of where to look for General Berger, he shook off the feeling, laid back in bed and turned on the TV.

When the picture faded into view, his tired mind was suddenly jolted awake by the image he saw before him, and the ominous feelings he'd had just moments ago were unexpectedly justified. The title at the bottom of the screen read, "Breaking News: 3-Alarm Fire at Fort Meade." Behind the reporter covering the story he could see a building engulfed in flames, and knew immediately it was Warehouse 1373.

He sprang up off the bed and tried to call J.R. and Valerie again. When they didn't answer, he slammed the receiver down and looked around, temporarily not knowing what to do. After telling himself not to panic, he quickly retrieved his truck's keys and made his way out of his apartment, not bothering to lock the door behind him.

He ran several red lights as he sped towards Fort Meade and managed to reach the main entry gate in less than five minutes. After producing his driver's license and the lease paperwork to the gate guard he was waived through, then he proceeded down Annapolis Road towards the shipping and receiving area of the base.

Approximately one-hundred yards ahead, he saw several military policemen standing in front of temporary barricades which were blocking cars from going any further. His heart sank when he also saw in the distance the still-smoldering remains of Warehouse 1373. Although it appeared as if the fire was now under control, three large fire engines were still spraying a full-bevy of water onto what was left of the burned-out structure. He could also see no less than six other vehicles, including two paramedic trucks, three police cars, and a red four-wheel drive truck emblazoned with the word "Chief" on the side; all parked around the warehouse but at a safe distance.

Driving down the blocked-off street anyway, he pulled over and got out, at which point he was immediately approached by one of the military policemen, a young private.

"Sorry, sir. Due to the fire this area of the base is closed. You'll have to get back in your vehicle and turn around."

"That's the building I'm leasing from the Army!"

"Could I see some identification?"

As Hank gathered his driver's license and lease papers, another military policeman, a lieutenant, approached and asked the private what was going on.

"Sir, this man says he was leasing the building that burned down."

Hank handed the papers and his license to the private, who gave them to the lieutenant. After thoroughly examining them, the officer walked over to one of the patrol cars and called in the information.

Five minutes later, which seemed like an eternity to Hank, the lieutenant finally returned from the patrol car and handed him back his license and the papers

"I'm sorry Mr. Stevens," he said. "we can't let you through until we get the okay from our commander and he gets the okay from the battalion chief of the fire department. I've informed my supervisor that you're here and they are sending someone out to talk to you."

"Could you at least tell me what happened? I just got back to Baltimore from a trip overseas, saw it on the news and rushed down here."

The lieutenant shook his head. "Right now we know as much as you do."

A dark-green military staff car drove up on the opposite side of the barricade and parked on the shoulder of the road. Mounted on the front bumper was a placard containing a polished silver eagle, which denoted the military rank of the officer inside. A tall Army colonel around fifty-five years of age got out of the passenger side carrying a walkie-talkie. Emerging from the driver's side was a younger, more muscular Master Sergeant, carrying an M-16 rifle. Both men, exuding an aura of power and authority, walked over and joined them.

"Thank you, LT," the colonel said, "I'll take it from here."

"Yes, sir." The junior officer rendered a salute, turned and left.

"I'm Colonel Lincoln Stillwater and this is Sergeant Paul Murphy," he said, addressing Hank. "We're from the Emergency Services Division. Mr. Stevens, is it?" He stuck out his right hand.

"Yes, Jim Stevens," Hank replied, shaking his hand. "Can you tell me what happened to the warehouse I was leasing?"

"Our records show that a Mr. Henry Stevens leased the building."

"He was my father."

"I see." The colonel started to say something, but stopped when he heard his call-sign on his walkie-talkie. After a short conversation with the man on the other end, he asked Hank, "The battalion chief wants to know if you stored any flammable liquids or toxic chemicals in the warehouse?"

"No, nothing more than a few cans of lubricating oil for machining metal parts."

"Give me a moment." The colonel made a quick call to relay the information, and after receiving a reply, his attention returned to Hank. "As you can see Mr. Stevens, we can't let anyone near the building until its safe and the investigations are over."

"Investigations? What investigations?"

"Fire and police. Until we know what happened the warehouse is a crime scene."

"A crime scene?"

"Yes, we received word less than ten minutes ago from the chief that his men found two people dead inside the building."

"Do you know who they were?" Hank's heart began to sink.

"No word yet, but I'd like to get some information from you."

"Sure, anything you need."

Just as the colonel reached in his shirt pocket and retrieved a small notebook and pen, his walkie-talkie came to life again. After stepping away for a few moments, he returned.

"They just identified the bodies. Lieutenant Colonel Benjamin Washington Jr. and his wife Valerie Washington. Did you know them?"

With his legs going weak and his vision narrowing, Hank dropped everything on the ground. He could tell Colonel Stillwater was trying to tell him something else, but he couldn't understand what he was saying.

For the next five minutes, Hank's thoughts were a blur. When he was finally able to focus on his surroundings, he realized he was sitting in the back seat of Colonel Stillwater's staff car. The tall Army officer was seated next to him, saying something about going over to his office to ask him some questions. Turning away from the colonel, he looked out the window just in time to see a close unobstructed view of what remained of the warehouse.

As his eyes fell upon the burned-out building his entire body began to tremble, and as the realization of what he was seeing became evident the tremor in his left pinkie finger increased in severity. It wasn't what he saw, but rather what he *didn't* see that made him shiver with fright, and its omission from where he'd last seen it was chillingly evident.

The piece of the device that he hadn't had time to dismantle before he'd left for Berlin, the large horseshoe-shaped field accelerator, was gone!

~ Now ~

A group of top-notch investigators and government professionals sat in Colonel Stillwater's office, ready to question Hank about the warehouse and his involvement with J.R. and Valerie Washington. These individuals (all experts in their professions) included Detective Phillip Evans from the police branch of Fort Meade's Emergency Services Division, Major Roger Thornton from the Civil Engineering Battalion, Fire Marshal David Green of the Baltimore Fire Department, Ms. Jenny Hancock, a Contracting Officer from the base's Procurement Branch, and Colonel Francine Kelso, special investigator assigned by Fort Meade's garrison commander. Master Sergeant Murphy, Colonel Stillwater's aide, also stood by with a staff of three enlisted troops known as "runners," in the event they were needed to retrieve information or check certain facts brought forth during the meeting.

The questioning lasted the better part of an hour, and the investigators touched on every subject pertaining to the lease of Warehouse 1373, ranging from what Hank did for a living to what business he conducted in the warehouse. They also asked him a bevy of questions about how well he knew Lieutenant Colonel Washington and his wife.

In response, Hank told them that his dad (Henry Stevens) went into business with J.R.'s father back in the 1940s, and for many years produced sheet metal tools and small engine parts in the warehouse. He had known J.R. for as long as he could remember, but hadn't met Valerie until a couple of weeks ago, after returning to Fort Meade to assist J.R. with disposing the old equipment in the warehouse. He also told them he'd spoken to J.R. on the phone from his hotel room in Berlin, and J.R. had informed him that he was going to stop by the warehouse later that day to inventory what was left.

As for what he did for a living, Hank told them that his dad (in addition to making tools and parts in the warehouse) was a physics professor, which sparked his interest in the subject. When his dad passed away, he inherited a large sum of money and was now independently wealthy. For the last ten years he'd been living abroad, studying physics at several different European universities and higher institutions of learning.

This line of questioning led to Hank explaining that he'd been in Germany finishing a physics-related research project, and had just returned to Fort Meade that afternoon when he learned of the fire. Colonel Stillwater, upon hearing this, nodded to Master Sergeant Murphy, who immediately left the office with one of the enlisted runners. (Hank later learned that the sergeant had sent the man to the airport to check his story.)

By coincidence, Colonel Kelso, the garrison commander's special investigator, commented that her major in college was Physics. She asked which area of the subject he studied, which Hank felt was more an attempt to see if he was lying rather than just a casual interest. He remembered some of the concepts he'd learned in the Firebird intelligence, and proceeded to recite the meaning of Einstein's Field Equations. He also threw in a few more complex physics terms that could only be understood by someone who had an advanced degree in the subject. When he was finished with the lengthy and incomprehensible answer, he had completely dazzled Colonel Kelso and impressed the other investigators.

As the line of questioning moved to the warehouse itself, he recalled the images in his mind and could tell them precisely where everything was positioned the last time he was there. The only sections he omitted were the placements of parts related to the device, including the now-missing field accelerator.

Since the Battalion Chief's preliminary investigation concluded that the fire had started in one of the circuit breaker panels, most of the questions were centered around the warehouse's electrical power, especially with regards to the additional high-voltage cable that was found running from the warehouse to the base's electrical substation. Major Thornton, the Civil Engineer, had no record of a work order to install the additional cable nor any other building modification information for the warehouse.

Hank informed them that (from what he remembered) the additional cable and high-voltage circuit breaker panel had already been installed when the building was leased. Since the building had always passed its annual safety inspections, he hadn't given it much thought and was at a loss as to why it wasn't in the construction records. The explanation (though incomplete) sounded plausible enough that the focus of the inquiry soon shifted to another subject.

When the meeting first began Hank felt as if he were on trial and under cross-examination, and that the panel of investigators were trying to find him guilty of negligence for causing the fire. From his exchange with Colonel Kelso, and the way he'd provided the articulate and truthful-sounding answers, he completely changed the direction of the investigation. By the time the runner returned from the airport with the passenger lists of the flights arriving that day from Germany (which proved that the plane Hank had flown in on hadn't yet landed when the first call came in about the fire) the meeting had been adjourned.

As everyone was filing out, Colonel Stillwater told Hank he wanted to have a word with him alone and asked if he could remain a few more minutes.

Just as both men sat back down, Fire Marshal Green ducked his head back in.

"Colonel, could I have a word with you?"

"Pardon me a moment Mr. Stevens." He stood up and quickly exited the office.

From the reflection on the glass of one of the award plaques on the wall, Hank could see the colonel conferring with the Fire Marshal and two other men. One was Detective Phillip Evans and the other was a fireman he hadn't seen before, much younger than the other men. Although they were well out of a normal person's earshot, his acute hearing enabled him to hear what the four men were saying.

The young fireman's name was Clarence Russell, an arson investigator who'd just come from the warehouse. He confirmed to Fire Marshal Green and Colonel Stillwater that the fire was deliberately set. Initially, he thought the fire was caused by an electrical short in the main circuit breaker panel, but upon closer examination found evidence that an accelerant was used, most likely gasoline.

Detective Evans next reported that the medical examiner had completed a preliminary examination of the two bodies. Pending a formal autopsy, there were no indications that Lieutenant Colonel Washington and his wife died from smoke inhalation, but instead their necks had been broken. Blood pools, swelling and bruising on their bodies also indicated that both had sustained a high degree of blunt-force trauma.

After overhearing this, Captain Hank searched his memory in hopes of pinpointing where he had compromised his identity. Up until today, he believed he'd taken all the necessary precautions in keeping what he was doing in the warehouse a secret. Somewhere along the way he'd made a mistake, and General Berger had found out who he was, located the warehouse, murdered J.R. and Valerie, and stole the field accelerator.

Returning to the office, Colonel Stillwater extended his hand.

"I know you've been through a lot today and I'm sorry that the questioning took as long as it did, but I'm glad you were able to remember everything. It will help us with our investigation."

"I'm glad I could be of some help," Hank said, shaking his hand.

"You've done more than just helped, Mr. Stevens. From what you've told us and from what the arson investigator and Detective Evans just told me, I think I know what happened. Colonel Washington and his wife stopped by the warehouse to inventory the equipment, just as he told you, but they interrupted a burglary in progress. It must've been more than one assailant, because the colonel and his wife were beaten before they were murdered."

"Murdered?" Hank asked, pretending he hadn't overheard the conversation.

"Yes, and to get rid of the bodies and destroy the evidence of who they were they set fire to the warehouse. In any case, I'd like you to stay on the base for a while, just as a precaution."

"On base?"

"If we're wrong about the perpetrator's motives, and they were looking for something else in the warehouse and couldn't find it, they might've gotten your name from Colonel Washington or his wife."

"I understand," Hank said, thinking the colonel was a very perceptive man.

"I'll call the lodging office and reserve you a room. Thanks again, you've been quite a help. Sergeant Murphy will give you a lift back to your truck." He handed Hank a card. "If you think of anything else give me a call."

Hank nodded and quickly exited the colonel's office.

Ten minutes later, as the staff car passed by the charred remains of Warehouse 1373, it was still hard for Hank to imagine he would never see J.R. or Valerie again. J.R. had reminded him so much of his father, Big Ben, that it seemed as if they were one-in-the-same person. And Valerie, who'd been so suspicious of him the first time they'd met, had subsequently welcomed him with open arms after she'd learned the circumstances of his arrival. In just a short amount of time, both J.R. and his wife had been a great help to him and he'd never had the opportunity to thank them.

As for the twins, Ethan and Evelynn, Hank wondered what was going to happen to them. He knew that J.R. was an only child and that Big Ben and Elizabeth couldn't have any children together. As for Valerie, he hadn't had a chance to ask her where she was from or whether she had any family in the immediate area. If she didn't, the courts would probably make the twins wards of the state and place them in a foster home. For a moment, Hank thought that if there were no other living relatives then *he* might be able to adopt them, but he soon realized the idea was completely out of the question.

He alone was responsible for the deaths of J.R. and Valerie, just as he was for Big Ben, Elizabeth, and (most-likely) Lana. If he hadn't phoned J.R. from his hotel room in Berlin and instructed him to mail the letter, then he wouldn't have even stopped by the warehouse with Valerie to retrieve it and avoided General Berger altogether. Similarly, if he hadn't called upon his best friend to help him build the device in the first place, Big Ben and Elizabeth wouldn't have been killed trying to get a message to him. And because of his obsession with the device, he lost Lana, the only woman he ever loved. Five people he cared about the most in his life were now dead, and the twins no longer had parents – *all because of him!*

When Sergeant Murphy dropped him off at his truck, Hank's mind was in a very dark place.

DALE C. GEORGE

* * *

News of the double homicide prompted Fort Meade's garrison commander to order Colonel Stillwater to raise the base's security threat-level to the highest state of force protection. Guards at the base's entry gates were doubled, and the beefed-up security contingent at the scene of the fire now included sixteen military policemen (half of whom were reservists called in on special orders) and four police dogs and their handlers on loan from the canine unit of the Baltimore Police Department. Four portable gas generators, powering lights normally used for war game exercises, were moved in to illuminate the site throughout the nights, while twenty bright orange drums, connected by yellow caution tape and signs denoting "No Admittance Unless Expressly Permitted by the Garrison Commander," circled the perimeter. Fully-illuminated, cordoned off, and with military policemen and dogs on patrol, the highly-secured crime scene was virtually impenetrable.

For five days and nights detectives poured over the charred ruins of what was once Warehouse 1373, looking for clues that might lead them to the person or persons responsible for the murders of Lieutenant Colonel Washington and his wife Valerie. While arson investigators examined ash and other burnt particles in the building, forensic teams searched for trace evidence on the victims' bodies and clothes. No stone was left unturned investigating the horrible crime that had rocked the once-tranquil Army base.

Hank spent most of the week in his room at the base's lodging facility, mentally reviewing the events while desperately trying to figure out where he'd made the mistake that had enabled General Berger to identify him, and subsequently find the warehouse. With each mental review of the events, his enhanced problem-solving ability came up empty. As his frustration level grew, so did his guilt and remorse for causing the deaths of J.R. and Valerie, Big Ben and Elizabeth, and for Lana.

313

He hardly ate, and except for one occasion only left his room when he'd reached a point where his body absolutely needed some type of nourishment. The one time he went out for something other than food occurred Tuesday, when he went off base to a local department store and purchased several shirts, pairs of pants and a large pack of underwear. Having worn the same clothes for several days, they were in desperate need of washing, and since he feared his apartment wasn't safe, he'd decided to simply go buy new ones.

On Saturday morning, August the third, Hank received a call from Colonel Stillwater.

"Mr. Stevens, could you meet me at the warehouse at noon?"

"Sure, what's going on?"

"The forensics teams and the fire department have completed their investigations, which means the garrison commander now has custody of the warehouse. He asked if we could get the lease contract terminated as soon as possible so that the site can be cleared."

"I understand. See you at noon."

With the sun blazing down in the cloudless sky and the temperature hovering near one-hundred degrees, Hank arrived at the ruins of Warehouse 1373 shortly before twelve o'clock. As he got out of his truck and his eyes traveled over to the scene of the fire, a profound sense of loss and sadness came over him. Seeing the blackened, burned-out shell of the place he'd once called home brought tears to his eyes, and he reached in his back pocket to retrieve his handkerchief.

A few minutes later a staff car pulled up, and much like before, Colonel Stillwater and Sergeant Murphy got out. Accompanying them was Ms. Hancock, the Contracting Officer from the Procurement Branch, holding a briefcase and a large manila folder.

"You remember Ms. Hancock," the colonel said, shaking Hank's hand.

Hank nodded to her.

"Mr. Stevens," she said, "I think I've got everything we need to terminate the contract."

The colonel pointed to one of the orange drums that was in the shade of a nearby tree.

"Let's go over there, out of this sun."

After reaching the drum, Ms. Hancock placed the manila folder on top of it and set her briefcase on the ground.

"First, I'll need to know if you are going to file a claim for any tools or personal property you had in the warehouse."

Hank looked over her shoulder at the remains of the warehouse.

"I don't think so. I already had most of the things moved out," he said.

"If you're sure, I'll need you to sign a couple of forms to make it official." She flipped a few pages over in the folder and showed him a document she had prepared, which already had her signature on it as well as Colonel Stillwater's, who was listed as an official witness. "This first one essentially says that you will not be filing a claim against the United States Government or the Army for tools, materials, or personal property that you had in Warehouse 1373 at the time the fire destroyed the building."

She reached down, obtained a pen from her briefcase and handed it to Hank, at which point he quickly signed the form above his printed name.

"This next one will forfeit your right of ownership to everything that was in the warehouse at the time of the fire, which will give the Army the right to dispose of it."

With his pen poised in mid-flight, Hank suddenly remembered the old gray toolbox with the false bottom. He had been so distraught over the deaths of J.R. and Valerie, wondering where he had compromised his identity, the old toolbox had slipped his mind. Looking up at the charred ruins of the building, he quickly recalled the images of the interior of the warehouse (as they'd looked before he'd left for Berlin) and made a mental comparison of what he was seeing now. The gray toolbox had rested on a wooden shelf, approximately ten feet from the front entrance of the building on the right-hand side. Looking at the same place now, he could see the wooden shelf it had been sitting on was now missing.

Walking the area with his eyes, he located the box approximately three feet away from its previous position; scorched black on the ground and half-covered by debris.

"Is everything all right, Mr. Stevens?" Ms. Hancock asked.

"I know it's a lot to ask, but I was wondering if I might have my dad's old toolbox? It's the only thing I have left of his and I would really like to hold on to it as a keepsake."

Colonel Stillwater motioned for Sergeant Murphy to accompany him, and both men proceeded over to a group of four military policemen guarding the site.

After a few moments, they returned.

"Show Sergeant Murphy where it is," the colonel said, "and he'll get it for you."

Hank walked over to the front of the building, stopped just before reaching the yellow caution tape, and pointed to the toolbox.

After a few minutes of grunting and groaning, Sergeant Murphy managed to work the heavy toolbox out from under the debris and drag it out of the burned down structure.

Hank offered to lift one end for him, and grasping the handles on each end, both men lugged the heavy toolbox over to the shade where the colonel and Ms. Hancock were standing.

Colonel Stillwater examined the contents, and after seeing it was just a collection of old tools, nodded to Hank.

"It's all yours."

Hank breathed a sigh of relief that neither the colonel or Sergeant Murphy had noticed the disparity in the thickness of the bottom of the box in relation to the shallowness of the bottom drawer. Returning to Ms. Handcock, he quickly signed the form releasing ownership of everything else that was in the warehouse and three other forms terminating the lease contract.

The colonel smiled. "Very good. I think we're finished here."

With Sergeant Murphy's help, Hank soon had the toolbox loaded in the bed of his truck.

"I guess this is goodbye, Mr. Stevens," Ms. Hancock said, shaking his hand. "And again, I'm very sorry for your loss."

"Thank you."

"I'm confident we will find the people responsible for this, Mr. Stevens," the colonel said, "and when we do I assure you they will be prosecuted to the fullest-extent of the law." He extended his hand to Hank. "You can stay in lodging for as long as you want. When something breaks, I'll be in touch."

"Thank you, Colonel. I appreciate that."

After exchanging a final handshake with Sergeant Murphy, the three made their way back to the staff car, and a few moments later the vehicle disappeared from Hank's sight. He looked back at the building one last time to set the scene to memory, then climbed in his truck and made his way out of Fort Meade's warehouse area.

As soon as Hank was parked back at the lodging facility, he proceeded to the rear of the truck and opened the tail gate. After removing the lower drawer of the toolbox and placing it off to one side, he slid back the metal lever which released the small piece of wood granting him access to what was hidden inside the false bottom. Reaching in, he pulled out the letter he'd prepared to the Simon Wiesenthal Center and the original photograph of General Berger – both undamaged and in the same condition as he'd left them. It was a miracle that neither the fire or the water from the firetrucks had penetrated the secret compartment.

Setting them to the side, he reached in again and found the little box that contained the ring he'd intended to give to Lana those many years ago, and opening it, stared at the still-glistening gold circle with the solitary diamond mounted in the center. *If I hadn't been so obsessed with the device*, he told himself, *and had properly tested those triodes, I wouldn't have gotten myself marooned in this time and all of my loved ones would still be alive.*

With his mind returning to the dark place, he reached back into the false bottom of the toolbox and retrieved the last thing he had hidden inside: the .45 caliber pistol that Big Ben had given him. Though Hank had carried it when he'd been in the device, after returning from the fourth dimension and regaining his senses he'd placed it in the toolbox for safe keeping. He remembered Ben telling him it was brand new and had never been fired, and examining it closely he could see there weren't any scratches or blemishes on the barrel or handle, nor was there any indication that the slide had ever been pulled back to cock it. It was as if the pistol had just come off the assembly line and had been saving itself for just this moment.

* * *

Early the next morning, Captain Hank sat quiet and motionless at the edge of the bed starring at himself in the large framed mirror that hung on the wall. For the past week, he'd reviewed the events in his mind over and over again, hoping to pinpoint where he'd left the clue that enabled General Berger to identify him, locate the warehouse, and kill J.R. and Valerie. No matter which way he assembled the mental jigsaw puzzle, the pieces didn't fit, and he was still at a loss as to where he made the fatal error. With the pain weighing heavy on his heart, his tired and tortured mind had reached the end.

The new handgun Big Ben had given him was laying no less than three feet away, easily within reach of his right hand. It could all be over in two seconds, he estimated, which was the time it would take him to pick up the weapon, place the barrel to his head and pull the trigger. In just two seconds he could atone for the deaths of Lana, Big Ben, Elizabeth, J.R., and Valerie, while at the same time make amends for leaving his mother Nora and his brother Robert back in 1952.

As he leaned over to pick up the gun, a ray of light pierced through the window and reflected off the mirror in front of him and back into his eyes. He stopped reaching for the gun and squinted to see if he could tell where the light was coming from. Through the mirror's reflection, he saw that the beam of light was from the sun rising in the eastern sky, and he unexpectedly became aware of how General Berger had found him.

That first time in the Ünterbunker, after his team had recovered the intelligence and exited up the access shaft, he'd gone back to the area of the laboratory where the Firebird device had been mounted, and it had felt like he was being watched. He'd held the lantern out in front of him for a few moments, trying to locate the source of the strange feeling. Even though the difference between real time and the time passing inside the aperture is significant, he must've remained in place long enough for Berger to identify his uniform and rank insignia.

Berger saw me through Firebird One's front window!

As if a huge dam had burst open in Captain Hank's mind, all the pieces of the mental jigsaw puzzle suddenly fell into place. Since General Berger had seen him, he must've also observed his reconnaissance team gather the files and what was left of the field accelerator, and place them in the duffel bags and footlockers. As soon as he escaped the fourth dimension, he'd used the bombs Sergeant Atkins left on the desk to hide all traces of his arrival in this time period.

Still obsessed with the device, Berger must've then set his sights on recovering the Firebird information. In a little more than two-and-a-half years, he had identified him as the commander of the reconnaissance team and traced him to the warehouse at Fort Meade. While he was gone to Berlin, Berger gained access to the base and made his move on the warehouse.

Because J.R. and Valerie hadn't retrieved the letter from the gray toolbox, Hank concluded that they must've surprised Berger while he was either searching the warehouse or stealing the field accelerator. He shuddered at the thought of what must have happened next, as both his friend's son and wife were beaten and murdered at the hands of the Nazi's White Wolf.

Hank then remembered something he hadn't thought about in a very long time. It was a phrase his parents had said to him and his brother while they were growing up, and the same thing he'd told Big Ben at intelligence school when his friend was passed over for deployment because of his skin color. When it came to Hank's mind this time, it seemed as if his parents were in the room with him, telling it to him again:

> *"We have no control over the things that happen to us in our lives, but whatever happens, good or bad, you must believe that they happen for a reason. We must have faith in God that those reasons are part of His plan for us. What you do have control over is the path you choose to take when things happen. The actions you take at those times will define you as a human being."*

A few moments ago that long-standing adage seemed old and out of date, but now with the sunlight striking his eyes it took on an entirely new meaning; more insightful and profound than ever before. The worst thing imaginable had happened to J.R. and Valerie, and what path was he planning to take? Suicide? At his life's defining moment, he was going to end his life by taking the easy way out? Was this how he wanted his life defined? As a coward?

After answering his own questions with a resounding "No," tears filled his eyes, and streamed out even harder the more he realized the magnitude of what he'd almost done. All the thoughts he'd had of killing himself withered away and evaporated, and he felt as if a great weight had been lifted off his shoulders. Those simple words his parents had told him those many years ago had rescued his mind from the dark place, and kneeling on the floor, he said a silent prayer – thanking God for his parents and thanking his parents for saying those words to him.

He rose up off the floor and walked out into the kitchen to get a glass of water. Thinking more about what his parents had told him, his mind zeroed in on the last sentence, and what actions he intended to take now that the warehouse was destroyed and J.R. and Valerie were dead.

With the mental image of the burned-out warehouse still hauntingly clear in his memory, he thought about how much it resembled the bombed-out buildings in Berlin at the end of the war. Comparing those images now suddenly made him realize that this was a war; an extension of the final confrontation of World War II that had not (as yet) been decided. If he had any chance of finding and stopping General Berger now, he needed to look at the mission in that context. His thoughts shifted to the lessons he'd memorized in the Army's intelligence school, and he began a tactical assessment of his enemy and his present situation.

In evaluating his enemy, he thought of General Berger as the commander of an opposing force. He was highly intelligent, ruthless, and had used the element of surprise to win the first battle in an utterly decisive fashion. Two things stood out where the general had a distinct advantage over him. First, Berger had returned from the fourth dimension more than two-and-a-half years ago and had learned all about this futuristic society. Second, Berger had obviously used some of the gold and silver bars he'd stolen to hire people to help him. Confirming that fact was the theft of the field accelerator; although the general was a huge and muscular man, he simply couldn't have gotten it down off the carriage by himself.

By stealing the field accelerator, Berger had tipped his hand as to what his plans were: to re-build the device and continue with the second phase of the Firebird plan. Hank shuddered when he thought of how that second phase entailed the rebirth of the Nazi regime, and a future Fourth Reich bent on global domination.

Evaluating his present situation, two things stood out. First, Berger didn't know he'd assumed the identity of "James" Stevens in this time period. If he had, he would've confronted him at his apartment and not taken the chance of breaching the security of a U.S. Army base. Second, Berger undoubtedly spent a lot of time and money tracking him down, which meant that he either needed the Firebird files to complete his device, or that he'd already finished it and was trying to find Hank to kill him and tie up a loose end. In either case, Berger didn't know he had a photographic memory and that he'd destroyed the Firebird files.

From his assessment, Hank concluded that if he was going to win this war he would need to do many of the things General Berger had done. First, he needed time to learn about this society, and catch up with the advancements that had been made in technology over the last forty years. Second, he needed to find people to help him; smart people he could trust. Since he was now a multi-millionaire, he could use his money to do just that. Finally, as far as a plan was concerned, he couldn't see any alternative to the one he'd originally embarked upon those many years ago: to build a device of his own and pursue General Berger into the future and stop him.

With his thoughts now free of the pain and guilt of self-recrimination, and his mind once again focused on the mission, Captain Hank knew with crystal-clarity what he needed to do.

* * *

The next morning, after checking out of his room at the lodging office and filling his truck with gas, Hank exited Fort Meade's main entry gate and made his way over to his apartment. It took him less than ten minutes to pack all his clothes and personal belongings into a suitcase. Once finished, he proceeded to the apartment superintendent's office where he terminated his lease agreement and turned in his room keys.

After returning to his truck, he drove several blocks down Reese Road until he reached the nearest branch of the U.S. Post Office, where he rented a small personal box and changed his mailing address from the apartment to the new box. He also filled out a request for the post office hold his mail, using "extended vacation" as the reason.

Hank's next stop was the bank where he changed his mailing address and set up automatic payments to the Oriole Self-Storage company. He also withdrew two-million dollars in the form of eleven cashier's checks; ten for the sum of one-hundred thousand dollars, and one for the remaining sum of one-million dollars.

While waiting for the teller to approve the large withdrawal, he noticed there was a small blue mailbox mounted to a stand just past the last teller station, and remembered the letter he'd written to the Simon Wiesenthal Center. (He'd been so absorbed in forming his plan, he'd forgotten to mail it when he was at the post office.) Once he received the cashier's checks, he proceeded over to the little mailbox, removed the letter from his shirt pocket and dropped it in. With his business at the bank concluded, he drove over to the brokerage firm where he changed his address and made a few adjustments to his stock account.

As Hank made his way back to Reese Road and turned south towards the interstate onramp, he mentally reviewed his plan again. He knew it all hinged on him buying enough time to adapt to this society and finding people he could trust to help him. As for the letter, he hoped it would spark some interest because if he had any chance of finding and stopping General Berger now, he needed all the help he could get.

* * *

Unknown to Captain Hank, when he mailed the letter to the Simon Wiesenthal Center he had put the wheels of a very large intelligence organization into motion. Even though the specific information he provided would be over two-and-a-half years old when they received it, it would give investigators the first solid lead to General Berger's possible whereabouts since before the end of the war. With the cold case suddenly thawing, authorities from the Mossad (the National Intelligence Organization of Israel) would reopen the investigation.

The copy of the photograph Hank had recovered in the Firebird intelligence also proved to be invaluable, as detectives now had a face to go with Berger's name. In less than a week, copies of the picture (including descriptions and artist's renditions of what an "older" Karl Berger might look like) would be sent out to the Mossad's global field offices, as well as to the FBI, CIA, Scotland Yard and Interpol. Within a month's time, eighteen major law enforcement agencies across the globe would be involved, and since many of Berger's victims in the Sachsenhausen concentration camps were Russian-born, even the Foreign Intelligence Service in Moscow would launch an investigation.

More than four-and-a-half decades after World War II had ended, the world-wide manhunt for the Nazi's White Wolf would resume!

Chapter Fourteen
The Letter

A massive pile of unopened mail sat on the small office desk, purposely spread out to obscure the telephone, writing instruments and open work folders. Small yellow sticky notes, with various funny faces drawn on and captioned "open me first" were sticking to some of these letters in a circular fashion, and formed a large round smiley-face. Completing the joke, were several similarly-sized sticky notes, pink in color, which formed a tongue protruding from the mouth of the face. Seated at the desk, smiling and shaking his head, was the newest permanent employee, Albert Greenbaum.

It was the third time this week that a load of anonymous mail had been left for him while he was at lunch, and although he was starting to grow tired of it, his good nature and sense of humor allowed him to laugh along with his coworkers. He knew from talking to some of them that there wasn't anything personal behind the prank, but instead was simply a hazing ritual for the new guy. What he didn't like was that he now had to spend an additional hour after quitting time and probably extra time early tomorrow morning going through all of them.

THE DEVICE

On Monday when it first happened, his coworkers informed him that as the newest permanent member of the team, one of his additional duties involved screening the anonymous mail. What they didn't tell him was that the unidentified mail was normally divvied out to the entire office staff, and everyone was supposed to share the cumbersome task of cataloging it. In that respect, all the anonymous mail that came in needed to be dated, numbered, and classified into one of three types.

The first type was the hate mail, consisting of anti-Semitic rants sent in by individuals who blamed the Jewish people for everything bad that was happening in the world, or for all the bad things that were happening to them. The second type were essentially extortion letters, where the person who'd sent it had some information about a war criminal, and would reveal what they knew for a price. The third kind were classified as "Potentials," containing legitimate leads or other information pertinent to one of the on-going investigations.

As Albert Greenbaum looked at the large stack of anonymous mail, he knew the early dinner plans he'd had with his girlfriend were now shot, and that the afternoon was going to be a long one.

~ Then ~

Albert started working at the Simon Wiesenthal Center a little over a year ago, just after graduating from high school. At the time, he planned to use the money he earned to go to college at night and earn a bachelor's degree with the long-term goal of becoming an officer in the military. With his small stature, energetic spirit, and dashing good looks, he thought he fit the mold of the ideal fighter pilot. Whether it be the Army, Navy, Air Force or Marines, it didn't matter; Albert wanted to fly jets.

His dreams of being the next "Top Gun" were short-lived, however, when his priorities unexpectedly changed. First, he started dating a girl named Justine, and after only a short period of time he'd fallen madly in love with her. They'd met on the day he started working at "The Center," as he called it, when he toured the facility and Justine happened to be the tour guide. Where he once had ideas of flying an F-16 into the wild blue yonder, his thoughts now centered around settling down with her and starting a family.

The second reason he'd abandoned his dream of joining the military was the love he had for his new job. When he'd first hired on as a part-time temporary office assistant, "Little Al," as he was affectionately called by his coworkers, was simply a gofer for the administrative staff. Instead of getting disheartened and quitting, he set about becoming the model employee, hoping to land a permanent position. In that regard, when the staff needed coffee, Little Al made the coffee. When Rabbi Hirsh, the assistant dean of The Center, needed a lift to and from the airport, Little Al drove him. If there was a job or a project no one else wanted to do, Little Al did it.

His friendly attitude, coupled with his willingness to do just about anything, didn't escape the notice of his supervisor Mr. Levinson, and in less than four months he'd received his first pay raise. Eight months later, he was assigned to a "Research Analyst" position, which led to new duty assignments; one of which involved taking notes at the monthly teleconference.

The main topic of the first teleconference he'd attended was an update of the status of all the current investigations going on around the world involving human rights violations, and included Nazi war criminals who were still at large. One of the men on the other end of the telephone line was the director of the Jerusalem Center, who coordinated the on-going searches and maintained the list of "Most Wanted" criminals. Other dignitaries in the teleconference included high-level directors and detectives stationed at the other Simon Wiesenthal Center offices in New York, Chicago, Miami, Toronto, Paris and Buenos Aires.

THE DEVICE

As Albert began taking notes, he became completely captivated with the stories he heard about these former Nazis, and the steps that were being taken to bring them to justice. Just as interesting was what he learned about the people on the other end of the telephone line. As each new voice came on, Mr. Levinson whispered in his ear who the person was and gave him a small tidbit of information about them. What struck him the most, in a sobering way, was the one thing they all had in common: all of them had lost loved ones in the Holocaust.

When the meeting was over, the thoughts Albert had of joining the military abruptly ended, and he knew he'd found his life's calling: he wanted to be a detective who hunted down war criminals. As soon as the meeting was over he approached Mr. Levinson to see how he could become one, whereupon he was told he needed to further his education. The next day he enrolled in night classes at the University of Southern California at Los Angeles, with his sights set on getting a degree in criminology.

Two days ago, his hard work paid off when he arrived at The Center and was astonished to find Mr. Levinson had changed his status of employment to "full-time permanent," and had assigned him his own desk and phone; both of which signified he had "made it." At the same time, a string of good-natured hazing incidents had begun to befall him, one of which involved a load of anonymous mail being dumped on his desk while he was out to lunch.

~ Now ~

As Little Al stared at the large stack of letters on his desk, he again laughed and played along with the gag. He knew if he reacted any other way than being a good sport, the hazing could escalate, and he didn't want to gain the reputation of a guy that couldn't take a joke.

By mid-afternoon he'd finished all the work in his inbox and began working on the stack of anonymous letters. After documenting and classifying four of them, all of which he found to be hate mail, he picked up one of the cleaner-looking ones from the middle of the pile.

He immediately noticed the address was handwritten, and with the most amazingly-perfect penmanship he'd ever seen. Looking more closely, he saw it was postmarked in Baltimore, and the date of the stamp was yesterday. Retrieving his pen, he assigned it the number 080791-05 and annotated the number and the postmarked location in the ledger. He picked up the letter opener and slid it into one end of the sealed flap, and after quickly tearing the envelope open down its top fold removed the papers inside.

He knew immediately that it was a letter all of his coworkers could only dream of receiving. Written in the same perfect handwriting that was on the envelope, the letter was from a witness who had seen SS Lieutenant General Karl Berger. The person who'd written the letter, wanting to remain anonymous, had also sent a photograph to prove they were telling the truth.

Moving the letter aside to see the picture, Little Al shook with nervous excitement. After hearing General Berger's name mentioned at one of the teleconferences, he'd later conducted some research of his own, and knew he was perhaps the most-notorious Nazi war criminal still at large. He quickly gathered the envelope and the two papers, and ran down the hallway to Mr. Levinson's office. Finding it empty, he remembered it was Wednesday and that the big-wigs held their mid-week staff meeting in the upstairs conference room.

Proceeding to the stairs, he ran up the flight until he reached the top then turned and sprinted down the narrow hallway.

Justine, working at the desk outside the conference room, sprang to her feet.

"Albert, what's wrong?"

"I have to go in there," he gasped.

"You can't go in there. That meeting is for the senior staff only."

"You don't understand, Justine. I just found something in the mail."

"Albert, Rabbi Hirsh is in there. Normally he doesn't attend the first meeting of the month, but today he decided to. You can't just barge in and..."

Before she could finish, he moved past her, pulled the door open and went inside. When he reached the large oak conference table, he stopped and loudly cleared his throat, which interrupted the Rabbi in mid-sentence.

"I beg your pardon Rabbi Hirsh, but you have to see this."

A hushed silence fell over the room.

The Rabbi stared at him for a few moments before replying.

"What is it?"

"I was going through the anonymous mail and someone has seen the White Wolf."

"What did you say?"

"Sir, someone has seen the White Wolf of Sachsenhausen, and whoever it was sent us this." He held up the photograph.

The quietness that had fallen over the room suspended itself in time, as no one uttered as much as a whisper.

* * *

Less than forty-seven hours later, a few minutes past twelve o'clock on Friday afternoon, the emergency meeting convened. More than one-hundred people, including senior staff members and investigators from the Mossad, now packed the Simon Wiesenthal Center's main conference room and outer office. Three times that number of people, stationed at other agencies and offices around the world, listened in on the telephone.

Inside the conference room, sitting at the head of the large oak table, was Rabbi Hirsh. Seated to his immediate left was Simon Wiesenthal, the famous Nazi hunter himself. Next to him sat Albert Greenbaum, pen and notebook in hand, ready to take notes. To the

Rabbi's right was Eugene Melnick, a senior investigator for the Mossad. On the large table in front of them lay numerous copies of Captain Hank's letter and the photograph of General Berger.

Addressing the crowd through a microphone, Rabbi Hirsh's voice boomed through the room's public-address system.

"All right, let us begin. First, I want to introduce our esteemed guest, Mr. Wiesenthal."

Wiesenthal raised his hand and briefly waved to the crowd.

"As to the events of the last two days, I have asked Eugene Melnick to give us an update on what we know so far."

Taking the microphone from Rabbi Hirsh, Melnick stood up.

"Thank you, Rabbi. As you all know, the day before yesterday we received an anonymous letter from someone claiming they saw SS Lieutenant General Karl Berger in Berlin, on or about the twenty-fourth day of December, 1988."

Pausing, he picked up a copy of the picture.

"Accompanying the letter was this photograph, who the letter writer says is General Berger. When Rabbi Hirsh told me about this I recommended we first make sure that this wasn't some sort of an elaborate anti-sematic hoax meant to embarrass either him, Simon, or the foundation. Fortunately, from what we learned yesterday and just a short time ago, this is not the case."

Side-bar conversations immediately broke out among the throng of listeners, at which point Melnick raised his hand.

"Please. May I have your attention?"

The talk died down.

"As I was saying, we learned some things yesterday, starting with what Josef Shapiro at our Paris office found out about the photograph." Leaning down to the little speaker box on the desk, he said, "Josef, tell everyone what you told me."

A deep voice with a pronounced French accent replied.

"When I received the fax, I remembered my father worked with a man named Oscar Wetzel who was an inmate at one of the Sachsenhausen concentration camps. After doing a bit of checking, I found Mr. Wetzel was still alive and lived just a short distance from our office here on Champs-Élysées. When I went to his home and showed him the photograph, he positively identified the man shaking hands with Hitler as SS Lieutenant General Karl Berger, the White Wolf of Sachsenhausen."

More sidebar conversations broke out, and again Melnick held up his hand to quiet the crowd.

"Are you sure he was not mistaken?"

"There was no mistake. Although Mr. Wetzel is quite elderly he still has a sound mind and an excellent memory. He lost his entire family at Sachsenhausen, and when he saw the photograph he became quite upset."

"Thank you, Josef," Melnick said, then stood to address the audience. "We also received word this morning from our New York office that they had located four other Sachsenhausen survivors, and all of them have positively identified General Berger as the man in the photograph with Hitler."

He held his hand up, stopping the talk before it started.

"Since we know now that the photograph is genuine, let us examine the letter."

Many people shuffled the papers they were holding and brought their copy of Captain Hank's letter to the top.

"The only thing we know for sure about the letter was that it was mailed either late Monday afternoon or early Tuesday morning in Baltimore. As for the person who wrote it, I'd like you all to meet Paul Eiffeld." He motioned to a man seated on the opposite side of the long table. "Paul is a handwriting expert and criminal profiler with the FBI here in Los Angeles."

Melnick walked over to him and handed him the microphone.

Remaining seated, Eiffeld gathered his thoughts for a moment before speaking.

"Let me start by saying this young man's handwriting certainly posed a challenge to both myself and my colleagues at the Bureau."

"So a young man wrote it?" a woman in the crowd asked.

"Oh yes, there's no doubt about it. We know it was a man because there aren't any common female characteristics or mannerisms present in his handwriting, and we know he is a younger man because his writing is steady. You see, when the average person reaches forty years of age their handwriting will begin to show signs of fatigue; shaky lettering, for example. On this letter there are none. Also, the paper is blank and not lined which normally means that the person used either an edge to make the lines straight, say a ruler or another piece of paper, or we're dealing with a very unique individual."

"What do you mean by unique individual?" A man sitting two rows back from the table asked.

"When my team and I examined the letter under a microscope and found it to be handwritten, there weren't any indications that a ruler was used nor any other mark to indicate that something was used to make the lines straight. Normally when people handwrite a letter on unlined paper, their writing tends to either go up or down at the end of each line. On this letter, every line on the page is perfectly spaced in relation to the one above it and below it. Even the left and right margins are equal in width."

He waited a moment, letting that thought sink in before continuing.

"Another thing that stood out was the absence of mistakes. Normally when a person writes a full-page letter by hand somewhere along the way they make a mistake. For example, they may start to write something and change their mind, then either scribble it out and start again or simply write over the mistake. Other common mistakes include the misspelling of words or running a sentence too long into the right margin, but in this instance there are no mistakes at all. Quite frankly, after I faxed it to

Virginia and had the Bureau's experts examine it, even they were astonished that this letter had been handwritten."

As Eiffeld momentarily stopped to take a drink from a can of soda, the murmuring and small-talk returned.

"But the team of experts in Virginia did offer one clue as to who wrote it."

His comment immediately quieted the crowd.

"They compared this unique style of handwriting to what they had on file, and in all cases the people whose writing was similar had one thing in common. They were all test subjects who scored high on an eidetic memory test." After receiving questioning looks from a few of those seated around the table, he clarified, "In other words, to some degree they all had a photographic memory."

As the side-bar conversations began again, another female voice rose from the crowd.

"What test subjects?"

As the room quieted, the woman repeated her question.

"You said similar handwriting was found in people who were test subjects. What test subjects?"

"People entering the military," Eiffeld replied. "The armed forces used to give such tests to new recruits if they suspected they had, shall we say, *special gifts*. Unfortunately, most of the records are classified, but the few that the FBI does have on file showed similarities to the handwriting in this letter."

"Are you saying that a member or former member of our military wrote the letter?"

"No, but what I *am* saying is that this handwriting is similar to samples taken from military members who scored well on the memory test. Therefore, I believe there is a distinct possibility that the person who wrote this letter has, to some degree, a photographic memory. This explains how they could handwrite it so perfectly and space the lines and margins the same distance apart. And as far as perfection is concerned, this letter surpasses any sample the FBI has on file from the other test subjects. It's the most-perfectly handwritten letter either myself or anyone at the Bureau has ever seen."

When he paused this time not a sound was heard.

"Now when we build a profile from a person's handwriting we look at everything you can imagine: writing style, line spacing, where they dot their i's and cross their t's, even the amount of pressure they exert on the paper with their writing instrument. Each of these things tells us something about the writer's personality. With anonymous letters like this one, we also look closely at what the person is telling us and what they are *not* telling us to ascertain their state of mind, and to determine whether they are being truthful. Lastly, we look to see if there are any clues as to their possible motive for sending the letter to begin with.

"After my colleagues and I examined this document, here's the profile we came up with. The man who wrote this letter is young, not much older than thirty-five years of age. He's very intelligent, articulate, and as I said has an incredible memory. He can organize his thoughts very well and has a strong sense of purpose in his life.

"As for his state of mind, the fact that he sent this letter anonymously tells us he is afraid; afraid of being found by the authorities, afraid of being found by General Berger, or perhaps both. If he's afraid of being found by the authorities he might be wanted, in which case he could be aiding and abetting General Berger. Another possibility is that he's a man of distinction, say someone who holds office or is the head of a corporation, who's checkered past is someway connected to Berger and he doesn't want that connection to be made public. Or it might simply mean that he doesn't want the notoriety of being involved in a case like this."

"Could he be someone who just happened to recognize General Berger?" A man standing near the door asked.

"The fact that he sent the photograph proves this is much more complicated than just a casual observance, which also brings up the possibility that he himself is afraid of being found by General

Berger. Perhaps he works for Berger and discovered his identity, or Berger might be after him for some other unknown reason."

"Can we believe what he is telling us in the letter?" Another man from the crowd asked.

"There's an old saying we use at the Bureau which states, *the more detailed the information someone gives you, the higher the probability it is reliable.* From the specific information this man provided to us in this letter, we have determined with a high degree of certainty that it is the truth."

Murmurs began again but immediately died down when Eiffeld raised his hand.

"This brings us to his motivation of sending us the letter in the first place. I can tell you, unequivocally, from his word choices and the inflections he uses in his grammar, that some event has occurred prompting him to write this letter and send it to us."

He started to hand the microphone back to Melnick and stopped.

"One more thing if I may?"

Both Melnick and the Rabbi nodded.

"I've done this kind of work for many years. Call it intuition or just a feeling I have, but I don't believe the man who wrote this letter has aided or helped General Berger at all. I do believe, however, that he's been trying to find him for some time. Whatever has happened, whatever event has occurred, it has now become too dangerous for him to proceed alone and he needs our help."

He handed the microphone back to Melnick.

"Thank you, Paul," Melnick said, turning to face the audience.

Before he could speak, Simon Wiesenthal was standing and motioning for the microphone.

"The only real question we have is why such an intelligent and gifted young man would send us this letter and the photograph without giving us his name."

He stopped and looked around the room.

"But have we not relied on anonymous tips before? Didn't we act upon a great amount of information that we couldn't completely verify when we captured Adolph Eichmann?"

Many of the older people in the room nodded.

"In my opinion, it doesn't really matter why this man has decided to remain anonymous. What does matter is the information he's given us in the letter and the photograph. As for the photograph, we've determined it to be genuine. As for the letter, we have an experienced FBI agent telling us he is almost certain the information is the truth. These are the first two pieces of evidence we've been able to gather about General Berger."

He paused and looked across the table at Paul Eiffeld.

"And if you believe the man who sent us this letter is in danger and needs our help, then in my opinion we must try to give it to him, in any way possible."

Wiesenthal handed the microphone back to Melnick and sat down.

Melnick picked up a piece of paper on the desk in front of him, took a moment to gather his thoughts, and addressed the crowd.

"By the power vested in me by the State of Israel, I hereby re-open this investigation. Wanted: SS Lieutenant General Karl Wilhelm Berger, aka the White Wolf of Sachsenhausen. Born February the twenty-ninth, 1912, in Munich, Germany. Description: Six feet eight inches tall, large muscular build, dark green, almost black eye color. Wanted for war crimes committed in World War II, including the willful torture and murder of inmates at the Sachsenhausen concentration camp and its sub-camps in or near Oranienburg, Germany. Date and location of last sighting: 24 December 1988, Berlin, Germany, around area of Gertrud-Kolmar-Strasse, the previous location of Hitler's bunker."

Setting the paper down, he began issuing instructions.

"I want the widest possible distribution of this, including airports, bus terminals, even taxi cabs if possible. Wherever people go to travel, I want them to see his face. I also want this story to flood the news media. Stan?"

A middle-aged man seated next to Albert Greenbaum scooted one of the extra phones on the table closer, and started dialing.

"I'm on it," he said, without looking up. "I'll have my staff start calling the major news organizations. I'll also call a couple of people I know at Fox and CBS. Who knows, maybe we can book a segment on America's Most Wanted or 60 Minutes."

"Good thinking," Melnick said, "and if anyone can think of something we might have missed let us know."

Melnick set the microphone down and walked over to Paul Eiffeld.

"Can we call upon your friends at the Bureau to provide us with some artist renditions of how Berger would look today?" he asked.

Eiffeld smiled. "Already ahead of you Gene. They should be here within the hour."

Melnick smiled back. "Paul, I believe you've earned your pay for the week."

Well after everyone else had exited the conference room, Little Al remained, frantically trying to finish the notes he'd been taking.

* * *

Albert Greenbaum went on to receive an avalanche of notoriety for bringing Captain Hank's letter and the photograph of General Berger to the attention of Rabbi Hirsh. When the spotlight finally faded, he returned to his regular duties as a research analyst even more excited about his life, his love Justine, and the successful career he hoped to build at the Simon Wiesenthal Center.

As the years passed, his involvement with the case of General Berger and anonymous letter number 080791-05 grew less and less, as more-pressing job assignments distanced him from the investigation. Fate would dictate, however, that the next solid lead would again come to him – at a time and from a source he least expected. The time would be a little more than twenty-three years later, and the source (of all places) a county sheriff's deputy in the nearby state of Utah.

In the weeks that followed the emergency meeting at the Wiesenthal Center, the story of Karl Berger gained a foothold, and eventually extended around the world to every major news organization. For a while, the haunting old photograph of the huge Nazi general shaking hands with Hitler seemed to be everywhere. Garnering equal interest was Captain Hank's perfectly handwritten letter, as people became fascinated with both the handwriting and the FBI's profile of the man who'd written it.

Despite the best efforts put forth by law enforcement officials, the elusive Nazi war criminal remained at large and the case would again go cold. From all outward appearances, the re-opened investigation looked to be a complete failure, but behind the scenes it was an unparalleled success. Not only would the pressure of the renewed manhunt drive the Nazi's White Wolf back into hiding, but it would also give Captain Hank the time he needed to adapt to the society, catch up with the modern technology, and find people to help him rebuild the time-traveling device.

Chapter Fifteen
The Wolf's Howl

Ten Days Later
Sunday, 18 August 1991, 18:01hrs
Inside the *Presidential Suite of the Dunes Hotel, Paradise, Nevada*

The sun shining through the west windows emblazoned the three vases full of fresh flowers, brightening the interior of the immaculate room with an array of floral colors. The white cushions on the dark natural-wood furniture, also awash in sunlight, seemed to emit an unnatural glow, giving the retro-style suite an almost ethereal appearance. The only sounds that could be heard were the soft air waves of the air conditioning system, a woman's voice on the television, and the heavy breathing of the sole occupant of the room: SS Lieutenant General Karl Berger.

Moments ago, after hanging up the phone, pouring himself a drink and turning on the television, he'd planned to relax the evening away by watching his favorite show, 60 Minutes. When the picture faded into view, however, and he saw his own face staring back at him, any thoughts he'd had of enjoying tonight's program were replaced with an ever-growing state of anger and rage. Turning up the volume, he could only look upon the screen helplessly as CBS reporter Lesley Stahl told the world his story:

"He was one of Nazi Germany's most brilliant officers, and the youngest to attain the rank of lieutenant general in Hitler's Third Reich. From eyewitness accounts, he was also one of the most brutal; a man who personally tortured and murdered over a hundred people in the concentration camps near Oranienburg, Germany. His name was Karl Berger, and for the survivors of those camps he was considered the 'worst of the worst' of the Nazis. In May of 1945, when Germany finally surrendered to the allies, General Berger was one of a handful of high-ranking Nazi officers left unaccounted for, and for more than forty-six years no clue as to his whereabouts had ever been found. Then eleven days ago someone sent this photograph to the Simon Wiesenthal Center in Los Angeles. Just as interesting as the photograph was the anonymous letter that accompanied it. This is the subject of our first segment – Who saw the White Wolf of Sachsenhausen?"

Twenty minutes later when the story ended, Berger's fury reached its melting point, and screaming in anger he picked up the nearest bar stool and threw it at the television. As it broke through the picture tube, the set exploded, sending sparks into the air and shards of glass cascading down onto the carpeted floor.

Thomas O'Malley immediately came running in from the adjoining room, at which point Berger, now in a blind rage, brutally kicked him in the groin and punched him in the face.

The Irishman instantly fell to the ground and doubled over into a ball, but managed to take in enough air to start pleading for his life.

"Boss don't kill me! Don't kill me! What happened?"

Red-faced and unresponsive, Berger moved in on him, and with his two large hands effortlessly pulled O'Malley up to his knees and encircled his neck with his huge, muscular arm. As he began to squeeze, he suddenly came to his senses, at which point he simply threw O'Malley to the side, retrieved his drink from the counter, and walked over to the window.

"Boss, what's going on?" O'Malley gasped.

"They know I am here! The Jews have my picture and know I am here!"

"How did…"

"The captain must have found my picture in the Ünterbunker and sent it to them!"

"How do you know?"

"It is all over the television, you dummkopf!"

"So what do we do now?"

"Shut up and let me think!"

O'Malley struggled to his feet and limped back to the adjoining room.

Berger stared out the window at Las Vegas Boulevard, but his thoughts were far from this place the Irishman called "The Strip." He remembered his good friend, Albert Speer, telling him he needed to be patient. "Your temper," he'd said, "will be your undoing."

THE DEVICE

After seeing the story about himself broadcast across America on 60 Minutes, it appeared as if he'd proven his friend right.

~ *Then* ~

Up until three weeks ago everything had gone according to plan. With the Irishman's connections and a few well-placed bribes, he had obtained a copy of the official report of the Alsos Mission's Task Force B operation, and identified the blue-eyed U.S. Army captain who had commanded the reconnaissance team that raided the Ünterbunker. He also learned that Captain Stevens had lied about his team not recovering anything. From the official report, he was able to trace the captain to his job at the university in Maryland and finally to the warehouse at Fort Meade.

At first, the two-and-a-half-year search to find Captain Stevens had been worth it; inside the warehouse, he found the place where he lived and where he'd built the device. A more in-depth search of the warehouse, however, had produced nothing; no Firebird files, nor any trace of the device's main structure. This told him that either the captain had died, was moving his operation, or that he'd activated the device and had gone into the future. Any one of these scenarios could explain why the warehouse was now mostly empty.

Just as he was planning his next move, the Army officer named Washington and his wife had entered the warehouse. Hiding behind some machinery, he overheard him tell her, "We've already moved the main structure. All Captain Hank and I have left are a couple of lathes and the field accelerator."

That was the only thing either of them said before the Irishman had stuck his gun in their faces, but with those two sentences the officer had given him three vital clues. First, he referred to Captain Stevens as "Captain Hank," so he knew they had the right man. When he had asked O'Malley why Stevens' former commander referred to him with that name throughout the official report, the Irishman had explained that "Hank" was a common American nickname of men with the first name of Henry. Second, Washington referred to the captain in the *present* tense, not the *past* tense, which meant that Captain Stevens was still alive. Third, Washington had told his wife that they had already moved the main structure, which meant that Captain Stevens was here in this time period.

When he began questioning them, he was sure he could make the Washington couple tell him where he could find the captain, but he'd completely underestimated their resiliency, and after murdering the man, his wife still wouldn't talk. When he made his move on her, she did the unthinkable and spit in his face! In a fit of blind rage, he immediately placed her in a headlock and snapped her neck. After coming to his senses, he realized that he'd killed them both too soon. He still didn't know where Captain Stevens was, nor the place where he'd hidden the stolen Firebird information.

Sensing time was short and that they might be discovered, he had O'Malley help him dismount the heavy field accelerator from its carriage and load it into the back of their moving van. Fortunately, it just barely fit at a slanted angle through the rear doors. Not wanting to leave any evidence, he then ordered the Irishman to burn the building down. That way when Captain Stevens did return, he would think his two friends perished in an accidental fire.

His plan was to have O'Malley watch over the place, but the extra security measures the military police imposed made it impossible for the Irishman to gain access back onto the base.

In any event, it now left him in the same dilemma he'd been in before he found the warehouse: where was Captain Stevens and where was the stolen Firebird information?

~ Now ~

As Karl Berger thought about his present situation, he knew it was not safe for him to be seen in public anymore. From what the 60 Minutes report said, law enforcement agencies all over the world now had his photograph and were looking for him. With modern technology, including the new World Wide Web that O'Malley showed him, someone could easily recognize him and alert the authorities.

The 60 Minutes story also touched on the letter that accompanied the photograph, and how the man who'd written it might have, to some degree, a photographic memory. Could this explain why he hadn't found any of the Firebird files in the warehouse? Had Captain Stevens set everything to memory and destroyed them? Not likely, he concluded, because no one person, no matter how gifted, could even begin to memorize the vast amount of complicated formulas and design specifications, nor would they destroy the files of the most important discovery in the history of mankind.

He sat down and stared at the suite's ornate marble chess set, and began thinking of the striking similarities of his favorite pastime. When he'd made the move on the warehouse and killed Washington and his wife, the captain had counter-moved and sent his photograph to the Jews. Therefore, to find Captain Stevens and recover the Firebird information, he was going to have to think of this little cat-and-mouse game in the same manner; move, counter-move.

He also realized that if he was going to win this game, he needed to follow Albert Speer's advice and control his volcanic temper. Killing Washington and his wife was a serious blunder and had cost him a chance of finding Captain Stevens. Silently promising himself to control his behavior until *after* he recovered the information, he spoke aloud to his dead friend.

"All right, Herr Speer. I'll do it your way."

As for the stolen Firebird files, he absolutely had to recover them. They contained the mathematical formulas to synchronize the power system of the device. Without them, they wouldn't be able to make the device work the way it was designed. Although he'd read the formulas several times when the two Jews, Eddleman and Kaufmann, had finally figured them out, they were simply too long and complex for him to remember. Even Mr. Hope, the very smart theoretical physicist the Irishman had recruited for the operation, hadn't been able to calculate them.

What made the recovery of the files even more imperative was the message he'd received just before turning on the television to watch 60 Minutes. Professor Hope had arrived at the Nevada site late last night with the moving van containing the field accelerator, and was already sketching the blueprints for the carriage it was to be mounted on.

The timetable to complete Firebird Two was proceeding well-ahead of schedule.

Part Three: The Journey

Chapter Sixteen
The Story (Part 5)

Eight Months and Eleven Days Later
Tuesday, 28 April 1992, 08:20hrs
Outside *Davis-Monthan Air Force Base, Tucson, Arizona*

The rows of decommissioned aircraft sitting side-by-side on the tan-colored desert sand disappeared into the distance as far as the eye could see. The morning sun, reflecting off of their old and dated airframes, highlighted their many shapes and colors, while at the same time masked their numerous flaws, giving them the false appearance of still being airworthy. Their engines, which at one time roared like thunder to complete flight missions for the United States' military, now hung motionless and quiet; victims of the advances in technology and the ravages of time. In their heyday, many of these planes were so innovative they were classified top-secret and guarded in hangars by an untold number of security forces personnel. Deemed obsolete and expendable, they now served as silent sentinels to bygone aviation eras, with only a tall and rusty chain-link fence left to protect them. Standing outside one of these fences, feeling a touch of melancholy, was Captain Henry "Hank" Stevens.

He'd spent the last few months living in a vintage hotel on East Congress Street in downtown Tucson, clearing his thoughts from the horrible events that had occurred at Fort Meade and fine-tuning his plans to rebuild the device. With his ideas in place, Hank was eager to return to his home state of Utah, but before exiting Tucson for good he'd decided to go out to the aircraft graveyard. During his previous visits, the abandoned aircraft hulks in their tranquil setting seemed to cast a spell on him and remind him of the loved ones he'd left in the past.

As he gazed on the old and decaying Douglas C-47 Skytrain troop transports, affectionately known as "Goony Birds," he thought back to the events that had brought him here, and hoped he was successful in hiding his whereabouts from General Berger.

~ Then ~

After departing Maryland on that hot August day, Captain Hank spent the next five months living on the road. While traveling, he took extreme precaution to make sure he wasn't being followed, which included staying off the interstate freeways as much as possible, not remaining longer than a week at a time in the same location, and always using a different name when checking into a hotel.

Using the money from one of the cashier's checks, he paid for his gas, lodging and meals in cash, and in doing so left no credit card trail behind him that could be used to predict the route he was traveling. Although he was quite sure he had escaped Baltimore undetected, to be on the safe side he kept to the same routine throughout the five months. Tired from the endless miles on the road, he'd finally decided to check in to a hotel in Tucson for a prolonged stay, and rest his weary body while lending more thought to his plan.

Hank had decided that the University of Utah was the perfect place to set up his new base of operations, *if* they had a suitable building or warehouse available. When he'd first enrolled there in the fall of 1941, he attended Welcome Week, which included a short tour of the school campus. During the tour, the guide had mentioned that many graduate students and alumni conducted on-going research projects at the school. This research, which the university encouraged and sometimes sponsored, entailed everything from physics studies to medical experiments, and was conducted in older buildings that were not being fully utilized.

Although it was now almost fifty years later, Hank concluded that the university would still be involved in such research, and were probably still making use of some of their older facilities for those purposes. As for a building, he hoped to find one configured somewhat like the warehouse at Fort Meade, where he could live at the site as well as have space for a machine shop and the polished-steel room for the device.

Having his base of operations at the university had other advantages. First, it was a place he thought General Berger wouldn't think to look for him. Even though it was fairly close to his hometown of Ogden, he concluded it was safe because of that short distance; like hiding in plain sight. Another advantage was its close-proximity to the professors and student body, a few of whom he hoped to recruit for the mission.

During his stay in Tucson, Hank visited a nearby bookstore and found an old book that contained physics theories, one of which was an early concept by Albert Einstein regarding time travel to the past. He remembered this theory from the Firebird intelligence, and that the Nazi's had researched it extensively at their Oranienburg think tank. When they had deemed it theoretically impossible for a person to return to the past (due to the laws of causality) they had subsequently abandoned this area of study.

The concept, presented by Einstein in 1907, hypothesized that it *was* possible for a massless particle (such as a radio beam traveling faster-than-light) to travel backwards in time. After thumbing through the book, Hank purchased it, and began studying the concept in depth to see if there was any way he could construct a mechanism that could produce such a beam.

THE DEVICE

His morning trips to the hotel's café for breakfast had led to him meeting several older gentlemen who had retired from Davis-Monthan Air Force Base. During one of these meals, he learned of the mammoth reclamation site that occupied hundreds of acres of the base, which led him to visiting the haunting aircraft graveyard.

~ Now ~

Heading north towards Phoenix, Hank adjusted his new truck's air conditioner, turned on the radio, and popped open a can of grape soda. His extended stay in Tucson gave him a newfound energy, and for the first time in quite a while he felt comfortable and relaxed. The only thing that still felt strange was the persistent tremor in his left hand, which had now spread to his entire arm. Attributing it again to a side effect of piloting the device through the fourth dimension, he dismissed it thinking it would eventually go away.

When he reached Salt Lake City the next afternoon, he immediately traveled up Second South Street to the University of Utah campus. Following the signs to the administration building, he made his way inside and memorized a campus map, then drove the short distance over to the James Fletcher Building, which was the location of the Physics Department. Entering, he proceeded to the area of the building where the professors' offices were located and found all but one of them closed. Checking the open one, he found a young Asian man standing behind the desk thumbing through some papers. He was short, around four feet ten inches tall, had straight black hair, and was very-well dressed. Hank also noticed he was wearing a very expensive-looking wedding band on his left ring finger.

"Can I help you?" the man asked

"Yes, I'm looking for a physics professor."

"Which one?"

"Any one will do."

The man sat down in the chair behind the desk and offered him a seat.

"Are *you* a professor?" Hank asked, thinking he was too young to have even graduated high school.

The man smiled. "Professor Daniel Lee, at your service."

Hank looked at the two frames on the wall behind him, and could see that one held a diploma from the Chinese Academy of Sciences. The other, oddly enough, held a photograph of an Asian man without a shirt on; his perfectly-toned body in a martial art pose.

"Stevens, Jim Stevens," Hank said, offering his hand. "I'm sorry professor, I guess I was expecting to find old men with gray beards."

Laughing, Dan shook Hank's hand. "That would be a few of my colleagues who are here during the day. So what can I do for you Mr. Stevens?"

Hank told him the same story he'd told to Colonel Stillwater: that his dad was a physics professor which sparked his interest in the subject. His dad, now passed, had left him a sizeable sum of money, making him independently wealthy, and he was now looking for a facility at the university where he could conduct some research. When Dr. Lee asked him what the research involved, Hank easily recalled some of the Firebird files he'd put to memory and informed him that it dealt with, among other things, Albert Einstein's relativity theories, Niels Bohr's studies of the structure of the atom, and Werner Heisenberg's quantum field theories. Much to Hank's surprise, Professor Lee specialized in those very subjects.

A ninety-minute conversation ensued, and by the time it was over Hank had developed complete respect for the professor's knowledge and felt as if he'd known him for a very long time. As far as that was concerned, Hank hadn't felt this kind of instant friendship with someone since intelligence school when he'd first met Big Ben.

THE DEVICE

He learned that Professor Lee was a child prodigy while growing up in Beijing, showing an aptitude for mathematics and physics. He'd completed the Chinese equivalent of a Master's Degree in Theoretical Physics at the age of eighteen, and by the time he turned twenty-one had earned his Doctorate Degree and Teaching Certificate from the Chinese Academy of Science. Despite achieving such illustrious academic goals at such an early age, he was unable to find full-time employment in China because he was the product of a mixed marriage; his father was Chinese and his mother was white Anglo-Saxon.

Not long after his graduation, his father passed away from a heart attack. Shortly afterward, his mother retired from her job at the American Embassy and decided to move back to the United States, and to her hometown of Salt Lake City. With no job prospects on the horizon in China, Dan decided to accompany her, hoping he might be able to find a teaching position in Utah. After dropping off his impressive resume at every educational institution along the Wasatch Front, the University of Utah called and he subsequently landed his present position.

As Captain Hank listened to his story, he felt as if he had struck gold by finding this professor. Not only was he friendly, personable, and had a great sense of humor, he was also very open, which gave him an aura of honesty and genuineness. As if that weren't enough, he was also an expert on the fundamental physics theories the Firebird operation was built upon.

"Would you mind staying a little while longer?" Professor Lee asked. "I only have one class tonight, and all I need to do is collect some assignments and answer questions."

"Sure, take your time. I've got all night," Hank said.

"I shouldn't be longer than thirty or forty minutes. Help yourself to the snacks and pop in the fridge." He showed him the small refrigerator he had behind his desk, and a box on top that contained a wide assortment of candy bars, bags of chips and packages of beef jerky.

"One question before you go. I noticed your diploma lists thirteen cities. Did you attend school at all of them?"

"Not really. The Academy of Science has thirteen campuses across China. I attended the one at Beijing." Pointing to the Asian man in the photograph, he smiled. "Oh, and that's my dad Bruce. He was a master of Wing Chun."

"Wing what?"

"Wing Chun. It's the art of fighting without fighting."

Hank merely nodded at the photograph and looked back at the diploma, more impressed with the young man's credentials.

Thirty-five minutes later, Professor Lee returned to his office to find Hank reading a periodical on molecular physics.

"I hope I didn't keep you too long."

Hank smiled. "Not at all, Professor. I was just thumbing through one of your magazines."

"Call me Dan. I only like to be referred to as *professor* by my students."

"All right Dan, and you can call me Jim."

"Okay Jim. So tell me, are you hungry?"

"I could eat something."

"Do you like pizza?"

"Only if it's got a lot of pepperoni and sausage on it."

"There's a place over by Kingsbury Hall."

"Let's go."

A short time later, they were seated in the loud and crowded underground pizzeria, sipping micro-brewed root beers while waiting for their order.

"When I invited you for pizza it was my intention to treat you," Dan said.

"How about you treat me next time?"

Dan smiled. "If I may ask, Jim, what's your research about?"

"I can't really tell you, I'll have to show you. What I *can* say is that it's quite advanced and could take years to complete. I hope to recruit some of the university's more-brilliant young minds to my

357

team. That's why I want to find a place on-campus, so that it would be convenient for everyone."

"How large of a place will you need?"

"Quite large, with at least two main rooms; one for a shop to manufacture some parts and the other for the research laboratory. It also needs to be very secure because I plan on living there."

"Large, at least two rooms, secure, and you want to live there. That may be a little hard to arrange."

The young man working behind the cashier's desk suddenly blurted out the name "Stevens" over the loudspeaker, and Hank immediately went over and retrieved their order. Returning, he sat the pizza down in the center of the table.

"This looks delicious," he said, "go ahead and dig in."

Dan thanked him again, and quickly pulled a steaming piece out of the tray and slid it onto his plate.

"You were saying it might be hard to arrange?" Hank asked. He removed a piece for himself.

Dan cut off the pointed end of the pizza slice and stabbed it with a fork.

"Are you affiliated with the school? Or do you know anyone here at the university?" He put the piece of pizza up to his mouth and blew on it.

"No, I didn't graduate from here, and right now you are the only person I know. Like I told you earlier, I've been away for quite some time."

"Where *did* you graduate from, if I may ask?"

Hank ignored Dan's question altogether.

"What if I were to make a donation to the Physics Department?"

"It would have to be a sizeable donation." He placed the cooled bite of pizza into his mouth.

"Would a million dollars be enough?"

Dan immediately started to choke, and after a few coughs grabbed his drink and took a couple of large gulps of the creamy root beer.

"A *million* dollars? Did you say a *million* dollars?"

Hank's penetrating blue eyes locked on the young professor.

"Do you think that will be enough?"

"For a million dollars, they'd probably let you use just about any building on campus except Rice Stadium and the Special Events Center."

Hank removed an envelope from his shirt pocket, pulled out the one-million-dollar cashier's check, and sat it down on a clear spot on the table.

"If you help me find a place on-campus I can use for my research project, I'll donate this to the Physics Department."

Dan's eyes grew wide when he saw the check.

"I guess I could ask the Department Chair at next week's staff meeting. You could come and introduce yourself and we..."

"I'm sorry," Hank interrupted, "but that would simply be out of the question. I cannot have my name associated with this in any way."

"Why not? If all you are doing is physics research?" When Hank didn't answer, he leaned in and asked, "It's not something that's against the law is it?"

"Oh, heavens no, Dan. It's just that the research I am planning to do is quite advanced, and like I said might take years to complete. As for why I want to remain anonymous, let's just say I have my reasons."

"Okay," Dan replied slowly, "but the university will know who you are when I take your check to the staff meeting."

"Not if I make it out to you, and you take it to the bank, deposit it, and have the bank make out another one with your name, payable to the University of Utah Physics Department."

"You would trust me to do that?"

"I think I'm a pretty good judge of character, so I'll say yes. I believe I would."

"If I take a check this size to the staff meeting, they're going to have a lot of questions. What do I tell them?"

"Tell them the truth. That a person you know, who wishes to remain anonymous, would like to make a sizeable donation to the department. All this person asks in return is a place to conduct some physics research. You can also tell them this generous donor plans to employ students and alumni on a part-time basis, and if everything works out there will be additional donations like this in the future."

Dan laughed. "When you put it like that it sounds like a good deal."

Hank smiled back at him and took a bite of pizza.

"But if the Department Chair and everyone agrees, they'll need the name of the person who is going to oversee the research."

"Give them your name."

"Mine?"

"Yes. You could tell them that the anonymous donor has placed you in charge of the research, which also might ease their minds if they have any apprehension about loaning a building to a perfect stranger."

"All right, say I'm able to make the donation and the university agrees to let you lease one of their unused buildings. If you're there all the time, working there and living there, won't people eventually figure out that you are the person who made the donation?"

"Not if you introduce me as Jim, the special assistant to Mr. H.

"Mr. H.?"

"Short for *has a lot of money*, or whatever name we decide on."

Dan laughed. "Mr. H. I like that."

"So what do you think? Will you help me?"

"I will, but only if you give me some idea of what your research is all about. I mean, it's not every day that a stranger comes into my office as knowledgeable about physics as you are and offers the university a million-dollar donation."

Hank thought for a few moments, retrieved a pen from his shirt pocket, and pulled a napkin out of the table dispenser. After unfolding it, he started writing out a long and extremely complex math problem. Once he'd completely filled up the space on the napkin, he plucked another out of the table dispenser, unfolded it, and continued where he'd left off. After completing the first problem, he thought for a moment, withdrew a third napkin and wrote out another problem. Even though his writing was very small, it ended up taking two more napkins to complete the second problem. When he finally finished, he reviewed what he'd written, made sure the five napkins were stacked in order, and slid them across the table.

As Dan started examining the problem, his mouth fell open and his eyes grew wide. Once he was finished with the first napkin he slowly looked up at Hank.

"Is this a joke?" he asked.

Hank smiled and shook his head.

Returning to the problem, Dan slowly followed the long equation again with his finger until he came to the end of the napkin. Without looking up, he pulled the first napkin off the second and set it aside; as if he was turning the page of an old and fragile book. He repeated this method with the second problem, and went back to the first problem and read it again. Once he was finished, he looked up at Hank.

"Have these been proven, or what I mean is, have these been validated?"

Hank leaned in. "Yes, as have a few other related equations."

"Related equations? What other related equations?"

"Let's just say they are very complicated. So much so, you'd almost have to be Albert Einstein to figure them out."

Dan's mouth fell open and his eyes grew wide again.

"Did *you* do these calculations?"

"You could say I put the pieces together."

"But this is unbelievable. These are groundbreaking. The possibilities are endless."

Hank nodded. "I think you can appreciate now why I would like a secure site for my research."

"Oh, I understand," Dan said, looking back at the napkin then back up to Hank. "Jim, may I ask you, do you have room for me on your research team?"

"I was hoping you would ask me that."

Hank retrieved the five napkins, and after refolding them, placed them in his shirt pocket.

* * *

The following week Dan attended the Physics Department's staff meeting, and when his turn came to comment or ask questions, he rendered everyone speechless with the anonymous donation. As the questions started flying at him, he stuck to the story Hank had given him and only revealed that the generous donor (Mr. H.) wished to remain anonymous and that he hoped to conduct physics research on campus, provided there was a building he could use.

When three of the older professors objected and voiced their concerns that the donation felt like extortion, a lengthy discussion ensued about whether the university should accept the gift. In pleading Hank's case, Dan told them that he'd met Mr. H. and found him to be a friendly person with an unparalleled knowledge of physics. He also informed them that Mr. H. said they could keep the donation even if there wasn't a facility available.

Hearing this, the Executive Assistant to the Department Chair, a stern-looking middle-aged woman named Rachele Carpenter, stood up.

"Do you know what the H stands for?" she asked.

Dan smiled. "Has a lot of money!"

Everyone at the meeting burst out laughing, even the normally stone-faced Ms. Carpenter.

After taking a few moments to regain her composure, she addressed the staff.

"Personally, I don't care why Mr. H. wants to give us such a sizeable sum, but I know that the Athletics Department accepts huge donations all the time, and most of them come from anonymous donors who just want to see the football team recruit the best college prospects. If Mr. H. is willing to donate a million dollars to our department, I say we take it and put it to good use. If all he wants in return is to use one of our older vacant buildings for his research lab, then as far as I'm concerned let him use one. It's not like we don't have any spare buildings on this campus."

After a quick vote, the department staff agreed to accept the gift and assigned Professor Lee the job of helping Mr. H. find a suitable facility.

* * *

It took less than an hour the next day for Hank and Dan to meet with an official from the university's buildings and grounds department and decide on a location. The building, number 3731, was located just off North Campus Drive, and was once used by the university's School of Medicine to conduct anatomical research on cadavers. With those functions now being performed at a newer facility, the older building stood vacant. Cementing the decision for Hank was the building number being 3731 – the exact opposite number of the warehouse at Fort Meade.

THE DEVICE

When Hank first examined the exterior of the white cinderblock building, it appeared to be too small and he wasn't sure if it would work. Once inside, however, he found the two main rooms to be more than large enough; the north one could be used for the polished-steel room for the device, the south for his living quarters and the machine shop.

A main hallway separated the two rooms, and there were two additional hallways traversing corner to corner in the front and rear of the building. In that respect, the floorplan resembled the capital letter "I." In the center of each end of these two main rooms, were a set of double doors which opened into the front and rear hallways. These were furnished with the standard push bars found on exit doors in most public schools. The only other ways in and out of the two main rooms were emergency exits, which were singular steel doors positioned in the center of each room's north and south walls. These heavy-duty doors, also equipped with push bars, had no handles on the outside, thus giving the rooms an extra layer of security. Each of the rooms also had 16-foot high ceilings and were equipped with numerous electrical power outlets that carried both the average household current of 120-volts, and the higher 220-volts.

There was a long and deep stainless-steel refrigeration cabinet in the room on the north side, which was where the School of Medicine used to store the cadavers. Mounted to the ceiling above was a 500-pound capacity hoist that ran the length of the room on two tracks, This hoist had previously been used to move the bodies in and out of the upper rows of the cabinet. Closely examining the hoist and the tracks, Hank immediately concluded it was the perfect place to mount the device's field accelerator. In addition, the long stainless-steel refrigeration cabinet (now unserviceable) could be dismantled and used to line the walls.

The building's restrooms were in the rear of the room on the south side, which Hank concluded would be ideal for his living quarters. The front, in turn, would also work well for the machine shop.

By mid-morning, an agreement was reached to loan the building to Professor Lee for a period of twenty years. Although Hank wanted Dan to secure the building indefinitely, the university official cited an administrative policy banning such agreements. Twenty years was the longest they could use the building, at which point the contract would be reviewed by the university.

Unfortunately, this meant that if Hank were to get the device working, he would only be able to go into the future to 2012, or within the specified dates of the agreement. Otherwise, he ran the risk of having the stewardship of the building change hands or the building torn down; both of which could result in the stationary plane being obstructed when he returned to real time. Aside from that drawback, the agreement did allow for them to upgrade the interior of the building as long as they remained compliant with fire and safety regulations. Resigning to the fact that it was the best deal possible, and that they would re-negotiate the term of the agreement at the earliest opportunity, Hank instructed Dan to sign the contract and list himself as "Jim S., Special Assistant to Mr. H." on the paperwork.

For the next six months, Hank set about refurbishing building 3731. Using more of the money from the cashier's checks, he paid cash to a bevy of contractors to upgrade the interior of the building to his specifications. By the time fall arrived, his living quarters and the shop were complete. With a state-of-the-art lathe and an array of other metal-forming tools, the shop took on the appearance of a modern sheet metal fabrication business.

While the contractors worked on the south room, Hank worked in the north one where he planned to build the device. Since Dan taught classes in the afternoons or at night, he stopped by in the mornings to see if he could assist Hank, and if there was a job that required more than two hands he gladly stayed to help. If Hank wasn't in the middle of a job, the two would either sit and talk or go to lunch and discuss everything from theoretical physics to life in general. As the two men got to know each other they became close friends.

Hank learned that Dan was a widower. Not long after he'd arrived in America with his mother, he started dating a girl named Audrey, who he'd met while searching for a job. He dated her for eight months before proposing, and shortly afterward they were married. A few months later, while he was teaching his first night class at the university, Audrey went shopping to a downtown mall and was struck by a vehicle while crossing the street. By the time Dan made it to the hospital she had passed away. Topping that tragedy with another, ten days later his mother had died from a brain aneurysm. With tears coming to his eyes while he recounted the events, Hank knew Dan was still coping with both losses.

At first, Hank only told Dan bits and pieces of his story, but after getting to know him, he opened-up about the baseball accident and how he'd developed certain gifts, including the photographic memory.

As for the two problems, Dan asked Hank numerous times about how he'd figured them out, but each time Hank would reply with the same statement.

"Trust me. If I told you now, you wouldn't believe me."

* * *

In late August, Hank asked Dan to accompany him on a road trip back east so that he could pick up some equipment for the research project. Along with clearing out the storage garages he rented in Baltimore, Hank also planned to change his permanent address at the bank and brokerage firm to his new post office box in Salt Lake City. Since fall classes at the university didn't start for a few more weeks, Dan eagerly accepted.

The next morning, Hank showed up at his house driving a semi with a full-sized trailer, and tooted the loud and obnoxious air horn.

"I forgot to mention," Hank said, "we have a lot of equipment to pick up. Some of it's kind of big."

"Does that mean I have to start calling you Mr. B. instead of Mr. H.?"

"Oh great, another nickname."

A short time later, they were eastbound on Interstate 80, headed to Baltimore.

On the second day of the twenty-one-hundred-mile drive, Hank exited the interstate and pulled into a rest stop near Lincoln, Nebraska, and parked the semi a discreet distance away from the other trucks. Reaching back into the sleeper, he retrieved his overnight bag, and after unzipping one of the side pockets, pulled out the napkins from the pizzeria and handed them to Dan.

"I've debated with myself, repeatedly, whether I should tell you where these came from."

Seeing the napkins, Dan's eyes grew wide.

"Be forewarned, though, what I'm about to tell you will probably be the most fantastic story you've ever heard."

Dan laughed. "As long as you don't tell me that some little green aliens landed and gave them to you, I'll keep an open mind."

Hank locked his eyes on the professor.

"Before I tell you, I want you to know that this knowledge is dangerous. It has already cost the lives of four people I deeply cared about. By telling you, I might be placing your life in danger. That being said, do you still want to know?"

Dan swallowed. "Yes."

Hank took a few moments to gather his thoughts.

"My real name is Henry Stevens, but my friends call me Captain Hank. I was born October the thirtieth, 1920. I am seventy-one years old, and in a little less than two months I will be turning seventy-two."

"Okay," Dan replied, drawing the word out.

"As I've already told you, I got hit in the head by a line drive while playing baseball and it gave me a photographic memory. What you don't know is that the accident also increased my cognitive abilities. Those abilities allowed me to read and learn things rather quickly, and as far as problem-solving goes, I developed the ability to put the pieces of complex problems together in my mind like a child's jigsaw puzzle."

Dan nodded. "Is that how you figured out the two formulas?"

"Not exactly. The two formulas on these napkins were found during an intelligence mission I was on at the end of World War II. They were used by the Nazis in a diabolical plot to change the future."

"Change the future? How?"

"By using a device that could create an aperture through the interdimensional plane of the space-time continuum, and carry a person into the fourth dimension."

Dan's eyes grew wide and his mouth fell open.

"I know it sounds impossible," Hank continued, "but after I finished memorizing the intelligence and put the pieces together, I realized that the device could actually transport someone into the future and return them to the present."

For the remainder of the trip to Maryland, Hank recounted the entire story. At first, from the multitude of questions Dan asked him, Hank could tell he was having a hard time believing him. The nonstop questioning finally ended when Hank pulled the semi into the Oriole Self-Storage business in south Baltimore, and showed Dan what they had come all the way across the country to retrieve: the dismantled main structure of the device.

* * *

The next morning as Hank drove out of Baltimore, Dan sat in the passenger seat not saying a word. Glancing over at him, Hank could tell from the way he was intensely staring at the road ahead and hardly blinking that he was deep in thought.

"Is everything all right?" Hank asked.

"You know, I didn't sleep a wink last night."

Hank remembered Big Ben telling him the same thing when he revealed to him the secret of the device.

"Sorry about that. When you think about what the device can do, it is a lot to comprehend."

Dan shook his head. "No, the reason I didn't sleep well wasn't because of the device. It was because of what you said about everything happening for a reason."

"I've always believed that."

"I haven't, but you've made a believer out of me."

"How so?"

"Ever since I was very young, I've been interested in science. When I attended my first class at the Academy in Beijing, I chose quantum physics as my major, which from what you've told me is the foundation the Firebird plan was built on."

Hank nodded.

"When I first met you in the physics building, on an afternoon when the other professors would've normally been there, it couldn't have been a coincidence. And quite frankly, ever since I lost Audrey and my mother my life has felt empty. Now, after meeting you and hearing your story, I feel as if I've got a new purpose. I now believe our coincidental meeting was meant to be, and that the reason we met is so that I can help you stop this evil man."

Tears came to Hank's eyes as he realized that he couldn't have recruited a better man for the mission.

* * *

THE DEVICE

Returning to Utah, Captain Hank went back to renovating building 3731 while Dan returned to his duties as a physics professor. The fall and winter terms passed, and in the early spring of 1993 the two men conducted an examination of the device's main structure and the burned-out triodes from the power distribution network. After going over the system thoroughly, Dan suggested they add two more people to their team: a couple by the name of Shelley and Roy Harrison.

The previous year, Dan had been assigned as Shelley's faculty advisor while she was working on her doctorate degree. Now graduated, she worked in the university's Physics Department teaching first year students. Her husband Roy, who Dan had met while mentoring Shelley, was an electrical engineer for a company that manufactured components for the Minuteman II missile defense system.

After listening to Dan talk about their credentials and letting him read Shelley's doctoral thesis on microwave communication technology, Hank agreed. A few days later Dan arranged a dinner at a local restaurant, where he introduced Hank to Shelley and Roy.

From the first moment he met them, Hank liked the attractive young couple. Both were in their early-thirties, with Shelley being the taller one (around five-feet ten-inches) with thick blonde hair that fell slightly over her shoulders. Roy stood just under Shelley's height, with brown hair cut high and tight over his ears and blocked in the back, military style. They looked to be in excellent shape, which confirmed what Dan had said about them both being long-distance runners.

Along with being courteous and respectful, they were also very quiet and reserved. At first, Hank believed that their lack of talking was a sign of standoffishness, but as the dinner progressed he realized that they were both introverts; quiet people who felt more comfortable listening than socializing. Hank knew from his Army leadership training that unless the subject was of real interest to them, introverts tended to stay to themselves and say very little.

Once everyone had finished eating, Hank reached into a small sack he'd brought along and produced one of the broken triodes from the device.

"So Dan tells me you are an outstanding electrician," he said, addressing Roy. "What can you tell me about this?"

He placed the part on the table, at which point the couple immediately opened up, confirming Hank's amateur personality diagnosis.

"Now there's a blast from the past," Roy said, "a vacuum tube triode."

"I haven't seen one of those since I was researching my doctoral thesis," Shelley added.

"Can you tell me what might've caused this triode to fail?"

Roy retrieved a pair of reading glasses from his shirt pocket to take a closer look

"It looks like there was an air bubble in the glass, see that dear?" He showed it to Shelley, and pointed to the spot.

Shelley took the triode from him, and after examining it, nodded.

Now very interested, Hank asked to see it.

"Right here," Shelley said, showing him the thin area.

"If I were to bet," Roy added, "I'd say it was in the glass when it was made. Probably a manufacturing flaw."

Hank reached back into the sack, produced another triode, and handed it to Shelley. After another short examination she handed it to Roy.

"Here it is again," she said.

"And this flaw caused it to overheat and explode?" Hank asked.

Roy examined the second triode for a moment before answering.

"Sure. Even the tiniest leak in the glass would mean no more vacuum. Without a vacuum, regular air leaks in, the mercury evaporates, and the filament will start to overheat."

371

"Eventually no more filament, no more electrons, and boom, no more triode," Shelley added.

Hank couldn't believe what he was hearing. Up until now, he'd thought he'd made a mistake in the wiring or had somehow misinterpreted the Firebird intelligence. Hearing Roy and Shelley's assessment, he knew the only mistake he'd made was not testing the triodes before installing them in the device.

"Forgive my ignorance on the subject," he said, "but what can you tell me about triodes? Are they still used today?"

"Not widely," Roy replied, taking his glasses off. "Transistors replaced them in the late 1970's when solid-state circuits came out."

"They only use them today in professional audio equipment," Shelley added.

"What do you mean by *professional audio equipment*?"

"Guitar amplifiers at concerts, or to mix different sounds together when a singer records an album."

Hank took a drink of water and looked over at Dan, who was smiling, and returned his attention to the couple.

"I don't know how much Dan has told you, but I am putting together a research team at the university and I'd like you both to join us."

"What kind of research?" Roy asked.

"It's based on physics, but I could use both of your expertise."

"Who's on your team?"

"Right now, just Dan and myself."

"Would we be paid?" Shelley asked. "And if so, how much?"

Hank smiled. "Of course you would. I would personally pay you for any time you put in, and at the hourly wage you are earning now. Oh, and this would be below the table, meaning that I would pay you in cash so we can avoid taxes."

"Isn't that illegal?"

"Not any more illegal than hiring a neighbor boy to mow your lawn and pay him in cash."

"How many hours a week?" Roy asked.

"You two can decide on that, but for starters I'd just like you to stop by our building and have a look."

"How come you're not paying me?" Dan asked.

Hank smiled. "You didn't ask."

After the four enjoyed a few laughs, he let Dan off the hook.

"I guess we'll have to negotiate your contract."

Throughout the rest of the spring and summer, Shelley and Roy assisted Hank and Dan in finishing the polished-steel room for the device. For the first few months, the quiet couple simply came in and did as they were told and didn't ask any questions. Then one Saturday morning, they noticed the large horseshoe-shaped piece of soft iron that was delivered the previous day, and asked Hank what (exactly) they were building, and what (if anything) did it have to do with physics research.

For the rest of the morning and into the late afternoon, Hank told Shelley and Roy his story, and when he was finished they wanted to help in any way they possibly could.

"You're already helping," Hank said, "from your analysis of the failed triode and what you've told me about the advancements that have been made in electrical technology, I believe we'll be able to get the device to work the way it was designed."

"Good," Shelley said, "because we plan to start a family soon, and if General Berger isn't stopped he could very well affect the lives of our children or grandchildren."

* * *

For the next twenty-four months, work proceeded on both the polished-steel room and on rebuilding the device. As far as the room was concerned, the team decided it needed to be more secure. On several occasions, members of the Physics Department, including the newly promoted Department Chair Ms. Carpenter, stopped by unannounced to thank "Mr. H." for his ongoing contribution. With each successive visit, it became harder and harder for them to explain what kind of research they were conducting. After a visit that barely placated Ms. Carpenter, the team decided to build a wall in front of the polished-steel room (sealing it off from the rest of the room) and mount the main structure further to the rear. Although this allowed less length of travel for the field accelerator, Hank calculated that it would still generate the needed power to initiate the activation sequence and deflect the main structure into the fourth dimension.

After constructing a reinforced wall to separate the room, they installed a steel door frame and state-of the-art security door like the ones used on bank vaults. This automatic door could only be opened from the outside with a key card and a coded number typed into a numeric pad. On the inside, it could be opened by using either an emergency button on the wall, or in the event of a power outage, manually by turning a large wheel on the door. As for the set of double doors exiting out of the rear of the room, they were locked, as were the emergency exits, which essentially made the room with the device inaccessible; the lone exception being the heavy-duty high-tech security door.

The team also decided that the front (unsecured) part of the room would remain open and be filled with work counters, microscopes and computers. That way, if anyone decided to drop in unannounced, the room would appear to be their research laboratory. From that day forward, the team referred to this unsecured area as the "Research Room." If people asked about the large security door and what was behind it, they planned to tell them that the large door was needed to protect expensive equipment as well as maintain a germ-free environment for their most-sensitive experiments.

Roy suggested they make the polished-steel room for the device a "safe room," which Hank learned was a fortified room that rich people were now installing in their homes. He also recommended they install cameras throughout the building, and place televisions both inside and outside the polished-steel room. That way, they could monitor the device from the outside or monitor the building from the inside. One of the polished-steel plates was then modified to make it easily removable with wing nuts, and a television was mounted on a shelf behind it. They also placed televisions in the research room, inside the slanted tops of each of the two work stations nearest the security door. Cameras were then mounted in the ceilings and synchronized with the channels on the televisions.

Along these same lines, Shelley recommended emergency buttons be placed in every room of the building, even the restrooms, which would immediately close the door to the polished-steel room and alert everyone in the building. She also suggested a small stainless-steel refrigerator be placed in the room with the device and stocked with food and water. Hank thought all of these ideas were excellent, especially after what had happened to J.R. and Valerie in the old Fort Meade warehouse.

While refurbishing the building, the tremors in Hank's left hand and arm became quite noticeable, as did a pronounced limp. On several occasions, Dan, Shelley and Roy asked him about it, but each time he explained it as being nothing more than a temporal side effect from traveling in the fourth dimension. On days when the tremors were most severe, he took measures to hide it from them by placing his left hand in his pants pocket, and choosing a project that involved the least amount of intricate work.

Completing the building modifications, the four immediately went to work on rebuilding the device, and as time passed they learned about each other and grew very close. Hank now regarded Dan, Shelley and Roy as members of his adopted family. Not only did they work on the device together, they ate most of their meals and socialized together; forging a strong bond of friendship.

THE DEVICE

During this time, Hank and Dan found out that the young couple had an exceptional talent: they were both fantastic chefs. They discovered this when Shelley and Roy invited them to their home for dinner. When the two men arrived, they were astounded to find that their favorite meals had been meticulously prepared. (Apparently, they'd overheard the two men mention their favorite places to eat, then used their culinary skills to prepare the meal as close as possible to how they liked it.) The evening was such a huge hit, the men looked upon Shelley and Roy's talents as unique gifts, rather than "just a hobby" as the couple described it.

Except for one occasion, the two men never asked the quiet couple to prepare these meals for them; Shelley and Roy always did so out of the kindness of their hearts. The one time they were asked occurred when Captain Hank requested it of them roughly nineteen years later, when he thought it would be a nice way to introduce himself to George and Madison d'Clare and recruit them for the mission.

* * *

It was now the first week of March 1995, and the rebuilt device was complete. Although the cylindrical shape of its main structure somewhat resembled a child's toy, its large size and shiny white exterior against the backdrop of the polished-steel walls gave it a clean and futuristic look; to the point of appearing ominous. Within the fuselage, eighty brand-new exciter-motors and their corresponding miniature electromagnets stood ready to energize the ferromagnetic metal, which would propel the main structure into the fourth dimension. Inside the cockpit under the seat sat Roy's new magnetic power distribution network; its state-of-the-art design and bank of integrated circuits hardly resembling the old one.

The front and side control panels, no longer equipped with only the minimum number of switches, now took on the appearance of a cockpit in a modern jet aircraft, complete with lighted control panels. On the front panel were several gauges showing the power distribution levels, with corresponding dials to control the current. Two digital chronometers were also installed, one which showed the time inside the cockpit, while the second displayed the time outside the polished-steel room. This was made possible by running a small wire down past the mounting points, across the floor and through the wall, then splicing it to a clock in the research room.

The side panel included the throttle, the main power switch and the all-important polarity-reversing switch. In addition, there was a set of new knobs and dials that controlled the field accelerator. These allowed the pilot to activate the device by himself, instead of having a second person standing by the circuit breaker panel; the job Big Ben used to do.

The right panel also contained a small receptacle to be used to plug in a communication headset. The wires from this receptacle ran out of the cockpit to the rear of the fuselage, and into a thin rectangular box whose other side was connected to a miniature aircraft antenna. A corresponding antenna, microphone and speaker were then installed in one of the slanted desks in the research room.

Perched majestically on the tracks above the main structure sat the shiny new field accelerator. The carriage wheels and tracks were perfectly aligned to prevent any binding while it traveled back and forth, and its eight high-powered electric motors and reverse-action cut-off switches (exhaustively tested) were now ready to achieve the near-supersonic rate of speed needed to attain the magnetic moment. Everything else, including more than enough uninterrupted flow of electricity to the field accelerator and the main structure, appeared to be ready.

The only thing left to do was for Hank to synchronize the power of the two main components, which he knew from the Firebird intelligence was simply a matter of calculating the gravitational waves of each, and plugging the results into a long mathematical formula. This formula would tell the team where to adjust the current levels in order to achieve the magnetic moment, stop the device in the future, hold the aperture open, and reverse the polarity to bring the pilot back to the present (taking into account the time-varying magnetic and gravitational fields).

Hank could tell by the way Dan, Shelley and Roy were acting, laughing all the time and giddy with excitement, that they knew the day was drawing near when they would activate the device. Unknown to his team, the impossible had happened: he couldn't remember the two critical synchronization formulas!

He hadn't felt well for the last few months, and things were happening to his body that he just couldn't explain away anymore. The strange tremors in his left hand and arm had spread to his leg, and on some days his left arm stopped swinging all together. His pronounced limp had also gotten worse, and upon paying close attention to the way he was walking, he could see that his left leg was moving at a slower pace than his right one.

In addition to the strange symptoms, forgetfulness and fatigue began to affect him. He would start working on one piece of the device in the morning, take a short lunch break, and return to find he had forgotten what he'd been doing. He would also become extremely tired in the afternoons, and could hardly function without an hour-long nap.

Attributing his physical problems to how hard he was pushing himself, he dismissed the strange symptoms and believed they would disappear when the device was complete. But when he shook uncontrollably as he made the announcement that he was delaying the testing stage, and later fell off a work stand, his three teammates sat him down and had a serious talk with him, insisting that he go have himself checked out by a doctor.

Finally deciding to heed their advice, Hank made an appointment with a general practitioner, who referred him to a neurological specialist at the university. After completing a battery of tests to check his motor-skills and cognitive abilities, the results showed why his body was acting so strangely, and gave him the reason for his recently-growing absentmindedness and fatigue.

"There's no easy way to put this, Mr. Stevens," the doctor said, "but it looks like you have early-onset Parkinson's disease. As for the forgetfulness, I'd like to run some more tests, but I suspect you're in the first stages of Lewy-body dementia."

Still thinking in terms of a war, Hank realized he was now in a battle on two fronts, and against a secondary opponent that was even more dangerous than General Berger. This other enemy had appeared slowly and without warning, and posed a greater threat to the mission than the burned-out triodes in the device. Although he couldn't see or hear this adversary, its shattering affects were no less demoralizing to his psyche and debilitating to his body than if he'd actually fallen in battle; mortally wounded and unable to go on.

Returning to building 3731 in a state of near-panic, Hank began writing down everything he could remember about the Nazi intelligence. But the formulas that were once so crystal clear in his mind were now unfocused, as if he were looking at them through a foggy windshield. Theories and mathematical problems of how the Firebird plan fit together (which were as easy as putting together a child's jigsaw puzzle) were now almost impossible to comprehend, and he was unable to place them in sequential order.

With Hank not answering any of his questions, Dan immediately called Shelley and Roy to come to the campus as soon as possible. Arriving at the building, they found Dan waiting for them inside the front door and Hank on the floor of the research room; his head buried in his hands and unresponsive. After more than twenty minutes, and only after Shelley coaxed him with her soothing voice, he was finally able to talk.

Tears of sadness came to Captain Hank's bright blue eyes when he told them about the devastating diagnosis, and how the doorway that had opened in his mind following the baseball accident those many years ago had started to close.

* * *

THE DEVICE

It took the team the rest of the afternoon and evening to finally get Hank into bed. It was now well past midnight, and after making sure he was asleep, Shelley crept out of his room and joined the others in the research room.

"There must be something we can do," she said. "The mission can't just end like this."

Dan shook his head. "What can we do? He knew the synchronization formulas, and without them we've just got a couple of cool-looking pieces of machinery in a polished-steel room."

"Dear, what do you think?" she asked, addressing Roy

"I don't know what to think. I'm now wondering whether…" His voice trailed off.

"Whether what?"

"Whether he's been telling us the truth, or if it's some delusion he's made up."

"How can you say that?"

"I know, I know, and yesterday I would've never said it. But think about it. He really hasn't provided us any proof."

Both Shelley and Dan started to reply, but Roy interrupted.

"Hear me out, okay? First, he gets hit in the head with a line drive while playing baseball and wakes up with a photographic memory. Now I'll grant you he is smart, but does that mean he has a photographic memory? Where's the proof? Then he joins the Army and goes on this mission and finds out about this device and that this Nazi, General Berger, got away. What does he do? He sets everything to memory and destroys the files, so we have no proof that any of this took place. Later, he gets out of the Army and builds the device at Fort Meade only to have it malfunction and leave him in our time period. What does he do? He goes back to Berlin and finds out that the Nazi is also in this time period, but before he can get back the Nazi kills his friend's son and wife and burns down the warehouse. So again, we have no proof that any of this happened."

Shelley started to talk, but Roy held up his hand and stopped her a second time.

"Then he comes here to Utah, and after we hear his story we agree to help him rebuild the device. And now, right at the time he needs to recall the critical formulas to get it to work, he finds out he's got Parkinson's disease with dementia and can't remember it."

Shelley stared at Roy for a few moments before finally replying.

"I still believe him. Nothing you say will ever make me change my mind."

"So do I," Dan said, "I know that the formulas he drew out for me when we first met were legitimate calculations on how to measure..." His voice trailed off and his eyes locked on Shelley and back to Roy.

"What's the matter?" Shelley asked.

"Those were the formulas," he replied, his voice rising. "One was how to measure gravitational waves around a stationary object, and the other was how the forces of magnetism could be manipulated to affect those waves!"

"Drew them out where?" Roy asked.

Dan jumped out of his chair.

"I'm saying that the keys to time travel are on five napkins, and hopefully in the last two years Captain Hank hasn't thrown them away!"

He ran out of the research room and down the central hallway with Shelley and Roy in hot pursuit behind him. As soon as Dan reached the door to Hank's room, he tore it open and flipped on the lights, instantly waking Hank.

"What is it? What's the matter?" he asked.

"Hank, where's your overnight bag?"

"My what?"

"Your overnight bag!"

"It's over there," Hank replied, pointing to a hook near the shower.

Seeing it, Dan jumped over the corner of the bed and grabbed it. Turning around, he brought it over and dumped its contents on the bed where Hank was still laying.

Not seeing the napkins in the spilled-out contents, Dan began searching the pockets. When he unzipped the last pocket and reached in, a big smile came to his face.

"What is it?" Hank asked.

When Dan pulled out the five napkins which contained the perfectly written formulas, all four team members started to cry, with Roy sobbing the hardest.

Two days later, with the power levels of the main structure and field accelerator synchronized, the team stood ready to activate the device.

* * *

"That's my final word on the subject," Hank said sternly, "and I sincerely hope you'll listen!"

"You can't be sure that's what caused it!" Dan said.

"As surely as I am standing here in front of you!"

Shelley and Roy walked in with the hot pizza box and sack of breadsticks, which interrupted the quarrel.

"What's going on?" Shelley asked. "We could hear you two all the way outside."

"He is not going to let any of us use the device," Dan said.

"I thought we were all going to get a chance to go into the future?"

"Yes," Hank replied, "I did say when the mission is over each of you will have a turn to use the device, but not now. Not after what's happened."

"He thinks the device caused his Parkinson's disease," Dan blurted out.

With everyone looking at him, Hank took a moment to gather his thoughts.

"When the device malfunctioned and I was catapulted into this time, I experienced an overwhelming headache with incredible dizziness and ringing in my ears. That's when the tremors started in my left finger, which have been getting worse and worse ever since. Before I ever used the device, I had no such symptoms. It is my belief that the device caused the Parkinson's, therefore we simply cannot take the chance of any of you getting the disease."

"Before we make any rash decisions, what do we know about Parkinson's?" Roy asked.

"Let's go look on the web," Shelley said, "maybe it will tell us what causes it."

When they reassembled in the research room, Dan booted up the computer and quickly typed the words "Causes of Parkinson's disease" into a search engine. Instantly, a page materialized containing a list of links on the subject; the first of more than ten thousand pages. Clicking on the first link brought up a lengthy article written by one of the lead neurologists at the Mayo Clinic, which both defined and described the condition. When it came to the causes of the disease, the doctor stated it was unknown, but researchers believed it was a combination of several different hereditary and environmental factors. Once the group finished reading the article, Dan closed the page and clicked on another link, which brought up another article that said essentially the same thing.

After everyone finished reading, Dan turned to Hank.

"See Hank? Even the best doctors in the country don't know what causes it."

"Did you read where it said the disease normally strikes people in their late-sixties or early-seventies? The fact that I am thirty-six years old proves that the device…"

"Oh no you're not. You told me yourself that you were born in 1920, which would make you seventy-five."

They all smiled, even Hank, which relieved some of the tension in the room.

"I don't think age even matters," Roy said. "The first article stated that the disease didn't discriminate and that it could strike anyone at any age."

"Do any of you understand what this disease could do to you?" Hank asked. "I've been looking on the web too, and the long-term effects of Parkinson's disease on a human being is not a pretty sight."

"Okay, for the sake of argument let's say the device caused your Parkinson's condition," Roy said. "Who's to say it wasn't from the device malfunctioning when the triodes blew apart? Maybe the sudden jump ahead in time and abrupt stop caused it. With the new power distribution network, we'll avoid that from happening."

"But the headaches and dizziness occurred *before* the device malfunctioned, when Big Ben and I were still testing it. I just don't think it's worth risking your health."

"We've all been risking our health ever since we agreed to help you build the device," Shelley said. "General Berger could be outside that door right now ready to kill us to get it."

Hank nodded. "That's true, he is a risk, but we don't have any control over him. *This* risk we do."

"All the choices we make in life are risky. If we choose to walk outside in a thunderstorm, we risk being struck by lightning. If we choose to stay inside during the storm, we risk the house getting struck by lightning, catching on fire, and killing us. My point is, we have a choice in the risks we take, so shouldn't this be *our* choice too?"

"I just don't want anything to happen to any of you. So please, just think about what I'm telling you."

That night, Captain Hank laid awake in bed worrying about his friends and what might happen to them if they used the device. He reached the conclusion that he was never going to change their minds, due to the simple fact that the lure of the device was too strong. From anyone's perspective, the chance of going into the future and returning to the present would be an opportunity of a lifetime; one they couldn't walk away from. He had to admit if the roles were reversed and he were given the choice, even with the risk of developing Parkinson's disease he would go.

Exhausted from lack of sleep, he rose out of bed the next morning and walked out into his small kitchen. After turning on his coffeemaker, he proceeded to the sink and filled a large glass with water. Picking up the pill holder and removing the top, he shook out two yellow tablets, popped them in his mouth and washed them down.

Twenty minutes later, sipping a hot cup of coffee, he could feel the medication go to work, temporarily calming the tremors in his left arm and leg. Setting the coffee cup down, he picked up the pill holder again and removed the top. It seemed like a miracle that these small yellow tablets actually worked, and for the most part magically made his Parkinson's symptoms disappear.

Suddenly, the enchanting similarities of the medication and the device hit him like a thunderbolt, and he realized the answer to his problem had been in front of him the entire time.

I can use the device to go into the future and bring back the cure for Parkinson's disease!

* * *

On Saturday, the team assembled in the research room. Captain Hank placed his key card in the reader and quickly punched in the numeric code. Almost immediately, the heavy security door unlocked and swung open revealing the device. Before going in, he turned to address them.

"I really can't thank you enough for assisting me with this project, but after careful consideration I've decided to temporarily change our mission objective."

Dan, Shelley and Roy immediately looked at each other.

"Before you get disheartened hear me out. I've always thought about the mission of finding and stopping General Berger in military terms. When I received the Parkinson's diagnosis, I thought about the disease in much the same manner. After we talked the other night, I realized that I needed to start thinking about what would happen if I were to become disabled. If that were to happen then one of you would have to take my place, and if one of you did take my place you would run the risk of getting the disease. Then it came to me. To defeat General Berger, we must first defeat the disease."

"How can we do that?" Dan asked. "From all we've read there is no known cure for Parkinson's disease."

"Today." Hank paused to let the idea sink in.

"Are you saying what I think you're saying?" Roy asked.

"The objective now is to go into the future and bring back the cure. That way, we will all be protected, and if something were to happen to me one of you could take my place."

"Is that even possible?" Shelley asked. "I mean, bringing something back that hasn't been invented yet?"

"As long as the majority of the atoms inside the main structure remain the same, I believe it is. Hopefully, after I bring it back I'll be able to regain my health. Once we're all protected, we'll be in a better position to go after our elusive Nazi general."

"So how do you intend to find it?"

"I'll follow the same plan I was going to use to find General Berger. I will test the device twice, and go forward in time a month and return, then six months and return. If all goes well, I will search in stages, starting with five years from now, ten, fifteen, and so on. If I arrive in the future and none of you are here, I'll immediately make my way to the library to check the medical news and see if they've found a cure for Parkinson's disease. If I don't make it back in three hours and fourteen minutes, then…"

"Then we'll know something happened," Dan interrupted, "and we wait it out, keep the door closed, and make sure the stationary plane stays clear."

Hank smiled. "One more thing. Call it a little bonus." He reached into his shirt pocket, retrieved three envelopes and handed one to each of them.

"You didn't need to do that," Shelley said.

"We can't take these," Roy added.

Dan shook his head, agreeing with the others.

"I insist," Hank said. "Besides, you may need it in the event something comes up we haven't planned for."

After a few minutes of debating the subject, Hank finally convinced them and the three begrudgingly accepted the envelopes.

"Oh, I almost forgot," Shelley said, "we have a surprise for you."

They moved past Hank to the front of the device, turned, and stood at attention.

"Drum roll please," Dan said.

Roy immediately pretended to play an imaginary snare drum, complete with his own brand of bad sound effects.

"Captain Hank, we hereby christen thee device, Four Freedom," Shelley proclaimed.

Dan pulled off a piece of cardboard covering the front of the device, revealing a freshly-painted white surface. In the center was a small American flag, over which was the number "4" and the word "Freedom."

"We think it represents us and what we stand for."

Hank beamed with pride. "It's the perfect name! Thank you all again from the bottom of my heart."

He embraced each of them, then walked over to the device and climbed in. Once he was settled in the cockpit, his team departed and closed the heavy security door. After securing the cockpit hatch, he placed the headset on and turned on the battery power to check communications.

"Dan, are you with me?" he asked.

"I'm here," Dan replied, "and you're clear to initiate the activation sequence."

Smiling about the way Dan sounded like an air traffic controller, Hank turned the main power switch on and the panel lights immediately illuminated the cockpit. A few moments later, the exciter-motors began powering-up, their low, distinct hum growing ever louder. Once the power level of the exciter-motors reached one-hundred percent, Hank radioed Dan.

"I'm at full power. Starting the accelerator."

"You're a go on the accelerator," Dan replied.

Hank activated the switch, and the huge electromagnet came to life above him and began to roll. When the carriage reached the end of the rails, it immediately bounced back in the opposite direction and started the process all over again. Less than a minute later, the accelerator reached the point where it was almost a blur, and the power of the generated field reached the magnetic moment.

"Ready for deflection!"

"Go for it!" Dan shouted.

Hank took a moment to check the gauges again and flipped the polarity-reversing switch. Much like before, when he'd activated the device with Big Ben, the gravity pressed him against the seat and his ears popped. From the new on-board chronometers, he could see the time inside the device was passing normally, while the time outside the device counted at a much faster rate. He eased the throttle forward until the outside date and time neared one month later, and slowed the exciter-motors down just enough to bring the main structure back into real time.

"Dan, are you with me?"

"It's about time you got back," Dan said, "What'd you do? Go on a vacation?"

Hank smiled. "Okay, I'll go back now and see if this thing works as advertised."

"Roger that."

Hank flipped the polarity-reversing switch again and the device hummed to life taking him back into the aperture, until finally coming out the previous month a minute after he'd originally departed.

After concluding that the first test was successful, Hank repeated the test, this time going forward in time six months before returning. Satisfied that the device was operating perfectly, he radioed to Dan that he was ready to start the search.

"Okay, but be careful." Dan said, sounding serious. "All you need to do is find the cure and bring it back."

"I understand."

"If you come across General Berger, don't confront him. Just come back and together we'll figure out what to do."

"Got it."

"And remember, you've only got three hours and fourteen minutes."

"Yes, mom."

"Okay, okay, I just want you to be careful."

"I understand, and thank you. Four Freedom's next stop, the year two-thousand."

Hank initiated the activation sequence, and a few moments later he disappeared again into the fourth dimension.

Even though they'd taken every precaution to make the polished-steel room safe, neither Captain Hank nor his team could've foreseen the unbelievable event that was destined to occur four years later.

It happened on August the eleventh of 1999, a few minutes before one o'clock in the afternoon, when a category F-2 tornado touched down in the heart of Salt Lake City.

* * *

Captain Hank knew immediately that something had gone wrong with the device – the dizziness and headache he was experiencing seemed even more intense than the last time the device had malfunctioned, as was the ringing in his ears. Warm fluid dripped off his earlobes and rolled down both of his cheeks, and wiping one of them away he discovered it was blood. From his stint in the Army, he'd seen soldiers bleeding this way; their eardrums had been ruptured from being too close to an explosion.

All he could do was sit on the floor of the polished-steel room, holding his head in his hands and wait for the pain to subside. When he'd first felt the harsh side effects of the device in the warehouse at Fort Meade, he could sit still and motionless, but this time his left arm and leg were shaking uncontrollably, as if he'd missed taking a week's worth of Parkinson's medication.

One thought he did manage to pull out of this sea of agony was the approximate date he came out of the fourth dimension, which he'd noticed on the chronometer just before it died: August of 1999.

A half-hour later, the intense headache finally abated and he was able to open his eyes and focus on his surroundings. The two dimly-lit lights over the emergency exits provided some illumination, but it was still difficult to see because of the smoke emanating from the cockpit. He struggled up to his hands and knees, then crawled over to the access panel and quickly removed the wing nuts. After setting the panel aside, he picked up the remote control but it wouldn't turn on the set, whereupon he realized that the power to the building was out.

Crawling over to the small fridge, he retrieved a bottle of water and washed down a dose of medication. Thirty minutes later, when he was finally able to stand, he returned to the device to investigate the malfunction. Obtaining the screwdriver kit and flashlight from the front console, he removed the seat and cover over the power distribution network and shined the light in. When he saw the mass of burned out circuits and still-smoldering wires, he instantly felt a sense of déjà vu. Whatever had happened, it had destroyed the entire network and fused the wires in the fuselage, which meant that the eighty exciter-motors and their corresponding electromagnets were probably burned-out too.

He sat back down on the steel floor and started asking himself questions, wondering if his faltering memory had forgotten something. He concluded that couldn't be the case, because after telling his team about the Parkinson's diagnosis, he'd insisted they check his work behind him. Even if he'd crossed a wire, it wouldn't have caused this much damage. Therefore, something else must have caused the device to malfunction.

He remembered the two atomic bombs the Allies had dropped on Japan, and began to wonder whether General Berger was responsible. If Berger had gotten his device to work, and subsequently obtained a bomb and used it against the United States, the explosion would've disrupted the forces of magnetism and gravity. This might explain why the device had malfunctioned again and why the power was out in the building.

As he began to play out more scenarios in his mind, the building lights suddenly came back on, and a few moments later the heavy security door unlocked and slowly swung open. Shelley, Roy and Dan immediately came rushing in.

Shelley reached him first. "Are you okay?" she asked. "Your ears are bleeding."

"I'm okay but I can't hear you very well."

"We knew something had happened when you didn't make it back within the three-hour fourteen-minute time limit, and now we know what it was," Dan said.

"What was it?"

"You're not going to believe it," Shelley said.

Rising to his feet, Hank suddenly felt dizzy again and he fainted. As Shelley faded from his sight, Hank wondered if he'd actually seen his team or if he'd been dreaming. He concluded that he must've been dreaming because of what Shelley had told him.

Everybody knows tornados don't happen in Utah.

* * *

THE DEVICE

Two days later, after determining the cause of the failure was from the forces of gravity and magnetism being disturbed by the freakish tornado, the team decided to rebuild the device. Shelley and Roy went back into their routine of coming to the building on Wednesdays and Saturdays, while Dan showed up every morning to help Hank before going to teach. While recuperating from the effects of the device, Hank went to work on procuring another eighty exciter-motors and manufacturing other parts that were needed.

This routine lasted over five months, and during this time the four conducted a more detailed examination of the entire electrical system of the main structure. Roy found many places where they could install safeguards, including a bank of small circuit breakers in the power distribution network. After completing the modifications, the device's rebuilt electrical system now had every conceivable protection against an inadvertent overload, and a battery back-up in the event of a power disruption. If the magnetic and gravitational forces were disturbed again while the device was in the fourth dimension, it wouldn't prevent the reentry into real time, but it would alleviate the sudden stop.

Shelley, conducting research on her own, concluded that the harsh side effects Hank had experienced were caused by sonic waves at the interdimensional plane, when the device entered and exited the aperture; much like a supersonic jet creates a sonic boom when it passes the speed of sound. Although normal hearing couldn't detect these waves (due to their oscillation at such a high frequency) they were heard by Captain Hank, whose ruptured eardrums were classic symptoms of being exposed to a loud and sudden noise.

Captain Hank agreed with her conclusion, except for one major point: he believed these sonic waves affected the "substantia nigra" part of his brain which develops dopamine, and had caused him to develop Parkinson's disease. Shelley didn't agree with his hypothesis, arguing that it was mostly conjecture on his part.

To protect the pilot from the sound waves, the team designed and constructed a special headset, like the ones used by crew chiefs on the flight line, which would still allow communications through the ear pieces. Although Hank believed this new headset would prevent many of the sound-related symptoms he encountered, he still believed it wouldn't work in masking the ultra hi-frequency waves that affected his brain and caused him to develop the disease.

As for Captain Hank's health, his eardrums healed and his hearing returned to roughly eighty-five percent of what it was before he'd piloted the device. His neurologist also gave him new medicine and dosage instructions, which miraculously alleviated his Parkinson's symptoms to the point that some days it was impossible to tell he even had the disease. He hadn't felt this good in a long time, and with the team sticking together to rebuild the device again, it made him feel even better.

On Monday morning, January the thirty-first of 2000, 4 Freedom was once again ready to travel into the fourth dimension. With the device operational and the building's lease contract renegotiated until the year 2020, the team assembled at nine o'clock in the morning to talk about the mission. At the meeting, Captain Hank agreed with the others that in his present condition he shouldn't make any more trips into the fourth dimension. Dan would take over as the pilot, with Roy as his alternate. Since Shelley was pregnant with their first child, the couple agreed he was the best choice.

As far as the mission objective was concerned, the plan hadn't changed: Dan was to travel into the future and obtain the cure for Parkinson's disease, and return within the three-hour fourteen-minute time limit. As soon as he made it back, they would administer the cure to everyone and begin the search for General Berger. When the mission was complete, everyone would have the opportunity to use the device once before they dismantled it.

At twenty minutes past nine o'clock, Dan climbed into 4 Freedom's cockpit and secured the hatch. Ten minutes later, with the team watching on the televisions from the research room outside, the device activated and the main structure successfully deflected into the fourth dimension. Approximately one minute later, Dan returned and radioed to Captain Hank that he'd gone into the future one month. With the first test successful he repeated the sequence, this time going six months into the future. After returning a second time, Hank gave him the go-ahead to begin the search for the cure. A few moments later, 4 Freedom vanished again from the polished-steel room.

Three hours and thirteen minutes later, Captain Hank, Shelley and Roy watched helplessly as the final minute ticked by, signaling to them that something had gone wrong. Much like the time when Hank had gone into the future and hadn't returned, Shelley and Roy silently exited the building and went home. Hank, realizing Dan wasn't coming back, sat in shocked silence staring at the television, hoping the main structure of the device would magically reappear.

* * *

To Captain Hank, being the one left behind was an entirely new experience, and he silently prayed for Dan's safe arrival wherever he was in the future. As he began a vigil at building 3731, waiting for Dan to return, he began to write his diary of what had transpired after he'd separated from the Army and began his decades-long mission to find General Berger. He also used the time to study the book he'd found in Tucson, which contained the early concepts of Albert Einstein – specifically with regards to sending a massless particle into the past.

To reacquaint himself with the Washington twins, he took several trips back to Baltimore to visit them. At the first meeting, which occurred on the eve of their eighteenth birthday, Hank told them the story and the truth of who'd killed their parents in the Fort Meade warehouse. Once he was finished, Ethan and Evelynn begged to join him on the mission, and he promised to send for them as soon as Dan returned from the fourth dimension.

The wait for Dan to reenter real time, however, would end up being a long one.

Chapter Seventeen
The Building

Fourteen Years, Seven Months and Fourteen Days Later
Saturday, 13 September 2014, 15:00hrs
Inside the *Country Boy's Store, Harrisville, Utah*

The large billboard sign next to Interstate 15 north of Ogden reads, "Five Acres of Adventure," and for any motorist who takes the bait and stops in at the massive retail store would find that slogan to be an apt description. Geared towards outdoorsmen, the business sells goods ranging from fishing and hunting equipment to vintage war-surplus items. On the second Saturday of every month, the store hosts a gun auction that attracts more than the usual number of customers, who are there to either purchase a cheap firearm or sell off one from their collection. It was here, amid this cauldron of western-clad bargain hunters, where Madison and I found ourselves this hot afternoon and where our adventure would continue.

We were in the store for only a couple of minutes when the auctioneer's gavel struck the podium, signaling the end of the final sale of the day. Almost immediately, the horde of hunters and firearm enthusiasts started making their way towards the exits. Unfortunately, Madison and I were now swimming upstream in a sea of humanity, and were stuck (ironically enough) in an aisle where fishing waders were on display.

As soon as the crowd thinned and the aisle somewhat cleared, we proceeded to the northeast corner of the building and weaved our way through a multitude of saddles until we'd reached our rendezvous point.

A few moments later one of the doors leading into a back room swung open.

"Come on back," Ethan whispered.

Proceeding through the door, we made our way through a maze of dusty boxes and storage racks until we reached another doorway leading out of the back of the building. Once outside, we hurriedly climbed into a car that Evelynn was driving.

Checking my watch, I noticed the total time it had taken Madison and I to enter the building and exit out the back had been less than four minutes – not too bad for a couple of amateurs. I thought back to the circumstances that had brought us here and led us to trying this James Bond-type maneuver.

~ Then ~

It took almost two hours for me to read the remaining pages of Captain Hank's diary, due to me being interrupted with a multitude of questions from Deputy Alvarez, Deputy Rivers and Albert Greenbaum. The questions posed to Ethan and Evelynn Washington (and to Madison and me) were both thorough and comprehensive, as the three investigators tried to piece together the chain of events and determine the validity of the story in Hank's diary. We also brought the twins up to date on the deaths of Shelley and Roy Harrison, our friend Gary, and how their deaths matched the killing method of General Berger.

When I reached the part in the diary where Captain Hank was waiting for Dan to return from the fourth dimension, the journal abruptly ended.

"Is that it?" Deputy Rivers asked.

I nodded. "That was the last entry, dated March the second of this year."

"That may be the last page of the diary," Evelynn said, "but it's not the end of the story."

Alvarez motioned for her to continue.

"Captain Hank was always writing things down in a little gray notebook. When he filled one up he'd get another one and start writing in it. I asked him once what he was writing about, and he told me his Parkinson's and dementia had caused him to forget many things, but sometimes he'd get flashes of insight and could remember. Since these times were only temporary, he carried around the notebook and wrote them down. Later, he'd try to piece them together and transcribe it to his diary."

"He did have a gray notebook on him when he was killed," Alvarez said. "I remember it was listed in the coroner's report as being empty."

"I'll bet there's a full notebook out there somewhere," Ethan said, "and when you find it you'll find the rest of the story."

"Just so I get this straight, when did Mr. Stevens, or I mean Captain Hank first come to see you and tell you about all of this?" Rivers asked.

"It was the day before our eighteenth birthday. December the thirty-first of 2000."

"I'll never forget it," Evelynn added. "We were at a Baltimore Ravens football game standing in line at the concession stand. I thought he looked familiar, but it'd been over nine years since I'd seen him and I didn't recognize him right away."

"I did," Ethan said, "but before I could say anything he passed me a note and disappeared into the crowd."

"What did the note say?"

"Something like, if you want to know who killed your parents meet me at the main entrance after the third quarter."

"I take it you both went?" Alvarez asked.

Ethan nodded. "He took us to a restaurant on the far side of town and told us the story."

"Did you think he was telling you the truth?"

"At first, we weren't sure what to think," Evelynn said, "but eventually we came to believe him."

"Why's that?"

"More than anything, it was the *way* he talked about our grandfather and parents. It's hard to explain, but we both felt he truly loved them as if they were his own family."

"How many times did you see him after that?"

"Three times," Ethan said, "and each time he'd hand one of us a note and we'd meet him later."

"He feared that if General Berger found out about us we'd be in danger, so he kept the meetings as clandestine as possible," Evelynn added.

"He was a very wise man," Albert said.

"Did he tell you about all of this at these meetings?" Rivers asked, motioning to the diary.

"Yes, but in much more detail," Evelynn said. "At the first meeting when he finished telling us his story, we wanted to help him with the mission, as he called it, but he wouldn't let us. He said it was too dangerous and that he wouldn't be able to live with himself if something happened to us."

"We finally reached a compromise," Ethan said. "We agreed to finish college and he agreed to send for us when Professor Lee reentered real time."

"I take it then that you did finish?" Alvarez asked.

He nodded. "Both Evelynn and I earned Bachelor's degrees in computer science."

"What do you do now?"

"We own a business, E and E Security Solutions, which is something else Captain Hank helped us with, in a roundabout way."

"How so?"

"He advised us to earn computer degrees."

"He thought it would help later when we joined him on the mission," Evelynn added.

"Did he tell you anything else at these meetings?" Alvarez asked.

"At the second meeting, he told us he'd hired a private detective firm to conduct an independent investigation of our parents' murders," Ethan said.

"Did he tell you if these detectives found anything?"

"Yes. Through their overseas contacts they identified the print that the arson investigator found at the crime scene belonged to the Irish mobster, Thomas O'Malley."

"And that they'd traced him to the United States," Evelynn said.

"Did he say where?"

"Somewhere in Nevada."

"Did he tell you anything else?"

"Mostly he'd just give us a quick update, and tell us he was still waiting for Professor Lee to come back," Ethan said. "Then at the last meeting, he told us the professor had come back, but that he'd almost died from a brain aneurysm."

"We both volunteered to use the device and find the Parkinson's cure for him, but Captain Hank wouldn't hear of it," Evelynn said. "He was adamant that the device had caused him to get the disease, and he would never forgive himself if one of us developed it or if something were to happen to us."

Alvarez nodded. "So with Hank stricken with the disease and unable to pilot the device, and him rejecting you two and the Harrisons as possible replacements, I see now where this led him." He looked over at Madison and me.

"Tell them what you said to him," Evelynn said, prodding Ethan.

"I told Captain Hank that it was too bad we didn't know someone who already had the disease but was still in the early onset stage, then they could pilot the device and we wouldn't have to worry about it."

I immediately realized how Captain Hank had come to involve Madison and me in his plan.

"When was that meeting?" Alvarez asked.

"In April. That was the last time we saw him."

"Did he contact you again?"

"Twice by texts. The first time was in May, when he told us that he'd found Mr. d'Clare and that he thought he was the perfect person to pilot the device."

"We didn't even know he was in Utah until he texted us the other night," Evelynn added.

"Do you still have those texts?" Alvarez asked.

"Yes, but the deputy outside took our phones."

A few moments later Alvarez returned their phones, and Ethan, unlocking his, brought up his text messages and handed the phone back to Alvarez.

After he'd finished reading them he handed it to Rivers, who read the messages aloud.

"Ethan, Evelynn, I've found someone to pilot the device. His name is George d'Clare, and I believe he fits our profile. Talk to you soon. Capt. H."

She paused for a moment and read the second one.

"Ethan, Evelynn, my failing memory has caused a security breach. Our enemy is close. I will need your help as soon as possible. Please catch the next flight to Salt Lake City and bring any electronic surveillance gear you have that detects bugs. Text me with your flight information and I'll meet you at the airport. Capt. H."

Evelynn began to cry again, at which point Ethan placed his hand on hers.

"This is the most fantastic thing I've ever heard," Rivers said. "What do you think, Bob? Is it possible?"

"Honestly? I don't know," Alvarez replied. "If you'd told me this story a week ago, I would've said you were crazy. Now I'm not so sure. Everything in the diary explains what's going on, from the man in the morgue with the forged birth certificate to the man who appears to be General Berger in the photographs Martineau took yesterday."

"I agree, but…"

"What photographs?" Evelynn asked, interrupting Rivers.

Alvarez quickly retrieved the pictures from the kitchen, then brought them in and laid them on the coffee table. The twins immediately converged to examine them.

"This proves Captain Hank was telling us the truth, and that Berger is alive in our time." Ethan said.

"You've got to do something!" Evelynn said, almost shouting. "That's the man who killed our parents!"

"Not to mention the hundreds of innocent inmates in the camps," Albert added.

"What *can* we do, Bob?" Rivers asked. "I mean, who'd believe all of this?"

"Good question," Alvarez replied. "After all, we can't just put out an all-points bulletin to be on the lookout for a hundred-year-old Nazi war criminal who just arrived in a time machine."

"May I say something?" Albert asked.

"Sure, we're all in this together. I'd welcome ideas from anybody."

"In my research of General Berger, I can tell you he was very smart at planning an operation. Did you know he assisted Heinrich Himmler in designing and building the system of concentration camps in Eastern Europe? That operation alone killed millions of people. As a scientist, he was extremely brilliant. He oversaw the development of Zyklon-B hydrogen cyanide that was used in the gas chambers. So you see, we are dealing with a very shrewd individual who places absolutely no value on the sanctity of human life. If the German scientists at Oranienburg perverted the discoveries of Einstein and the other great physicists of that time to create a device that could breach the fourth dimension, such a device in the hands of General Berger would be catastrophic.

"I agree with Deputy Alvarez that as implausible as the story seems to be, it appears to be true. But let's examine this entire affair a little more closely. Assuming the diary is a true account of everything that happened to Captain Hank, then we know General Berger intends to rebuild the device and continue the Firebird plan. We can therefore assume that in the years since Hank discovered Berger escaped the Ünterbunker alive, he's built a new Firebird device."

"But he needs to recover the intelligence to get the device to work right," Alvarez added.

"Precisely, and if I were to guess I'd say it has something to do with the formulas that were necessary to synchronize the power system of the device's two main components, the main structure and the field accelerator."

"Hank did say in the diary that those formulas were long, complicated and critical to making the device work the way it was designed," I said.

"Which explains why Berger and his gang were after him," Alvarez said, "but what Berger didn't know was that Hank set it all to memory and destroyed the intelligence."

"So why kill him?" Evelynn asked.

"He must've found out about Hank's affliction and that he'd written it all down in the diary," Albert said. "If he possessed the diary, Hank would've been expendable."

"And the only person in this time who could identify him," Ethan added.

"That's true, but don't you think he would've made sure he'd recovered the diary *and* made sure his device worked *before* killing Hank?" Rivers asked.

"Perhaps something went wrong with his plan," Albert speculated. "In any event, Berger found out Hank was in Utah." He thought for a moment and addressed Deputy Alvarez. "When was Mr. Tomkins found?"

"Wednesday morning, September the third."

Albert looked over at Madison and me.

"Would you say your friend was computer-savvy?"

"Definitely," Madison replied. "When I showed him the equation from the diary he spent over an hour and a half at my desk searching for it on my computer."

"*That's* how Berger and his gang found out Captain Hank was in Utah."

Alvarez's eyes grew wide. "Dennison, she's a computer expert."

Albert smiled. "Exactly, and if I were to guess I'd say she found a way to track the internet searches."

"Probably by inserting a tracking cookie into some of the more popular search engines," Evelynn said.

"A what?" I asked.

"Tracking cookies are small programs that can be used to follow someone's internet search history. Online businesses use them all the time to track people's browsing habits and then bombard their computers with shopping ads for things they might be interested in."

"All she would've had to do is track the searches of key words," Ethan added.

"Such as Einstein's Field Equations?" Madison asked.

"Right."

"But wouldn't hundreds of college students who are taking physics courses search for that?" Rivers asked. "I mean, how did they identify him out of all those searches?"

"Duration and location." Evelynn said.

"Could you explain that?"

"She could've set up a cookie to alert her when someone searched for those words for a very long time, or conducted multiple searches for the same information and looked to see where the searches had originated from. And since it is still very early in the fall semester of most colleges right now, there probably wouldn't be as many searches for Einstein's equations as other times, say before mid-terms or finals."

Ethan nodded. "If I were doing it, that's what I'd do."

"When Gary used your computer for an hour and a half," Evelynn continued, addressing Madison, "he must've alerted Dennison, who found the long search had originated in Utah."

"He had to have gotten his hands on a copy of Hank's records to track him to Fort Meade, so he knew he was from Utah." Alvarez said.

"He might've even had Dennison set up the cookie to alert her to *all* searches originating in Utah," Ethan said. "Then later, when your friend was home and figured out the equation, Dennison must've got a second alert of another long search originating in Utah."

"We can therefore assume at this point, General Berger moved in on your friend, but before murdering him obtained your name," Albert said, addressing Madison and me.

"Then he must've ordered his people to watch you two and planted the bugs in your house," Alvarez added.

"Poor Gary," Madison said sorrowfully, "and to think I was the one who talked George into contacting him to see what the equation meant."

I placed my hand on hers. "You can't blame yourself for that, sweetheart. Besides, at the time we were just seeing if Captain Hank's story about the device was true. We had no idea all of this was going on behind the scenes."

"Still, if I'd only believed Hank to begin with…" Her voice trailed off.

"Your husband is right, Mrs. d'Clare," Albert said solemnly, "the person solely responsible for the death of your friend is General Berger."

Everyone sat without saying a word, until Albert finally ended the long silence.

"Deputy Alvarez, you mentioned that Shelley and Roy Harrison were also murdered in the same fashion. When was that, exactly?"

"Detectives found them on Monday, but they were killed much earlier than that." He thumbed his notebook until he found the page. "The coroner put their time of death sometime late Saturday afternoon or early evening."

"We received a text from Hank early Saturday afternoon," I said.

I quickly retrieved my phone and read it out loud.

"Dear George and Madison, I would very much like to talk to you both as soon as possible. This is extremely urgent! Let me know what day/time will work best for you. Very respectfully yours, Jim Stevens."

"He must've learned of your friend Gary's death and wanted to warn you about General Berger," Albert said, "but then that presents the problem of how Hank came to know Berger killed him, and why he waited so long to warn you."

"I think I might know part of the answer," Ethan said. "This is just a guess, but he might've found out from his police scanner."

"If I remember right, the Davis County boys found one in his truck at Station Park," Alvarez said. "He must've heard Wilson talking about the suicide on the radio."

Rivers nodded. "Deputy Wilson is new and was the first responder to Mr. Tomkins' home," she explained. "He's an excitable young man to say the least, and everyone in the office has had to caution him about what he says on the radio."

"Which brings us to why Captain Hank waited so long to send George and Madison the texts," Albert said. "I mean, if he heard the deputy on the scanner on Wednesday, why did he wait until Saturday to try and warn you two?"

"Maybe he heard about the suicide on the scanner but wasn't sure if Berger was involved," Madison speculated.

Albert turned and addressed Deputy Alvarez.

"When do you normally release autopsy information to the public?"

"As soon as the findings are official, usually the next day."

"Do you post them online?"

"Yes, but you have to have an account to our secure site to see them." Alvarez's eyes grew wide again, and he quickly thumbed through his notebook. "Which in this case, was Saturday, September sixth."

Albert smiled. "We can assume then, with quite a bit of certainty, that Captain Hank did have an account to your secure site and checked the autopsy results of Mr. Tomkins on Saturday. When he learned of his injuries, he immediately sent George and Madison the text."

"Did you reply to him?" Albert asked, addressing me.

"Yes. I told him we were going to a late movie at Station Park, and that we'd meet him Sunday at noon at his home in Mountain Green." I read the text aloud.

"So now, if I may speculate further, Captain Hank knows that General Berger has murdered this man, but since he agreed to meet you at his home in Mountain Green the next day, he must've felt he was still somewhat safe."

"Which means that sometime on Saturday, Hank went to Mountain Green and found the Harrison's dead," Rivers said.

"Or maybe he found General Berger and his men there," Alvarez added.

"Whichever the case," Madison said, "he then went to Station Park and waited for us to come out of the movie."

"We can also assume," Albert continued, "that when General Berger murdered the Harrisons he learned about Captain Hank's affliction and that he'd written everything down in the diary."

Alvarez nodded. "It makes sense, but it now brings us back to the question as to why he killed Hank before recovering the diary."

"I guess we won't know that until we have him behind bars." Evelynn said.

"Agreed," Albert said, "which brings us now to George and Madison's incarceration."

He looked over at us.

"Since your house was bugged, they must've overheard you say you were going to go to Hank's home in Mountain Green."

"And followed us up there knowing we would find the bodies of the Harrisons," I said.

"And what better way to scare people into talking," Rivers added, "than to arrest them for murders they didn't commit?"

"What bothers me," Alvarez said, "is how they fooled almost all our night staff into believing they were FBI agents, present company excluded."

Rivers smiled at him.

"You're forgetting that identity fraud is one of the many talents of Ms. Dennison." Albert said. "I'd say she used that talent to forge FBI identifications for Berger and all his people."

"He's good Bob," Rivers said.

"I agree," Alvarez replied. "I'm glad he's on our team."

Albert smiled. "Up until now, we've been assuming Captain Hank's diary is a true account of everything that happened to him. I take it then, we agree that it is."

"Of course it's a true account!" Evelynn said, almost shouting.

"Captain Hank wouldn't lie to us," Ethan added, calmly but firmly.

Alvarez concurred next. "I agree. The story in the diary explains the bodies we have in the morgue and the photos that were taken yesterday."

Rivers nodded. "I never thought I'd say this, but I agree too."

I looked at Madison and received a nod from her to answer for us both.

"We agree," I said. "What other explanation could there be for the attacks on us?"

"As implausible as the story sounds, I agree," Albert said. "Which now brings us to the problem at hand, which happens to be the same problem Captain Hank had. Where do we find General Berger?"

"We know he's bent on getting his hands on the diary so he can continue the Firebird plan," Alvarez said.

Albert nodded. "Which presents us with another problem. How do we find him and stop him, *and* keep people from finding out about the time-traveling device? Because in my opinion, this device is as dangerous as the atomic bomb."

After Albert's comment, everyone stopped talking. The only sound was the continuing click of the second hand of our wall clock, which was an appropriate sound effect for our dilemma.

"We have something he wants," Albert said, finally breaking the extended pause. "So maybe we need to look at this from a different angle."

"What do you mean?" Madison asked.

"How does a rancher stop a wild bear from killing his livestock?"

He looked around at each of us.

"He sets a trap and attracts him with bait." Alvarez said.

Albert smiled. "Exactly, and with the diary as bait we shall set a trap for the White Wolf of Sachsenhausen."

The plan Albert and the two deputies devised was simple. Madison and I would go out to the Country Boy's Store on Saturday afternoon, making sure we were being followed. I would be carrying my old college book bag containing a three-ring binder that resembled the diary. Once we were in the building, we would proceed to the back of the store on the northeast side and meet Ethan and Evelynn. Deputy Alvarez, whose brother was a manager at the store, would make sure the door alarms on the back of the building were turned off. Once outside, the four of us would proceed down to building 3731 at the University of Utah – all the while making sure we were still being followed. Albert and the two deputies would be waiting inside the building to spring the trap when Berger and his gang arrived behind us.

* * *

Later that night, I couldn't sleep. I kept thinking about Captain Hank, and how the earth-shattering secret he'd discovered in the Ünterbunker had cost the lives of people in his time and ours. As for the diary, I wondered what would happen to it once General Berger and his gang were under arrest. The government would surely want to see it, study it and learn the secret of time travel. Captain Hank believed the Firebird intelligence was so dangerous it could destroy the world; he'd even risked his career to keep it from the Army.

Trying not to wake Madison, I crept downstairs and retrieved the diary from under the dishwasher. After proceeding to our den, I removed the pages that contained the equations, refilled the binder with blank typing paper, and placed it back in its hiding place. Returning to the den, I closed the door and turned on the paper shredder. Five minutes later, the time travel formulas were gone.

Back in our bedroom, feeling satisfied I'd done the right thing, I laid back in bed and quickly fell asleep.

~ Now ~

THE DEVICE

As Madison and I sat in the back seat of the twins' rental car, I hoped that the first phase of our plan had worked and that General Berger and his gang were following us.

I looked over to see if Madison was okay and she was grinning at me. I could tell from the false way she was smiling, however, that she was still in a great deal of pain. When I asked her to stay home and give her shoulder a chance to rest, she wouldn't hear of it; she wanted to see the device.

It took Evelynn only thirty minutes to cover the distance between Harrisville and Salt Lake City, and to weave her way up First South Street to the University of Utah. When we reached the white building numbered 3731, the black SUV stopped a short distance away and pulled off to the side of the road.

Although the building was old, the cinderblocks and eves had been painted recently. There were also new aluminum shingles on the roof, along with new rain gutters and downspouts, and the small signs on the corners of the building containing the numbers "3731" looked as if they'd been stenciled on that morning. I could tell from the clean outward appearance that Captain Hank had worked hard preserving the building; most likely to keep it off the university's demolition list.

I quickly retrieved my book bag and followed Madison and the twins through the main doors on the southwest side. The interior of the I-shaped building was as spotlessly clean as the outside. The white wall on our left looked as if it had just been painted, and the tan carpet running the length of the long hallway still had a newly-installed smell to it. The windows in the entrance doors, as well as the floor-length ones in-between, looked as if they had been professionally cleaned; not a streak or smudge could be seen, even with the late afternoon sun shining in.

To our right, the inner wall of the hallway was alive with an abundance of poster-sized calendars advertising the university's sporting events. Also along this wall, every ten feet or so, was a hinged box made of clear plastic. The boxes covered red buttons,

412

which I took to be the building's alarm system Captain Hank had described in his diary.

When we reached the first set of interior doors on the right-hand side, which were propped open, we found Hank's workshop. The walls were peg board, and on the left side a variety of sheet metal tools were hanging on hooks. On the right side sat an industrial-sized lathe, a metal bender and a drill press. Between each of the machines were toolboxes sitting atop heavy-duty roll-away carts. In the center of the floor, six work tables had been pushed together and ran lengthwise through the room. Several more plastic boxes, covering over red alarm buttons, were also evident throughout the shop, strategically placed between the tools and the machines.

Except for one of the tables, everything in the shop seemed to be in perfect order. On the one that was different, there was a small toolbox with its top open and three of its drawers pulled out. A few electrical tools sat on the table next to the toolbox, which I recognized from my days working as an aircraft electrician. These tools included wire strippers, a set of crimpers, a voltage meter, a small set of diagonal plyers and a couple of stubby screwdrivers. There were also several lengths of spare wire and terminal connectors scattered about. It appeared as if someone had just been working at the table and had momentarily stepped out.

"This is where Captain Hank rebuilt the device," Evelynn whispered

The eerie quietness of the building suddenly gave me the feeling that something had gone wrong with our plan, and I walked back out into the hallway.

"Deputies? Albert?" I yelled.

No answer.

I rushed back to the doors where we'd entered the building and glanced up the street at the black SUV.

"Is it still there?" Madison asked.

"Yes, but I don't like the deputies and Albert not being here."

"Maybe they're in the room with the device," Evelynn said.

Ethan nodded and led us past the main hallway that split the building in two; each of us taking turns to look down the long corridor that ran to the rear of the building.

"Deputies? Albert?" I yelled again.

Still no reply.

When we reached the next set of double doors, Ethan pulled one of them open and the four of us proceeded into the research room.

At first glance, I thought it resembled Mission Control at the Johnson Space Center. The room was roughly forty feet square with four rows of old-fashioned fluorescent light fixtures providing overly-bright lighting. The first fifteen feet of the room were absent of furniture, after which there were six work stations, three rows of two, with chairs facing away from us. A center aisle split the rows down the middle and led to a large vault-like door in the center of the far wall.

The two closest work stations were stainless steel-topped tables upon which sat several microscopes, glass beakers and other assorted laboratory equipment. The two center work stations were metal desks. On the right side of each of these desks sat a computer monitor, keyboard and mouse, and on the right, a pad of blank paper, a pencil and an old, heavy-duty stapler. Each of the two stations farthest from us, which were closest to the large security door, had a slanted top containing a small built-in television. Protruding up from the station on the right was a thin, flexible microphone, which I concluded was for communicating with the pilot of the device.

In each corner of the ceiling above the far wall, two surveillance cameras pointed back at us, which I remembered from Captain Hank's diary fed images to a television monitor inside the polished-steel room. More alarm buttons with the clear plastic covers, like the ones in the hallway and shop, were on each wall of the room, placed roughly ten feet apart. Hanging high on the wall and to the left of the security door was a large black-and-white clock, while underneath it, approximately halfway down, was a card reader and key pad.

Ethan immediately proceeded past the work stations until he reached the door.

"George," he said, "give me the key card."

I set my book bag down on one of the work tables, reached down and retrieved the key card from inside my left sock and walked over and handed it to him.

"What about the numeric code?" I asked.

"One of the last things Captain Hank told us was that he was starting to forget things, but he'd found a way to remember our birthday."

"Which we thought was rather strange, because at the time it wasn't our birthday," Evelynn added.

After inserting the card into the reader and punching in the code 0-1-0-1-8-3, the large security door unlocked and swung open.

Once the door had opened all the way, we stood in awed silence staring at the incredible time-traveling device. The cylinder-shaped main structure appeared larger than I'd first imagined it, roughly ten to fifteen feet long, and the white paint on the flat front end (scorched black in several places) reminded me of a space capsule that had reentered the earth's atmosphere. Although it was hard to discern, I could still make out the charred outline of an American flag on the flat front end, as well as the "4 Freedom" inscription above it.

In contrast, the field accelerator looked pristine and new, its seemingly flawless bright white color and copper wire windings sparkling in the light. It reminded me of something a medieval artist could've chiseled out of a piece of pure granite, while at the same time it appeared menacingly frightful, as if the magnitude of the power it generated was not meant for mortal man.

415

After proceeding through the threshold, Madison, who was nearest to the open cockpit hatch, stepped up and looked inside.

"Wow!" she exclaimed. "It looks like something out of a sci-fi movie."

We crowded together behind her to see.

The inside resembled the cockpit of an aircraft, but with every switch, knob and indicator light labeled with Captain Hank's perfect handwriting. There was also a laminated sheet of paper containing instructions on how to operate it taped to the forward wall; undoubtedly placed there to help Hank's friend, Professor Lee.

"Oh, there's a notebook," Madison said.

Reaching in, she pulled out a small, circular-bound gray notebook from off the seat.

I suddenly remembered the SUV that had been following us. The device was so captivating, I'd forgotten about the immediate threat to our safety. Hurrying out of the room to the outer hallway, I looked through the window and found the vehicle still sitting there.

A moment later, Madison and the twins joined me.

"I wonder what they're up to?" Ethan asked.

"And I wonder where the deputies and Albert are," Evelynn said.

"So what do we do now?" Madison asked. "This just doesn't feel right."

"How about we stay out here in the hall and keep an eye on things outside," Ethan suggested. "If something happens, we'll call 9-1-1, fall back into the room with the device and lock ourselves in."

"While we're waiting," Evelynn added, "let's hear what Captain Hank wrote in his notebook."

* * *

For the next thirty minutes, we listened to Madison as she read the final chapter of Captain Hank's story; the emotionally-charged ending causing all of us to dry our eyes several times. While she read from the notebook, Ethan, Evelynn and I stared out the windows of building 3731, hoping we would soon see General Berger, Thomas O'Malley, and the rest of their gang (having fallen into our trap) arrested and taken away in handcuffs.

At the time, we had no way of knowing that it was the four of us who had actually fallen into a trap, and that Deputy Alvarez, Deputy Rivers and Albert Greenbaum would not be coming to arrest anyone this afternoon.

Chapter Eighteen
The Story (Part 6)

Five Months and Twenty-Seven Days Earlier
Tuesday, 18 March 2014, 08:32am
Inside the *Emergency Reception Wing of University Hospital, Salt Lake City, Utah*

Two emergency medical technicians rushed the gurney carrying the critically-ill patient down the crowded hallway, yelling at everyone within earshot to get out of their way. When they reached the end of the corridor they quickly turned and narrowly missed hitting an elderly man being pushed in a wheelchair by his equally-aged wife. The speed and momentum that was built up before the turn, coupled with the lead technician now being out of position from the near-collision, caused the gurney to careen out of control and start to tip over. Thankfully, the blue-eyed man was still awkwardly running after them, and he hooked the bed with his cane and prevented it from falling. Once they'd regained control of the gurney, the men sped up their pace again and quickly traversed the connecting hallway leading to the operating rooms.

The nearest operating room's double-doors were already open when they arrived with the patient, at which point the head nurse emerged from within.

"We'll take him from here," she said.

THE DEVICE

Two orderlies joined her and they maneuvered the gurney in, then the set of double doors slammed closed behind them.

Panting heavily, one of the technicians turned to the blue-eyed man with the cane.

"Thanks for helping us out back there," he said.

The other technician, also gasping for air, only nodded.

After a few moments, Captain Henry "Hank" Stevens caught his breath and was finally able to reply.

"Thank you both for getting my friend here so quickly."

As Hank walked back to the waiting room, he called Shelley and Roy Harrison.

It was a waiting game now, with the outcome resting in the skilled hands of a University of Utah trauma surgeon.

Back inside the operating room, Professor Daniel Lee clung to life by a thread.

~ *Then* ~

Approximately thirty minutes ago, Captain Hank had just finished reviewing his small gray notebook (which contained reminders and other remembrances he'd wrote to himself) and wondered if the recent security improvements he made to the building were sufficient. Yesterday, the workmen had installed five auxiliary generators in the rear wall of the polished-steel room. If there happened to be a power outage now, or if someone deliberately cut the electricity to the building, he and his team could retreat to the room and still barricade themselves inside. The only thing he wasn't sure of was whether the new system would generate enough voltage to activate the device (if future circumstances warranted doing so). On paper, his calculations told him they could, but he wouldn't know for sure until they tested the device using the new auxiliary power system, and he couldn't do that until Dan returned from the fourth dimension.

After reviewing his notes, he sat back in his chair, put his feet up on the desk, and enjoyed a morning cup of coffee while reading the newspaper. He also kept a close eye on the built-in television in the desk, which showed the interior of the polished-steel room. Ever since Dan had gone into the future and hadn't returned, he'd gone through this same morning routine, the few exceptions being when he'd traveled back to Baltimore to visit the twins.

As for Hank's health, it was evident now that his body was in decline because of the disease. Even though he was following a strict exercise regimen, he now needed a cane to help support his left leg when he walked. To stay mentally sharp he worked the daily crossword puzzles in the newspaper, but the simple word games that used to take him mere minutes to complete now took hours, if completed at all. Although he could still drive, for safety's sake Shelley and Roy gave him rides wherever he needed to go.

The Lewy-body dementia had also taken its toll, and as each month passed more of his memories slipped away from him. His neurologist had told him at his last checkup that in normal cases Lewy-body dementia progressed quite rapidly, but for him it was extremely slow-moving. Since he could still take care of himself, Hank considered it a blessing and hung on to his faith that the disease and the dementia were all happening for a reason.

His incredible photographic memory was now a thing of the past. Still, from time to time, he'd get flashes of recollections that would pass by his conscious thoughts, like a fast-moving train that he couldn't fully-focus his eyes on. On rare occasions the train slowed down, and he would retrieve his little gray notebook and write down what he thought the memory was telling him; all in hopes that he might later connect the dots and see where the memory fit in his ever-growing diary.

He'd just returned from refilling his cup of coffee when the picture on the television screen turned snowy with static, and the faint but familiar low-pitched hum of the device filled the research room. When the television image finally cleared, the large cylindrical shape filled the screen, glowing a deep shade of pure blue. Although the number, word and flag on the front of the main structure were now burned off, their vague outlines could still be seen.

After more than fourteen years, 4 Freedom had finally reentered real time.

Hank thought he would soon see Dan's smiling face on the television screen, but after a few minutes, when the cockpit hatch still hadn't opened, he hurriedly opened the large security door and rushed in. Since the exciter-motors were still generating power and holding the time aperture open, it made the task of opening the hatch from the outside both dangerous (from the super-heated fuselage) and difficult (because of the over-powering magnetic force holding it in place).

When Hank finally got it open, he found Dan awake but unresponsive – his eyes not recognizing him at all. As he tried to pull him from the cockpit, Dan's right arm slipped out of his hand, and his elbow inadvertently struck the main power switch, turning it off. With the power off, the time aperture instantly closed and the bright blue fuselage began to dim. Although Dan was now free from the fourth dimension, he could never return to the time he'd started his journey fourteen years ago.

On the second try, Hank managed to wrestle Dan completely out of the cockpit and lay him gently down on the floor. Still not getting a response, he pulled his phone from his pocket and immediately called 9-1-1. While giving information to the emergency operator, he thought he'd better hide the device, and after carefully dragging Dan out of the polished-steel room, he opened the closest plastic box on the wall and pressed the emergency button underneath whereupon the large vault-like door slowly swung closed.

Amid a cauldron of flashing red lights and wailing sirens, a bevy of campus police, fire trucks and emergency medical technicians arrived at building 3731. Once the lead technician had established communications, the trauma physician at the hospital recognized the symptoms of a severe brain injury; possibly an aneurysm or a stroke. There was also the possibility that Dan was experiencing an "acute subdural hematoma," or in layman's terms, his brain was bleeding on the inside from a ruptured vein or artery. If that were the case, the pressure the escaping blood was placing on his brain, if not relieved soon, would surely kill him. The physician ordered the technicians to get Dan to the hospital as soon as possible. An operating room would be standing by when they arrived.

Captain Hank, having heard the exchange between the medical technicians and the physician at the hospital, asked if he could accompany them. Less than three minutes later, after breaking every speed limit on campus, the ambulance pulled up to the rear entrance of University Hospital and Dan was rushed to emergency surgery.

~ *Now* ~

The trauma surgeon walked into the waiting room, and after checking with two other groups of people approached Captain Hank.

"Are you the friends of Mr. Lee?" he asked.

"Yes, Jim Stevens, and this is Roy Harrison and his wife Shelley."

"It looks like he's going to be all right."

Hank felt so relieved tears came to his eyes, and he quickly retrieved a handkerchief from his back pocket to dry them.

"He suffered what we call a ruptured saccular aneurysm, which in most cases is caused by an inherited weakness in the wall of a cerebral artery. This rupture leaked blood into his brain, which confirmed the suspected subdural hematoma. To repair the aneurysm we performed a craniotomy, which relieved the pressure, and inserted a small clamp around the artery to stop the bleeding."

Not being familiar with the medical terminology, Hank quickly took out his gray notebook and jotted the terms down.

The doctor waited for Hank to finish before continuing.

"Although it's still early, he's responding well and showing no signs of permanent brain damage. We are, however, going to keep him in a medically-induced coma until the swelling goes down and the artery heals."

He stood to leave.

"By the way, which one of you called 9-1-1?"

"I did," Hank said.

"And you came with him to the hospital?"

"Yes."

"You are to be commended, Mr. Stevens. Another minute and Mr. Lee would've died. You saved his life."

After the surgeon departed, the three sat for a few moments not saying a word.

"This is all my fault," Hank said, finally breaking the extended silence. "I should've never let him pilot the device."

"You didn't know this was going to happen." Shelley said.

"She's right Hank," Roy added, "the doctor said it was an inherited condition."

"Precisely my point. Dan told me his mother died from a brain aneurysm, but I'd forgotten. Had I remembered, I would've disqualified him."

"As unresponsive as you said he was, I wonder how he managed to slow the device down enough to reenter real time?" Shelley asked.

"We may never know that answer. I can only guess that when the aneurysm happened, he felt some pain or realized what was happening and had a few seconds to pull back on the throttle."

"And those few seconds to him were fourteen years to us," Roy concluded.

"It's a good thing he did," Shelley said, "otherwise he would've died and the device would still be taking his body forward in time."

Hank nodded. "And we would've been left waiting here forever, wondering what happened to him."

"The important thing is, he's back," Roy said, "and hopefully, is going to be all right."

"So what do we do about the mission?" Shelley asked.

"How about I just go?" Roy suggested.

"No," Hank said, "we've already talked about this. You and Shelley have those three kids to think about now."

"I agree with Hank, dear," Shelley added sternly. "Besides, your father died from an aneurism."

"In his heart, not his brain."

"Thank you for the offer Roy, but no," Hank said. "The side effects of traveling in the fourth dimension are simply too obvious to ignore now, and your family medical history disqualifies you. Why don't we mull this over for a while and see if we can come up with some ideas, okay?"

"Okay," Shelley said, and looked at Roy. "Dear?"

"Okay," Roy echoed, "you're probably right."

"Now that Dan is back, I've got to go see the twins and tell them," Hank continued. "Who knows? Maybe they'll have some ideas of how we can proceed."

"Ethan will want to go," Shelley said.

"I know, but that is also out of the question. I've already caused the death of their parents, and if something were to happen to them I'd never forgive myself."

* * *

March rolled into April, and with Dan still unconscious in the medically-induced coma (due to the swelling in his brain

425

receding back to normal at a snail's pace) Hank paid a visit to Ethan and Evelynn Washington in Baltimore.

Sitting in the same restaurant he'd taken them to the first time he'd contacted them, Hank recounted the events that had taken place, and that Dan was now back but seriously ill.

Just as Shelley had predicted, Ethan begged Hank to let him pilot the device.

"You've just got to let me go!" he said.

"I simply will not allow it, and that's all I'm going to say on the matter."

"Then let me go," Evelynn pleaded.

"Try for a moment to put yourselves in my shoes. How do you think I'd feel if something were to happen to you? That's why I kept you at a distance all these years. The threat of General Berger is real. The device is unpredictable. It's side effects caused both my Parkinson's disease and Dan's brain aneurysm."

"You don't *know* that," the twins exclaimed in unison.

Hank suddenly remembered something he'd written in his notebook, then quickly flipped through the pages until he found what he was looking for.

"Neither of you can pilot the device because your family's medical history disqualifies you."

"How so?" Evelynn asked.

"Your father told me when Big Ben died he had Parkinson's and several other medical problems that strike the elderly. In recent studies, many researchers believe Parkinson's is hereditary, which makes the two of you more susceptible to acquire it – just like Dan inherited the arterial condition from his mother that caused his brain aneurysm."

The twins remained quiet, which told Hank his reasoning was getting through.

"Now do you understand why I won't let you go?"

"Well if you're not going to let one of us pilot the device or either of the Harrison's, who are you going to get?" Evelynn asked.

"I was hoping you two might be able to help me with that dilemma."

"It's too bad we don't know someone who already has the disease but is still in the early on-set stage," Ethan said, "then we wouldn't have to worry about it."

"That's it!" Hank yelled, startling a few of the nearby patrons. "We find someone who already has the disease!"

"I thought you might've already thought of that."

"No, and I feel like a complete fool for not thinking of it sooner."

"It's not like you haven't had a lot on your mind," Evelynn said.

Although Captain Hank heard her, his mind was now busy thinking of where he could find a group of Parkinson's patients, and how he could pick one to join the mission.

"He or she would have to still be rather young," he said, "probably not much older than fifty or fifty-five."

"Someone you could trust with the secret of the device," Ethan said.

"And not have a medical history that disqualifies them," Evelynn added.

"I think I know where to look," Hank said, jotting the idea in his notebook.

After thinking for a moment, he addressed the twins again.

"There might be something else you can help me with."

"Anything," Evelynn said. Ethan simply nodded and leaned in.

"As far as covert listening equipment goes, what do you recommend?"

"You mean like bugs?" Ethan asked.

"No, I don't want to break any laws. Is there something that can be casually used to eavesdrop on someone's conversation, say from across a street?"

"They've got some pretty snazzy parabolic microphones out on the market now," Evelynn suggested.

"What, exactly, is a parabolic microphone?" Hank asked, writing the name down.

"They're quite common," Ethan explained. "They use them to capture field audio at football games. Have you ever seen those replays where you can hear what the players are saying in the huddle?"

Hank nodded.

"That's what they're using, a parabolic microphone."

"Are you planning on eavesdropping on someone?" Evelynn asked.

"If I can locate someone who fits our profile to pilot the device, then I'll need to make sure I can trust them."

"Oh," the twins said in unison.

"Although I think I'm a good judge of character, I just want to be sure."

"And what better way is there to learn about someone than eavesdropping on them?" Evelynn asked.

Hank smiled. "When you put it like that, it sounds almost criminal. I just want a way to quickly determine if I can trust the person with the secret of the device. And the longer we forestall the mission, the better General Berger's chances are of completing his device and continuing on with the Firebird plan."

After they'd provided him with a few of the more-reliable brand names of the eavesdropping microphones, and where he could go on the internet to purchase them, Hank placed his pen and notebook in his pocket.

"I'll need to leave immediately."

"Won't you stay just a little while longer?" Evelynn asked.

"No, I really should get going. You've both helped me out immeasurably and I can't thank you enough."

Ethan shook his hand. Evelynn gave him a hug.

"If you need any help, anything at all, you'll call or text us?" Ethan asked.

Hank nodded.

"Promise?" Evelynn asked.

"I promise," Hank said, wiping a tear from his eye.

* * *

Returning to Utah, Hank checked in on Dan at the hospital, then met with Shelley and Roy for dinner to tell them his plan. Although the couple agreed it was a good idea, they were at a loss as to where they could go to locate a Parkinson's patient to pilot the device.

"The answer really is quite simple," Hank said. "Where do you go to find a lot of people who have Parkinson's disease?"

"The clinic at the university?" Shelley asked, while Roy simply shrugged his shoulders.

"If you mean the Movement Disorder Clinic, you're partially correct." After letting them ponder the question a few more moments, Hank said, "A support group."

Shelley turned to Roy.

"Why didn't *you* think of that?"

"I didn't know."

Hank smiled. "Quite simply, you both didn't think of it because neither of you have the disease, and therefore weren't aware that Parkinson's support groups even existed. Am I right?"

They both smiled and nodded.

"Do these support groups meet at the clinic?" Roy asked.

"If I remember right one of them does, and another one just formed not that long ago up in Davis County. They have information about all of them on the clinic's bulletin board, and as it just so happens I have an appointment there tomorrow morning with my neurologist."

429

THE DEVICE

* * *

On the seventh of May, Captain Hank attended the meeting of the Wasatch Front Parkinson's Support Group in Davis County. Although many of the attendees were somewhat older and didn't fit his profile, he was immediately drawn to the couple he found running the group, George and Madison d'Clare. George looked to be about fifty to fifty-five years of age, and in good physical shape; so much so, that at first it was hard for Hank to tell he even had Parkinson's. This told him that George was still in the early stages of the disease, and that he could control his symptoms quite well with the medication. Thinking he might've just found the man to pilot the device, he jotted his name down in his notebook and left the meeting before it was over.

Not wanting to limit the candidate pool to just one person, Hank attended several more Parkinson's support group meetings throughout the month; traveling as far as Brigham City. The few people he investigated at those groups were later ruled out due to their family medical history.

With his search leading him back to the d'Clares, he began eavesdropping on them. He learned that both were retired military veterans who had served in the Air Force Reserve at Hill Air Force Base. Madison was still working, while George (when he wasn't doing things for the support group) spent his time writing memoirs of his Air Force career, golfing with friends, or in his workshop restoring old jukeboxes and arcade machines.

The eavesdropping continued for the next two months, and on one occasion Hank heard the story of how the d'Clares formed the support group. Learning they were doing it for the sole purpose of helping Parkinson's patients, and not for personal notoriety, he knew he had found the right man to pilot the device. Helping cement the decision was the rank that George had attained before retiring from the Air Force Reserve: Captain.

Hank was also impressed with how personable George and Madison were. They even tried to trick him into coming forward and introducing himself at the support group's June meeting. The episode ended rather comically when Madison chased him into the men's restroom.

He didn't want to come forward just yet, however, until he had completed investigating George's family medical history. When he finally obtained the information and knew for certain that George d'Clare fit the profile of the man he was looking for, Hank decided to introduce himself at the support group meeting in August. He realized (too late) that he should've heeded the twin's advice of not being so paranoid, when he scared the man half-to-death in the men's restroom, but he didn't want to take the chance of anyone overhearing their conversation.

Later that night, while watching from a dark office window inside the Senior Center, he saw the d'Clares drive away and called the Harrisons. Five minutes later they arrived to pick him up.

"How did it go?" Shelley asked.

"Perfect. I believe we've found ourselves a pilot for the device."

"Are you sure?"

"As sure as I can be at this point."

"So what's our next move?"

Hank smiled. "I'm glad you asked me that. I think it's time for you two to prepare a luncheon for our new friends." He removed his notebook from his pocket. "And from listening to them these past few months, I just happen to know their favorite foods."

As for where to hold the luncheon, Hank had secretly bought a house in Mountain Green that he intended to give to Shelley and Roy as a gift for helping him with the mission. Since the house was still empty, he felt it would be the perfect place to have a secluded, uninterrupted dinner with the d'Clares. At the same time, he could see if Shelley and Roy liked the home and whether there was enough room for their expanding family.

THE DEVICE

On Saturday afternoon, the first part of the luncheon with the d'Clares went rather well. While George and Madison feasted on their favorite dishes, Hank began telling them his story. He pretended that his dad was the one in the picture who possessed the photographic memory, and that he had subsequently discovered the Firebird intelligence in the Ünterbunker. By framing the story in this fashion (at least to begin with) he thought it might be easier for George and Madison to believe the rest of it.

As he was about to tell them how his "dad" had set the Nazi documents to memory, his phone started to vibrate, and checking his messages, immediately excused the couple. Once they were gone, he called the Harrisons to come back to the house and pick him up, and a few minutes later they were on their way to University Hospital. Although he hated leaving George and Madison hanging like that, the message he'd received was just too important to ignore.

After fourteen years in the fourth dimension, and another five months in a medically-induced coma to allow his brain to heal, Professor Daniel Lee had finally regained consciousness.

* * *

The five-foot tall machine that measured intracranial pressure sat silently next to the bed, its cord attached to Dan's head three inches above his left ear. Next to the pressure monitor was another machine commonly referred to as a "Christmas Tree." This modern technological marvel, attached to the monitor on one side and an intravenous tube in Dan's arm on the other, could recognize minute changes in his condition, and instantly inject his body with a myriad of chemical compounds intended to stabilize his nervous system.

After a brief consultation with the physician on duty, and promising not to stay more than five minutes, Hank, Shelley and Roy entered the room.

As the three approached the bed, Hank spoke first.

"Dan? How are you doing?"

Dan looked over and replied in a loud, agitated voice.

"I'm hungry, but they won't let me eat. My back hurts, but they won't let me get out of bed. I've got a headache, but they won't give me any aspirin. The catheter they put in me hurts like hell, and I've got an extension cord plugged into my head. *That's* how I'm doing!"

Not believing how normal Dan sounded, Hank's eyes watered with tears of joy.

"Why didn't you tell me the device was going to put me in the hospital?"

"You didn't ask," Hank said.

All four laughed, easing the seriousness of the situation.

"You gave us quite a scare," Shelley said. "What do you remember?"

"I remember right after the magnetic moment and the deflection happened, my ears popped. Then I must've passed out, because the next thing I knew I was here."

"You were away for quite some time." Roy said.

"How long?"

"Fourteen years" Hank said, "give or take a few months."

"You're kidding me, right?"

"He's not," Shelley said. "It's now 2014. August the sixteenth of 2014, to be exact."

"What happened?

"You had a brain aneurysm. Captain Hank saved your life."

Dan's eyes focused on Hank.

"Really?"

"That's not entirely true," Hank said, "I did have some help from a couple of emergency medical technicians."

"A brain aneurysm. That's strange. I don't feel any different."

"You wouldn't, because you've been in an induced coma for months," Shelley said.

"For a while it looked like we were going to lose you," Roy added.

Dan turned to address Hank again.

"Thank you for saving my life, but when can I get out of here? Have they said? I'm ready to get back in the device and continue the mission."

"I'm sorry Dan, but your days of piloting the device are over."

"Over? I feel fine. I just need them to unhook me."

"Believe me, I'm pleased to see you're doing so well, but if I'd remembered that your mother had died from a brain aneurysm I would've never let you pilot the device to begin with."

"But now that I'm all right, doesn't that make me the perfect pilot?"

"No, and I'll tell you why."

Hank retrieved his notebook and thumbed through the pages until he found what he was looking for.

"The trauma surgeon told us he performed a craniotomy on you, and placed a tiny clamp around the artery in your brain to stop the bleeding. In researching this procedure, I found these clamps are made from cobalt. If the field accelerator were to affect the clamp in your head like it affects the main structure of the device…"

"I get the picture," Dan said, interrupting him, "I just thought that since I was all right now..." His voice trailed off sadly.

"And I thank you, but we've already found someone else to pilot the device."

"Who?"

"A man who already has Parkinson's but is still in the early-onset stage. When you get out of here, check your email. I've been sending you updates."

"Okay, but what can I do to help?"

"Get better, and by that I mean do what the doctors and nurses tell you."

Hank checked his watch and motioned to the other two that they should leave.

"Hank's right," Shelley said. "You need to get better."

"Get some rest my friend," Roy added, "you'll need it."

"Haven't I rested enough?"

"What he means is, you have a lot of rehabilitation to go through," Hank said. "All those muscles you haven't used in a while are going to be sore when you start to use them again."

"Did they say how long it would take?"

"No, but you could always approach it like Bruce Lee."

"What do you mean?"

"Pretend you are in a fight against the pain," Hank said, starting to laugh, "and practice the art of fighting without fighting."

Hank ducked out of the room just in time to avoid being hit by a pillow.

* * *

The following Monday afternoon Captain Hank received a call from Shelley, who asked if she and Roy could stop by the building and see him, which he thought would be the perfect time to present them with the keys to the house in Mountain Green.

When the couple walked in, Hank said, "I'm glad you wanted to stop by. I have something for you." He reached into the false bottom of the old toolbox, removed a small gift-wrapped box, and handed it to Shelley.

"This is for all the help you've given me on the mission and for driving me everywhere."

She tore the wrapping off, and opening the small box found two keys.

"I know you two have been looking for a house, so I'd like to give you the one up in Mountain Green, if you want it."

"We can't accept it," Shelley said, "you've already given us so much."

"Oh nonsense, of course you can."

"Shelley's right, we can't accept it," Roy said. "That house must've cost you a small fortune."

"Please try to look at this from my side. I have a lot of money and I'm not getting any younger. This disease and the dementia will soon take away my ability to manage my affairs. Since I cannot take it with me, I want it to go where it will do the most good, and what better good than my two dear friends? Please accept it as a token of our friendship and let's just leave it at that."

After looking at each other, they turned back to Hank.

"Please?" Hank asked, his blue eyes pleading as much as his voice.

"Thank you," Shelley said, giving him a hug.

"Yes, thank you," Roy repeated, shaking his hand.

"Oh, by the way, what did you want to see me about?"

"We've solved your problem," Shelley said.

"What problem?"

"We'll have to show you. It's on the computer."

A few moments later they were in the research room, with Shelley sitting at one of the computer desks and Hank and Roy standing on each side of her.

"Remember when you asked me if there was a way to convert a typed message to Morse code?" Shelley asked. "Well, after searching on the internet, we found a free app."

"App?"

"Application," Roy said, "you know, a computer program."

"Of course." Hank replied, suddenly remembering.

After finding the website, Shelley downloaded the application.

"Watch this," she said.

After typing the sentence, "Hello Captain Hank, how are you today?" she clicked a little box titled "convert," and the message instantly blared out from the computer's speaker with the dot-dot-dash of Morse code.

"Isn't that cool?"

"And you can save it to a file and download it to any portable audio device, just like a song," Roy said.

Hank turned to one of the last pages of his notebook and found a note he'd written to himself, explaining why he had asked them to find the program.

"This is perfect," he said, "absolutely perfect."

"What are you going to use it for?" Shelley asked.

"Remember a few months ago, when we were talking about Einstein's physics theories? The one I thought was particularly fascinating was the theory of generating a massless particle, like a radio beam, to speeds faster than light. You told me all we needed to do was to figure out a way to enhance a Klystron Amplification Tube."

"Yes, I remember. *Theoretically*, I guess it's possible."

Hank smiled. "I've figured out a way to enhance the tube, and now with this app I have a way to attach a message to the radio beam."

"Really? How did you manage to do that?"

"Oh, never mind. It's just one of my hobbies to pass the time. By the way, I'd like another dinner with the d'Clares, and was wondering if either of you would be available to drive me this Saturday night?"

Shelley checked the calendar on her phone.

"That's the day of Meredith's dance recital. How about the next Saturday? We don't have anything going on."

"Saturday the thirtieth it is," Hank said. "I'll send them a text next week and let you know what time."

* * *

THE DEVICE

Captain Hank climbed into the front seat next to Roy and set the large three-ring binder containing his diary on the floor next to his feet.

"Thanks again for taking me, he said. "I truly appreciate it."

"Not a problem. It gives me a chance to get out of the house. Shelley would've come too, but the kids wanted to have some friends sleep over. So where are we headed?"

"Do you know where the old Hotel Utah is?"

Roy smiled. "I'm afraid not. A little before my time if you know what I mean."

Hank chuckled. "It's called the Joseph Smith Building now. Just go down to Main Street, then over to South Temple."

"Got it."

They'd only traveled a few blocks and were nearing the Seventh East intersection, when a black SUV passed them on the left side and suddenly swerved into their lane. To avoid the collision, Roy slammed on the brakes, but some loose gravel caused the car to go into a skid, and they struck the curb and jumped over it. Having forgotten to buckle his seat belt, Hank's head slammed into the upward bound dashboard. After landing on the grass next to the sidewalk, the car slid several more feet before being stopped by a towering oak tree.

They sat there for a moment, not saying a word.

"Are you all right?" Roy asked.

"I'm okay, I think," Hank replied, rubbing his head.

A small crowd of concerned citizens gathered around the car, and after Roy assured them they were all right he turned to Hank.

"Let's get out and check the damage."

Hank gathered his hat, cane and the binder.

After walking through the plume of antifreeze steam and seeing the crumpled front end, Roy turned to Hank and shook his head.

"Shelley's not going to like this. Of the two cars we have, she likes this one the best."

"Not to worry my friend. I'll see that it is repaired. And if the damage is too extensive, I'll simply buy Shelley a new car."

"Thanks Hank, but we do have insurance."

Just then, a Salt Lake City police cruiser pulled up and two officers got out. While one remained in the street directing traffic around the scene, the other approached Roy and Hank.

"Are either of you injured?" the officer asked.

"My friend bumped his head," Roy said.

He immediately went to Hank, and seeing the large bruise sat him down on the grass and called for an ambulance.

"So how did this happen?"

Roy explained how the SUV had cut him off.

"Did either of you catch the license plate?"

"All I know is that the vehicle was black with tinted windows," Roy said.

Captain Hank, sitting silently on the grass, wondered if General Berger had finally discovered his whereabouts.

* * *

During their short ride in the ambulance over to Salt Lake Regional Hospital, Hank checked his watch and suddenly remembered that George and Madison were still waiting for him at the Roof Restaurant. He retrieved his cell phone and sent them both a text, apologizing for missing their dinner. As an added gesture, he quickly found the restaurant's phone number on his phone's internet browser, and called and paid for their meals. He hoped that later, after he'd had a chance to explain, they would understand why he was unavoidably detained.

After a lengthy examination and determining that he hadn't suffered a concussion, the attending physician released him. Even though Hank thought it completely unnecessary, the demanding nurse insisted he sit in a wheelchair, and finally losing the argument, she wheeled him out into the waiting room.

Seeing him, Roy stood and gathered up Hank's hat, cane and the diary.

"How are you doing?" he asked.

"I'm fine, just a minor bump, but *she* insisted on *this*." He slapped his hands on the armrests of the wheelchair.

"Hospital policy," she said, winking at Roy.

Roy smiled. "Thank you. I'll take him."

As soon as she'd walked away, Hank stood up, took his hat from Roy and put it on.

"Are you sure you're okay?" Roy asked.

He nodded and motioned for him to hand him his cane and the diary.

"The rental car is on its way and should be here in a few minutes."

"Good, then we shall proceed to George and Madison's home," Hank said. "I simply cannot postpone the mission any further. I've got to tell them the rest of the story and get George ready to pilot the device."

* * *

The following Wednesday morning Captain Hank was sitting in the research room, finishing the message he was going to convert to Morse code while thinking about the late-night conversation with George and Madison. Although he wasn't able to finish telling them the entire story, he thought the evening went rather well. Madison's non-verbal signals told him she believed him, but George was going to take more convincing; his easily-discernable body language betrayed his doubt. He decided to give the couple one week to think about what he'd told them, update his diary and mull over the offer he'd made to George. At the next meeting, he would tell them the rest of the story and reveal his true identity.

Suddenly, his police scanner came to life with chatter. He turned it up and found it was the familiar voice of Deputy Wilson.

"I'm at the Tompkins house," Wilson said excitedly, "and I've got a body. It looks like a suicide!"

"Remember your radio protocols," the female dispatcher said.

Wilson continued, ignoring her warning.

"It looks like he tried to hang himself, but the rope broke and he fell all the way down the stairs!"

A harsh male voice replaced the female's.

"Wilson! How many times do we have to tell you? Watch what you say on the radio! We've dispatched another unit to your location, so stand by!"

"Yes, sir," the deputy whimpered.

Hank immediately retrieved a large notebook from the desk and after opening it to the last page added the name "Tompkins" to the long list of other names.

Going back to the message he was working on, he reread it several times before clicking on the "convert" button that changed it to Morse code, then listened intently to the playback. Satisfied that the app had transposed the message correctly, he downloaded it to a small audio player. Taking it into the shop, he retrieved a small tube-shaped component from the hidden compartment of the old toolbox, along with the book he'd purchased in Tucson.

Remembering why he'd painted the component black, he wrote "e-KAT" across the front with a white permanent marker, and after checking the twisted pair of wires sticking out of each end, labeled one end "input," and the other end "output."

He took a few moments to review a few pages of the book, then examined the component and audio player.

"I agree with you Shelley," he said, aloud and to himself, "*theoretically* it just might be possible."

441

THE DEVICE

* * *

On Saturday morning, Hank rose out of bed and washed down his Parkinson's medications, then made himself a pot of coffee and proceeded into the research room to send Dan an email. Even though his friend had awoken and seemed to be recovering quite rapidly, he still sent him the weekly update; a habit which also served Hank as a good brain exercise when he typed-up the message.

After sending the update, he started thumbing through the newspaper, and reaching the obituaries found the one for Gary Tompkins. With the name ringing a bell, he retrieved the large notebook from the drawer, and after turning to the back, found that he'd added the name "Tompkins" to the bottom of the list. Remembering the conversation he'd overheard on the radio, he quickly logged in to Weber County's secure website.

A cold chill ran through Hank's body as he read how the injuries to Mr. Tompkins coincided with the killing method of General Berger. After a few moments, he reasoned that it must be a coincidence. Why would General Berger come to Utah to kill a federal employee?

Returning to the obituary, he was suddenly alarmed again when he read that Mr. Tompkins had previously worked in the Depot Maintenance Facility at Hill Air Force Base. Now starting to panic, Hank couldn't remember if he'd told the d'Clares to keep what he told them confidential.

He quickly retrieved his phone and sent them both a text, urgently requesting they meet with him. As soon as he'd sent it he regretted it, thinking that his paranoia was again getting the best of him. By the time he received George's reply, he'd calmed himself and agreed to meet them the next day at the house in Mountain Green.

Thinking more about the house in Mountain Green, Hank remembered Shelley and Roy were going to check it out that afternoon. Since they'd been so busy preparing the food for the luncheon the last time they'd been up there, they hadn't had a chance to look over the rest of the house. He quickly sent them both a text to see how they liked the place, and proceeded to his bedroom to take a shower. Thirty minutes later, now dressed and feeling somewhat refreshed, he retrieved his cane and hat and walked down North Campus Drive to the nearby restaurant.

Normally he found the walk refreshing and invigorating, but today's jaunt seemed gloomy by comparison. Although he couldn't put his finger on it, he felt something was terribly wrong. Attributing it again to his enhanced paranoia, Hank made his way down to the cozy little restaurant, thankful that they served breakfast all day long.

* * *

Later that afternoon, Hank woke abruptly from a bad dream. In it, he thought General Berger had discovered his whereabouts, and in the form of a real white wolf, was silently creeping up on Building 3731. Accompanying the general was a legion of henchmen also in wolf-form, their jowls dripping with saliva in anticipation of the upcoming kill. After realizing the vivid dream was just that, he rose off the bed and cursed himself for taking a nap after eating such a large stack of pancakes.

Checking his cell phone, he found Shelley and Roy still hadn't replied to his message, which he found rather odd, especially as far as Shelley was concerned; no matter what message he sent her, she would always reply within minutes. He immediately tried to call her, and when she didn't answer, he tried Roy's number. Not getting a response, he started thinking about General Berger. The more he thought about him, the more scenarios raced through his mind, and the more the feeling grew that something wasn't right.

He wondered again whether he was having another episode of his overblown paranoia, when suddenly the two conversations with George and Madison became crystal clear in his mind. It was one of those rare occasions when the passing train of memories slowed down long enough for him to focus on it. The instant the memories sharpened with clarity, he realized he'd neglected to tell the d'Clares to keep his story a secret. He'd told them that he was conducting highly-sensitive and cutting-edge research, but had completely forgotten to have them promise not to share his story with anyone!

As the scenarios played out in his mind, the pieces of the mental jigsaw puzzle began falling into place. If for some unknown reason the d'Clares had involved Tompkins, then General Berger must've discovered his location and murdered him. If that happened, the possibility was high that Berger also obtained the name of the d'Clares from Tompkins. The next step for Berger would've been to place George and Madison under surveillance (and possibly follow them or bug their home) in an effort to find him. He shuddered to think that this scenario might explain why the Harrisons weren't answering their cell phones. Granted, it was a lot of "ifs," but he'd underestimated General Berger before and he was not about to make the same mistake again.

He tried to call Shelley and Roy again, and not receiving an answer at either number slammed his fist down on the desk. After telling himself to calm down, he opened his phone and quickly typed a message to the twins asking them to come to Utah as soon as possible. As soon as he'd sent it, the thought occurred to him: *What if I'm wrong? What if Shelley and Roy aren't answering because of the bad reception in Weber Canyon?* The only way he could be sure was to go to Mountain Green and find out for himself.

Grabbing his hat and cane, he proceeded out the door to his truck.

* * *

One hour later Captain Hank arrived back at Building 3731, still in a state of shock at seeing Shelley and Roy dead in the house at Mountain Green. He went directly to the shop, where he retrieved the enhanced Klystron Amplification Tube, the small audio player, and several wires from the hidden compartment in the bottom of the old toolbox. After laying them all out on the workbench, he opened a smaller toolbox that contained his electrical tools. It took him less than five minutes to solder the wires, and once he was satisfied the connections would hold, he carefully picked up the component and audio player, grabbed a screwdriver and a piece of duct tape, and hurried into the polished-steel room.

Reaching the device, he made his way to the rear of the main structure and opened an access cover. Removing the thin rectangular communication box, he quickly replacing it with the e-KAT component. After plugging in the power cable from the distribution network, he connected the communication wire from the cockpit and the wire leading to the antenna. Knowing he was prone to making mistakes because of the disease, he double-checked the connections to make sure he'd hooked it up the right way.

Using the piece of duct tape, he secured the audio player to the inside of the panel and closed the access cover. Stashing the old communication box and screwdriver in the refrigerator, he pressed the nearest emergency button and locked himself in the room with the device.

Climbing into the cockpit, he turned on the main power switch, and as soon as the exciter-motors reached their self-sustaining threshold, he turned on the field accelerator. A few moments later, the green light came on indicating that the magnetic moment had been reached, and that the device had initiated enough power for the deflection.

The second he placed his thumb and index finger on the polarity-reversing switch, something stopped him. What was he forgetting? The d'Clares! If the e-KAT didn't work, what would happen to George and Madison? They didn't ask to be recruited for the mission, *he'd involved them!* General Berger had obviously found Shelley and Roy through the d'Clares, which meant they were also in danger – a loose end that Berger would undoubtedly tie up. Knowing he couldn't leave now (at least not until after he warned the couple) he turned off the power and the electrical current slowly drained from the device.

Climbing out of the cockpit, he opened the security door and walked out into the research room. After trying to call the d'Clares again and not getting an answer at either of their numbers, he remembered George texting him that they were going to a late movie, and quickly reviewed the message.

Retrieving his small gray notebook from his pocket, he scribbled a few notes on the last page and threw it into 4 Freedom's cockpit. Closing the security door, he retrieved a new blank notebook from a nearby desk and hurried back into the shop. Not bothering to put away the tools, he returned the second key card to its hiding place in the false bottom of the old toolbox, gathered his hat and cane, and proceeded out of the building.

A short time later, Captain Hank was speeding north towards Farmington Station Park, hoping he would reach George and Madison in time.

* * *

Captain Hank was unaware that his decades-long mission would soon be over, and that it would end both prematurely and unsuccessfully. The life of the man who had breached the fourth dimension to stop the sadistic Nazi war criminal now hung precariously inside a different type of chronological device. This particular timepiece happened to be an older type of clock known as an hourglass – one whose upper teardrop-shaped globe was nearly devoid of sand.

While racing down the freeway, Captain Henry "Hank" Stevens unknowingly hurried toward the final minutes of his life.

Chapter Nineteen
The Wolf On The Trail

Three Days Earlier
Wednesday, 3 September 2014, 01:46hrs
Inside *White Pines Army Air Station, Sixty-Seven Miles Southwest of Ruth, Nevada*

The full moon shining down on the faded white World War II-era buildings gave them the eerie look of being haunted. Enhancing their otherworldly appearance were the strong gusts of wind blowing across the abandoned airfield, which rattled the metal chain against the rusty flag pole and made the roof rafters groan like bodiless spirits. From all outward indications, the seventy-five-year-old military base was deserted, but in truth, the installation had been active for quite some time.

In the lower level of the antiquated headquarters building was a large briefing room that had once been used by the base commander to meet with his staff. The room resembled the dimly-lit work stations of air traffic controllers, but instead of a group of well-trained professionals directing an assigned number of aircraft flights, this hub of operations was manned by only one person, whose given task was to monitor untold millions of internet searches. Amid the plethora of state-of-the-art computers and electronic equipment was an equally-sophisticated projector, casting a crimson outline of the United States against the wall. Inside this outline, two yellow lights blinked over the northern part of the state of Utah.

Not believing what she was seeing, computer expert and white-collar criminal Dannielle Marie Dennison refreshed the alert page of the tracking cookie, which removed one of the blinking lights and re-plotted it on the projected map. A few seconds later, when the second blinking light reappeared over the same location, her excitement boiled over and she stood and kicked the chair out from under her.

"Yes!" she yelled.

After staring at the screen for a few more moments to admire her work, she moved to another computer and verified the numeric code of the internet protocol address, which told her whose computer had initiated the search for Einstein's field equations. Moving to yet another computer, she quickly found the local address of the owner by hacking into their online account. The instant the information appeared on the screen, she clicked the "print" button and hastily retrieved her cell phone to text her boss and the Irishman.

Less than three minutes later, the entry door of the command center burst open and in stormed SS Lieutenant General Karl Berger – his large frame and muscular physique still sweaty from his early morning workout.

"What do you have?" he snapped.

"The trace finally came through, General. In the last twelve hours, there have been two extensive searches originating in Utah. The first one was initiated yesterday from a building at Hill Air Force Base, and a second a few moments ago from a residence in Ogden." She pointed to the wall projection.

Berger smiled. "We have him then?"

"I believe so, sir."

"We have him!" he yelled triumphantly.

At that moment, Thomas O'Malley came limping through the door, clad in his western wear and carrying his boots and phone.

"What is it?" he asked.

"Captain Stevens has finally made a mistake. Contact the pilot and assemble the men. We leave as soon as possible!"

O'Malley immediately turned and exited the room, still carrying his boots while dialing the number.

Berger's attention returned to Dennison.

"Are the new credentials ready?"

"Yes, General. I just finished them." She quickly handed him his from the top of the stack, and another piece of paper. "Here's what a real one looks like."

After watching him compare his forged FBI identification with the one on the paper and seeing him smile, she pointed to a cardboard box on another desk.

"I also have seven phones, handguns and sets of handcuffs that are undistinguishable from the ones they issue to new agents."

"Very good work, my dear."

"Thank you, sir," she said, looking directly into his eyes. Although she'd seen him many times without his contact lenses, this time, within the confines of the glowing red command center, his dark eyes looked even more soulless. Shuddering at the sight, her skin instantly broke out in goose bumps.

"When you pack, don't forget your little bag of tricks."

"General?"

"If the person who searched for the information is not Captain Stevens, we may need to employ some of your unique tools to find him."

"I understand, sir."

Berger looked up at the projected map.

"It appears you were right, Herr Speer. Move, counter-move. And this time, my good Captain Hank, you shall not escape me."

"General, if I may be so bold, who is this man Speer you keep talking to?"

He smiled, which made her break out in goose bumps again.

"An old friend who once told me I needed to have more patience. But we need not dwell on the past, my dear. Get your equipment and report to the aircraft."

He turned and exited the room, while Dennison stood motionless watching him leave.

Approximately thirty minutes later, the small plane lifted off from the abandoned airfield and turned north towards Utah.

~ *Then* ~

Seven years and three months earlier, General Berger was sitting in the cockpit of Firebird Two looking forward to the third test. When the magnetic moment was reached and the deflection occurred, everything seemed to be working correctly, but when he increased the power to exciter-motors, the magnetic force immediately ejected the main structure from the fourth dimension. Realizing he was being thrown out of the aperture, he jammed the throttle fully-open, firewalling the electrical current. Instead of reentering the time opening, the power system winked out and closed his doorway back to the past forever. He immediately checked his on-board chronometer, which had a battery back-up, and took note of the date.

This was the third test of Firebird Two since 1993, and the third instance where he'd skipped ahead seven years and was not able to return. With another unsuccessful attempt to get the device to stop and return to its starting time, he was now furious beyond reason. Helping carry his volcanic temper to the boiling point was the pounding headache he was experiencing.

Getting out of the cockpit, he threw his communication headset as hard as he could against the polished-steel wall, shattering it into more than a dozen pieces, then sat down on the floor holding his head in his hands.

Twenty minutes later, when the throbbing somewhat dissipated, he focused his dark and menacing eyes on the man he felt was responsible for the failed test: Professor Hope. Standing up, Berger moved toward him.

"Professor, may I speak to you for a moment?"

Hope stood motionless.

O'Malley readjusted his cowboy hat, stepped behind the professor and shoved him forward. Once Hope was within an arm's reach, Berger reached out and grabbed him by the shirt collar and harshly yanked him closer.

"Give me one good reason why I should not kill you Mr. Hope! Just one!"

Suddenly remembering he'd promised himself not to let his temper get the best of him, Berger abruptly released him and walked back toward the device. After a few moments, he returned to the professor.

"There must be something we can do."

Hope picked himself up off the floor and cleared his throat.

"The root cause of the failure is our inability to synchronize the power system of the main structure to the field accelerator."

"Tell me something I do not know!"

"We *must* have the two formulas."

"But we *do not have* the two formulas, professor!"

"General, ever since we entered the testing phase twenty-two years ago, I have been working on it. The gravitational wave formula is still considered one of the greatest unsolved problems in modern physics. Where you previously had an army of Germany's most-brilliant scientists working on the formula, I am only one person."

Berger started to interrupt and remind him that the scientists at Oranienburg had only worked out part of the equations, and that the two Jews had completed the calculations in the Ünterbunker. Instead of correcting him, he decided to hear him out.

"While you were gone this time," Hope continued, "I researched an untold number of books, consulted with dozens of former colleagues, and even traveled to Denmark to ask a group of world-renowned physicists attending a conference at the Niels Bohr Institute in Copenhagen. Not finding an answer, I took the liberty of recruiting someone who might be able to recover the formulas for us."

"Who is he?"

"He is a she, General, and her name is Danielle Dennison."

"And where is this woman? Why is she not here?"

O'Malley stepped forward and interrupted.

"She's in the headquarters building, Boss. I think you'll be impressed."

Berger looked at his second-in-command, then back to the professor.

"I'd better be, because right now I'm not impressed with either of you."

"What did I do?" the Irishman asked.

"Look at yourself in a mirror. The attire you have chosen makes you look like a complete imbecile."

O'Malley frowned and followed him out the door.

Upon meeting Danielle Dennison, General Berger couldn't help but be enthralled with the quirky and attractive little woman, whose technical knowledge and high-tech gadgetry truly fascinated him.

After hearing how she intended to find Captain Hank using the tracking cookies, Berger instructed her to concentrate her search in Maryland and Utah. Dennison acknowledged the order and informed him she could keep the cookie alert running as long as needed. Hacking into the internet search engines and going through all the historical data, however, could take up to six months. He ordered her to proceed and walked out of the headquarters room, pleased with Professor Hope's new and competent recruit.

Three months later, General Berger found himself even more elated with Danielle Dennison when she called him from his early morning workout to inform him she had pinpointed the Utah locations of two extensive internet searches: one originating from an office complex at Hill Air Force Base, the other from a home computer belonging to Gary Tompkins.

~ *Now* ~

Approximately five minutes after the plane taxied to a stop at the open-air gate of the Ogden Municipal Airport, Karl Berger was in full "General" mode. He first ordered the pilot to remain on stand-by until the team returned, then turned to O'Malley and instructed him to go out and rent three vehicles, preferably large SUVs with tinted windows. Once the Irishman had departed the plane, he called together the rest of his team and reiterated his orders.

Glaring first at the short professor, the general's dark and sinister eyes moved slowly to the other larger and more-muscular men: William Slone, Alex Benoit, and Lance Petri. Although they were normally assigned to bodyguard duties, Berger added them to this incursion because of what Dennison found in their background investigations: they were all ex-military, had no qualms about killing, and knew how to follow orders.

"Remember," Berger said, addressing the team, "this is an *extraction* operation, nothing more, nothing less."

He handed each of them a copy of Hank's photograph, along with an age-enhanced picture Dennison had prepared.

"We are here to find and capture Captain Henry Stevens. The first photograph is from his Army record that Mr. O'Malley obtained some years ago. If he built a device and came forward in time, he will still look somewhat the same. If not, he may look like the second. One distinction he will *not* be able to hide, even if he is older, is his piercing blue eyes."

He paused for a moment to let his remarks sink in.

"Under no circumstances are you to kill Captain Stevens. Do you understand?"

After hearing only a few murmurs of acknowledgement, he screamed the question again.

"Yes, sir!" the team yelled in unison.

"Once we recover the information and Firebird Two works to my satisfaction, I will deal with the captain myself. Understood?"

"Yes, sir!"

"Good. Now remember to act the part. From this point forward, when we step off this aircraft you are all agents of the FBI. Now pick up your credentials and equipment from Miss Dennison and wait outside."

He looked over to her and nodded, at which point she called out their names one at a time, handing them their identifications, cell phones, handcuffs and firearms. When she got to the last individual, the name "Crosby" flew from her lips, whereupon Professor Hope stepped up.

Berger, who was putting in his contact lenses, immediately turned around, and seeing Professor Hope receiving the identification, walked over to investigate.

"What is the meaning of this? Why was I not told of the name change?"

The professor smiled. "Hope and Crosby, General. I thought you'd be familiar with the famous names from your time and find it amusing."

Berger glared at him menacingly.

"It might interest you to know, Professor, that I am in fact, quite familiar with the names of the two American movie stars. At the time, I found their singing to be childish and their comedy quite boring. Just as I am finding you, right now."

Frowning, the professor quickly retrieved his equipment and made his way out of the aircraft.

Berger looked over at Dennison, smiled, and winked.

At that moment, O'Malley ducked his head back into the plane.

"Boss," he said, "our transportation is here."

"Let us be off then. We have a lot to do today."

* * *

When the team reached Gary Tompkins' house, it took the general less than fifteen minutes to extract the d'Clares' names from the odd-looking government worker. After beating and murdering him, he ordered O'Malley to make it look as if Tompkins had taken his own life.

While O'Malley corrupted the crime scene using a mostly-rotten rope he'd found in the garage, Professor Hope and the other men searched the rest of the house. When they located Tompkins' home computer, they also found a piece of paper containing a part of a complex mathematical problem that solved one of Einstein's field equations. Walking out of the house, Hope showed the paper to Berger.

"Does this look familiar, General?" he asked.

Berger examined it, and recognized it as being one of the ones the Jews had worked out on the chalkboards in the Ünterbunker.

"Good work, Professor."

Returning to his command vehicle, the general immediately ordered Dennison to find the address of George and Madison d'Clare.

"How do you want to handle them, Boss?" O'Malley asked.

Berger thought for a few moments. He was hoping Tompkins would tell him where he could find Captain Stevens, but instead he'd only disclosed the names of the d'Clare couple. Even after beating him within an inch of his life, the man still hadn't changed his story – he didn't know Captain Stevens. Since this was an unexpected development, he decided precautions were in order.

"This is a lot deeper than I first imagined. We must be careful, otherwise the good captain will slip through our fingers again. Let us proceed to the d'Clares and employ some of Miss Dennison's tricks."

For the rest of the morning, Berger and his team watched George and Madison's home. Since the house was situated on a corner lot of the subdivision, it made the surveillance rather easy. O'Malley and Slone sat two doors down and across the street, which gave them an unobstructed view of the front of the house. Professor Hope and Benoit parked down the adjoining road, where they could watch over the rear of the home. The general, with Dennison and Petri, sat one block away in an empty church parking lot. Even though Berger couldn't directly see the d'Clares' house from this location, he was still close enough in the event they needed to quickly move in. In addition, he didn't want another black vehicle being noticed by nosey neighbors.

A few minutes past six o'clock in the morning, the team observed the d'Clares' garage door open and Madison depart in a silver SUV, whereupon Berger instructed O'Malley and Slone to follow her. Approximately fifteen minutes later, the Irishman called to report that she'd just passed through one of the entry gates of Hill Air Force Base.

Four hours later, O'Malley informed him that George had also entered the base, and after checking with Professor Hope to make sure no one was in the area, Berger ordered Dennison to go to work.

She immediately exited the command vehicle and made her way down the sidewalk to the d'Clares' home. When she reached their front porch she rang the doorbell, and after waiting a few moments retrieved a small electronic instrument from her book bag. Turning it on, the garage door opened, whereupon she calmly stepped off the porch and made her way inside.

Twenty minutes later, she climbed back into the command vehicle.

"How did it go, my dear?" Berger asked.

"Like clockwork, General."

DALE C. GEORGE

* * *

For two-and-a-half more days, General Berger and his team conducted round-the-clock surveillance on the d'Clares. From the listening devices, they learned George was retired from the military, while Madison still worked as a civil servant. They also overheard them talk about a man they'd recently met named Jim Stevens, who was purportedly the son of Captain Henry Stevens. Berger speculated if Captain Stevens had built a device of his own and had come forward in time, the man the d'Clares were referring to might be the captain himself, masquerading as his own son. If that were the case it was a brilliant move, but he wouldn't know for sure until he captured him.

Another piece of information Berger collected had to do with Einstein's solved field equation, and how a piece of it happened to be in Tompkins' possession. He overheard the d'Clare couple say they'd asked Tompkins to try to figure it out for them, to see if this man, Jim Stevens, was telling them the truth about the device. As for the equation, it came out of a diary Jim Stevens left with them to review. Berger immediately suspected that the diary might also contain the stolen Firebird files (including the synchronization formulas) and when the time came to move in on the d'Clares, one of the top priorities would be to recover the diary.

Nothing stood out in the general's mind as to why Captain Stevens or Jim (if it was his son) would involve the d'Clares to begin with. Although they were both educated, their knowledge base did not include physics, mathematics, nor any other natural science that would be of any help to the project. Berger decided this would be an area of questioning when he had either the Captain (or his son) in custody.

While he listened to the couple's conversations, the general developed a complete hatred for the husband George. Since he already believed the shaking palsy condition was a sign of

459

weakness, listening to this do-gooder talk about his insignificant support group made him loathe the man. As far as the disease was concerned, Berger agreed with Hitler that the physically weak and frail of mind were nothing more than a burden and a hindrance to the Fatherland, and should be eradicated from society. He looked forward to the time when Captain Stevens (or his son) was in his custody, at which point he would also tie up a loose end by putting an end to this over-age boy scout and his doting wife.

The clue to the whereabouts of Captain Stevens came late on Friday afternoon. Berger overheard the d'Clares say the luncheon they'd recently attended was at the Stevens home in Mountain Green, which Dennison found on the internet was a small rural town, fifteen miles northeast of their location. He immediately ordered her to find an address, but with every search she'd reported coming up empty; of the twenty-five hundred people who lived in Mountain Green, no one had the last name of Stevens. Finally, late Saturday morning, Dennison reported that she had identified the home.

"When I couldn't find anyone named Stevens in the Mountain Green records," she said, "I turned to real estate companies selling property in the area and hacked into several of their agent's accounts."

She showed him the address on her computer's screen.

"Very good work, my dear."

He immediately placed two calls, the first to O'Malley and the second to Professor Hope, instructing them to remain on surveillance at the d'Clare home, and ordered Petri to drive him and Dennison to Mountain Green. Twenty minutes later, the command vehicle pulled in to the hilly wooded subdivision and parked along the side of the road. A short distance ahead of them, at the end of the picturesque street, sat the house owned by James Stevens. With no vehicles parked in the driveway it appeared as if no one was home, but to be sure, Berger ordered Dennison to investigate. A short time later, after breaking in the same way she did at the d'Clares, she called and confirmed that no one was there. Exiting the vehicle, Berger ordered Petri to proceed back to the entrance of the subdivision. If anyone approached, he was to immediately call and let him know.

Once inside, Berger and Dennison began searching for the Firebird files. When they reached the dining room, they found three photographs sitting on an end table. Picking up the two smaller ones, Berger smiled at the pictures of the Ünterbunker.

"What is it, General?" Dennison asked.

"Nothing, my dear. Just a place from the past that is long since gone."

He set the two photos down, and picked up the third and largest one. Even though the picture was quite faded, he could still see enough of the officer's face to recognize Captain Stevens.

"Just as I remembered you," he whispered.

The ring of his phone took his eyes away from the photo, and he quickly set the picture down and answered the call.

"Boss, it's Petri. There's a car pulling into the driveway."

Berger snapped his phone closed, withdrew his firearm, and nodded for Dennison to do the same.

After taking up positions in the kitchen, Berger began to shake with nervous anticipation. He'd waited a long time to confront Captain Stevens, and now that moment was upon him. The different ways he planned to torture him began to play out in his mind, as did the many questions he intended to ask. Realizing he was agitating himself into a rage, he quickly talked himself down. He couldn't afford to let his volcanic temper kill the captain, at least not until he had recovered the files and had synchronized the power system of Firebird Two.

When the kitchen door opened and the ordinary-looking couple walked in, all thoughts of controlling his violent temper swiftly evaporated.

Instead of enjoying a nice afternoon exploring the new home Captain Hank had given them as a gift, Shelley and Roy Harrison learned first-hand why the inmates at the Sachsenhausen concentration camps had nicknamed General Berger the White Wolf.

* * *

The general decided to try a different method of interrogation this time, and it worked better than he expected. When he questioned the Harrison couple, he quickly identified the wife as having the stronger personality of the two and decided to kill her first. With Dennison holding the husband at gunpoint, he unmercifully beat the wife; tossing her around the room and smashing her into the walls as if she were a dog's play toy. Long after rendering her unconscious, he finished his appalling ritual by placing her in a headlock and breaking her neck.

As Shelley's lifeless body was still falling to the floor, Berger turned to Roy and found him sobbing like a baby.

He smiled. "Now Mr. Harrison, are you going to tell me what I want to know?

Five minutes later, after only a few well-placed punches, Roy's willpower cracked and he started answering his questions. The only stumbling block Berger encountered was when he asked Roy the location of Captain Stevens' laboratory. No matter how many blows he administered, the man must have sensed he was going to die, and from that point on steadfastly refused to answer any more questions. With his volcanic temper aroused again, Berger snapped Roy's neck and threw his body across the room into a wall, where it crashed through the sheetrock before landing on the floor. As an afterthought, he retrieved Roy and Shelley's corpses and placed them side-by-side on top of the dining room table.

"Move, counter-move, Herr Speer," he said. "We shall now see how the good captain counters this move."

As he smiled at the Harrison's dead bodies, he thought about the information he'd extracted from the husband. He knew now that there was no "Jim" Stevens, and that Captain Stevens was pretending to be his own son. In addition, when the captain built his device in Maryland and traveled forward in time, he'd developed Parkinson's disease, and attributed his health condition to using the device. This also explained why the captain had involved the d'Clares: he hoped to recruit George to pilot the device into the future and recover the cure.

What impressed the general the most was the confirmation that Captain Stevens had a photographic memory, and that he'd memorized all the Firebird files before destroying them. This disclosure also explained why he later wrote everything down in the diary: with the Parkinson's disease and dementia overtaking his mind, the captain simply couldn't let the greatest scientific discovery in the history of mankind be lost.

Even though he hadn't been able to elicit the location of Captain Stevens laboratory, the information he'd obtained was useful, and made the recovery of the diary imperative.

He immediately retrieved his phone and tried to call O'Malley. When the Irishman didn't answer, he tried to call Professor Hope. Not getting an answer from him either, and thinking something was wrong, he called Petri to come pick them up.

Approximately five minutes later, as the command vehicle weaved its way down Weber Canyon, Berger's phone rang; it was O'Malley.

"Why have you not been answering?" Berger asked.

Before the Irishman could reply, the transmission suddenly became garbled.

Handing the phone to Dennison, she listened for a moment.

"Bad reception," she said, "probably because of the canyon."

Cancelling the call, she immediately redialed the number, and when the Irishman answered she handed the phone back to the general.

"Mr. O'Malley, are you there?"

"Yes, Boss."

"If the d'Clare couple leaves their home, you are to follow them, but have Professor Hope and Mr. Benoit stay there in case the captain shows up at their house. If the d'Clare couple meets the captain, capture them, but under no circumstances are you to kill them. We must recover Captain Stevens' diary. It contains the Firebird information. Do you understand?"

"Got it."

"We will stay up here, in case the captain visits the Harrisons."

After hanging up with O'Malley, the command vehicle cleared the canyon, at which point the general's phone rang again; it was Professor Hope. Berger quickly repeated what he'd told O'Malley.

Now confident that he had covered every contingency, Berger ordered Petri to return to the home in Mountain Green.

* * *

General Berger had no idea that in the span of ten minutes he'd made two critical errors, the first occurring when he temporarily abandoned his surveillance of the rental home in Mountain Green. If he'd remained there for merely three more minutes, he would've intercepted Captain Hank as he was arriving to check on Shelley and Roy Harrison.

His second mistake was using his cell phone to relay important orders to O'Malley while still traveling within the steep walls of Weber Canyon. Unknown to either man, the communication stream was interrupted several times, and those intermittent lapses resulted in the Irishman receiving an entirely different set of orders.

From O'Malley's perspective, the general had given him the green light to kill George and Madison d'Clare, *and* Captain Hank.

* * *

It was half past two-o'clock on Sunday morning when the last emergency vehicle left the scene of the hit-and-run at Station Park. Thomas O'Malley, who had been watching from a darkened side street, walked back toward their vehicle and found William Slone smoking and pacing nervously.

"What's the matter with you, Slone?"

"I think you should've waited for the boss."

"You heard the order."

"Yeah, I heard it, but I also think you should have waited."

"You worry too much."

Just then, the command vehicle pulled in to the deserted lot, and General Berger got out and approached O'Malley.

"Did you locate Captain Stevens?" he asked

"I took care of him, Boss."

"Explain. What do you mean, you took care of him?"

"I killed him."

"What?! I distinctly told you *not* to murder him! Captain Stevens was to be mine, and mine alone to kill!"

"But you ordered me to take care of him and the d'Clares."

"I never gave such an order!"

O'Malley stepped back and ran into Slone, who was also trying to move away from their infuriated leader. In one quick sweeping motion, Berger caught the Irishman by the throat and pulled him toward him, his cowboy hat falling off his head in the process.

"Give me one good reason why I should not kill you right now, Mr. O'Malley! Just one!"

"Boss," he replied, struggling to talk, "I swear on my mother's grave I heard you give the order."

"He's not lying, Boss," Slone said, "I heard it too."

Berger stopped to look at Slone for a moment, then turned to Dennison.

"What do you think, my dear? Is it possible?"

"We were in the canyon at the time," Dennison said. "I suppose the interference could've affected the transmission."

After hesitating a few moments, Berger finally released O'Malley, but stood in place scowling at him.

"Since you've seen fit to kill the captain, then tell me my Irish friend, what are we supposed to do now?"

"What else is there, Boss?" he asked, rubbing the circulation back into his throat. "We've got the diary…"

"But we *do not* have the diary, you dummkopf!"

Both O'Malley and Slone remained quiet. From their large eyes and startled expressions, Berger could tell they were astonished at the news, which confirmed Dennison's theory that their conversation over the phone had been interrupted by the steep canyon walls.

"May I make a suggestion, General?" Dennison asked.

Berger nodded.

"Until we come up with a plan, I say we go back and continue surveillance on the d'Clares."

"Thank you, my dear," Berger said, still glaring at O'Malley. "At least *someone* is still using their brains."

* * *

Later that morning, the general received a call from Professor Hope, informing him that a young couple had knocked on the d'Clares' front door, and that they appeared to be selling something. Dennison, who was eavesdropping, immediately relayed that she'd heard George d'Clare say they'd left a brochure advertising free energy.

"Explain. What does he mean by free energy?" Berger asked.

"They're probably trying to sell him some insulation for his home," Dennison replied.

"Continue the surveillance."

Less than a minute later, Dennison reported that the d'Clares were planning to go to Mountain Green to inform the Harrison's of Captain Hank's death. Berger immediately called O'Malley and ordered him to follow them up there.

A few minutes later, O'Malley's SUV pulled up alongside the command vehicle. Berger, who had somewhat calmed himself from the events that had occurred earlier, instantly became irritated again.

"Is there a problem, Mr. O'Malley? Did you not understand my order?"

"Boss, I've got a plan," the Irishman said.

"Does your plan involve recovering the diary?"

"Yes."

"Then tell me."

After listening to O'Malley outline his scheme to arrest and interrogate the d'Clares, Berger thought it was a good idea.

"Where will you take them?"

"I was hoping Denny could look on her computer and tell me where the nearest local jail is."

"A local jail? Explain."

"I saw it in a movie once..."

"Need I remind you, Mr. O'Malley, that this is not a movie, a show or a play."

"I know, but hear me out. In this movie, the bad guys dressed up as cops, then took this stooge to a local jail to try to make him talk. Scared he was going to be put in prison, the man told them everything. Now, to everyone around here, we're FBI agents, which means we outrank every officer at the local jails."

Berger turned to Dennison.

"Where is the nearest jail?" he asked.

She typed in a quick internet search.

"The Weber County Jail in Ogden," she replied, "on Kiesel Avenue."

467

"Where's that again?" O'Malley asked.

"Go with him and show him, won't you my dear?"

"Yes, General."

"You have my permission to use the entire team," Berger said, addressing O'Malley. While you are interrogating the d'Clares, I will be at their house searching for the diary. Once you have extracted the diary's location, call me immediately. If they have lied to you and I cannot find it, you will increase the pressure. Do you understand?"

O'Malley nodded.

"Between the both of us, we should be able to find out where it is."

* * *

One day later, in his posh executive suite at the elegant Ogden hotel, General Berger sat contemplating his next course of action. He knew the diary was in the d'Clares' possession, but he hadn't been able to finish searching their home. He was only there for a short time the previous day when the front doorbell rang. Peeking through the blinds of the window, he'd watched a couple carrying briefcases, and surmised they were the salesmen that Professor Hope had reported seeing. After what seemed like a long period of time waiting for someone to answer the door, they finally left. While watching them walk away, he saw a police car drive up and stop at a neighbor's house. Sensing it was no longer safe to continue searching for the diary, he exited the home and quickly made his way back to the command vehicle.

As upset as he'd been with his unsuccessful search of the d'Clares' home, listening to the Irishman tell him how his interrogation plan had failed sent his temper to the boiling point.

"Boss," O'Malley said, "George d'Clare is a tough nut to crack. I worked him over pretty good, but he still wouldn't talk."

"You've seen my methods, why did you not start with his wife?"

"We couldn't get to her. There was this woman deputy named Rivers who…"

Berger stood and slammed his fist down on the bar counter.

"You're telling me that one female deputy kept you from the d'Clare woman?"

"There were more deputies than just her."

"Shut up and let me think!"

Berger paced back and forth several times then stopped and addressed O'Malley again.

"Anything from Professor Hope and Mr. Benoit?" he asked.

"Nothing, except that the two salesmen came back."

"What? Why did you not tell me?"

"I didn't think it worth mentioning."

"*Everything* that is happening at the d'Clare home is worth mentioning! Is Miss Dennison still monitoring the home?"

"Yes."

"I want to talk to her."

A few moments later, O'Malley handed his phone to Berger.

"Mr. O'Malley has informed me that the salesmen returned. Did you hear what they talked about?"

"Yes, General. Their names are Ethan and Evelynn Smith. They were selling solar panels."

"Explain. What are solar panels?"

After Dennison had provided him with a brief description, Berger thought it strange these salesmen were so persistent. Thinking about their names, he remembered reading about the Washington couple in the Maryland paper after he'd murdered them, and that they had twins named Ethan and Evelynn.

"Have they left?" he asked.

"Yes, General. About ten minutes ago."

"Let me know immediately if they return."

Berger handed the phone back to O'Malley.

"This is another unforeseen circumstance we will have to deal with."

"What do you mean, Boss?"

"The salesmen who keep coming to the d'Clares' home are the Washington twins, which means Captain Stevens must have involved them and perhaps others."

"So what do we do now?"

"Continue monitoring the d'Clares, and let me know if anyone else comes to their home. *Do not* make any moves without informing me first. Do you understand?"

"Yes, Boss."

"We shall wait a day and see what happens. If no one else comes to meet them and the police are not around, we will storm the home and capture the d'Clares. One way or another, I will find that diary."

* * *

Late Tuesday night, hidden behind the church near George and Madison's home, General Berger called his team together to give them their final instructions.

"Our objective is to capture the d'Clare couple and recover Captain Stevens' diary. If they refuse to cooperate, I will deal with them. Remember, the key to unlimited wealth and power is in that diary, so even if we have to tear the entire house down piece by piece we will not leave here tonight without it. Do you understand?"

"Yes, sir!"

"Good, then let us begin."

Berger led his people down to the end of the church and looked around the corner. Glancing over at the neighbor's house, which was the same house the police car had stopped at yesterday, something appeared different. When Dennison had run a check on that neighbor earlier, she'd found that the owner, Randy Johnston, was a Weber County Sheriff's deputy who lived alone. Ever since they'd started surveillance of the d'Clare couple, this deputy had always kept a light on at night, but now his home was dark. In addition, the police car that was normally parked in the front driveway was gone.

He signaled the team to hold, unzipped the cargo pocket on his pant leg, and removed a pair of binoculars. Examining the house, he found the windows of the ground floor closed, but the ones on the upper level open. He thought it strange that a law enforcement officer living alone would leave his windows unsecured, even if they were on the second floor. Returning to the open windows, he caught the reflection of a nearby streetlight inside one of the rooms. A second later, the reflection was gone. It appeared as if someone had moved out of the way of a mirror and then moved in front of it again. Lowering the binoculars, he saw that it could've been the wind blowing a tree limb into the path of the light, but he wasn't sure.

With his intuition on alert, he motioned for the Irishman to join him.

"I have decided to give you a chance to redeem yourself, Mr. O'Malley," he said.

"What do you mean, Boss?"

"I want you to lead the team and recover the diary. Do whatever it takes."

"Did you say *whatever* it takes?"

"Yes. Do what you need to do, but get me that diary."

The Irishman smiled proudly and turned to Dennison.

"Denny, could you please find me George d'Clares' phone number?"

After a quick internet search on her cell phone, she read it to him, whereupon O'Malley quickly typed the number into his phone and prepared a text message.

"If we can surprise them, we might just catch them trying to hide the diary."

Berger nodded.

"All right, you heard the boss," O'Malley said, addressing the others, "let's be off now."

As his people departed, the general walked toward the street (just far enough to get a clear view of the d'Clares' home) then knelt behind some thick shrubbery to observe the operation. When they reached the d'Clares' front porch, O'Malley signaled them to hold and sent the text, after which he withdrew his gun, and motioned Petri and Slone to kick open the d'Clares' front door.

Just as Berger began to think that his intuition might've been wrong, a large contingent of policemen came running out of the neighbor's house. An instant later, six police vehicles, their lights flashing but without sirens, rushed down the street to the d'Clares' home. Berger watched helplessly as the leader, a large muscular man brandishing a shotgun, entered the house, followed by seven other officers. A short time later, his team emerged one at a time from the house; each handcuffed and escorted by a policeman.

* * *

Two hours later, back in the command vehicle, General Berger retrieved Dennison's laptop computer. Since the majority of police vehicles around the d'Clares' home were marked with Davis County markings, he quickly typed in an internet search and found the location of the jail. Closing the laptop, he placed it in the back seat next to his small suitcase. Seeing the suitcase, he suddenly had an idea how to gain the release of his people. Retrieving the laptop again, he brought up the previous page, and found the name of the officer in charge of the jail, Sherriff Richard Sanders. After another quick search, he located Sanders' home address and typed it into the command vehicle's global positioning system. Retrieving his suitcase, he unzipped one of the side pockets and removed a bar of gold. Deciding to wait until daybreak before trying to exit the neighborhood, he sat back in the command vehicle with his eyes closed, mentally reviewing the story he intended to tell Sherriff Sanders.

Shortly after seven o'clock, Berger drove to Sanders' home, and a few moments after ringing the doorbell, the man came to the door.

"Can I help you?" Sanders asked.

Berger immediately noticed intimidation in the man's eyes, and knew he would be easy to manipulate. Confirming his assumption was the way the short man kept nervously changing his weight from one leg to the other.

He retrieved his forged credential from his pocket and handed it to him.

"I am Deputy Director Kurt Schmidt from the Criminal Investigation Office in Wiesbaden, Germany, currently on special assignment with the FBI. Could I have a moment of your time?"

Hardly examining the identification, Sanders nodded.

"Certainly, Director Schmidt. Please come in."

Berger followed him inside.

Twenty minutes later, the general had convinced the Sherriff that his team had been unjustly incarcerated, and that both the Davis and Weber County Sherriff's offices had interfered with a federal investigation involving the theft of over two-hundred bars of gold from Germany's Central Bank. The trail to recover the stolen gold had led his team of investigators to France, where they'd learned from an informant that the mastermind behind the theft was a man named John LeClair, who was now living in the United States under the assumed name George d'Clare. Then last night, just as his team of investigators were about to move in on d'Clare and his wife, they'd been arrested by the Sherriff's department. If Sanders helped his people recover the gold, his department would be entitled to part of the reward being offered by the Central Bank. Helping Berger sell the story was the bar of gold he'd brought with him, and the d'Clares' name being French.

Seeing the gold bar and hearing about the reward, Sanders immediately called his office at the jail, and the deputy on duty confirmed to him that five men and one woman had been brought in several hours ago by Deputy Alvarez. Much to the general's delight, Sanders had a not-too-friendly history with Alvarez, and didn't like the Weber County deputy operating outside his jurisdiction.

Less than an hour later, Berger secured the release of all six members of his team, with Sherriff Sanders promising his department would be standing by to assist, if needed, with the arrest of the d'Clares and the recovery of the stolen gold.

* * *

At noon, the general and his people reassembled at an indoor-outdoor restaurant at Farmington Station Park. Preferring to eat outside, Berger sat alone at the end of a row of tables with Petri, Slone and Benoit taking up their normal positions as bodyguards, standing and facing away from him. At the table next to the general sat Danielle Dennison, nibbling a sandwich and working on her laptop computer, while O'Malley and Professor Hope sat across from her, sipping at glasses of Irish-brand beer.

Staring intensely at the park's square, Berger's mind was hard at work on a plan of what to do next. Even though he was able to gain the release of his team from Sherriff Sanders, he knew it was just a matter of time before background checks identified them and the police were dispatched to arrest them again.

Finishing his meal, he stood up and stretched, at which point the Irishman got out of his seat and approached him.

"What should we do now, Boss?" O'Malley asked.

"*You* are to do nothing."

"What do you mean?"

"What I mean, my Irish friend, is that you are to do absolutely nothing unless I tell you otherwise. Do you understand?"

"But Boss, it wasn't my fault that the..."

"No, it was not *your* fault you disobeyed my orders and killed Captain Stevens before we'd recovered the Firebird information. It was not *your* fault you botched the interrogation of the d'Clares because of *one* female deputy. And certainly, it is not *your* fault the listening devices that Miss Dennison planted in the d'Clares' home were discovered by the police, is it Mr. O'Malley?"

Just as the Irishman was about to reply, William Slone, who was watching the square, interrupted.

"Boss, I think someone is taking pictures of us."

Berger slowly turned away from O'Malley and casually walked over to join Slone.

"Where are you looking?"

"Left of the playground, ten o'clock position, against the shop on the other side of the square."

Berger immediately spotted the long telephoto lens and walked back to O'Malley.

"I am going to tell you to do something, and I expect you to obey my orders."

"Yes, Boss. Anything you need…"

"Shut up and listen. Take Slone and Benoit and find out who that person is."

Ten minutes later, the three men returned and O'Malley reported to the general.

"Whoever it was, they were gone when we got there," he said.

"I must assume then that someone has followed you here," Berger replied, "and now knows you have contacted me. Probably a law enforcement officer working for Deputy Alvarez."

Before the Irishman could muster up another apology, Dennison interrupted.

"Yes!"

Berger and O'Malley immediately walked over to investigate.

"Sir," she said excitedly, "I have established a link to the LD-5000. I *knew* that deputy hadn't found it."

"What's that?" O'Malley asked.

Before she could answer, Berger held up his hand and stopped her, then turned and addressed O'Malley.

"You may go and rejoin the professor until you are needed."

O'Malley walked away, giving Dennison a dirty look.

As soon as he was out of earshot, Berger turned to face her.

"Do not worry about Mr. O'Malley, my dear," he whispered. "He has almost outlived his usefulness. As soon as we recover the diary and take care of some loose ends, I believe he will be worthy of my attention. Now, you may continue."

"As I was saying, sir, I have established a satellite link to the LD-5000."

He remembered her telling him she'd planted the sophisticated listening device in the d'Clare home (in addition to the other ones) and that it was virtually undetectable because of its small size. Up until now, her efforts to connect to it had been unsuccessful.

"Then we will still be able to listen in on the d'Clares?"

"From just about anywhere, sir."

"Excellent, my dear. I knew you would not disappoint me."

Berger immediately proceeded to the table where O'Malley and Professor Hope were sitting.

"Let's go!" he ordered.

"Where to?" the Irishman asked.

"Back to the airport. By now Sherriff Sanders has discovered his mistake, and with Deputy Alvarez's people taking our pictures it is no longer safe for us to be out in the open."

* * *

Twenty-four hours later, back onboard the aircraft, General Berger leaned back in his chair satisfied that he now knew almost all of Captain Hank's story. With Dennison's laptop computer linked to the LD-5000 eavesdropping bug, he listened to George d'Clare read over half of the diary, and he and his wife tell what they knew to Deputy Alvarez, Deputy Rivers and Albert Greenbaum. When the Washington twins arrived, they supplied even more information; first-hand accounts of their meetings with Captain Stevens. After George finished reading the rest of the diary, the only thing Berger didn't know was what happened after the captain's friend, Professor Lee, had returned from the fourth dimension. But that didn't matter. He now knew the location of Captain Stevens' laboratory and where George d'Clare had hidden the diary.

As if hearing the captain's story wasn't enough, the general thought he'd struck gold when he listened to Albert Greenbaum admit he was one responsible for bringing his photograph to the attention of his superiors, who subsequently leaked it to the news media in 1991. Smiling with glee, Berger thought of the different ways he was going to torture the Jew before murdering him.

A short time later, when he overheard Greenbaum describe his puny and unsophisticated plan to capture him, Berger laughed.

"No, my clever little Jewish friend, it is *you* who will be trapped!"

As soon as the meeting at the d'Clares had concluded, the general spoke briefly with Dennison and called his team together at the bottom of the aircraft's boarding ladder. After giving them quick summary of the situation, he issued his orders.

"Mr. O'Malley, you will take one vehicle and go with Mr. Slone, Mr. Petri and Mr. Benoit, and secure building 3731 at the University of Utah. Take the explosives with you."

"Yes, Boss," the Irishman replied sullenly.

"Miss Dennison has something for you to take along."

Stepping forward, she handed O'Malley a small black box.

"What is it?" he asked.

"It's a cell phone scrambler. It won't affect our phones, but it should work on just about any other type. All you have to do is turn the switch on."

The Irishman nodded.

"I don't want anyone calling for reinforcements, so turn it on as soon as you secure the building," Berger said.

When O'Malley morosely acknowledged the instructions and turned to leave, Berger grabbed him by the throat and jerked him back.

"I do not need your surly attitude, Mr. O'Malley. Do you understand?"

"Yes, Boss," he squeaked.

"When Deputy Alvarez, Deputy Rivers and Mr. Greenbaum get there, you are to *capture* them, *not kill* them. Do you understand?"

"But what if they start shooting?"

Berger tightened his grip.

"I am paying you to obey my orders. If the four of you cannot overpower one man, one woman and a Jew, then you do not deserve the riches the device will bring."

The Irishman nodded, at which point Berger released him.

"You must leave immediately."

O'Malley stood for a moment, gulping in air and rubbing the circulation back into his neck.

"Why so soon, Boss?" he asked. "It's only Thursday, and if they're not planning on being there until Saturday..."

"Because we do not know when the deputies will arrive," Berger interrupted, "and I want you and the men in place *before* they get there. Do you understand?"

"Yes, Boss."

"Call me once you have secured the building, and again after you have captured the deputies and Mr. Greenbaum."

"What about Hope and Denny?"

"As a ruse, Mr. Hope will be following the d'Clares, while Miss Dennison and I recover the diary."

One hour later, Berger received the first call from the Irishman, reporting his team had secured the building and were now in position to capture the deputies and Albert Greenbaum.

"What about the device?" Berger asked.

"It's here. We can see it on the TV monitors."

"The security door is closed then?"

"Yes, Boss, and what a door it is."

"What do you mean?"

"It looks like a bank vault protecting Fort Knox."

* * *

A few minutes past two o'clock on Saturday afternoon, General Berger received word from O'Malley that his team had successfully captured deputy Alvarez and Albert Greenbaum, but not without casualties.

"What has happened Mr. O'Malley?" Berger asked, instantly irritated.

"Boss, we did exactly as you told us to do. When the deputies and Greenbaum got here, we jumped them, but when Petri tried to take Alvarez's gun away they started to fight. That's when..."

"Tell me!"

"That's when Alvarez kicked Petri and broke his leg."

"You mean to say Alvarez is free?"

"No, Boss. With Slone's help I knocked him out, but while we were getting Alvarez under control, Deputy Rivers kneed Benoit between the legs, wrestled his gun away from him and shot him dead. I had to put a bullet in her eye."

"What about the Jew?"

"Slone already had him handcuffed. He's alive, but looking scared."

Berger thought about the entire situation as if it were a giant chess game again, and that his first move had resulted in *acceptable* losses. Although Benoit was a good bodyguard, he could easily recruit another, and as for Deputy Rivers, she really didn't matter because he was going to kill her anyway.

"How bad is Petri injured?"

"He's in a lot of pain, but he's handling it pretty good."

"Now listen to me. I want you to hide the bodies and the two captives."

"Where will we put them?"

"Take them to the latrine and have Mr. Petri watch over them. You and Mr. Slone are to continue monitoring the building. Report to me immediately when the d'Clares and the Washington twins arrive."

"When they get here do you want us to capture them too?"

"No. We do not know if Captain Stevens has involved anyone else or if the deputies have either. For the time being, just keep watch and report. Do you understand?"

"Yes, Boss, you can count on…"

Berger closed his cell phone, not wanting to hear any more of the Irishman's meaningless promises.

* * *

Approximately ninety minutes later, having retrieved Captain Steven's diary from the d'Clares' home, Danielle Dennison climbed into the passenger side of the command vehicle.

"Everything is going according to plan," Berger said. "While you were gone, Professor Hope and Mr. O'Malley called. The d'Clare couple and the Washington twins have arrived at Captain Steven's laboratory, and no one else has approached the building. This will all be over very soon, and by tomorrow morning we shall be back in Nevada testing Firebird Two."

When she didn't answer, he looked at her and immediately noticed she was trembling. "What is it, my dear?"

"Sir, the formulas are not here."

Ripping the diary out of Dennison's hands, Berger quickly examined the contents.

"The d'Clares," he whispered. "It *must* have been the d'Clares."

With his temper starting to rise, he called O'Malley.

"Capture the d'Clares at once!"

"Okay, Boss, but what about the twins?"

"Kill them if you have to, but I want the d'Clares alive!"

He threw his phone into the back seat followed by the now-worthless diary.

"Buckle your seat belt, my dear. We have business to attend to."

Like a slow-burning fuse making its way toward a keg of gunpowder, General Berger followed the command vehicle's global positioning map to the University of Utah campus. As each mile passed, any thoughts he'd had of controlling his volcanic temper diminished, while conversely, his anger and rage grew exponentially towards its boiling point – reaching a crescendo when he arrived at Building 3731.

"Now, Herr Speer," he said, aloud and to himself, "we shall do things *my* way!"

Chapter Twenty
The Confrontation

One Hour Later
Saturday, 13 September 2014, 17:40hrs
Inside *Building 3731, University of Utah Campus, Salt Lake City, Utah*

Five dead bodies lay side-by-side near the two entrance doors, as if they were nothing more than pieces of oversized trash waiting their turn to be taken out to the dumpster. The growing pool of bodily fluids on the floor beneath them gradually crawled outward, which reminded me of the way slow-moving magma oozes from a volcano and melts everything in its path. Enhancing the grisly sight were the dimly-lit emergency lights, which colored the room a dark shade of crimson red. Even in the shallow lighting, I recognized the dead as being Deputy Rivers, Ethan and Evelynn Washington, Albert Greenbaum, and my beloved wife Madison – all now victims of General Berger and his men.

As the tears welled up in my eyes, I remembered what happened just before the Irishman had struck me with his gun, and how Captain Hank's research room had been transformed into this gruesome human slaughterhouse.

~ Then ~

I was still watching the black SUV that followed us to the building when Madison finished reading the final passages of Captain Hank's notebook.

"Was that the last thing he wrote?" I asked. "Torn Fu?"

"Right after he wrote, *must warn George and Madison.* He underlined it several times."

"How is it spelled?"

"Capitol t, o, r, n, then a period, capitol f, u."

"If he underlined it, it must have been important."

Ethan and Evelynn Washington, who were sitting on the floor of the main hallway, simply stared down, their tear-filled eyes reflecting their emotions of losing Captain Hank.

"I wonder," I said, getting their attention, "this e-KAT transmitter he wrote about. Do you think something like that is even possible?"

"I'd have to say no," Evelynn said. "For it to work, it would have to break one of the fundamental laws of physics."

"The law of cause-and-effect?"

"Yes."

"I agree," Ethan said. "Besides, if it did work, Captain Hank would've used it and we wouldn't be standing here."

"What if he didn't have time to use it?" I asked.

"I guess we'll never know for sure."

"Well I know one thing for sure," Madison said. "He got killed trying to warn us about General Berger."

I glanced out the window at the SUV, and noticed the driver's door was now open.

"Something's happening."

"Is it Mr. Greenbaum and the deputies?" Madison asked.

When I shook my head, she joined me at the window along with the twins, and we observed the man who called himself Agent Crosby (whom Deputy Alvarez identified as being Professor Hope) exit the vehicle.

484

A moment later, the squeaking hinges of a door opened from the long hallway leading to the rear of the building. Walking over, I stuck my head around the corner and saw O'Malley, gun in hand, emerge from the room on the far right-hand side.

As he limped toward me, I ran back to Madison and the twins.

"Something must've gone wrong," I whispered. "It's O'Malley."

"Maybe the deputies are waiting until General Berger gets here before they move in," Ethan said, also whispering, "but in case I'm wrong, let's get into the polished-steel room. If we have to, we'll lock ourselves in."

Following him, we quickly made our way through the research room and into the polished-steel room with the device. Proceeding immediately to the wall on the left side, Ethan raised the clear plastic cover over the alarm button. The instant he touched it, however, the worst possible thing happened: the lights went out.

In the darkness, I heard Ethan frantically pushing the button several times.

"The power's been cut," he said.

A moment later the light from Evelynn's phone came on and her fingers moved quickly over the numbers.

"And I can't dial out," she said.

Ethan, Madison and I immediately retrieved our phones too, and found they wouldn't work either. I looked around for a moment and remembered something Captain Hank had written in his notebook.

"The auxiliary generators. Captain Hank just had them put in."

"The switches must be here somewhere," Madison said.

Using our phones as flashlights, we frantically searched the walls. Suddenly, dim red emergency lights came on, faintly illuminating the polished-steel walls and the research room.

Before we could return our attention to looking for the auxiliary power switches, one of the doors to the outer hallway opened and closed. The twins immediately reached behind them and withdrew guns from the back of their belts. Between Madison reading the notebook and us retreating into the room with the device, I'd completely forgotten they were armed.

Now somewhat assured we were protected, I motioned to Madison to stay back, crept over to the security door and peeked around the corner.

The Irishman was crouched just inside the door with his gun drawn. Next to him, was another man I recognized from the night of the interrogation, carrying a rifle. Taking a second look, I noticed that it wasn't just an ordinary rifle the other man was holding, but a very modern military assault weapon, complete with a laser-targeting scope.

"You four had best come out of there now," O'Malley yelled, "before I order Slone to shoot you!"

Ethan tapped me on the shoulder.

"Get back George, we've got this."

"All right but be careful. That Slone guy has some heavy-duty firepower."

I moved back out of his way, at which point he took up my previous position, while Evelynn stood behind him.

Very cautiously, Ethan knelt and peeked around the corner. Just as he moved his gun out to take aim, I noticed a red dot appear on his hand, but before I could warn him a deafening shot rang out.

In an instant, Ethan's gun flew out of his hand and he fell to the floor writhing in pain. Realizing that his head was still out in the open, I moved forward to try to help him.

"No George, stay back," he said.

Evelynn, who'd frozen at the sight, quickly recovered, holstered her gun, and grabbed his ankles to drag him to safety. The moment she started pulling him, a red dot appeared on his forehead and a second shot rang out. Ethan's body immediately relaxed and went limp.

"No!" Evelynn screamed.

Quickly pulling her gun back out, she moved toward the open door.

"Evelynn!" Madison and I yelled in unison, but she wasn't listening.

Stepping out into the open, she fired her weapon wildly into the research room. Once she was out of ammunition, several rounds of return fire struck her and she fell to the floor; her eyes vacant and staring.

In the span of ten seconds, both twins were dead, and gone with them was our only means of protection.

Footsteps approached, and O'Malley stepped through the doorway and pointed his gun at us.

"Well I do declare," he said, grinning from ear to ear, "it's the d'Clares."

After searching us thoroughly and removing everything we had in our pockets, the Irishman forced us into the research room. Once we'd reached the open area near the entry doors, he handcuffed us with our hands behind our backs and made us get down on our knees.

As soon as he was satisfied we weren't going anywhere, he ordered Slone to retrieve the twins' guns and watch us, at which point he proceeded to the nearest work table, and went through my wallet and Madison's purse. Finishing, he tilted his cowboy hat back on his head and smiled.

"Good shooting, Slone. I think the boss will be pleased."

Before Slone could answer, one of the entry doors exploded open, and in stormed SS Lieutenant General Karl Berger, the White Wolf of Sachsenhausen! Having previously read his description and seeing his photographs, I expected him to be tall and muscular, but up-close and in-person I couldn't believe how big he was. Madison had said he reminded her of one of those professional wrestlers you see on television, but her comparison was a gross understatement; his chiseled muscles on his large frame were developed well-beyond any wrestler I'd ever seen.

From his red face and serious look, I could tell he was livid about something. Proving my theory was O'Malley, who walked over to greet him and was instantly swatted aside by the general's huge right hand.

Berger looked around for a moment, letting his eyes get accustomed to the dim lights, and locating Madison and me, proceeded toward us. When he was less than five feet away, he stopped and looked at Madison for a moment, then stepped over to me.

"Mr. d'Clare, you are either going to tell me where the Firebird formulas are, or you are going to watch everyone die, including your wife. Do you understand?"

His thick German accent, coupled with his dark and menacing eyes, paralyzed me.

"Do you understand!" he screamed.

I could feel my Parkinson's symptoms emerge, and my right arm and leg began to tremble.

"There aren't any formulas. I shredded them all," I said, barely getting the words out.

"We shall soon see."

He stood and turned to O'Malley.

"Bring in the deputy and the Jew."

As the Irishman and Slone departed, Danielle Dennison entered the room carrying a laptop computer, followed by Professor Hope. Berger, seeing her, pointed to Captain Hank's two computers.

"See if you can extract any information."

"I'll need the power back on to do that, sir,"

"Then stand by, my dear. This shouldn't take long."

With Professor Hope following, she made her way over to one of the desks, while Berger walked back into the polished-steel room and examined the device; touching it and nodding a few times, as if he was impressed with Captain Hank's work.

"George," Madison whispered, "did you really shred the formulas?"

"I got rid of them while you were asleep."

"What about the flash drive?"

I looked back at her in a state of disbelief. With everything that had gone on, I'd completely forgotten about it. To top it off, I couldn't remember where I'd hidden it.

"George, what about the flash drive?" she asked again, slower this time.

"I don't know where it is," I confessed.

Before we could say anything else, the entry doors opened and Albert Greenbaum walked in, handcuffed with his hands behind his back, followed by O'Malley and Slone dragging Deputy Alvarez, unconscious and secured in the same fashion. A third man, who I recognized from the interrogation, came in behind them; limping so badly he needed his assault rifle to help himself walk.

After the Irishman ordered Albert to kneel next to me, he and Slone dropped Alvarez next to Madison. In the dim light, I thought the deputy was dead, but after a moment his chest rose and fell. From his torn and disheveled uniform and the many contusions on his face, I could tell he'd put up quite a fight. I also noticed a large bump in the temple area of the left side of his head, undoubtedly where they'd knocked him out.

Returning from examining the device, Berger ordered O'Malley and Slone to bring in Deputy Rivers.

"What happened?" I whispered to Albert.

"They were waiting for us when we got here. Deputy Rivers managed to kill one of them, but unfortunately she's dead too."

I was stunned at the news, as was Madison, who let out a gasp.

"If I'd only brought my gun," Albert added, his voice trailing off.

THE DEVICE

Before I could ask him any more questions, O'Malley and Slone returned, dragging the body of Deputy Rivers. After instructing the two men to lay her down on the other side of the room across from us, Berger ordered them to move the twins' bodies next to hers and position them shoulder-to-shoulder. Once they were situated to his liking, he instructed Slone to take up a position in front of the entrance doors and O'Malley to do the same on the opposite side, thus blocking the center aisle that led to the room with the device.

Returning to me, Berger knelt.

"As you can see, Mr. d'Clare, three of your friends are dead. We shall now see how many more people will die before you tell me what I want to know. And believe me, before this night is over, you *will* tell me what I want to know."

Much to my surprise he walked over to the nearest work table, removed his shirt, and started doing a series of exercises, including deep knee bends and leg stretches. As soon as he'd completed a few repetitions, he stopped to look at something on the table; it was my wallet and Madison's purse.

"You searched them?" he asked, addressing O'Malley.

"Yes, Boss. That's all they had on them."

"What about this?" He held up my bookbag.

"I'll check it out."

Berger tossed it to him and continued to exercise.

As I watched O'Malley unzip and empty out each compartment, my heart suddenly sank when he pulled out Madison's barrette containing the flash drive. I instantly remembered stashing it there when Madison was in the hospital. Trying to act calm I looked away, while at the same time, I silently cursed myself for being so absentminded.

Laughing, O'Malley held up the barrette and looked over at me.

"Tell me Mr. d'Clare, with that bald head of yours, where exactly do you wear this?"

"It's mine, you dope," Madison said. "Or maybe you're just too stupid to know that?"

The Irishman, fully enraged, threw the barrette on the ground shattering it to pieces, and with his face now a bright shade of red, locked eyes on Madison and started towards her. He hadn't taken more than a couple of steps, when the massive arm of the general stopped him.

"Get back to your position, Mr. O'Malley," Berger said, coldly and business-like. "I will deal with the d'Clare woman."

The Irishman stared at her for a few more moments before finally stepping back, whereupon Berger walked back over to me.

"Now I ask you again Mr. d'Clare, where are the Firebird formulas?"

"Like I told you before, I shredded them."

"Very well, I shall now kill your friend."

He immediately turned to O'Malley and ordered him to remove Albert's handcuffs. Still glaring at Madison, the Irishman walked over and harshly pulled Albert up to his feet. A moment later the handcuffs dropped to the floor, at which point O'Malley pushed Albert out into the center of the open area.

Like a boxer sizing up an opponent, Berger began circling him, striking him several times in the face and stomach as he went around. Even though Albert managed to block and dodge a few of the blows, the general countered quickly and delivered devastating punches to his abdomen and kidney area. In a short amount of time, Albert was writhing on the floor completely at his mercy.

Berger laughed. "I see you are as good a fighter as your countrymen at Sachsenhausen."

Wobbling, Albert stood back up and defiantly cursed, calling him a name I didn't understand but took as being a Hebrew insult.

In response, Berger pretended to yawn, withdrew the gun from his belt, and shot Albert point-blank in the head. As his body fell to the floor, I felt nauseous and thought I was going to throw up.

Even though I'd heard the stories, seeing the general take a life so indiscriminately was truly horrifying.

Holstering his gun, Berger dragged Albert's body over next to Evelynn's, and slowly walked back over to Madison and me.

"That makes four, Mr. d'Clare. Are you ready to talk now?"

"I told you, I destroyed the formulas."

"Very well then, say goodbye to your wife."

He motioned to the now-grinning O'Malley.

As I looked at Madison, tears came to my eyes. Although she was shaking too, she had a calmer look on her face, as if she were silently telling me not to worry and that everything was going to be all right.

Once the Irishman had her handcuffs off, he harshly shoved her out in the open area of the room and stepped around behind me.

Berger circled Madison much like he had Albert. Completing one full circle, he abruptly stopped and began again in the opposite direction.

I started to stand up, but O'Malley moved around in front of me and slugged me in the stomach, knocking the wind out of me and sending me back down to my knees. After a moment, I'd gulped in enough air to plead for Madison's life.

"I've told you everything! I shredded every math and physics equation that was in that diary! The formulas are gone! Killing her won't get them back!"

Ignoring me, Berger began hitting Madison, and after a series of well-placed punches she doubled-over and fell to the floor; her nose and lip bleeding profusely.

Quickly moving in, he took hold of her belt, and using only one arm effortlessly picked her up off the floor. Grabbing a handful of her hair with his free hand, he pulled her head up and turned to me.

"Are you ready to tell me now, Mr. d'Clare, or would you like to see your wife die in front of you?"

With tears in my eyes, I sat there speechless, not knowing what else I could say to make him stop.

Returning his attention to Madison, he pulled her close until her face was less than a foot away from his.

"Say goodbye to your husband, Mrs. d'Clare."

In response, Madison did the bravest thing I'd ever seen. On the brink of death and in a final show of defiance, she inhaled deeply and spit in his face. Not an ordinary "sunflower seed" spittle, this one was quite voluminous and red in color, undoubtedly gathered within the last few moments from her bloody facial wounds.

Temporarily blinded, Berger let go of her and tried to clear his eyes with his hands. Realizing he was only smearing it and making matters worse, he looked around for something to wipe his face with and spotted the shirt he'd left on the work table. As he made his way over to retrieve it, his foot happened to kick one of the broken pieces of the barrette, and it slid across the floor and struck the leg of the chair occupied by Danielle Dennison.

Dennison, who'd been watching the murderous spectacle in a trance-like state, jumped when the piece hit her chair. Looking down to investigate, she picked up the broken piece of the barrette and moved it into the light of her laptop computer. My worst fears, not only for myself but for the entire world, were realized when I saw the piece she was holding was the hidden flash drive!

I looked back at Berger just as he tossed his shirt aside.

"No one does that to me, Mrs. d'Clare! No one!" he snarled.

In an instant, he was back to attacking Madison, and after several more crippling punches to her face and midsection he placed her in a headlock.

Knowing what was going to happen next, I started to stand up again, but the Irishman stopped me with a hammering blow to the back of my head. Before losing consciousness, the last thing I remember was O'Malley standing over me, grinning with his gun in his hand, and hearing the sickening sound of Madison's neck breaking.

~ Now ~

Having regained my senses, the true impact of what I was looking at sunk in and I laid my head back down on the floor and wept uncontrollably. Captain Hank's mission of stopping this evil man had now taken five more casualties, but none more important to me than my beloved Madison. The one person I cared about most, the beautiful woman who had agreed to share her life with me was gone – the latest victim of the Nazi's White Wolf.

As the thought of never seeing her again overwhelmed me, I suddenly felt alone and afraid, like when I'd received the Parkinson's diagnosis. At the same time, I was overcome with survivor's remorse and wished that I was the one laying motionless on the floor instead of her.

Pulling my teary eyes away from her, I looked around the dimly-lit research room to see if anything had changed while I'd been unconscious. O'Malley, grinning, was standing next to me pointing his gun at my head, while Slone, the man who'd killed the twins, was still in position in front of the entry doors, his assault rifle ready. General Berger, Dennison and Hope were huddled together, staring at her laptop computer.

"Unbelievable, this is truly unbelievable," Hope said. "When I thought this area of study couldn't be proven, I thought it was a dead end and abandoned it."

"In your estimation, Professor, will these formulas enable you to synchronize the power system of Firebird Two?"

"Definitely General. Once we get back it should only take a few hours."

Berger smiled. "Very well then, you and Miss Dennison help Mr. Petri to the vehicle and stand by. We won't be long now."

"What about the captain's computers, sir?" Dennison asked.

"Take them. They may have more information we can use."

Dennison and Hope gathered up the two machines, and helped the injured man out.

"Boss, Mr. d'Clare is back with us," O'Malley said.

Berger looked at me and smiled. "Unlock him, Mr. O'Malley. It is his turn to die."

O'Malley jerked me to my feet, removed the handcuffs, and shoved me out into the open area. My right leg, weak from Parkinson's, immediately gave out and I fell to the floor.

As I stood back up, Berger began circling me. Even though I wanted to die and join Madison, my instinct for self-preservation kicked in and I backed away from him. Darting in, he struck me with a barrage of punches to my face and abdomen. When I finally fell to my knees, he moved around behind me and placed me in a headlock; his huge right arm encircling my neck like a giant boa constrictor.

"Very clever hiding the information in the hair piece, Mr. d'Clare. Very clever indeed," he said, "but now, my weak little do-gooder, it is time for you to join your wife."

As his giant arm squeezed, I grabbed it with both hands and tried to pry it off me. As the pressure increased, my windpipe pinched closed, and in state of panic, I thrashed around in hopes of breaking the hold.

Suddenly from behind me, I heard the voice of Deputy Alvarez.

"Is that all you know how to do?" he bellowed. "Kill those who are weaker than you?"

Berger immediately relaxed his arm, which allowed me a few precious breaths of air, and while still holding me, he turned around.

No longer on the floor, Alvarez was standing upright - seemingly uninjured and steady as a rock!

Berger laughed. "You think you can defeat me, Spaniard?"

"On my worst day, I could take you down."

"Very well then, I accept the challenge."

Berger shoved me away, and after stumbling a few steps I crashed into one of the work desks; toppling it over as I fell to the floor.

Disoriented from the beating and still trying to catch my breath, I looked around to get my bearings. I'd landed in the center aisle, roughly fifteen feet away from the large security door and the room with the device.

The Irishman started towards me, but after taking only a few steps, the general stopped him.

"Unlock the deputy Mr. O'Malley."

"Are you sure, Boss?"

"Unlock him! Do not make me ask you again!"

O'Malley moved behind Alvarez, and a few moments later the handcuffs dropped to the floor. When the Irishman tried to force him out into the open area, the big deputy spun around and delivered a solid right fist to the side of his head, which sent O'Malley reeling into the wall behind them.

Returning his attention to Berger, Alvarez stripped off his torn shirt and readied himself for the fight.

As he'd done with Albert, Madison and me, Berger began circling him.

"First you break one of my men's legs, now you injure my second-in-command. What am I to do with you, Spaniard?"

"Take your best shot," Alvarez replied, unwavering.

Like ultimate fighters vying for a championship, the huge Nazi general and Weber County deputy engaged in the most violent fight I have ever seen. For every punch or kick Berger delivered, Alvarez countered with hits and kicks of his own; each combatant seemingly unfazed by the pounding their body was taking from the other.

After several lengthy exchanges, Berger backed away and immediately began circling him again.

"I see you've had some training, Spaniard. Military?"

"Hundred and First Airborne," Alvarez replied.

"A screaming eagle? Some of my friends killed hundreds of you cowards at Bastogne."

"Better check your history, Nazi. *We* won the Battle of the Bulge. As for cowards, why weren't you there helping your friends?"

Berger's face grew red at the insult and he charged, tackling Alvarez like a pass rusher sacking a quarterback.

Thinking I could help, I looked around to see if I could find something to use as a weapon, and my eyes happened to catch sight of the left wall inside the room with the device. Except for one small rectangular piece of metal directly underneath the alarm button, the polished-steel walls reflected the red emergency lights like a mirror. Looking closer, I saw it wasn't just a piece of metal, but a small door that resembled a home's circuit breaker panel. Suddenly it hit me: it must be switches for the auxiliary generators! When the lights had gone out earlier, Madison and the twins and I hadn't been able to find them, but from the angle I was at now, its polished-steel finish wasn't as reflective as the rest of the wall and it stuck out like a sore thumb. If I could somehow reach it, I might have a chance of activating the security door and locking myself inside.

Leaning up to get a better look, my knee contacted something on the floor, and reaching down found it to be one of the old heavy-duty staplers that had been on the desk. Since there wasn't anything else within arm's reach, I took hold of it and slowly tucked it up close to my stomach.

Returning to the fight, General Berger had gained the upper hand and was now on top Deputy Alvarez, pummeling him with series of punches to the side of his head where he'd been previously injured. A few moments later, the deputy's arms dropped, and he appeared to be on the verge of being knocked out. After delivering a few more punches, Berger stood and circled him again.

THE DEVICE

With everyone distracted watching the fight, I thought I might be able to silently crawl into the room with the device, but before I could move a muscle, O'Malley walked over and stood next to me.

Alvarez tried to stand up but Berger leveled him with another powerful hit to the head, and after quickly moving in behind him, pulled the deputy up to his knees and screamed in his face.

"Don't pass out on me yet, Spaniard, the fight is far from over!"

Remaining unresponsive to Berger, Alvarez's right hand moved down, ever so slowly, and removed something from the inside of his boot. Squinting, I could see it was a switchblade knife. Since Berger was facing the same direction as the deputy, he couldn't see it, nor could Slone because the two were blocking his line of sight. Glancing up at O'Malley to see if he'd noticed, I found him with his eyes closed and rubbing his head; still woozy from the surprise punch Alvarez had given him.

When I looked back at Deputy Alvarez he was staring at me, at which point he gave me a slight and almost-imperceptible nod.

"I'm not Spanish, General," he said, his voice growing louder, "I'm a Mexican and damn proud of it!"

In a lightning-fast move, he clicked open the knife and stabbed Berger in the right thigh – burying the blade to the hilt! Not done, he pulled the knife out, and while rising to his feet slashed it at the general's throat. In a swift defensive move, Berger threw his arm up just in time to deflect it, but in doing so, the blade passed by his face and sliced open his left cheek.

Back-pedaling away, Berger reached up to feel the cut, and seeing his own blood, went into a maniacal rage. Rushing Alvarez again, he managed to grab hold of the deputy's arm holding the knife. Struggling for control of the weapon, both men fell to the floor where the fight became a savage life-or-death wrestling match.

With O'Malley now absorbed in watching the fight, I slowly stood up next to him, trying not to make a sound. With all the strength I could muster, I swung the heavy stapler into his head and the blow sent him to the floor.

As I made a break for the polished-steel room, Berger screamed.

"Slone, stop him!"

A split-second later a shot rang out, and the bullet struck my right shoulder. The impact of the bullet coupled with my weak right leg made me to lose my balance, and I fell through the threshold, landing on the floor in front of the device. Realizing I was still out in the open, and an easy mark for Slone's deadly aim, I swiftly rolled to my left. The instant I moved another shot rang out, followed by the sound of the bullet as it passed by my right ear.

Crawling as fast as I could to the left wall, I reached the small metal door, tore it open, and found a bank of five circuit breaker switches. Quickly flipping them all on, the wall behind the device suddenly came alive with the sound of the auxiliary generators powering-up. A few moments later the main lights came back on, which illuminated both the polished-steel room and the research room in a blinding sea of light.

Reaching up, I worked my hand under the clear plastic cover and pressed the red emergency button underneath. Almost immediately, sirens blared and red lights flashed, then the heavy security door began to swing closed. As the door made its way toward the threshold, I prayed that Deputy Alvarez's distraction of pulling the knife on General Berger and the blow I'd delivered to O'Malley had given me enough time to lock myself in.

Once the door was roughly twelve inches from closing all the way I felt relieved, but my hopes instantly evaporated when O'Malley, gun in hand, came diving through the shrinking door opening. Unfortunately for him, his trailing left leg was a second too late and the closing door caught him by the ankle. For a moment, I thought the modern and sophisticated-looking door might have safeguards installed (such as sensors) and detecting an obstruction would either stop its travel or open again. My worries were put to rest when the door continued to close, and the Irishman's ankle snapped like a dry tree branch.

Screaming in agony, O'Malley dropped his gun and began thrashing around on the floor; all the while, being held in place by his trapped leg.

I pulled myself up to my feet, then walked over and retrieved his gun. As I approached his eyes grew wide, and for the first time his normally pompous expression was replaced with the look of fear.

"I told you one day I was going to kill you for what you did to Madison."

"Please Mr. d'Clare, don't kill me! I'll talk to the boss! I'll see if…"

I didn't let him finish the sentence.

Turning away, I slowly walked back to the left wall and took a moment to gather my thoughts. Although I seldom attended church, I still consider myself a spiritual person, and up until now had believed all life was sacred. But Madison's death, as well as the deaths of the others, had done something to me. In that moment, I felt no remorse for taking O'Malley's life.

Now that I was armed, the thought crossed my mind to reopen the security door and kill Berger, or at least try to help Deputy Alvarez, but remembering the sharpshooter Slone was also outside I thought better of it; a novice like me using a handgun wouldn't stand a chance against an experienced marksman with a laser-targeting assault rifle.

Remembering what Captain Hank had written about the room's surveillance system, I located the polished-steel plate being held in place with wing nuts. Quickly removing the panel, I found a medium-sized television, on top of which sat a remote control for the outside security cameras.

Turning the set on, the picture of the research room slowly faded into view. Much to my dismay, General Berger was alive and standing in the center aisle near the tipped-over desk. Using the controller, I moved the camera around until the gunman Slone came into view. He was standing at the keypad of the security door, frantically pushing the buttons trying to get it to open. Next to him, still wedged between the door and the threshold, was O'Malley's left foot. Panning back from the gruesome sight, my heart sank when I saw Deputy Alvarez laying motionless in the background, his switchblade knife protruding from his chest. The fearless deputy had bought me the few precious seconds I needed to escape into the room with the device, but had paid the price with his life.

Returning the camera to General Berger, I watched him limp over and retrieve his shirt, and after tearing it in two, he tied one of the pieces around the wound on his right thigh. Folding the other piece into a small square, he pressed it against the cut on his cheek.

"Mr. Slone, go tell Miss Dennison and Professor Hope I want to see them," he said, "and bring the explosives back with you."

Slone immediately exited.

A few minutes later Danielle Dennison returned, carrying her laptop computer, followed by Hope and Slone, each carrying a duffel bag.

"I need you to get this door open, my dear," Berger said, addressing Dennison.

After acknowledging the order, she immediately proceeded to the keypad.

"Slone told us what happened," Hope said, staring at O'Malley's foot.

Berger nodded. "That dummkopf Irishman let Mr. d'Clare get the drop on him."

"Do you think he's dead?"

"We shall soon see."

"What about d'Clare? What if he activates the device?"

"It does not matter. Once Miss Dennison opens the door we will destroy the building and everything in it."

"Why not just blow it up now?"

THE DEVICE

"Because I do not know how well the room is fortified, and I want to make sure *everything* is destroyed."

Before I could hear Hope's response, I felt a surge of pain in my right shoulder. A sea of lightheadedness followed, and thinking I was going to pass out, I leaned against the wall to steady myself. Closing my eyes for a moment, I regained my balance and started to feel a little better, but upon opening them felt lightheaded again. Looking down, I noticed the blood dripping off me had already formed a small pool on the floor where I was standing.

Since reopening the security door was not an option, and I didn't have enough strength to make it to one of the exit doors in the back of the room and run to safety, I tucked O'Malley's gun in my belt and hobbled over to the device.

As I neared the round front of the cylinder-shaped main structure, I noticed blood spatter on it and a small hole at the nine o'clock position. Examining it for a moment, I realized that the blood was mine and that the bullet must've passed through my shoulder and lodged itself somewhere inside the fuselage.

With my pain telling me to get going, I staggered the last few steps to the open hatch of the cockpit, and used my good left arm to pull myself inside.

After settling in the seat, I located the main power switch and turned it on. A moment later, the cockpit lights illuminated and the exciter-motors came to life; their low-pitched hum becoming more audible as the system energized itself with electricity. The only thing that appeared not to be working was the on-board chronometer, and I realized from its position that it might've absorbed the bullet. Proving my theory, I leaned up to take a closer look and found the back of it completely shattered, with a small hole in the forward wall directly behind it.

Satisfied everything else was working, I leaned over and secured the hatch, then retrieved the headset from the right-hand console and put it on. Following the instructions on the laminated card, I located the gauge on the forward console that indicated the combined power level of the exciter-motors, and found the needle at fifty-percent and climbing. Just before the level reached the seventy-percent mark, a green light came on which meant that the motors were now self-sustaining.

Suddenly, General Berger's voice came blaring through the headset.

"If you activate the device Mr. d'Clare, I will blow up the building, and when you come back to real time you will merge with the rubble. Save yourself a horrible death and come out now. I promise I will kill you quickly."

When I didn't answer he screamed my name a few more times, and I reached over and unplugged the headset.

With the exciter-motor gauge now touching one-hundred percent, and another green light indicating full power, I located the switch labeled "FLD ACCL" in the front console and turned it on. In an instant, the field accelerator began to move back and forth across the tracks above me, emanating a rumbling sound as it traveled. As the accelerator's speed increased, so did the volume of the rumble, until it sounded as if I was sitting beneath the roaring engine of a diesel locomotive. Approximately ten seconds later, another green light came on indicating the generated field had reached the magnetic moment, and after checking the instructions one last time to make sure I hadn't missed a step, I flipped the polarity-reversing switch and entered the fourth dimension!

Much like Captain Hank had described in his diary, I felt an unseen force press me back into the seat, and as the pressure increased both of my ears popped. Almost immediately, the thunderous sound of the field accelerator was gone, leaving only the low hum of the exciter-motors. When the pressure finally eased, I leaned up and looked out the window; everything in the polished-steel room was as it had been a few moments ago.

Suddenly, a bright flash of light passed in front of the window followed by a loud booming sound, and a shock wave rocked the main structure. For a moment, the low steady hum of the exciter-motors cut out and the cockpit lights went dim, but both soon recovered to their previous state.

I leaned up and looked out the window again, but couldn't see anything; no polished-steel room, no building, no General Berger – nothing.

It was as if the world outside had completely disappeared.

* * *

A short time later, I came to the horrifying realization that my getaway had been in vain; only a temporary reprieve from my inevitable fate. The blood from my shoulder wound had completely saturated the seat, and from the sleepiness I was feeling I knew that I didn't have long to live. From the earlier disturbance, I concluded that Berger and his henchmen must've destroyed the building, and from the blackness outside the window I surmised that the stationary plane was now blocked, preventing me from safely reentering real time. The device had successfully transported me into the fourth dimension, but in doing so had left me in a no-win situation with only two possible choices: bleed to death while waiting for the stationary plane to clear, or return to real time and die upon reentry.

How ironic. I was sitting at the controls of the most technologically advanced machine in the history of mankind, but it couldn't help me. Then again, since its inception at the Nazi think tank in Oranienburg, the device hadn't been about life at all; death had always followed it. And even though Captain Hank had constructed this particular device with the noble intention of stopping General Berger, the original design had been based on a diabolical plan with a sinister purpose.

Thinking about all the lives that were lost because of the device, I was overcome with feelings of remorse and the bitter taste of defeat. Madison and the others were dead and there was nothing I could do to bring them back. Not only had I broken the promise I'd

504

made to Captain Hank, but my forgetting about the barrette flash drive had allowed General Berger to recover the synchronization formulas, and he was now free to implement the second phase of the Firebird plan.

The Nazi's White Wolf had won. I was out of time and out of options.

After checking the instructions again, I took a deep breath and eased the throttle back just far enough to reenter real time. Closing my eyes, I sat back and waited for death to envelope me, but instead of experiencing any of my preconceived notions of what death would feel like, nothing happened; no suffocating as my lungs starved for air; no excruciating pain as my body merged with the debris field; no looking back at my deceased body – nothing at all.

Opening my eyes, I found everything the same as it was before: the cockpit lights were still on and the exciter motors were still humming with power. Realizing I had survived the reentry back into real time, tears of joy ran down my face.

I was still alive, but for how long? I'd arrived in the future beaten, shot and bleeding to death, and from what I could see through 4 Freedom's small cockpit window, the world outside was nothing but darkness.

Chapter Twenty-One
The Dark Future

Unknown Years, Months and Days Later
Inside the *405th Contingency Hospital, Salt Lake City, Utah*

I was asleep in a very comfortable bed experiencing one of those rare instances where I knew I was dreaming. In this particular dream, I was preparing for my graduation from basic military training. Standing to my right was Madison, motioning to me that my tie needed straightening, and my dad, with his arms folded and looking concerned; as if hoping I wouldn't make a mistake during the ceremony. To my left stood Captain Hank, the entire three-generations of Benjamin Washington's family, Roy and Shelley Harrison, Deputy Alvarez, Deputy Rivers and Albert Greenbaum, all of whom looked worried too. Many other people stood around us wearing striped prison attire, but I couldn't see their faces.

When my attention returned to fixing my crooked tie, I found Madison had moved over to help me and was straightening it herself. With her darker hair and smooth wrinkle-free skin, she looked twenty years younger, like she had the day I'd married her. It occurred to me that my dad and the others also looked younger, as if they'd discovered the fountain of youth and were in the prime of their lives.

THE DEVICE

My uniform service coat had my retired rank of captain on the shoulders, which made me wonder why I was wearing rank at my basic training graduation.

"Madison, what's with my uniform?" I asked.

"You need to remember," she said.

"Remember what?"

As she began to explain, I woke up to the loud and rhythmic sounds of soldiers marching in cadence. My eyes were suddenly filled with disturbing images of Nazi-like troops marching in goose-step fashion, with their right arms raised rendering the "sieg hiel" victory salute. At first glance, I thought it was an old film clip from World War II, and the man they were paying respect to was Adolph Hitler. A few moments later, however, the camera panned and reversed its angle. The person in front of them was General Berger.

He was in uniform, standing at attention on a platform and saluting a seemingly endless procession of soldiers as they marched by. Next to him, clad in similar uniforms, were Danielle Dennison and Professor Hope. They were all wearing black arm bands on their sleeves, emblazoned with the symbol of an eagle with fiery wings. This same design was on a multitude of flags hanging in the background, as well as smaller hand-held ones being waived by thousands of onlookers, including small children.

The footage was being projected on the ceiling above me in the clearest three-dimensional image I'd ever seen. In the upper left-hand corner were the words, "Live from Wembley Stadium." Across the bottom in large red letters, the headline proclaimed, "Scores dead as Great Britain falls!" A smaller line underneath the headline explained, "London surrenders to the forces of the New Socialist Order." Understanding what this meant, I started to tremble in fear.

I suddenly became aware that I couldn't move. My wrists were secured to the bed with straps, as were my legs at the ankles. An intravenous tube was protruding out of the top of my right hand, and another one was coming out of the inside of my left arm; the only difference being that the tube on my left was colored red, and the one on my right was clear. The other end of the tubes were connected to odd looking machines on both sides of me, which in a peculiar sort of way resembled robots.

Realizing I was in a hospital room I began to relax, and looking around again, noticed how different the room looked than those in my time: it was virtually spotless. The floor was covered with tiles of polished steel, much like the room with the device, and the walls, gray satin in color, looked as if they'd been painted that morning. The clean and antiseptic appearance resembled a sterile scientific laboratory, instead of a room where patients convalesced. There was also a small placard attached to wall next to the door inscribed with the 405th unit designation, which immediately told me I was in a military hospital.

Returning to the projected image of General Berger, I remembered how I got here.

~ *Then* ~

With the device's onboard chronometer not working, I had no way of knowing how long I'd traveled in the fourth dimension or what year I'd reentered real time. All I knew for certain was that I'd survived the time-traveling voyage, and if I didn't receive medical attention soon I was going to die.

Following Captain Hank's instructions, I eased the throttle back to the one-quarter position above idle, which allowed the exciter-motors to remain running at the minimum level needed to keep the time aperture open. That way, if I found the world outside to be a hostile environment, I could quickly retreat back into the device and reenter the fourth dimension; my tired mind rationalizing that bleeding to death inside of 4 Freedom's cockpit would be preferable to meeting my end in some other horrific fashion.

I took off the headset and placed it on the right-hand console. Surprisingly, my ears weren't ringing, nor did I have a bad headache; the modified headgear had protected me from the harsh side effects Captain Hank had experienced.

With my left hand, I unsecured the cockpit hatch and pushed it open. Although the bright blue glow of the device provided some lighting, it was still too dark outside for me to see anything, so I retrieved the flashlight from the front console and clicked it on. Much to my amazement, I was inside a large room. It looked to be roughly the same size as the one I'd left in the past, but instead of the walls and floor being lined with polished-steel plates, this room was covered with black padding.

"Hello? Is anybody here?" I yelled.

Nothing.

Feeling my blood squishing in the cockpit seat, I knew I needed to hurry, so I grabbed the handle near the opening and started to climb out. No sooner had I moved my legs over to step down, my strength gave out, and with my right arm not able to catch myself, I fell the rest of the way to the room's padded floor.

The instant I landed machinery turned on, followed by a bevy of lights illuminating the room. After waiting a moment to allow my eyes to adjust to the brightness, I stood up and looked around to see if anyone was there.

"Hello?"

Still no response.

Looking back at the device, I was immediately struck by how much it resembled a UFO. Glowing a pure shade of blue, the cylinder-shaped fuselage hung motionless in mid-air, with its aft end dissipating waves of electrical current into a large bright-yellow sphere directly behind it. It reminded me of a rocket ship expelling exhaust gases, except that the current was traveling in *both* directions. Remembering what Captain Hank had written in his diary, I realized I was looking at the magnetic forces holding the time aperture open, which would allow me (for the next three hours and fourteen minutes) to return to the past.

I turned my attention back to the room and noticed there were several rows of green-colored arrows painted on the padding on the floor, which directed me to a large sign posted on the wall. Tossing the flashlight back into the cockpit, I hobbled over see what it said, and much to my surprise, found the message on the sign was addressed to me.

Welcome to the future, Mr. d'Clare.
The button to your right
will enable you to exit the room.
We have been alerted of your arrival,
and will be here momentarily.
Friends of Captain Hank

Knowing it wasn't possible for someone in the future to know both myself and Captain Hank, I thought I might be falling into one of General Berger's traps, so I withdrew the gun from my belt and checked it to make sure there was still a bullet in the chamber. After taking a quick look to see how far I was from the device (in case I needed to hurry back to it) I took a deep breath and pressed the exit button.

In an instant, the entire wall to the left of the sign lifted and disappeared into the ceiling. The suddenness of it opening startled me, making me take a step backwards, and in my weakened condition I almost fell. Regaining my balance, I shuffled over and peeked around the corner.

The research room looked spotless, as if a janitorial crew had spent the week scrubbing the floor and wiping down the walls. The rows of workstations also looked brand new and dust-free, and their stainless-steel surfaces were polished to a mirror-like finish. Down the center aisle past the work stations, the open area was empty; not a trace remained of Madison or the other dead bodies, nor any other indication that anything violent had occurred there.

THE DEVICE

As I moved my eyes left to right, taking in the picture-perfect (yet eerie) sight, I caught sight of a reflection, and I realized that the open area was separated from the rest of the room by a sheet of heavy-looking glass. This glass, approximately five feet high, was anchored to the floor by a metal frame, and except for a small access door on the far-right side, the glass ran the entire width of the room.

Just past the last workstation there was a sign facing the other way, and curious as to what it said I proceeded toward it. The moment my trailing right foot cleared the threshold and I was all the way out of the padded room, the wall came back down again – cutting me off from the device. Freezing for a moment, I again yelled out to see if anyone was there, and not hearing a response, my attention returned to the sign.

As I made my way down the center aisle, my objective of reaching the sign suddenly became an almost insurmountable goal, the distance seeming longer and longer with each step. When I finally made it to the pane of glass I was so exhausted I could no longer hold on to the gun, and it slipped out of my hand, hit the floor, and slid out of sight underneath the last work station. Panting heavily, I waited a few moments to catch my breath, and when I started forward again my body gave out and I fell to the floor.

Landing in front of the sign, I looked up and read:

This building is dedicated to the memory of the heroic men and women who died here on September 13th, 2014, and to all the victims of violent crimes whose cases remain unsolved.

Weber County Sheriff Deputy Robert Alvarez
Weber County Sheriff Deputy Crystal Rivers
Mr. George d'Clare
Mrs. Madison d'Clare
Mr. Ethan Washington

DALE C. GEORGE

Ms. Evelynn Washington
Mr. Albert Greenbaum

"May your souls find solace in the belief that
those who committed these egregious crimes against you
will ultimately be brought before a higher court,
and be made to answer for the sins they committed against their
fellow man."

- *Professor Emeritus*
Daniel Lee

13 September 2018

Realizing I was in a memorial, I laid my head down and started to fall asleep, at which point I unexpectedly began hearing voices in my head.

"Mr. d'Clare, can you hear me?" a woman asked.

"Stay with us, Mr. d'Clare!" a man's voice yelled.

I felt a sharp slap to my face.

"Mr. d'Clare, look at me! Look at me!" the woman's voice said, now also shouting.

Opening my eyes, I saw the man and the woman were both Asian. The woman was holding my head in her hands, staring at me intensely, while the man behind her was frantically digging into the lower cabinet of the nearest work station, pulling out handfuls of bandages and other medical supplies. They looked to be roughly sixty years of age, and were wearing dark green clothes that resembled military uniforms, with identification badges clipped to their shirt pockets.

"How do you know my name?" I asked.

"The bullet has pierced your right subclavian artery, Mr. d'Clare," she said. "We have to open the wound and clamp it off to stop the bleeding. This is going to hurt. Do you understand?"

513

She didn't have anything in her hands, but instead was looking at her forearm.

"How do you know that?"

"We'll explain later," the man yelled, ripping my shirt open, "but you have to stay awake!"

"Do you understand Mr. d'Clare?" the woman said. "You have to stay awake!"

"Yes, I understand, but General Berger has recovered the Firebird formulas. He's going to try to..."

"It's all right Mr. d'Clare," she interrupted, "you need not worry about him now. You are safe now."

The man and woman looked at each other, as if they knew something but didn't want to tell me.

"I'm safe?"

"Yes, but you must not fall asleep!"

Using their knees to pin my arms down, the woman leaned over and moved her arm in front of my face so that I couldn't see what they were doing. A moment later, I felt a sharp pain in my right shoulder, which soon became so excruciating I thought they were removing my arm at the socket. Now in a state of agony, I began thrashing around trying to get them off me, but the two were well-experienced at subduing a patient, and the more I tried to get away the more I remained pinned in place. Finally, after a few more tortuous seconds, the pain abated.

"We've got it clamped off Mr. d'Clare, but again, you must stay awake!" the man said.

For the next few minutes, while I lay prone on the floor fighting to keep my eyes open, the research room became a hub of activity; people streamed in wearing the same strange military uniforms as the Asian couple.

They lifted me up and placed me on the top of the nearest workstation, after which I felt the stings of needles being placed into my left arm and right hand. I also heard a bevy of medical terms being shouted out, which reminded me of my days in the Air Force

514

Reserve when I'd assessed mock-casualties during war game exercises. Some of these terms, such as "class-four hemorrhage" and "hypovolemic shock," I was familiar with, while others, like "artificial crystalloid induction" and "platelet regeneration infusion," were completely unknown to me.

While this was going on, the woman kept yelling at me and slapping my face. As much as I tried, I couldn't keep my eyes open.

The last thing I remember hearing, just before I slipped into unconsciousness, was the woman screaming.

"We are losing him!"

~ Now ~

Waking up to the sight of General Berger in the stadium, feelings of guilt and survivor's remorse overwhelmed me. Even though the doctors in this time period had saved my life, I wished they hadn't. I had nothing here; no Madison; no friends – nothing. Adding insult to injury, my absentmindedness with the barrette flash drive had obviously enabled Berger to continue the Firebird plan, and a world war was now underway.

In an instant, the projected images of Berger dimmed and the overhead lights came on, which suspended my bout of self-recrimination. A moment later, the woman who'd found me in the research room came in, followed by the man, and they proceeded to my bed and undid my restraints.

"We're sorry, Mr. d'Clare," the woman said. "We were only gone for a short time to get something to eat."

"What happened?" I asked.

"You had a hypersensitive reaction to one of the medications, and the orderlies had to subdue you so you wouldn't hurt yourself."

"Or anyone else," the man added.

"What medication?"

Ignoring my question, they took my straps off, and when I tried to lean up they both reached out and stopped me.

"Easy Mr. d'Clare, you've just gotten out of surgery," the woman said. "We almost lost you twice."

"I don't remember them strapping me down."

"You wouldn't, because the medication they used to counteract the reaction induces brief periods of memory loss. When the drug dissipates you should be able to remember."

"Who are you people, and how is it that you know my name?"

"My name is Mary and this is my brother Mark."

For the first time, I was able to focus my eyes enough to read their identification badges. Not only were they both physicians, they also had the same last name as Captain Hank's friend.

"I take it Professor Lee is your father?"

"You've been gone for a very long time, Mr. d'Clare. Daniel Lee was our grandfather."

"He told us about you and the device," Mark said.

"*Was* your grandfather? Has he passed away?"

"Oh yes, many years ago," Mary said sadly, "from causes incident to age."

"I'm sorry for your loss."

"It was a blessing. He was very aged and ill."

"So he told you about me?"

"Repeatedly, until we could recite the story in our sleep," Mark said.

"You see, our parents died when we were very young, and we went to live with him," Mary explained. "A few years before he died, he told us the story."

"He also kept a comprehensive journal," Mark said. "So we know all about you, Captain Hank, and the device."

"How many years have I been gone?"

"A little more than one hundred."

"A hundred years?"

516

"Today is November the first, 2114," Mary said.

"How did you know I came out of the fourth dimension?"

"Our grandfather never stopped believing you would come back."

"But I've never even met your grandfather."

She smiled. "We know."

"But how…"

She held up her hand. "It is a long story, Mr. d'Clare, and in your present condition, you're not up to hearing it. We'll let you rest for now and come back later."

"Please Mary, or I mean doctor, won't you stay?"

"You may call me Mary and my brother Mark. We do not insist on professional titles in our time."

"Thank you, Mary, but I'm wide awake now. Won't you both please stay for just a while and catch me up on what has happened?"

She looked at her forearm.

"I don't go on duty for another hour, so I guess I can stay for a short time."

"And I just got off duty for the day," Mark said, also looking at his forearm.

For the first time, I noticed that it wasn't just their forearms they were looking at, but rather an image of a computer screen being projected *onto* their forearms; emanating from tiny holes in the sides of their small wristwatches.

"That's quite a watch," I said.

"This old thing? I'd much rather have the new Advantage Two model like Mary's. They can do so much more than the Advantage One."

"How do you feel, Mr. d'Clare? Are you comfortable?" Mary asked.

"I'm fine, but my throat's a little sore. Could I get some water?"

While she retrieved a cup from a sophisticated-looking dispenser, Mark pulled two modern-looking chairs up to the right side of my bed.

I was about to ask them another question about their grandfather when a large brown cat jumped up on the bed next to me. Its sudden appearance startled me so much, I forgot what I was going to say.

Mark smiled and began petting it. "Say hello to Cleopatra, Mr. d'Clare. She's one of our therapy animals."

"Therapy animals?"

"To comfort sick patients."

As he was petting her, the friendly feline nestled in and began rubbing her head on my hand.

"I thought they didn't allow cats in hospitals because of people's allergies?"

"We've made significant advances in the medical sciences, Mr. d'Clare," Mary said. "Domestic pets no longer carry allergens."

"I hope not, because normally when I'm around cats I break out in hives."

Relaxing a bit, I began to pet the rather pretty cat, at which point she flopped over on her back, wanting me to scratch her belly. For some strange reason, she reminded me of something, but for the life of me I couldn't remember what.

"My brother and I are anxious to know how you managed to get away from General Berger."

After taking a sip of water, I gave them a misty-eyed summation of what had happened in the research room, and how I'd found the switches for the auxiliary generators, closed the security door, and escaped in the device.

"That confirms much of what our grandfather believed happened," Mark said.

"We are sorry for *your* loss, Mr. d'Clare," Mary said, sympathetically. "Did you know that after you left the building was destroyed?"

"Yes, I saw the flash and felt the shockwave."

"Our grandfather was still in the hospital recovering from the aneurysm when he learned about the explosion. When he couldn't get in touch with Captain Hank or the Harrisons, he became so upset the doctors had to sedate him."

"And since he leased the building from the university, detectives came and questioned him about the murders," Mark added.

"Unfortunately, they were quite hard on him," Mary continued, "and the questioning went on for hours."

"Wasn't he still a patient in the hospital?" I asked.

"Yes, but at the time the police were focused on finding out who killed two of their fellow officers."

Thoughts of O'Malley came rushing back to me. I hoped Professor Lee's interrogation sessions weren't as horrific as mine had been.

"Shortly afterward, he learned of the Harrison's deaths and that Captain Hank had been killed."

"Which resulted in yet another session of harsh questioning by the police," Mark said.

"Why so?"

"Captain Hank left a will, instructing his fortune be split evenly between our grandfather and the Harrisons. With the Shelley and Roy Harrison dead, he was the sole beneficiary of over forty million dollars."

"Forty million? So what did he do?"

"About a month after the building was destroyed, he finally got released from the hospital and went home," Mary said.

"Home? After fourteen years of being away, he still had one?"

"During the time he was gone, Captain Hank had paid off his mortgage and completely remodeled his house. He also deposited a salary in his bank account every month, paid his taxes for him, and even went as far as hiring a company to take care of his yard in the summer and snow removal in the winter; all to make it appear as if he was still living there."

"But didn't the neighbors eventually start to wonder?"

"Oh, they did. Captain Hank would come by twice a week to check on things, posing as our grandfather's brother-in-law," Mark said. "Whenever he was asked, he would tell them Professor Lee was fulfilling a teaching obligation in Beijing and that he planned to return when his tenure was over."

I wondered how Captain Hank had explained Dan's fourteen-year disappearance, and was amazed at all the steps he'd taken.

"Captain Hank had sent him email messages, keeping him informed of what had happened while he was away. In one of those messages, he learned that Hank had hired a private detective company to investigate the Washington's deaths at the Fort Meade warehouse, and that they'd identified Thomas O'Malley's fingerprint."

"That's exactly what Hank told Ethan and Evelynn," I said, "and that the detectives had tracked O'Malley to Nevada,"

She nodded. "In one of the last messages our grandfather received from him, Captain Hank informed him that the detectives had traced O'Malley to the White Pines area of Eastern Nevada."

"What did your grandfather do with this information?"

"He immediately contacted the detective company, who sent some of their people to question him."

"Question him? Why?"

"Because two of the detectives they'd assigned to the case were found murdered."

"Let me guess, they were beaten and their necks were broken?"

This time they both nodded.

"From stolen credit card receipts, the company traced O'Malley to a small town near an abandoned Army base," Mary continued, "but by the time they figured out he'd been staying there and alerted the authorities, the base was deserted."

"And since O'Malley's body was among those found in the building at the university, the lead to General Berger's whereabouts came to a dead end," Mark added.

"What did your grandfather do then?"

"There wasn't anything further he could do as far as General Berger was concerned, so he turned his attention to two things, the first being to take care of the Harrison's children."

"Sounds like your grandfather was a very noble man."

"He felt guilty for not being there when his friends needed him," Mary explained, "and since he'd developed such a close personal friendship with the Shelley and Roy Harrison, the least he could do was make sure their children were taken care of."

"The second thing he did was figure out a way to save you," Mark said.

"How did he even know about me?"

"When the police recovered the bodies, yours was missing, and when grandfather was finally allowed to examine the building ruins, the main structure of the device was not among the debris," Mary said. "The forensic investigators recovered some of your DNA, and since you were missing they determined your body had been pulverized in the explosion. Even though they listed you among the dead, our grandfather believed you had somehow gotten away in the device, and that you were still alive in the fourth dimension, traveling forward in time."

"Which explains why my name is on the plaque in the research room."

She nodded.

"As for the research room, the only thing grandfather could think of to save you was to turn the building into a memorial," Mark said.

"When I first saw it, I thought it looked different. Too clean and perfect, if you know what I mean."

"He spent an exorbitant amount of time and money annexing the property from the university, locating the original plans, and obtaining the necessary permits to build it. The entire project took almost four years to complete."

"That long?"

"Our grandfather was a very meticulous man, and he oversaw the entire construction himself," Mary said. "He wanted it to be as close to the original design as possible, so that when you did return the stationary plane would be clear when you reentered real time. Knowing he wouldn't be able to position everything exactly as it was, he lined the room with padding. That way, when you did return, you would have a soft landing."

I was stunned that their grandfather had taken such extreme measures to save me.

"As for how we knew you had returned, there are sensors underneath the padding on the floor. The moment you touched it we were immediately notified," Mark said, pointing to his watch. "And since our grandfather suspected you might be hurt, he pre-positioned medical supplies everywhere in the research room."

I sat there for a few moments, petting Cleopatra and digesting what they told me.

"In any event, your timing is impeccable. If you had taken any longer, we wouldn't have been able to save you."

"What do you mean?"

"They just ordered the evacuation of Utah, Idaho, and Arizona. We've been ordered to fall back to the underground facility at Cheyenne Mountain in Colorado."

"Evacuate?"

He hesitated before answering and looked at Mary. When I looked too, I saw that she had tears in her eyes.

"You have arrived in a time of war, Mr. d'Clare," she said, struggling to get the words out. "A global war we cannot win."

The images of the general came rushing back.

"Berger."

"Yes," Mark said, patting his sister on the hand. "He's using the device to conquer the world, one nation at a time. And now, with Great Britain's collapse, only the Allied Forces of the North American Continent are left to oppose him."

"Allied Forces?"

"Formerly Mexico, the United States and Canada," Mary replied, "and from the intelligence reports we received late last night, *we* are now in jeopardy."

"When did it start?"

"A little more than five years ago, in Germany again."

I shook my head in disbelief.

"What began as a peaceful demonstration against their unpopular government soon turned violent, and several of the demonstrators were killed. Then General Berger arrived, preaching his nationalistic rhetoric, anti-Sematic hatred, and telling everyone how they needed to get back to the fundamentals that made Germany strong. Since they had the world's poorest economy at the time, his words hit a chord that resonated with the masses, which eventually gave rise to a fascist movement called the New Socialist Order."

"Whatever they're calling themselves, they're still Nazis. The only difference being the Firebird symbol instead of the swastika," Mark said.

I looked back and forth at them, stunned at what I was hearing.

"The last day of February 2112," Mary continued, "they installed Berger as the new Chancellor of Germany, and he immediately began his conquest to capture the world."

"Are you sure he's using the device?"

"Oh, quite sure. When he rose to power, his political opponents disappeared, and from the way he always knows where to concentrate his forces in battle, leaves little doubt."

As the impact of what they told me sank in, I stared at the wall, speechless and not knowing what to say. Cleopatra, sensing something was wrong, rolled back over and rubbed her head against my hand.

"Are you all right Mr. d'Clare?"

"This is all my fault. I caused all of this to happen."

"How could this be your fault? You were in the fourth dimension when Berger rose to power."

"Because I should've opened that door and killed him when I had the chance."

"From what you've told us, you were outnumbered," Mark said, "and in your condition, either Berger or his gunman would've killed you."

When I didn't respond, they looked at each other and stood to leave.

"We've stayed too long and overwhelmed you," Mary said.

"No please, won't you stay just a little while longer?"

"We really should be going, Mr. d'Clare, but I'll be by in a while to check on you."

I nodded, thinking she was probably right, and laid my head back down on the pillow.

As they proceeded out of the room, Mark stopped at the door.

"While you rest enjoy Cleopatra," he said. "There's no finer therapy animal in this hospital than our Egyptian cat."

Looking down, I found the cat staring at me, then suddenly, as if an invisible hand had reached out and slapped my face, something about what Mark said sounded familiar.

"Wait. What did you say?"

"I said, while you rest enjoy Cleopatra."

"No, after that."

"There's no finer therapy animal than our Egyptian cat?"

Hearing the name again triggered my memory, and the recollection came flooding back.

"That's it!" I yelled.

"What?" Mark asked, and motioned for Mary to come back.

"What time is it, or I mean, how long ago did you find me?"

They both pressed a tiny button on the sides of their small wristwatches, and checked the projected images on their forearms.

"The alert came in at one twenty-three this morning," Mary said, "and it is now two minutes past four o'clock, so roughly…"

"Two hours and thirty-nine minutes ago," Mark interrupted, beating her with the math.

"Then there's still time!"

"Time for what, Mr. d'Clare?"

"Time for us to change history and defeat General Berger!"

* * *

It took me over ten precious minutes to explain to the two doctors what Madison had read in the last pages of Captain Hank's notebook, and to convince them to take me back to the memorial. As we sat in the back of the sleek and modern-looking ambulance, I prayed we would get there before the three-hour and fourteen-minute time period had elapsed. Even though I'd talked Mark into believing my plan had a chance of succeeding, Mary remained skeptical, and the argument escalated the closer we got to the building.

"This is suicide, Mr. d'Clare! You are risking your life on a handful of assumptions!"

"But if there is even a remote possibility that it could work, don't you think I should at least try?"

"No, because there is no way you can change one of the fundamental laws of physics! What has happened has happened! You must move on!"

"Move on to what? To a world taken over by General Berger and his new Nazi regime? Move on knowing that because of my shortsightedness, I caused the deaths of millions of innocent people? No ma'am. Not if I have a chance to stop it."

"But you're too injured to go back! Even though we've repaired your artery and replenished your blood supply, you need to rest! Not only that, you could easily tear the incision open and start to bleed again."

"How about I just go?" Mark suggested.

"You can't! Captain Hank told Madison and me that when the device achieves the magnetic moment, it aligns the atoms of the main structure and everything inside it. Later, when the pilot wants to return to his own time, the majority of those atoms must still be in alignment. If they aren't, the device will malfunction and the aperture will close. So you see, I *have* to be the one to go back."

"But what if this e-KAT thing doesn't work and you return to the building?" Mary countered. "It is now three hours later, and General Berger will be waiting for you."

"With the big security door closed, I should be safe."

"You could also reenter real time after he detonates the bombs, in which case your atoms will merge with a fiery debris field."

"For what it's worth, I'm willing to take that chance."

As she started to protest further, I held up my hand and stopped her.

"Let me ask you a question. Would you say your grandfather trusted Captain Hank?"

"Of course he trusted him. The captain saved his life."

"Well I didn't, at least not at first. When Madison and I met him, I thought he was a nut. A crazy kook with Parkinson's disease and Lewy-body dementia, and that his ailing mind had invented this wild story about the device. But after the hit-and-run, as he lay there dying, I looked into his eyes and *knew* he'd told us the truth. Don't ask me how I knew, I just knew. It's the same feeling I have now!"

She started to say something, but I interrupted her again.

"Please, let me finish. Captain Hank believed all things happened for a reason, and I believe that now too. What other explanation could there be for me surviving Berger and his men, while Madison and all the others died? I was put in this position for this reason. You said your grandfather trusted Captain Hank. Won't *you* trust him now too?"

"It's not a matter of trust or beliefs, Mr. d'Clare, it's a matter of science!"

"I respectfully disagree," I said, meeting her intense gaze with my own. "Listen, when we first got to the building, it looked as if Captain Hank had been working on something in his shop. From the tools he had out, I could tell it was something electrical, or at least electrically-related. I believe he completed the e-KAT component, but didn't get the chance to use it because he left to warn Madison and me about General Berger."

"Still assumptions, Mr. d'Clare."

I suddenly remembered the last thing Madison read in Captain Hank's notebook.

"Do those wristwatch computers have internet access?" I asked.

Mark nodded and turned his on.

"Search for this: torn, with a capital t, then a period, capital f, and a small u."

"What?"

"Just type it in. It was the last thing Captain Hank wrote in his notebook and Madison said he underlined it several times."

Mark quickly typed it on his forearm and his eyes grew wide.

"What is it?" Mary asked.

"A Torn.Fu is the model name of a series of wireless receiver-transmitters the Germans used in World War II," he replied, his voice rising, "some of which were capable of receiving hi-frequency radio transmissions!"

"What?" Mary asked, and grabbed his arm to look.

"See?" I said. "This proves what Captain Hank was trying to do."

After reading it, Mary looked up at me with a more-astonished look than her brother's.

"If you are correct Mr. d'Clare, it could change the entire timeline."

I smiled. "That's what I've been trying to tell you."

She immediately checked her watch, then turned around and yelled at the ambulance driver.

"Step on it! This is a matter of life and death!"

* * *

When we reached the memorial, Mark and Mary rushed me inside. Even though I was still extremely sore and weak, we managed to traverse the short distance to the building rather quickly, and soon made our way into the research room. We found the room still a mess from the events that had transpired three hours ago: empty packages of gauze, bloody towels, and other medical supplies were strewn all about.

Reaching the first row of workstations, Mark projected the image of the computer screen on his forearm and started typing, while Mary retrieved O'Malley's gun from under the work station. The right side of the forward wall instantly rose and disappeared into the ceiling, like it had before, and the three of us proceeded into the room with the device.

The glowing cylinder-shaped main structure was still there, suspended motionless in mid-air, but the stream of electrical current was smaller now and not as bright as before. Sensing time was running out, I motioned for O'Malley's gun, tucked it in my belt, then the two helped me over to the cockpit hatch.

"Wait!" Mary yelled, and ran back to the research room.

"I can't wait! I think the aperture is closing!"

After quickly pulling myself inside, I reached down to close the hatch but Mark stopped me.

"Just one moment, Mr. d'Clare. Please."

A few seconds later, Mary rushed back in holding a thick spiral notebook and handed it to me.

"Our grandfather wanted you to have this," she said.

"What is it?"

"It's the cure for Parkinson's disease."

"What?" I didn't believe what I'd just heard.

"The cure for Parkinson's disease, including the formulas of all the medical breakthroughs leading up to it. We would've put it on a flash drive for you, but the computers of your time wouldn't be able to interface with it."

"You'll also find the cures for Huntington's disease, Alzheimer's, ALS, and even some forms of cancer," Mark added.

My eyes began to water.

"All of those research projects that patients took part in back in your time eventually paid off," Mary said. "When the breakthrough finally came, they were able to cure the other diseases my brother mentioned. In our time, children merely require an inoculation when they are born that will prevent them from getting the disease. It has a ninety-eight percent success ratio."

She started to say something else, but abruptly stopped and looked down. When she looked up again, tears were streaming down her face.

"What's the matter?"

"After we stabilized your condition and transported you to the hospital, we administered the serum, but your body's immune system rejected it."

"That's why the orderlies tied you down," Mark said.

"Scientists in our time were on the brink of discovering why the cure wouldn't work for some patients," she continued, "but when the war started, the government transferred all research funding to the defense department. Please take it with you, Mr. d'Clare. If the e-KAT transmitter doesn't work and you somehow get away from General Berger, then you can take it to the university. Perhaps the scientists in your time can discover why people like you are allergic to it."

"At very least, it will help almost all of the people in your time who have the disease," Mark added.

Not knowing what to say, I simply nodded and stuffed the notebook inside my shirt. Just as I was about to say goodbye, she took off her small wristwatch and handed it to me.

"Here, put this on."

"What for?"

"If you are attacked, push the little red button at the nine o'clock position. You'll have five seconds to close your eyes and cover your ears."

"What will it do?"

"It will release an airburst of electrically-charged particles, and for a short time disorient your attacker. Similar weapons in your time are called stun grenades."

"It seems too small to…"

"No worries, Mr. d'Clare," Mark interrupted, "it's not called the Advantage Two for nothing. Last summer at the Milwaukee Zoo, a man wearing one of these watches happened to fall into one of the ape exhibits and the AAPD feature stopped a four-hundred-pound gorilla from mauling him to death."

"AAPD?"

"Anti-assault personal defense," Mary said, "but remember two things. It will only work once, and it will only stun your attacker for a short time."

"How short?"

"Two to three minutes, depending on how close they are to you."

"It will have the full effect if they are within two feet," Mark said.

"Why so close?"

"It was originally developed to stop sexual assaults."

As I slipped the band over my left wrist, my eyes began to water again.

"Thank you both for saving my life."

"You can thank us by saving us from this world," Mary said, as more tears streamed down her face. "Godspeed to you, Mr. d'Clare."

"Yes, Godspeed," Mark repeated.

Reaching down, I pulled the hatch closed and retrieved the headset from the right console. After quickly reviewing Captain Hank's instructions, I took a deep breath and flipped the polarity-reversing switch.

As the fuselage groaned and the device returned to the fourth dimension, I looked out the small cockpit window just in time to see the two sibling doctors, Mary and Mark Lee, disappear into the darkness.

* * *

Having remembered Captain Hank's idea to change the timeline, and that I now had a chance to complete the mission, my mood was bright and my optimism was restored. I eased the device's throttle forward to the midway position and waited for the exciter-motors to stabilize to the increased speed. As soon as the low hum steadied, I located the small switch on the forward console labeled "e-KAT" and turned it on.

The cockpit lights dimmed for a moment and returned back to normal. Not knowing what to expect, I braced myself but nothing happened.

I waited a few more seconds, then turned the switch off and back on again.

Like before, the lights dimmed momentarily and brightened.

I cycled the switch several more times, praying that something would happen, but each time I got the same result. The

531

optimistic feelings I'd had merely seconds ago instantly evaporated, and as my anxiety intensified my Parkinson's symptoms emerged.

With the e-KAT transmitter apparently inoperative and the device hurtling me back to the past, I started to pray with all my might that I would reenter real time *before* General Berger destroys the building.

As if on cue, a shock wave rocked the main structure and a loud booming sound emanated around the device. An instant later, a blinding light flashed outside the window. Once it dimmed, I leaned up and looked out; I was back in the polished-steel room. Everything appeared to be the same as it was when I'd left three hours ago, except for one striking difference: the heavy security door, which afforded me my only means of protection, was now open.

I looked at the cockpit hatch for a moment, wondering what fate awaited me outside, and remembered something Captain Hank had written in his diary. It was an old saying that his parents had told him when he was young, that years later prevented him from committing suicide. Even though I couldn't remember the exact words, the main idea went something like, "all things happen for a reason, and the actions you take when things happen will define you as a human being."

The situation I was in now, however, was a lot more serious: depending on what I did or didn't do, my actions would not only define me as a human being, but also determine the course of history for the next one-hundred years.

To complete Captain Hank's mission, and fulfill the promise I'd made to him before he died, I had to face and defeat the Nazi's White Wolf.

Chapter Twenty-Two
The Return

Ten Minutes Later
Saturday, 13 September 2014, 21:55hrs
Inside *Building 3731, University of Utah Campus, Salt Lake City, Utah*

The glowing blue fuselage of the device, coupled with the shining yellow sphere of the time aperture, added untold wattage to the already-bright florescent light fixtures, illuminating the polished-steel room to a near-blinding intensity. The only sound in the room was the low and steady hum of the device's exciter-motors, smoothly running on as they generated the voltage needed to keep the aperture open. The combination of lights and sound created a futuristic backdrop, and set a fitting stage for my final confrontation with General Berger.

Seeing him now, up-close and in the bright lights, he looked even more threatening than he had in the red dimly-lit research room three hours ago. His tall frame and large muscular physique, combined with his dark menacing eyes, made it appear as if he was born from a race of demonic giants. And the Cheshire cat-like grin he had on his face seemed to grow more malevolent the longer I looked at it.

His cheek was cleaned and bandaged with clear medical tape, and the torn shirt around his leg wound had been replaced by adhesive medical gauze. Other than a slight limp, there weren't any other signs of impaired physical movement, which told me that even though Deputy Alvarez had plunged the knife in his leg to the hilt, the blade had somehow missed his femoral artery, resulting in only a minor injury.

Moving toward me, he quickly delivered several punches to the side of my head, and I fell to the floor. After returning to my feet, he repeated the combination to my abdomen, and I was soon back on the floor writhing in pain and gasping for air. Now completely at his mercy, I found myself in the same predicament I'd been in three hours ago, the only difference being this time I didn't have the fearless Deputy Alvarez on hand to save me.

As General Berger prolonged his attack, I thought about the plan I'd devised several minutes ago, and prayed I wouldn't be killed or knocked unconscious before implementing it.

~ Then ~

When I'd reentered real time, I didn't know if the device's main structure could go back into the fourth dimension again without the added power of the field accelerator. In the event it could, I eased the throttle down to the one-quarter position, which like before, kept the exciter-motors running and the time aperture open. I reasoned that if events dictated I needed a quick escape route, the device could possibly give me one.

Thinking back to my military training, I conducted a quick threat assessment of my enemy and strategized a makeshift plan. The general had four people helping him: Slone, Dennison, Hope and Petri (who was most-likely a non-factor because of his broken leg). Since Berger posed the greatest threat, to both the present and to the future, he was target number one. My secondary target was the sharpshooter Slone. If I could somehow take him out and get my hands on his high-powered rifle, the playing field would definitely tilt to my favor. From all outward indications, neither Hope nor

Dennison seemed a likely threat, but since appearances can be deceiving, I still prioritized them third and fourth on my target list.

In the event the general (or one of his people) overpowered me, then the possibility was high that Berger would enact his sadistic ritual and beat me up before breaking my neck. If that happened, I was assured at some point he would be within two feet of me, whereupon I would use the stun feature in Mary's wristwatch, retrieve a gun and kill him.

With my impromptu plan in place, I removed O'Malley's gun from my belt, checked the clip and found eight rounds left. Not much of an arsenal, but if I aimed well and conserved my ammunition, I had more than enough bullets to get the job done.

Holding the gun in my right hand, I began to experience tremors again, and quickly placed the gun in my left hand. (One advantage of growing up left-handed in a world of right-handed people: when I became old enough to shoot a handgun, I'd learned how to aim and fire with *either* hand.)

After checking the gun again to make sure the safety was off, I leaned up and looked out the window. Not seeing any movement, I took a deep breath, unfastened the cockpit hatch, and quickly pushed it open.

Much to my surprise, I found myself face-to-face with the gunman Slone! With my sudden appearance startling him, he hesitated for a fraction of a second not knowing what to do. Since my gun was already pointed at him, that delay gave me all the time I needed, and I squeezed off two shots in succession. As he fell away from me, I jumped out of the cockpit on top of him, but before I could retrieve his rifle, a crushing blow to the back of my head sent me to the floor.

Turning over, I found General Berger towering over me, confidently pointing his gun at my face. For a moment, I thought he was going to shoot me on the spot, but instead he stepped down on my left wrist. With my gun-hand and the wristwatch pinned, he proceeded to apply pressure until the pain was so great I opened my fingers. Quickly kneeling down, he retrieved my gun and threw it out into the research room.

Standing back up, he holstered his own gun, and smiled.

"Welcome back, Mr. d'Clare. You've arrived just in time for me to kill you."

~ *Now* ~

After enduring a succession of punches, one of which reopened my shoulder wound, I struggled to my feet, whereupon Berger moved in close, faked a jab, and quickly stepped away again. He did this several times, and every so often throw in a real punch that connected.

"I knew you were stupid, Mr. d'Clare, but I did not think you were a complete imbecile."

"What do you mean?"

He laughed. "To return within the three-hour and fourteen-minute time limit, you dummkopf. Oh, and thank you for taking care of Mr. O'Malley and Mr. Slone for me. You saved me the trouble."

"I thought they were your loyal lap dogs."

"They were loyal for a time, but like you, O'Malley was stupid. As for Slone, he was expendable."

He moved in, delivered a quick punch to my face, and moved away again.

"You're probably wondering how Miss Dennison was able to open the door, eh?"

I didn't reply.

"Like chess, Mr. d'Clare. Move, counter-move."

"How's that?"

"You told me."

"*I* told you?"

"Yes. When you read the good captain's story, Miss Dennison had a sophisticated bug planted in your house that the deputy didn't find, and I heard the whole thing. I remembered you mentioning the toolbox with the false bottom, so after you left in the device we searched the workshop and found it. You'll never guess what was inside."

"Another card-key?"

"Precisely, and with the second card key in place, it took Miss Dennison only ninety minutes to pick the electronic lock. Move, counter-move, you see?"

"Why was it so important for you to get in here? There's nothing in here but me and the device."

"That is exactly why I wanted to get in here, to make sure that there is nothing left of you or the device. You see, after I kill you I'm afraid there will be a terrible accident and this building will be destroyed by an explosion."

He pointed behind me, then toward the security door. Following his finger, I saw there were five modern-looking explosives planted along the arc of the field accelerator, with many more on top of the work stations outside in the research room. I also noticed their digital displays were synchronized and counting down – each showing less than five minutes until detonation.

He lunged in again, this time striking me with a kidney punch, and stepped back.

"Now that I have the formulas, which you so graciously provided, Professor Hope will be able to synchronize the power system of Firebird Two. Once it is fully operational, I will be able to complete the plan I started all those years ago."

"*Your* plan? I thought it was Hitler's plan?"

He laughed again. "How little you know, Mr. d'Clare. Except for approving the reichmarks for the project, Hitler had nothing to do with it. I was the one who developed it. I was the one who tested it, and as far as escaping into the future to build the Fourth Reich, that too was my plan. I was never going to allow that little Austrian Corporal to get his hands on my creation!"

As he rambled on, his dark eyes went into a trance.

"Firebird Two will enable me to go into the future, learn who my enemies are, and return to the present and eliminate them. I shall build a vast army of loyal followers, so large that the combined allied army that defeated Germany will pale by comparison! I shall shape events to my choosing, and outmaneuver any opposing force on the battlefield. Then one day, I shall rule the world!"

"But aren't you forgetting something? I've seen the future and you will be destroyed."

"That is not possible, Mr. d'Clare. You are the only one left who can identify me. The final opposing chess piece that will soon be tipped-over and out of my way."

"Captain Hank knew where you were and sent messages to the authorities. Somewhere in the White Pines area of Nevada, isn't it?"

"We have already planned to move our headquarters once Firebird Two is operational. So again like chess Mr. d'Clare, move, counter-move."

He darted in and threw a punch, but I succeeded in turning to the side and dodging it. Frustrated, he swiped his huge right hand at me, but was only able to take hold of my shirt. As I struggled to get away the buttons of my shirt tore open, and the notebook containing the Parkinson's cure fell out onto the floor.

He knelt and picked it up, and after examining it for a few moments, tossed it over his shoulder and began to laugh again.

"You think the cure for your disease is going to help you? Nothing can help you now, Mr. d'Clare, nothing! When I build my new empire, there will be no room for the weak, or the diseased, or the disabled. Only the strong shall have a place in my new socialist order!"

"After the police find all the people you've murdered, they'll come after you."

He smiled confidently. "Now it is you who are forgetting something, Mr. d'Clare. Nobody knows I am here. And in the event

538

I have left any evidence, it will be destroyed in the explosion. So once again, move, counter-move."

He looked over at the bombs and checked his watch.

"And now, as you Americans are fond of saying, all good things must come to an end."

Suddenly, Danielle Dennison came running into the room carrying her laptop computer, followed closely by Professor Hope.

"General, there's a storm coming!" she yelled.

"Not now, my dear. Can't you see I am in the middle of killing Mr. d'Clare?"

"You don't understand, General," Professor Hope said nervously, "this is unlike any storm I have ever seen!"

"What are you talking about, professor? A storm is a storm."

"Not like this one!"

He turned to address them directly, and abruptly stopped and looked down.

Following his line of sight, I glanced down too, and a cold chill instantly traveled down my spine.

The pages of the notebook containing the Parkinson's cure were turning on their own!

Before I had a chance to guess whose ghost was thumbing through the pages, a warm breeze cascaded into the room and soon built itself up into a moderate gust. Feeling relieved that it was only the wind blowing the pages (and not some spirit from the great beyond) I looked around to see where the wind was coming from, but there weren't any windows in the room, nor was the air conditioning on.

Berger, Dennison and Hope must've been thinking the same thing, because they began looking around too.

"Look General!" Dennison yelled, showing him her laptop computer.

The picture on the screen was a live news report, showing what appeared to be gigantic black tornado approaching Salt Lake City. As it drew closer, I realized it wasn't a tornado at all, but instead looked more like a massive airborne whirlpool. As the unbelievably large twister moved over the city, the camera zoomed in, at which point we beheld a truly frightening sight: the swirling mass was enveloping everything in its path, including buildings, cars and people!

The connection to the remote camera was suddenly lost, and the news station went to a live feed from inside their studio. The visibly-shaking meteorologist was pointing to a map of the city, showing the trajectory of the storm – a path that was headed directly toward the University of Utah and our location!

I realized that I might actually be watching the timeline change, but before I could think of what to do, the screen on Dennison's computer went blank and the wind inside the room intensified.

Turning back to face me, Berger's menacing self-confident look was gone.

"What have you done, Mr. d'Clare?" he asked.

This time it was my turn to smile.

"Like chess, Herr General. You know the game. Move, counter-move."

He glanced over to the device and the still-glowing time aperture.

"We shall soon see."

Shoving Dennison and Hope out of his way, he started toward the device, and in an effort to block his path I threw myself in front of him. In a quick move, he sidestepped me altogether and delivered another crushing blow to the back of my head. Before I could recover, he moved around behind me, and in one swift motion placed me in a headlock.

"Move, counter-move, Mr. d'Clare?" he snarled. "Let's see how you counter-move this."

Quickly locating the small button on Mary's watch, I pushed it, closed my eyes and placed my hands over my ears.

"What are you doing?" he asked.

"Checkmate!"

A thunderous boom rang out followed by a concussion wave that was so strong it knocked me to the floor.

Opening my eyes, I found Berger laying next to me in a catatonic state; his eyes were open, but he wasn't moving, and from his blank expression it seemed as if he was completely unaware of his surroundings. On the floor behind him, also in a state of shock, were Dennison and Hope; both apparently having been too close to avoid the stunning airburst.

Getting back to my feet, I quickly retrieved Berger's gun from his holster, but before I could aim and pull the trigger a massive shock wave struck the building. A hundred times stronger than the self-defense feature in Mary's watch, this new wave threw me into the air, and I bounced off the wall and landed on the floor a few feet from the device.

Looking out into the research room, I saw the entire outer wall was now ripped away, and in its place the spinning black whirlpool. Coinciding with its arrival was the increased severity of the wind – now blowing at near-hurricane velocity.

The black spinning mass began moving toward me, and in the blink of an eye Madison and the other bodies were gone.

Turning my attention back to General Berger, I rose to my knees, aimed the gun and pulled the trigger. As the bullet struck his still-prone body, I thought about Madison and the others, and fired again and again until I was out of ammunition.

Remembering the explosives, I glanced up at the bombs attached to the field accelerator and found their digital displays now reading less than thirty-five seconds to detonation.

Thinking the explosives would go off before the whirlpool reached me, I decided to take my chances in the device, and I crawled over to the main structure and climbed inside. As I was closing the hatch, I watched helplessly as the notebook containing the Parkinson's cure lift off the polished-steel floor and disappear into the epicenter of the twisting black mass.

Returning my attention to the controls, I flipped the polarity-reversing switch, and much like before, the exciter-motors groaned and the cockpit lights dimmed. As 4 Freedom labored to reenter the fourth dimension, I looked out the cockpit window just in time to see the black whirlpool enveloped the security door, along with Dennison, Hope, Slone and the bodies of O'Malley and General Berger.

An instant later, the exciter-motors steadied and the lights brightened, followed by the familiar blinding flash of the bombs detonating. But instead of hearing the explosion and feeling the shock wave, everything came to a complete standstill – as if someone had clicked a stopwatch and suspended time.

As the device disintegrated around me and the spinning black whirlpool pulled me in, I prayed I was right about it being the changing the timeline, and that I would be reunited with Madison on the other side.

* * *

Several months later, after many late-night hours of research on the internet, I pieced together my theory of what must've happened.

When I'd activated the enhanced Klystron Amplification Tube (or "e-KAT," as Captain Hank referred to it) the communication system onboard the device initiated a radio beam. This beam traveled through the audio player, acquired the Morse-code signal, and proceeded to the e-KAT component. Entering, the beam struck a series of small mirrors, charged with an untold amount of electricity drawn from the exciter-motors, causing the beam's speed to accelerate. Exiting, the beam sent a signal to the device's antenna beacon, before being reflected back and starting the cycle all over again.

Since normal radio beams travel at the speed of light, the accelerated beam arrived back at the beginning *before* the original beam had gotten there, thus proving Einstein's theory that a faster-than-light massless particle (like the radio beam) could travel *backwards* in time. As the successive beams repeated the cycle, the signal repeated – each time broadcasting the signal earlier than the one before it.

Activating the e-KAT component while in the fourth dimension had an exponential effect on the range of the broadcast, and sent the signal into the earth's ionosphere. This "sky wave," as it is called in radio jargon, enabled the signal to reach virtually every location in the world.

With the audible frequency of the transmission well-above the normal upper-range limit of human beings, only cats, dogs and other select species in the animal kingdom could hear the signal, and only if they were standing close to a hi-frequency radio receiver tuned to the same frequency. These limitations made it near-impossible for the signal to be heard and understood by anyone, man or animal – with one notable exception.

The only one capable of hearing and interpreting the signal was a man who'd acquired the ability from an accident playing baseball; an accident that also (oddly enough) had given him a photographic memory.

THE DEVICE

Chapter Twenty-Three
The Signal

Sixty-Nine Years, Four Months and Four Days Earlier
Thursday, 10 May 1945, 01:15hrs
Alsos **Mission-Task Force B Reconnaissance Team**
Inside the *Ünterbunker, Berlin, Germany*

Like heavenly orbs caught in an invisible net, the four lights shining down from the U.S. Army-issued flashlights hung motionless in the darkness. The masked soldiers holding them were also silent and still, making it appear as if their muted voices and immobile bodies were either trapped in suspended animation, or imprisoned in time. Having been in this position for the last five minutes, it was natural the men would now need to stretch or move around, but instead they remained steadfastly in place; frozen by a halting hand gesture from the man who'd led them down here.

In the prime of his life, with his perceptive gifts at their peak, Captain Henry "Hank" Stevens sat in the chair behind the desk of the central room, listening intently to the Torn.Fu receiver-transmitter. For the men holding the flashlights, which included Sergeants Phillips, Sergeant Atkins, Sergeant Southerland and Private Jenkins, the sound emanating from the small speaker was barely-audible static, but from Hank's perspective, it was much, much more.

THE DEVICE

~ Then ~

Approximately twenty minutes ago, Captain Hank and his team had breached the access shaft leading down to the secret lower level of Hitler's underground bunker. After fifteen minutes of searching each of the rooms thoroughly, Atkins reported finding three unexploded bombs. Walking out of the polished-steel room to take a closer look, Hank found that the fearless sergeant had removed them from wherever they were planted, and had placed them on the top of the desk next to the receiver-transmitter.

"Looks like the whole level was wired, sir, but only two of the bombs went off," Atkins said. "The one in the room above, and the other against the far wall in there." He pointed back into the room the captain had just exited.

Hank took his handkerchief off and smiled.

"I'm assuming these are safe now, Sergeant?"

Atkins casually picked up one of the bombs.

"As safe as any bomb can be when its igniter fuse is soaking wet. As you can see, they were all wrapped in cloth rags, which soaked up the seeping groundwater like a sponge. If they'd stayed dry and all the charges had gone off, we wouldn't be standing here because this level wouldn't be here anymore."

Hank shined the flashlight on the bomb Atkins was holding and back to the other two on the desk.

"For the record, where were they planted?"

Atkins pointed his flashlight over the exit leading to the access shaft.

"One was on the ceiling over that door where we came in, and the other two were against that main support beam." He moved the light over to the spot.

"Anything else, Sergeant?"

"I don't know if this is important or not, sir."

"Try me."

"Well sir, these are very sophisticated explosives with a lot of firepower. By sophisticated, I mean they could be set off by either connecting them directly to a detonator, like these were to the one I found upstairs, or by a timer."

He showed Hank the small box, and the clock face taped to one end of the bomb.

"The two they planted in here on that main support beam would've been more than enough to bring the entire ceiling down in all three rooms," he continued, "but why would the Nazi's go to all the trouble of digging this place out, and place all these high-powered explosives down here to blow it all up, when there's nothing down here *to* blow up?"

"Good question," Hank replied, pondering the scenario.

Phillips reported next, informing Hank that Sergeant Southerland and Private Jenkins had finished searching the two dead bodies, and found papers identifying them as civilian scientists assigned to the "RFR." From the intelligence he'd previously gathered, Captain Hank knew the letters referred to the "*Reichsforschungsrat,*" or Reich Research Council, which was the entity in charge of the Nazi's weapon development programs.

"What were their names?" Hank asked.

"Jakob Eddleman and Abraham Kaufmann," Phillips said, handing him the papers. "And I know my German is a little rusty sir, but doesn't Juden mean Jewish?"

Hank took the papers from the sergeant and examined them. *Now that is strange,* he thought, *Jewish guys down here dressed as laboratory assistants? It didn't make sense.* After examining them for a few moments and putting them to memory, he re-folded the papers and stuffed them into his breast pocket.

So far, the information provided by the dying German scientist and the other documents they'd found in the sewer were true; there was an Ünterbunker, and what appeared to be a laboratory. But what were the Nazi's up to? And as Atkins pointed out, why did they try to blow it all up when there appeared to be nothing of value down here at all?

Thinking he needed to further investigate the larger room that resembled a laboratory, Hank turned to walk back. Suddenly, he heard the familiar sound of Morse-code coming from the receiver-transmitter on the desk. He immediately noticed his men were oblivious to it, due to its high frequency, but with his improved hearing he could make out the words. After deciphering a short portion of the signal, he raised his hand in a halting gesture, which instantly froze the men and told them to be quiet.

With his bright blue eyes now locked on the Torn.Fu receiver-transmitter, he slowly sat down in the chair behind the desk, not believing what he was hearing.

~ *Now* ~

After listening to the repeating signal three times, Captain Hank slowly stood and walked back into the polished-steel room that resembled a laboratory, lost in thought as he decided what course of action to take. When he reached the mound of debris, he stopped and realized Phillips had followed him.

"What did you hear, sir?" the sergeant asked

"I'm not sure."

Hank suddenly remembered an old adage he hadn't thought about in a while. It was a phrase his parents repeatedly said to him and his brother while they were growing up, and the same thing he'd told Big Ben at intelligence school. When it came to his mind this time, it seemed as if his parents were right there in the Ünterbunker with him.

Could *this* be the reason he was given the mental gifts after the accident? So that he would be in this position, at this exact moment in time, to hear the signal? *It had to be! It just couldn't be a coincidence!*

548

Looking away from the mound of debris, he stopped noticed a bundled file of papers on the floor, which happened to be laying on a dry section. He leaned down, picked it up and slapped it against his leg to knock off the small rocks and dust. Shining his flashlight on the cover page, it read, *Unternehmen Zunden Vogel*, or in English, Operation Firebird, and had a large red-lettered stamp across the top stating *STRENG-GEHEIM*, German for TOP-SECRET.

After translating a few of the pages, he knew without a doubt that the Morse-code signal was from *himself, and from the future!* This was one of the times in his life that would define him as a human being, and the next order he gave to his men would determine the course of history for the next seventy years!

"Are you all right, sir?" Phillips asked.

Hank simply nodded and continued to stare at the paper.

"Sir, may I make a suggestion?"

Phillips' direct question snapped his thoughts back to the present.

"What's that?"

"Let's pack up the intel and get out of here. This place gives me the creeps."

Hank looked past the sergeant for a moment, and seeing the bombs on the desk, knew precisely what he needed to do.

He hurried back into the central room, with Phillips following closely behind, and set the small bundle of papers on the desk. Turning to Sergeant Atkins, he pointed to the bombs.

"Can these still be detonated?"

"I don't see why not, sir. I've got a few dry igniter-fuses that'll turn the trick."

"How far ahead can you set the timers?"

"Forty-five minutes, give or take a few."

"And if that main support beam goes, it will bring down the ceiling in all three rooms?"

Atkins nodded.

Hank locked his penetrating blue eyes on the sergeant.

"Are you absolutely sure?"

"Definitely, sir. You see where the ceiling is uneven?" He pointed the beam of his flashlight to the spot.

Hank nodded.

"That's a planer fracture, or fault in the sandstone."

Sutherland and Jenkins started to laugh, whereupon Hank silenced them with another halting hand gesture.

"Back home, my dad's a geological surveyor and demolition man for the Bureau of Public Roads," Atkins explained. "I was working with him part-time when I got drafted. Whenever we'd have to cut through a mountain, we'd always try to plant the explosives in the fractures. As for this fracture, it runs the length of the ceiling in all three rooms."

With his photographic memory, Hank immediately recalled the images in his mind from when he'd first walked through the level a few minutes ago, and remembered seeing the uneven rock in the ceiling of both the small living quarters and in the larger room, where the polished-steel plates had come off because of the explosion. Examining it further, he saw that the uneven ceiling in the larger room was directly over the raised platform, and immediately in front of the mound of debris containing the wrecked equipment.

"I remember it," Hank said.

Atkins moved the beam of his flashlight to the main support beam.

"Look at the way the Germans kept adding more and more wood to shore up that beam. That was to keep the ceiling from collapsing."

Although Hank had previously set the image to memory, he looked at it again and confirmed Atkins' analysis; the supporting beam had numerous pieces of wood nailed to it.

"But if they were having so much trouble keeping the ceiling from coming down, why didn't the bomb that went off in the other room cause it to cave in?"

Atkins pointed to the ceiling above.

"Because *this* area is the weakest point of the sandstone's planer fracture."

Hank, with his enhanced ability to quickly solve problems, mentally concluded Atkins' explanation.

"The groundwater."

"Exactly, sir. The seeping groundwater, concentrating for who-knows-how-long on this spot, eroded the sandstone and weakened this point of the fracture. So like I said before, if the two bombs they'd planted in here had gone off, it would've brought the entire ceiling down in all three rooms."

"Good detective work, Atkins. Start getting the bombs ready."

"Yes, sir."

Hank turned to Phillips.

"Sergeant, we are leaving."

"What about the intel, sir?"

Hank pointed to the small bundle of papers on the desk.

"We have all we need right here. Southerland, Jenkins, take off and wait topside with the others. Tell them to get ready to go. We'll only be a few more minutes."

The two junior-ranked men immediately turned and exited through the doors leading to the access shaft.

As Hank gathered the bundle of papers from the desk, one of them dropped from the bottom of the pile. Sergeant Phillips, picking it up for him, shined the beam of his flashlight on the paper and found it to be a photograph of a very big and muscular Nazi officer shaking hands with Adolph Hitler.

"Jeez," Phillips said, "Look at the size of that Nazi. I wonder who he was?"

Examining the photograph for a few moments, Hank remembered the ornate German uniform insignias from intelligence school, and saw that the man was Waffen-SS with the rank of lieutenant general. From his large muscular build and dark eyes, he immediately remembered the description from one of the intelligence briefings, and realized he was looking at a photograph of General Berger. Seeing what the man looked like for the first time, and that Berger was shaking hands with Hitler, Hank was somewhat captivated with the haunting photograph, then recalling the Morse-code signal, Berger's picture took on an entirely new persona – more evil in appearance.

"I don't know," Hank said, finally replying to Phillips' question. "Hopefully someone we no longer have to worry about."

Fifteen minutes later, with the dry igniter fuses installed in the explosives, Atkins set the timers to forty-five minutes and planted them around the Ünterbunker's main support beam; carefully making sure they were out of the way of the seeping groundwater.

Hank smiled at Phillips. "Sergeant, let's get out of here."

After Atkins departed up the ladder, Hank instructed Phillips to go ahead of him, and walked through the Ünterbunker one last time to set the scenes to memory. When he reached the area of the polished-steel room that had sustained the most damage, he had the strangest feeling he was being watched, and he paused for a moment in front of the mound of debris.

Shining his light on the uneven ceiling, he smiled at General Berger's predicament.

The last image Hank memorized before leaving was the Torn.Fu receiver-transmitter, still on and picking up the same sound as before, but with the hi-frequency Morse-code signal fading into static. Closing the door behind him, he walked over to the ladder and looked one last time at the two dead lab assistants. Pointing his flashlight up, he placed his foot on the first ladder rung and climbed out.

When the men emerged from the bunker's main entrance, the two young Russian guards stationed at the doors were visibly relieved that they hadn't taken too long. As a token of appreciation for allowing them to go in, Hank presented them with a German luger pistol, a Nazi dagger, and a couple of small swastika-laden flags that the men had secretly brought along for bribery purposes, leaving the two men completely delighted.

A short time later, with the team and their gear now loaded in the deuce-and-a-half, Hank ordered Sergeant Phillips to send a coded radio message to the Alsos Forward North Headquarters, informing them Task Force B was leaving Berlin. He cautioned all the men that when they got back to their headquarters in Aachen, Germany, they were to use "utmost discretion" when talking about the incursion with the other members of the Alsos mission team. The men nodded their acknowledgement of the code words, which to them simply meant: keep your mouths shut.

Since the departure was made very early in the morning, half of the checkpoints the men passed through were abandoned. The captain had assumed correctly that the Russian celebration would take its toll on their occupying forces, and for most of the slow drive out the men saw many Red Army troops asleep alongside the main road, some still clutching empty bottles of vodka. Twenty minutes later, after disbursing a few more bribes at the last Russian checkpoint, the truck carrying the reconnaissance team was out of the city.

As their truck drove away, Captain Hank heard the faint but unmistakable rumbling sounds of the bombs going off deep underground – forever sealing Operation Firebird and General Berger in the secret lower level of Hitler's bunker.

* * *

Nine and a half weeks later, the Douglas C-47 Skytrain taxied to the end of the runway, and sat in line behind four other troop transports awaiting takeoff. When the plane lurched forward and abruptly turned around, Colonel Boris Pash, sitting in the seat farthest forward, ducked his head around the cabin wall and addressed the radio operator.

"What gives, Sergeant? Why are we turning around?"

The man pulled his headset away from his ear.

"Sir, we've just received orders to return to station and let you off."

"Let *me* off?"

"Yes, sir, and is there a Captain Stevens in your group?"

"Yes, Captain Henry Stevens."

"He's getting off with you."

"I don't understand."

"Me neither, sir, but a general named Groves in the Pentagon wants to see you both ASAP, and there's a flight back to stateside leaving in ten minutes."

As soon as the aircraft parked, Colonel Pash and Captain Hank retrieved their duffel bags and disembarked the aircraft. When they reached the bottom of the stairway and were out of earshot of the men, Hank stopped the colonel.

"Sir, before we leave I have to tell you something."

"What is it?"

"As you've probably noticed, I haven't been myself for the past couple of days."

"I've noticed. What's going on?"

"The accident that gave me the photographic memory also gave me flashes of insight."

"Sir, we have to leave!" the plane's navigator yelled.

Colonel Pash motioned for the navigator to hold and returned his attention to Hank.

"Can't we discuss this later?" he asked.

"Please bear with me, sir. I've never told anyone about this."

"Okay, go ahead."

"As I said sir, the accident that gave me the photographic memory also gave me flashes of insight, or perhaps a better term for it is – premonitions. They don't happen very often, but every time I've experienced one of these premonitions they've come true. *Every* time. I know this sounds crazy sir, but you can't let the men go on this flight."

Colonel Pash looked up at the navigator and back to Hank.

More passionately, and with tears in his eyes, Hank said it again.

"Sir, you can't let the men go on this flight!"

* * *

Twenty-four hours later, Colonel Pash and Captain Hank were seated in the sparsely decorated Pentagon briefing room, getting a thorough tongue-lashing from their heavy-set commanding officer, Major General Leslie Groves. Before either man could respond to the general's rant, there was a knock on the door.

"What is it?" Groves yelled.

A second lieutenant came into the room and nervously approached the general.

"Pardon me, sir, I was told to inform you that the first planeload of Alsos personnel arrived in Manila, and Dr. Goudsmit has already met with General MacArthur's staff."

"Very well."

The junior officer stood in place, not moving.

"Anything else, LT?"

The lieutenant nodded.

"Well, spit it out!"

"Just this, sir."

He handed him a note.

After studying it for a few moments, General Groves looked up and replied in a much calmer voice.

"Thank you, LT. That will be all."

After the lieutenant exited the briefing room, General Groves addressed Colonel Pash.

"Tell me Colonel, are you Irish?"

"No, if I recall my ancestors were all English."

"You must have some Irish blood in you."

"What do you mean, sir?"

"You're as lucky as a leprechaun. Two hours ago, that plane you and your men were supposed to be on reported engine problems, and didn't make its scheduled landing. Search planes just reported seeing floating wreckage twenty miles off the Philippine coast. And to think, I was just about to chew you out for pulling your men off that flight. Which reminds me, *why did* you pull your men off that flight?"

Before Colonel Pash could answer, the general looked at his watch and stood up.

"Never mind. I've got another meeting to attend. Submit your report as soon as possible Colonel. Meeting adjourned!"

As General Groves and his staff exited the room, one of his aids, a major, paused and handed Colonel Pash two pieces of paper stapled together.

After he was gone, the colonel and Hank sat for a few minutes in stoned silence. Finally, the colonel's attention turned to the papers, and as he read them his eyes grew wide.

"What is it, sir?" Hank asked.

"Some info just came back on those two bodies you found, Eddleman and Kaufmann. Just as you thought, they were pretty famous Jewish guys, quite well-respected in the scientific community. They managed to locate some surviving members of their families, who sent along their heartfelt thanks for providing them closure."

Hank took the two papers and instantly memorized them.

"You'll immediately let me know if you have any more of these premonitions?"

Hank smiled. "Yes, sir. When I know, you'll know."

* * *

The next evening, after finishing dinner, Hank cleared the empty Chinese food boxes and silverware from the table, while Ben took J.R. into a corner bedroom and started singing lullabies.

A few minutes later, Ben tip-toed back into the kitchen, and whispering, asked Hank if he wanted another Grapette.

"Sure," Hank whispered back, "but I've got to ask you, what was that awful caterwauling I heard just a minute ago?"

"You don't like my singing?"

Hank smiled. "Oh, that's what it was."

"Man, you just don't appreciate a great singing voice when you hear one. Let's go out on the porch so that we don't wake the little man. Besides, this part of the house is just too hot in the summer."

"At least you get to live in base housing for free while you're stationed here."

"Yeah, I can't complain too much."

They sat down and took turns popping the tops off their sodas with a bottle opener.

"You have a beautiful son, Ben," Hank said.

"Thanks, man. He's all I have left of Amy, and I'm going to make sure he grows up right and stays out of trouble. That's the promise I made to her before she died, and I intend to keep it."

"Well I, for one, am sure you'll keep that promise."

"What about you, man? How did the war go? Did you see any action?"

"Not really. For the most part, the unit I was assigned to just followed the guys on the front lines, looking for enemy intel after they'd cleared the towns."

Ben grinned. "Sounds like the perfect assignment."

"It was for a time, but my priorities have changed."

"How so?"

"I plan on leaving the Army."

"What?"

"You heard me."

"You can't leave the Army, because in case you haven't heard, there's still a war going on."

"I don't mean *right now*. As soon as we defeat the Japanese and the Army has a draw-down, I'm getting out."

"What makes you so sure there is going to be a draw-down?"

"It's a matter of record that after every major war the Army cuts back its personnel, and when they do I'm resigning my commission."

"Don't tell me something's finally gotten to you? What happened to the Hank who said he was going to be a lifer, and stay in until he made general?"

"Like I said, my priorities have changed."

"What happened? Did you screw something up?"

"No."

"Did an officer chew you out for something?"

Hank shook his head.

Ben grinned again. "Is it a girl?"

"You're way off base."

"So tell me, what would cause my good buddy, Captain Hank Stevens from Ogden, Utah, the one with the photographic memory, to leave this man's Army?"

"Before I answer that, I want to ask you something."

"All right, shoot."

"And I'm asking you this as a friend and not as a fellow Army officer."

"Okay," Ben replied, dragging the word out slowly.

"Let's suppose that you went out on a mission, and found…"

"Impossible. The Army doesn't send black captains out on intelligence missions."

"I know my friend and I'm sorry about that, but for the sake of argument, let's say this time your commander is color blind and he sends you out."

"Okay, for you I'll suspend my disbelief."

"Say you're on this mission, and you find a magic radio that was sending you a signal from the future. Oh, and let's say that no one else can hear this signal but you."

"From the future? What's the signal saying?"

"It's telling you that your time on this earth is so short, you'd better not waste any of it, and use the time God gives you to be with those you care about the most."

Ben thought about it for a moment and laughed.

"If I heard something like that, man, I'd do it. No need to tempt providence too often, if you know what I mean."

Hank smiled. "That's exactly what I thought."

"So after you get out, what will you do? For a living, I mean?"

"I was thinking about opening a shop that restores old jalopies."

"You're kidding me, right?

Hank looked directly into Ben's eyes and shook his head.

"You'll need money to get started. So if you don't mind me asking, how will you get it?"

"Oh, you could say I've taken an interest in the stock market recently, and I believe I can make some money at it. Then, after I make a bundle..."

"Do you need a business partner?"

"My friend, I was hoping you would ask me that."

Ben smiled.

"Who knows," Hank continued, "maybe after we get it started, we'll meet a couple of nice gals we can marry and settle down with."

"Did the magic radio tell you that too?"

Instead of replying, Hank sat back in the lounge chair and smiled.

Ben's booming laugh roared, waking up J.R., as well as half a dozen dogs in the neighborhood.

Chapter Twenty-Four
The New Timeline

Seventy-One Years, Three Months and Thirteen Days Later
Wednesday, 2 November 2016, 17:45hrs
Inside the *Wasatch Front Senior Citizen Center, Layton, Utah*

There were more than fifty people seated around the tables in the large assembly hall, talking with each other or sitting quietly, while waiting for the meeting to begin. At the center of each table sat a different display of Halloween decorations, left over from the party two days ago. The setting sun, casting the day's final rays of light through the west windows, enhanced the colors of these centerpieces, which bathed the room in a bright hue of orange and created a warm fall ambiance for the support group meeting.

As I gathered my notes and prepared to make a few announcements, I looked around the room and noticed six people near the entrance, one of whom was pushing a seventh person in a wheelchair. Since the sun was shining in at such a low angle, it made it impossible for me to see their faces, so I proceeded over to greet them. The second I passed into the shaded part of the room, I immediately recognized five of them as being Deputy Alvarez, Deputy Rivers, Ethan Washington, his twin sister Evelynn, and the man in the wheelchair, Captain Henry "Hank" Stevens.

Although Hank was much older than the first time I'd seen him in the other timeline, he was still wearing the same style of clothing: black slacks, white dress shirt, black overcoat and tie, fedora hat and white sneakers. He was also wearing an oversized pair of wrap-around sunglasses, which almost hid his gaunt face and overabundance of wrinkles.

"Welcome to our Parkinson's support group. I'm George d'Clare."

Ethan offered his hand.

"Pleased to meet you, Mr. d'Clare, I'm Ethan Washington and this is my sister Evelynn, my dad J.R. and my mom Valerie."

I shook hands and exchanged pleasantries with them, and stepped over to greet the two deputies, at which point Deputy Alvarez introduced himself and Deputy Rivers.

"Are all of you together?"

"No," Alvarez said, "we were on our way to work when we found these out-of-towners lost, so we showed them how to get here."

"I *told* you to pack the GPS," Valerie said, comically scolding J.R.

"Why are you complaining?" he replied. "We're here, aren't we?"

As everyone laughed at their remarks, I smiled and knelt to Hank.

"This is our friend, Henry Stevens," Evelynn said.

"Pleased to meet you, Mr. Stevens."

He slowly took off his hat and glasses, placed them on his lap, and reached out with his trembling arm to shake my hand.

I immediately noticed how much his bright blue eyes contrasted with his aged physique, and knew that a much younger man still existed inside this older man's body.

Madison, who had been visiting other members of the group, walked up.

"And who do we have here?" she asked.

"Sweetheart, I'd like you to meet J.R. and Elizabeth Washington, their daughter Evelynn and son Ethan, Deputy Alvarez and Deputy Rivers, and last-but-not-least, Mr. Henry Stevens."

"You can call me Captain Hank," he whispered, "everyone else does."

~ Then ~

A little more than two years ago, when the front wall of 4 Freedom's cockpit dissolved, I lost consciousness and woke up in bed next to Madison. Realizing where I was, and that she was still alive and laying next to me, I sobbed like a baby. When I'd composed myself enough to tell her the story, she had no memory of Captain Hank coming to the support group, nor any of the other subsequent events regarding O'Malley, General Berger or the device. Although she thought I'd remembered everything with precise clarity, she concluded it was all a vivid dream, triggered (most likely) by my Parkinson's medications.

In the months that followed, I gave quite a bit of thought as to why I could remember. Since the timeline had changed while I was in the fourth dimension (and inside 4 Freedom's cobalt-metal fuselage) I believe that it must've shielded me from the full effects, which in turn allowed me to retain all of my memories.

I've also often wondered why the timeline didn't immediately change when I turned on the e-KAT component, and concluded that it must've been because the signal had taken some amount of time to travel around the world to Germany, and go back to the moment in history when Captain Hank and his team had entered the Ünterbunker. In any case, my final confrontation with General Berger could've been avoided had I only stayed inside the cockpit after I'd returned from the future.

Although these two minor points are only conjecture, they do explain the events as I experienced them, both when the timeline changed and afterward. Even though it would be easy for me to dismiss the entire story as a vivid dream, I know that it happened. Even now, years later, I can still recall the events with precise clarity, which is something I'm currently unable to do even when my Parkinson's medications are working overtime.

~ Now ~

With the meeting adjourned, the members of the support group made their way to the exit. Wanting to say goodbye to Captain Hank and the Washington family, I hastened over to their table. Madison followed close behind.

"Thank you all for coming. I hope to see you again next month."

"I'm afraid we won't be here," J.R. said, "We are actually on vacation and only visiting."

"We live in Maryland," Valerie added.

"I've never been to Maryland," Madison said, and engaged the four in chit-chat.

While they were talking, I knelt down to Hank.

"I was the one who sent you the signal," I whispered.

"I know," he replied softly, "your name was in the message I sent to myself all those years ago."

Madison and the others stopped talking, and Hank and I suddenly found ourselves the center of attention. When I reached out to shake his hand, he grasped it with both of his and locked his penetrating blue eyes on me.

"Always remember that your time on this earth is short," he said, "and you'd better not waste any of it. Use the time God gives you to be with those you care about the most."

I smiled. "Thanks Captain Hank. I'll remember that."

A short time later, after Hank and the Washington family had departed, Madison and I were straightening the chairs in the assembly hall and getting ready to go home.

"So that was him?" she asked.

"That was him."

"While you two were talking, Valerie told me his wife Lana, died some years ago, and they've been taking care of him ever since. He celebrated his ninety-sixth birthday the other day, and when they asked him what he wanted to do, you know what he said?"

I shook my head.

"He said before he died, he wanted to come back to his home state of Utah and shake the hand of Mr. George d'Clare."

"They must've thought he was losing his mind."

"They did, but he'd been such a good friend to them over the years they thought it was the least they could do."

* * *

Captain Hank's parents once told him that everything happens for a reason, and that the path he chooses to take when things happen to him will define him as a human being.

When I received the diagnosis of Parkinson's disease, my life's path changed drastically, and led me to meeting a strange man with an incredible story; an unbelievable tale about a device that could do the impossible. The ensuing events gave me a brief glimpse of the future, where I learned (for certain) that scientists will someday discover a cure for the disease. I now have faith that the reason I survived and remembered this adventure was so that I could write this account, and give hope to others who are also afflicted.

As for Operation Firebird, I am reminded of a quote by the famous Spanish philosopher George Santayana, who once said, "Those who cannot remember the past are condemned to repeat it."

While Madison and I follow our life's path toward the now-unknown future, I pray that there are no other malevolent spirits in the world like SS Lieutenant General Karl Berger, the White Wolf of Sachsenhausen.

Epilogue

Unknown Years, Months and Days Later
Inside the *Ünterbunker, Berlin, Germany*

The loud popping sound of the first vacuum-tube triode blowing apart instantly wakened the pilot of Firebird One. Looking out the small cockpit window, and seeing the main structure still covered in rocks and debris, he broke out in a trembling sweat. With the power-distribution system now overloaded, one by one the other triodes began to fail, crippling the eighty exciter-motors supplying power to their corresponding electromagnets.

As the main structure of the device reentered real time, its molecules immediately fused with the objects occupying the same stationary plane, forever altering both sets of particles at the sub-atomic level. Once merged with the debris field, the device's bright blue glow instantly faded to black, followed by an ear-splitting scream of mortal agony, lasting only a second, and then – silence.

THE DEVICE

Dale C. George

During my Air Force Reserve career, nothing gave me more pleasure than documenting the actions of the men and women who wear our nation's uniform, and to subsequently see them presented with a medal or an award for their accomplishments. After my Parkinson's disease diagnosis, and a great deal of encouragement from those close to me, I decided to channel my skills toward a more-personal (albeit ambitious) goal, and the first pages of The Device were born. Since I enjoy reading about military history, and my favorite genre is science fiction, combining them turned out to be a fun experience; one that has rekindled my love of writing, as well as sparked my imagination.

THE DEVICE

Made in the USA
Middletown, DE
24 March 2018